Armed and Glamorous

"Whether readers are fashion divas or hopelessly fashion-challenged, there's a lot to like about being *Armed and Glamorous*." (*BookPleasures.com*)

Shot Through Velvet

"First-rate... a serious look at the decline of the U.S. textile and newspaper industries provides much food for thought." (*Publishers Weekly*, starred review)

"Great fun, with lots of interesting tidbits about the history of the U.S. fashion industry." (*Suspense Magazine*)

Grave Apparel

"A truly intriguing mystery." (*Armchair Reader*)

"A likeable, sassy, and savvy heroine, and the Washington, D.C., setting is a plus." (*The Romance Readers Connection*)

Veiled Revenge

"An intriguing plot, fun but never too insane characters, and a likable and admirable heroine all combine to create a charming and well-crafted mystery." (*Kings River Life Magazine*)

"Like fine wine that gets better with age, *Veiled Revenge* is the best book yet in this fabulous series." (*Dru's Book Musings*)

Hostile Makeover (also a movie)

"Byerrum pulls another superlative Crime of Fashion out of her vintage cloche." (*Chick Lit Books*)

"As smooth as fine-grade cashmere." (*Publishers Weekly*)

"Totally delightful... a fun and witty read." (*Fresh Fiction*)

Designer Knockoff

"Clever wordplay, snappy patter, and intriguing clues make this politics-meets-high-fashion whodunit a cut above the ordinary." (*Romantic Times*)

"A very talented writer with an offbeat sense of humor." (*The Best Reviews*)

Killer Hair (also a movie)

"Girlfriends you'd love to have, romance you can't resist, and Beltway-insider insights you've got to read. Adds a crazy twist to the concept of capital murder." (Agatha winner Sarah Strohmeyer)

THE
WOMAN
IN THE
DOLLHOUSE

a novel of suspense by

ELLEN BYERRUM

Author of the Crime of Fashion Mysteries

Lethal Black Dress Press

Acknowledgments

Ideas for books spring up anywhere and everywhere. While I cannot pinpoint exactly how and where everything came together for *The Woman in the Dollhouse*, several people provided inspiration at various key stages of this work. I'd like to thank Juan Chavarria, Kathy Irving, Dr. John Howard, Dr. Julia Frank, Diane Byerrum, Rosemary Stevens, and most of all, Bob Williams, who has been with me through every book, many plays, and various endeavors. Our odyssey is not over yet.

Any errors you may find in this book are the author's, but please remember: This is a work of fiction, and the events described may not necessarily reflect reality.

But, ah, I dream!—the appointed hour is fled,
And hope, too long with vain delusion fed,
Deaf to the rumour of fallacious fame,
Gives to the roll of death his glorious name!
With venial freedom let me now demand
Thy name, thy lineage, and paternal land.

The Odyssey of Homer, translated by Alexander Pope

Chapter 1

IN MY MEMORIES, my eyes are always green.

As green as the dark and dangerous sea, my grandfather used to say. Mermaid's eyes, he called them. Eyes that changed, from the color of seaweed, to sea glass, to the green of troubled water. Yet I was never troubled, when my eyes were green.

There are huge gaps of time, years, when I don't remember anything about my life. Still, I am quite convinced that my eyes were always green.

Even in my double memories, they are green. Even though I seem to remember being two people, they are green. It doesn't matter if I recall being a child with blond streaks in my braids, collecting shells with my grandfather at the stony edge of the sea, or if I think I was a dark-haired girl riding a new pony, under the watchful eye of my pretty mother. My eyes are always green.

These days the mirror tells me my eyes are not green. They are brown. As brown as leaves that die in the fall.

I'm writing down these words because I don't know if tomorrow I will remember what I know today. I have too many memories. Like the memory of my eyes. But I also have memory losses. Great chunks of time are missing. Frankly, I'm terrified of losing more pieces of myself, no matter how small.

"Green eyes are a false memory, Tennyson," according to Dr. Embry. "You never had green eyes."

His words interrupted my mental rambling. His specialty is memory loss and recovery. And apparently—*me*. Giles Embry is the head of "the Campus," the facility where I am lodged. He is both a scientist and a medical doctor.

He studies disorders of the brain.

It seems I possess one of those pesky disordered brains. But why would I have false memories? How could they have taken root?

The first time I saw a stranger with brown eyes staring back at me in the mirror, I shrieked. It was the wrong reaction. Dr. Embry took away all the mirrors for a week. I learned not to react. I learned to stop flinching at the unfamiliar eyes reflected there.

But my eyes are not all that's changed.

Something happened to my hair.

When did it become so dark, so brown, so short? I often reach for my hair, my long blond hair, to braid it, to put it up, to brush it. My brown locks barely reach the bottom of my ears. Someone cut it. I don't know why.

When I steel myself to look in the mirror, my facial features are similar to the ones I remember, but I can't be positive, because of the brown eyes and the short dark hair. I try not to look into mirrors for very long anymore.

Men used to call me beautiful. Or did they? I suppose that could be a false memory too.

Dr. Embry tells me certain memories have been implanted, changed, and distorted. Perhaps an aftereffect of the accident.

From what he has told me, even if I could be sure of who I am, I could never trust my memory. Our memories are fluid. They change. We start editing them as soon as they are completed. We make them better, more interesting. We lace things together so they make a story out of the puzzle of our lives. We crave stories that have meaning.

But my memory is a hopeless liar and I am broken into pieces.

When I'm awake, people call me Tennyson.

In my dreams, I hear voices calling me Marissa.

"Your name is Tennyson," the doctor tells me with great patience. "You're not a woman called Marissa. She is something your brain has constructed."

Couldn't my brain have constructed Tennyson instead of Marissa? Besides, what kind of name is Tennyson? I'm not a poet, although I recently emerged from the Valley of Death. My fancy name, I'm told, is a *Southern* thing.

The doctor calls me Tennyson frequently, knowingly, intimately. He stands, superior, a slight smile on his lips, as he explains.

"Your life is complicated, Tennyson. Your mind has invented a simpler one."

"Why, Dr. Embry? Why do I need a simpler life?"

"It's Giles, Tennyson. You do remember that?"

"Yes, I remember that. Giles. Why?"

He doesn't answer my question. "The important thing is that you continue to discover and recover who you really are. Your therapy has been tailored specifically to your needs. You can tell me anything, Tennyson."

How can I tell him it feels as if someone is trying to kill me?

Blot me out, erase me a little bit at a time? Someone who started with my eyes.

Dr. Embry—Giles—never flinches when I protest that I am not Tennyson. He ticks off facts like a statistician.

"Your name is Tennyson Olivia Claxton. You are twenty-four years old, we are engaged, and you are going to marry me, Tennyson. We are going to be very happy."

Marry Giles Embry? That has got to be a joke. Except that he doesn't joke. We couldn't possibly have anything in common. He must be at least ten years older than I am. He is a doctor and I'm— What am I? Who am I? I seem to be a blank slate.

Dr. Embry is quite mistaken about an "us," crazy even, yet I don't say so. We don't say crazy here, even though we might be as crazy as blue loons under the full moon.

How could I be his patient *and* his fiancée? Is it some cosmic coincidence that I have lost my memory and he is a leading expert in this field? I've told him and told him that I am his patient, only his patient.

"You're a resident, Tennyson, not a patient. And it may be a coincidence, but it's a lucky thing for both of us."

"What are you talking about?"

"You know what I am talking about."

"I don't remember you, Giles."

"You will. All you have to do is trust me, Tennyson."

How can I trust Giles when I can't even trust the mirror? And my own eyes?

The absence of my memory seems to make his heart grow fonder. Not mine. Giles is merely the head doctor in a pale blue lab coat with embroidered navy script over the pocket: Dr. Embry, followed by a string of initials. He is the handsome doctor who keeps me from my freedom.

"You know what you did with your freedom, Tennyson."

I've heard rumors.

When he talked about us together, I closed my brown eyes. When I opened them, he was still observing me, never blinking.

"You and I, Tennyson, we have a history. And a future. You are the most important case I will ever have."

"When can I leave the Campus?"

"Soon."

Soon in Giles's world is eons in mine. "How soon?" I asked.

"We've just completed your Phase One: Phoenix."

"You call it Phoenix? Out of the ashes?" I'm just trying to emerge from this Fog that surrounds me.

He inclined his head, *yes*. "I've tailored this therapy protocol to your particular needs. Phase Two is a little more—intensive. It's code-named Pegasus."

"But I thought—" More intense than what I've been through? I cannot bear it.

"This is the interim phase, Tennyson. A breather. I am giving you time to rest, to integrate all the memories you have recovered. Don't worry. Pegasus will erase all thoughts of your mythical Marissa."

"How many phases are there?" I wasn't sure I wanted to lose Marissa. I've only just found her.

"As many as it takes." He almost betrayed some irritation, but looked as if he thought better of it. "Listen, Tennyson, your physical injuries took time to heal. We had to go slow with your cognitive therapy. I had to take it easy on you."

"Easy?" I strangled the scream making its way up my throat. "What are the programs for the other patients?"

"Well, there's Icarus, of course. But that doesn't concern you." He put his hand on my shoulder and squeezed. "Nothing to worry about."

With his specialized research at the Campus, Giles hopes to find the answers to where memory lives, where it retreats, whether from trauma or disease, and how it can be retrieved—or jump-started with cables made from drugs and therapy. It must be very expensive. Giles tells me not to worry about that either.

The Campus is not its real name. Unofficially, it is "The Hunt Country Campus, a C&B Institute Memory Project." A research institute, it also has long-term care for lost souls like me, we who might yet hold the keys to memory recovery.

I assume everyone here on this side of the pastel lab coat has been poked, prodded, and provoked, as I have been. Our gray matter is massaged with transcranial magnetic stimulation to encourage lost history to be rediscovered. Our brains are mapped by MRIs and subjected to other machines with long names, like the "quantitative electroencephalograph," which I'm told measures brainwaves.

We are the bugs under the microscope. The frogs dissected, skin flayed open, and pinned back in wax-lined trays for all to see.

We are the "residents" with holes in our minds—holes that used to be filled with people, places, and things. Some of us have traumatic brain injuries or PTSD, some have inexplicable memory loss, and some have Alzheimer's disease or other types of dementia.

Then there is me, Tennyson Olivia Claxton. Poor Tennyson and her disordered brain. Missing years, as well as people, places, and things. But somewhere down Memory Lane, I picked up a hitchhiker whose name is Marissa— Marissa Alexandra Brookshire, who has green eyes. I may have Tennyson's eyes, but I have Marissa's memories, as well as Tennyson's.

Giles insists the Campus is not a hospital, yet there are doctors and nurses and various assistants on staff. They all wear pastel lab coats, coded to their ranks and specialties: doctors in blue, nurses in green or pink, lab techs in yellow, research assistants in lavender, and orderlies in white. Pale colors that do not excite the brain or raise blood pressure. The guards wear gray jackets or gray lab coats.

Instead of clipboards and pens, staff members carry digital tablets to record their observations of the "residents." Instead of jewelry, they wear microphones and body cams to capture interactions, as if they were policemen on patrol. Instead of humans, they act like machines, without emotions or empathy. Giles says they are simply trained professionals doing their jobs.

There is no place to hide from Dr. Embry or his minions. His guards follow me at a discreet distance. Giles calls them assistants, but they are clad in gray. Some come and go, but one is the most constant. Giles told me his name was Roy Barnaker. *Barnacle* would be more apt, because I can't scrape him off.

Giles's cameras are everywhere. In every room, on every rooftop, over every door. They are mounted on poles in the gardens. Motion sensitive, they turn, lenses focusing on us as we walk by. I have observed it all, like one of the cameras.

Oddly, amid this wonderland of computers and cameras and digital surveillance, there is one oversight. Giles has neglected to provide me with a phone or a computer. Of course I wouldn't dare use one. He could listen to my calls, trace my keystrokes, stalk even more of my thoughts. Am I paranoid? Giles assures me that I am.

I have started a journal where I pray he will never find it. Writing in an old book in a corner of my suite, between the bed and the wall, where the camera lens doesn't see. At least I hope it doesn't. I write in tiny print between the lines, and sometimes in the margins, of an ancient book that looks as if no one ever cracked it open. *This* book. I found it on the bookshelf in my room, placed there as a decoration, nothing more. Many of the gold-tipped pages have to be carefully pried apart for the first time.

I've hidden my thoughts in this book. Under a line of poetry, I pen a line of my diary. Like this:

> **Saved from the jaws of death by heaven's decree,**
> My name is Tennyson Claxton. My eyes are brown.
> **The tempest drove him to these shores, and thee**.
> I survived a terrible accident that I can't remember.
> **Him, Jove now orders to his native lands**
> My name is Marissa Brookshire. My eyes are green.
> **Straight to dismiss: so destiny commands:**
> One of us might not actually exist.
> **Impatient Fate his near return attends,**
> I am stuck in a prison called the Campus.
> **And calls him to his country, and his friends.**
> I have no friends. I am alone. No one visits me but the doctors.

Jotting down words in this book, which no one else will ever read, is safer than talking to Giles, and certainly more honest. This is *The Odyssey* that only I will know. My Odyssey.

After the nightmares wake me up, on the nights when I'm sure he's gone home, I scribble my words in the dim light. I don't want him to know what I am thinking. I don't want his kind solicitations, or his unkind suspicions. I don't want to hear him call me Tennyson.

How can I be that Tennyson?

Giles makes my skin crawl.

What is he doing in my bed?

Chapter 2

GILES IS NOT in my bed all the time, it's true. Sometimes he simply sleeps beside me, without sex. I think. He says it gives me comfort and company. What it gives him—I don't know. When he wants sex, I go blank. I refuse to remember what he must have felt like before the accident. What he feels like now. All I want is to be left alone.

"There is nothing wrong with me being here, Tennyson," he said. "We are a couple. I am not forcing you to do anything."

"If I can't remember, how would I know?" I said. "It doesn't feel right. It's like sleeping with—"

A stranger, I think, but do not say. You might think that there would be objections raised by the staff to this arrangement, but I do not reside with the other patients. Residents. Because Tennyson Olivia is the notoriously irresponsible spawn of the infamous Claxton clan, I am housed in a special cottage, a duplex which mimics the architecture of the main building, claustrophobically close to Giles.

Giles keeps two offices, one in his laboratory and one in the other half of the duplex. There are connecting interior doors. It is so easy for him to slip into my bed every night. I wonder if he turns the cameras off when he visits me? Or does he leave them on to study my reaction to him? Or does he watch them later to get—what? To get turned on? Giles is so cold I can't imagine him being excited by anything. Even his fiancée.

Everyone at the Campus knows we are engaged. Everyone knows all about me, which leaves me at a loss. I know nothing about myself. And I know too much.

Surely if we were engaged, I would feel something for him, other than revulsion. He reaches out to hold me and I pull away. He shrugs, glances at me, and reaches for his tablet, as if to record his observations of my behavior the instant I misbehave.

Maybe I should be attracted to him. Perhaps I was once. Objectively speaking, Giles is almost pretty, in a stereotypical square-jawed way. Straight features, dark hair, and blue eyes that I wish would look at someone other than me.

Giles wears horned-rimmed glasses over those blue eyes for reading, or maybe for show, perhaps just to enhance his intellectual aura. He smells of rubbing alcohol and antiseptic soap. Hs touch is cool and dry. Professional.

The female staff—even the older women who serve meals in the dining room—flirt with him endlessly, and I wonder how successful they are. I wish them well, because heaven knows I have entirely too much of his attention and I'm more than willing to share.

I don't want to sleep with Giles, although people seem to think I do, and I assume many women would. He keeps his skin lightly tanned and his body fit. He exercises in the early morning as if demons were after him. He doesn't have to tell you he runs obsessively: Several framed Marine Corps Marathon medals hang in his office as proof.

For weeks, I have been obsessed with getting away from him.

Wherever I go, I am under surveillance. When Giles leaves, I am locked in, one of his guards outside the door or in his office. Usually the Barnacle, also known as Creepy Roy.

Roy always seems to be on the edge of my vision, a few steps behind or to the side, watching me. When Giles isn't stalking me, the task of surveillance is left to the omnipresent cameras—and creeping, crawling, Creepy Roy. The others are interchangeable. But the Barnacle is different.

He stares at me when I walk in the garden. He ogles me in the hallways when I speak with one of the psychologists. He lurks everywhere, always gazing with those oddly blank eyes. Even when I don't see Roy, I sense that he's there, skulking around the dining room, or following me into the library in the main house to borrow a book. I know he reports back to Giles, but I have no idea what he reports or why it's so important. "Tennyson reads another book." Big deal.

Creepy Roy is tall and thin. His inch-long gray crewcut stands like a somber halo over those shadowed round blue eyes and sunken cheekbones. Those eyes seem to look beyond me. His voice emanates from somewhere deep in his chest. His uniform is a gray lab coat over a blue oxford cloth shirt and blue jeans.

And even though Giles hands me pills to make me sleep, pills to make me alert, pills to make me remember, pills to make me docile, he insists that one of his "aides" stays close by. Why do I merit all this attention? Am I that dangerous?

I detest the Fog the pills bring. They are fast-acting and fast-dissolving. In self-defense, I've started performing a classic sleight-of-hand trick. Something imaginary Marissa's grandfather taught her. Me. Someone. At least I think he did. Instead of coins, I palm pills before they reach my mouth. I don't want to feel drugged and doped.

"You can't sleep here anymore, Giles," I told him this morning as he was getting dressed. I stopped short of telling him he made me cringe, but I'm sure I flinched anyway. "Not with me."

In his detached way, tying his tie in the mirror, he considered my request. "What brought this on?"

"You're asking me to accept you from ground zero. I don't remember you before the Campus."

He turned toward me, putting his hands on my shoulders, moving them down my body. He touched my face with his fingers. I assume he was touching me in a way he used to, a touch calculated to make me melt. I shook my head.

"Don't."

He was quiet for a while. I fully expected him to take out his iPhone and make a note.

"Very well, Tennyson. I realize you have a lot on your shoulders right now. Let's say I will acquiesce to your request. Let's see if you can concentrate on your memories if I put our romance on the back burner for now."

Romance? Who was he kidding? It's like having a romance with a surveillance camera.

But did I detect the slightest hint of relief in his poker face? My gut—Tennyson's or Marissa's?—tells me he's changed toward me as well.

 og

I am housed at the Campus because I was in a horrific car accident and nearly died. Giles has shown me pictures of the wreck and they haunt me. How could anyone have survived that smashed heap of steel and glass?

He tells me the crash was my fault. I don't remember the night of the accident, or the wreck, or the weeks afterward. But I have discovered bit by bit that I'm a terrible, irresponsible person. Lucky to be alive. Or maybe not so lucky.

After I begged him to leave my bed, he told me more about the crash. Why? Did he decide I was strong enough for more details? Was it in retaliation for pushing him away? I didn't care. I retreated into the living room of the suite, waiting for him to leave.

"I tried to stop you from driving that night," he said. "Do you remember?"

Remember. The word I hear so often, it might be my real name. I stood very still. "The night of the accident?"

"You were inebriated. We argued. You grabbed your keys and left. You wrapped your Porsche around a tree."

He went on. Drinking and drugs and anger and a reckless disregard for seatbelts were all involved, ending in broken glass, crumpled metal, a shattered Porsche—and a shattered me. I listened, horrified. He took my hand.

But not to comfort me. Dr. Giles Embry is very big on account-ability. I was being held accountable. My faults were duly ticked off one by one: I was selfish, careless, forgetful, thrill-seeking, self-destructive. What wasn't my fault? The weather? The ice storm that turned the streets into a bumper-car ride that night?

"I was drunk?" I wouldn't drink and drive, I thought. And a Porsche? He might as well have told me I was piloting the Starship Enterprise. A Porsche. Have I ever even ridden in a Porsche? Tennyson, yes. But Marissa?

"More than drunk. There were drugs too, we found out, when they did the tox screen." That's how Giles talks. Very clinical. "I didn't realize how out of control you were. I'm sorry, Tennyson."

"Was I driving too fast?"

"You always drove too fast. And the roads were icy. Especially at the curve where you left the road and flew into the tree."

At least that night I could fly. I pulled my hand away and folded my arms. It wasn't easy to listen to my endless shortcomings all the time, especially when there seemed to be so many of them.

"What did we fight about?"

"I don't remember," he said.

He didn't remember the argument that ended in my storming out and nearly dying in an accident? Giles was lying. I wasn't shocked exactly, though a bit surprised that he would bother. The memory expert remembers everything. Yet he doles out facts like bitter little pills on a daily schedule. This was just one more, perhaps the worst.

"Exactly how long have I been here?" That is one of the fuzzy aspects of my brain. Time collapses and expands with my memories and my mood and the Fog. It feels like forever. Or a day.

"Since January. You totaled your car in January. Right after New Year's."

"For God's sake, Giles, it's April! The flowers are in bloom." I could feel tears spring to my eyes. I blinked and refused to let them fall.

"Yes. It's been months. You were in an induced coma for a time. It was touch and go. You were hanging in the balance, between life and death."

I told him to leave me alone, I wanted to sleep.

ଔ

January is an empty page in the calendar. February never happened at all. I started to wake up in March, along with the forsythia bush that grows outside the bedroom of my suite at the Campus. Before that, time is a blur. Not just January and February. My entire life. Aside from the shadows in my dreams and an occasional voice, the bright yellow flowers of late March on stark brown stems are the first things I remember clearly, as if I had just been born. Every day the blossoms grow thicker and the green leaves push through bare stalks. It's the forsythia that told me to start living again. That and my nightmares. I started to look for the magnolias, the daffodils, the tulips. I remembered tulips. If they could erupt out of the dormant soil, maybe I could as well.

Giles insists it was the constant care of the superior medical staff at the Campus who tended to me after the accident that brought me back to the land of the living.

I was heavily medicated, he says, and I needed to recover from my physical injuries, as well as the injuries to my soul. There were hours and hours of physical and mental therapy. But my mind was still caught by the Fog. Slowly, Dr. Embry says, he's trying to wean me from the heavier drugs, though there are still the "maintenance" meds, which he insists are necessary. Pills that dull my brain and my senses, the pills I now ditch on a regular basis. Pills whose names I don't recall or want to recall.

He holds the threat of more medication over my head. I want to throw something at him that would wipe that smug expression off his face.

"You may not believe it, but you're healing now." A trickle of praise, yet his blue eyes remained as cool as a robot's. If there were depths in Giles's eyes, I couldn't see them. I couldn't detect any warmth in them. "You're remembering who you are, Tennyson. I'm very pleased."

Giles repeated the litany that I am lucky to be alive, lucky to be here.

Lucky me. How can you feel lucky when you don't know who you really are? When your eyes are brown and not green? I don't feel particularly lucky.

Every damn day someone reminds me of how fortunate I am to be in this place! And every day, I find it difficult to show my gratitude. I'd say I was getting a reputation, but my reputation precedes me.

If I could figure out a way, I would flee. But where would I go? What would I do? Giles promises I won't have to stay here forever.

"Everything depends on your memory," he says.

He means my performance. "I'm not a moron, Giles."

"I never said you were."

Not in so many words, no. I'll ask a question and Giles will draw me a diagram. He is always grading me. Marry a man like that?

Because of my double memories, I worry that I have multiple personality syndrome. After all, I've seen the movies, like everyone else has. Haven't I? I have a lot of general knowledge of the world at large. I know about movie stars, presidents, 1776, state capitals. It only gets fuzzy the closer it comes to me.

"Am I crazy, Giles?" I ask him that question a lot. I asked again.

"You're being dramatic, Tennyson," he says.

"I am not being dramatic, I am scared to death. I just want to know. That's all. Where did Marissa come from? Why does she haunt me?"

"You're not crazy, you're just confused."

"Confused?"

Giles likes things that he can explain away. "There is something called a fugue state, where you lose time and memory, usually related to stress, and there are states called misidentification syndromes. In your case, if this is a type of fugue state, it could be related to the trauma you suffered in the accident."

"And voila—Marissa?"

"There is no Marissa." He graced me with a rare smile. "Don't worry, Tennyson, you're improving every day."

Or am I simply getting better at jumping through his hoops?

"Tell me, what do you remember about us?" It's his favorite quiz question.

"I don't know what I remember and what I've been told."

He doesn't like this answer. He can't assemble his Tennyson like a jigsaw puzzle, one piece at a time, even though he tries. Some of those pieces belong to Marissa and they just don't fit.

Dr. Embry stared at me. "You will. I promise."

Promise or threat?

ೞ

Giles Embry is the public face of the Campus. He looks good on film and on paper. He is the one who raises funds for all this important research. It's at those times, when he becomes animated by what he does and what he cares about, that I don't mind listening to him. He seems almost human.

Tennyson Claxton's memories, what I have of them, stop before he entered the picture. But if I really knew him, why did I love him? If I loved him, why don't I remember him? If I loved Giles once, shouldn't I be able to love him again?

To help me remember, Giles, or someone from his staff, has collected pictures, mementos, film, and news clippings of me into a digital scrapbook, a constant slide show and video collage. In the virtual reality lab, I am submerged in total immersion in this data stream. Screens in my sitting room and bedroom play this material continuously. Playing on my nerves. Images flicker on and off.

I call this onslaught *The Big Show of Tennyson O*. And much worse than the digitized clippings and photos are the interspersed home videos of Tennyson's dubious achievements, such as living to another birthday without being blackmailed, jailed, sued, or lying on a slab in the morgue. The family looks on with forced smiles. Then they look away.

My family. You may have heard of my family. My grandfather, Abercrombie Foxhall Claxton, was a senator for many years. Now, Giles says, he has "business interests." His pictures make him look very distinguished, both the Senator and his wife, Octavia Standish Claxton. My grandmother. Occasionally I hear the staff refer to me as "the heiress." I don't even know what that could mean. Except that I had a Porsche to wrap around a tree.

The star of this show looks a lot like me. Tennyson Olivia

Claxton, with her brown eyes and short dark hair. I can't avoid her. She smiles out of the videos and slide shows and the photos of her with Giles. They look like the perfect pair, a golden couple, in evening dress, at a picnic, at a gala, caught posing in a "candid" moment. There is even an oh-so-artistic black-and-white studio portrait of their profiles side by side. It's very big and hangs over the fireplace. It's embarrassing.

I've amused myself wondering whether the eyes in that portrait hide peepholes, the way portraits do in old movies. I wonder if I'll detect a pair of human eyes staring back at me. With all the cameras around here tracking me, there is no need for human eyes to watch me.

Worse than the portrait is a life-size marble bust of me with an expression as blank as a death mask. Apparently, I just couldn't get enough of me. It's a miracle I didn't bore myself to death. I must have bored everyone else. And yet there are times when I have a grim fascination with all this.

There are no mementos for Marissa Brookshire, no images, moving or still. But I can see her in my mind. She's the one I look for in the mirror, with her green eyes and sun-streaked hair, her big grin. Is Marissa merely a ghost in my mind? The fictitious woman with the simpler life, the ghost I'd rather be?

Every so often, when I smell coffee or a whiff of rain or spring air, I feel I'm on the edge of a real memory. I feel the anticipation that something will fall into place, and I will know without a doubt who I really am. I'll be able to pick up my keys and go home. I just don't know where home is right now.

But ah, Ulysses! Wert though given to know
My life is like a word I can't think of, right on the tip of my tongue.
What Fate yet dooms these still to undergo,
I almost catch it, but there it goes, flying away from me.
Thy heart might settle in this scene of ease,
I close my eyes and try to call it back, but it's gone.
And e'en these slighted charms might learn to please.
I am stuck here at the Campus. With Giles edging ever closer.

Chapter 3

THE CAMPUS WAS once a big Virginia horse farm. Giles says I should remember the area very well. I do, and I don't. On the outside, the public spaces look more like an exclusive private college than a costly, privately funded medical prison for brain-impaired problem people like me.

Near Middleburg, the Campus is just one turn off a narrow country road called the Snickersville Turnpike. Appropriately enough, so the Fates can snicker at me. I'd laugh myself, if I felt up to it.

The Campus is deceptively lovely. The sun casts spring-green shadows through the tall oak trees leafing out as the days grow longer. It's especially beautiful just before dusk, when the coral-colored flames of sunset lick the coming purple night. Sometimes I can pretend it's just one of the lovely antebellum estates on the Virginia landscape. I remember some of them. But not this one.

The purpose of the Campus is camouflaged by its facade. What were once horse stables and service buildings now serve as laboratories. Earthy aromas have been supplanted by the astringent smells of metal and meds.

Instead of the main offices and resident care facilities, I try to imagine parties in the three-story manor house. The brick is painted pale yellow, the trim is white, and the shutters on all the many windows are black. Giles allows me to walk around the large circle drive and down to the gardens, discreetly followed by his robotic aides, the Barnacle, and the ever-present cameras. But I'm not to go all the way down the half-mile lane that leads to the road. And freedom.

I can feel time pass. As I emerged from the pharmaceutical Fog I watched the magnolia trees explode and then lose their blossoms, followed by the dogwoods, which are now in full bloom. The white azaleas and the rhododendrons in their riot of pinks and lavenders have turned green.

Walking across the Campus to the Research Wing is like leaving one world and emerging in another, the way skyscrapers in the city burst from the edifices of old townhouses.

Someone wanted to preserve the presumed gentility of the past. But walls of glass and granite walkways have been added, beyond the old brick walls, down a sloping hill. It's as disorienting as the split hemispheres of my brain.

Inside the research laboratories, there is always a chill in the air and the quiet hum of machinery. There is also a state-of-the-art infirmary where I was housed when I was first brought here. I don't remember any of that. I've been told about it, the way a child is told about the hospital where she was born.

Everything in the Research Wing is as spare and antiseptic as Giles Embry.

The laboratories are where I undergo the virtual reality therapy and take endless tests, about what I remember and what I don't remember and what I should remember. They are mixed in with the more mundane tasks of recalling numbers, and words, and sequences of facts and dates. Dates no more personally meaningful to me than 1066 or 1492. It is an endless classroom from which I can never advance. Yet I think I loved school, once upon a time. Somewhere.

While there are various people who take turns testing me, Dr. Embry is the constant. My days feel busy, but Giles says I am more or less on Spring Break right now. I can look forward to more intensive sessions with him. Soon. Where can I disenroll?

Though it feels like I am the lone student in the glass-and-chrome Research Wing, there are others. A few days ago, I ran into an old woman preparing for a brain MRI. Eyeing the cylinder-shaped contraption, she confided in me, "I'm having my hair done today."

I hope she liked the way it turned out. As for me, I've never confused the testing lab for a beauty parlor, the machines for an old-fashioned hood dryer. But let her have her fantasy. Beats reality. Another time, just outside Giles's high-tech lair, I overheard two orderlies talking about me.

"She's the one, I'm telling you," the first one said.

I walked slowly, head down, hoping to be enlightened.

"No," the other one said. "Really?"

"Yeah, trust me. The Claxton chick on that video. You know, the sex tape? Big scandal."

Oh my God, a sex tape? That bit of information wasn't in *The Big Show of Tennyson O.* I was mortified. It couldn't be true.

"I don't know," the other said. "I mean, look at her. Tennyson Claxton's supposed to be a total babe. That one, she's a scarecrow."

Scarecrow? Me? I wouldn't know. I'm not interested in looking into mirrors anymore. I ran away, my face burning. Giles found me in the gardens and dragged me back to the lab without a word. I performed badly on the tests that followed.

C03

Faint screams occasionally come from behind locked doors. Mostly I hear the screams in the night, and once in a while when the sun is out. And one time while I was in the testing lab.

"Who was that, Giles?" I asked.

"One of the men," he answered. "A soldier."

"Is he trying to remember?"

"No. He's trying to forget. Concentrate, Tennyson."

I worry about the soldiers who scream in the night. They live on the other side of the glass-and-steel laboratories in their own glass-and-steel boxes. They do not mingle with the rest of us. But I have caught sight of them, hollow-eyed and tormented. According to Giles, they are capable of doing grave injury, to themselves and others. I am to stay away from them, as if they were time bombs.

After the tests, when I've had enough, I am returned to my suite. Sometimes I walk back, accompanied by an ever-present aide. On days when I am exhausted and my brain is tired, the Barnacle drives me back in a golf cart bearing a Campus logo.

If you saw my suite, you might think I was living in a very nice resort. My two rooms and a bath are decorated tastefully, if anonymously, in pale yellows and tans, with horse country prints on the walls. I don't hate it, but I know it's not to my taste. Whoever I am. My suite has a living room, bedroom, bath, and a kitchenette with a petite refrigerator that holds bottled water and yogurt. A few plates, dishes, and plastic forks. No sharp knives. Did I have a problem with sharp knives? Did I stab people? Was I a self-cutter? I've checked my body for scars, from the accident, from self-harm, from falling off a bike when I was a kid, from anything. Only my left arm is marked.

I heat tea in the microwave. My meals are generally delivered to the door and set up on a table in the sitting room. Recently Giles has been letting me go to the dining room in the main house, where I can eat with the other residents who have permission to walk the grounds.

As you can imagine, there is no sparkling conversation in either location. Are they all as drugged as I was? As depressed as I am now?

My days are filled with batteries of therapies to help me remember. In a simplistic way, I could say it's working. More and more vivid memories of Tennyson's childhood come bubbling up. Recollections of a mansion, manicured gardens in the summertime, parties, women wearing extravagant hats, talk of races and horses. I have mental pictures of private school uniforms and a gaggle of silky blond girls, with me, the dark-haired child, among them. Tennyson was never the outsider among all those blondes. Tennyson was the ringleader, the troublemaker, the alpha girl.

I have been taught the outline of my life. Tennyson's life.

For high school, having exhausted the patience of my by-then-divorced parents, I was sent to Foxcroft, the girls' boarding school in Middleburg, with its famously unheated dorms and riding lessons and glossy-haired students. The school was not far from the estate of my grandparents, the Senator and Mrs. Claxton. They still had some good will toward me when I was a child. Until inevitably, as I did with everyone but Dr. Giles Embry, I wore them out.

These memories crowd me and push thoughts of Marissa to the side. But I can't let Marissa go so easily, and she refuses to leave me. She sits on my shoulder, watching all this as if it were a foreign movie. Before I go to sleep at night, I return to her childhood, splashing in the cold seawater at some rocky beach. I think about her—me—following her grandfather, his gray hair covered by his navy blue sailor's cap, her little legs trying to match his long strides. He wasn't a senator, but he explained about shells and stars and tying a sailor's knots. And he knew a few magic tricks as well, the corny sleight-of-hand tricks I enjoyed so much.

"Look up, Marissa. See the Big Dipper? Follow those pointer stars. That's the North Star. You find that star, you'll find True North, and you will always know where you are."

These days I find myself looking up at night, searching for the North Star to know where I exist—beyond the Virginia countryside. But the nights here are cloudy. Like my brain.

Today I suddenly remembered one moment very clearly, and I couldn't wait to tell Dr. Embry, thinking he would be happy, though I really don't know why I try to please him. Still, I hold on to the hope that the sooner I remember things, the sooner I can leave.

I knocked on his adjoining door before entering. He looked up and arched his brow, waiting. A little surprised, but pleased. I rarely go into his office voluntarily. He gestured for me to enter.

"My grandmother painted murals! She wore her hair in a silver braid down her back," I told him. I could see her long, graceful fingers with faint blue veins dip the brush into the paint and onto the wall of the dining room. I could almost see her face, her smile. "She painted murals all over our dining room. She gave me my own set of watercolors and a large sheet of white butcher paper. I was hopeless at it, but she was a real artist."

"Your grandmother did no such thing." Giles sat back in his leather chair and stretched his arms. He considered for a moment. "Well, there are murals of country scenes in the hallway and the dining room at Foxgrove Manor. Of Williamsburg, I believe. Perhaps that's what you're remembering. Yes, of course. That's it, Foxgrove." He lowered his voice. "Your grandmother Octavia is not an artist. She is, however, quite taken with gardening. Perhaps you saw an artist working at the estate and fused the two. Or in school, where your teacher gave you paints. See how the memory can work? You conflate two disparate events and your mind tries to make the pieces fit. Two different jigsaw puzzles."

"Everyone has two sets of grandparents," I protested. "Maybe it was my other grandmother."

"Yes, everyone does. But Tennyson, your maternal grandmother died before you were born. She did not paint, to my knowledge. No one in your family was ever an artist."

Marissa. It was Marissa's memory, I realized, not Tennyson's. The murals I remembered were not colonial, not horses and fox hunts. They were of the sea and sailboats and islands and blue skies.

I felt as deflated as a punctured balloon. I looked out the window, at nothing I could remember.

"I'm tired, Giles. I'm going to lie down."

I wanted to remember Marissa's grandmother's murals in the quiet of my room. I urged the memory to come back to me. Yet, after Giles mentioned it, I could also describe the painted pictures of Williamsburg in Grandmother Octavia Claxton's front hallway, in soft greens and colonial red and blue.

"Yes, you should rest." Sometimes even Giles can tell when I've had enough.

He accompanied me to the relative safety of my bedroom, past the sitting room, his hand pressed against my back. He waited until I slipped my scuffed loafers off and settled back into my bed, scrunching the pillow under my head. I closed my eyes to shut him out.

I proceeded to worry, which I often do, about whether I have insurance to pay for all these treatments. They are radical and experimental and surely not on any HMO's list of approved therapies. I've gone through so much more than the usual annual physical exam and flu shot. Who is going to pay for all of it?

Giles thinks this is amusing. He tells me there is nothing to worry about. But worrying seems to be part of my ingrained nature. No one could afford this place on a teacher's salary.

A teacher's salary? Where did that come from? One of those pesky little implanted memories, or a real one? I hung on to it.

"Did I have a job?" I opened my eyes. He was still there.

"Only if you count shopping and partying." He almost smiled.

"But the money—"

"Tennyson Olivia Claxton will never have to worry about money," Giles assured me. "You never considered money before. Not once in your life. And you'll never need to."

"This kind of place could eat up a lot of money."

"You're an heiress. Do you realize what that means?"

"By definition, an heiress is rich. How rich? Mildly rich or stinking rich?"

I could hear my imaginary grandparents saying, "If we were rich, we could go to the circus." And I would answer, "If we were *stinking* rich, we'd *buy* the circus!" It was one of our jokes. To be stinking rich would solve all our problems. Now I wasn't so sure.

"Let's say you have nothing to worry about, except getting better. Get some rest, Tennyson."

I closed my eyes. He kissed my forehead and returned to his office, through the bedroom, through the sitting room and the connecting door, shutting it with a click.

The image of a woman flashed across my mind. I recognized her from a nightmare. I've had more than one. The woman looks like me, but she's cold and pale and stretched out on a long metal table. Her eyes are open, but she's not breathing. The woman haunts me, but I haven't told Giles about her. She comes from my dreams. Could she be a hallucination, a false recollection, a nightmare? Or a memory?

I slipped out of bed, over to the bookcase, and grabbed my

journal. The camera posted on the ceiling could see the back of the chintz-covered wing chair and a slice of the window. If Giles spied on me, he would only see the back of my head sitting in the chair. He would assume I was staring out the glass, watching the world go by. I could always tell Giles that I was reading. That would bore him.

I checked in with Ulysses before I started writing. He was never very cheerful.

Wretch that I am! What farther fates attend
This life of toils, and what my destined end?
Too well, alas! the island goddess knew
On the black sea what perils should ensue.

ↅ

The more I wake up out of my Fog and explore the Campus, the more I notice that everywhere I turn, I read the initials "C&B." A brass plaque mounted at the side of all the front doors proclaims, "The Hunt Country Campus. A Memory Project, Supported by the C&B Institute." The Campus's annual reports and journals scattered on coffee tables and side tables in the front lounge are written by, and furnished by, and funded by, the C&B Foundation or the C&B Corporation or the C&B Institute, a think tank headquartered in Washington, D.C.

"What does it stand for? C&B?" I asked Giles. I was on my way to the reading room in the main house where I find books and magazines to fill my mind with something other than myself.

"Checks and Balances, of course. The name was the Senator's, your grandfather's, idea." Giles was referring to former United States Senator Abercrombie Foxhall Claxton. "He is by far our biggest supporter, and the man behind all the C&B corporate entities." Giles often sounds like a press release.

"My grandfather pays for this place? Is that why I'm here?"

"As it happens he does, Tennyson, in part. But you're here because you need to be here."

He went on to explain that Senator Foxhall "Fox" Claxton and my alleged father, Porter Quantrell Claxton, sit on the boards of directors of all things C&B: the Foundation, the funding arm; the Corporation, a major defense contractor; and the Institute, which oversees research projects like the Campus.

Abercrombie Foxhall? Porter Quantrell?

More grandiose Southern names, as grand as Lee's generals.

The Claxtons have always taken a great interest in the work of the Campus, Giles said, and even more now that I am here. But I pointed out that they have not taken an interest in me. They do not visit me, or call me, or seem to know I even exist.

"You have to understand, Tennyson," Giles said. "We agreed it would be best for your recovery. Not to have any distractions."

"Not to have any visitors? Or friends? Do I even have any friends?" Despite the massive media displays in my room, there wasn't a single old-fashioned card or letter. If I had calls or texts or e-mails, I wouldn't know. I couldn't even remember a phone number.

"You have me."

"How comforting."

"You're very fragile," Giles said. "More than you realize. Other people would wear you out."

"You are wearing me out."

According to Giles, I have "fallen out" with all of my family at one time or another. Everyone—mother, father, grandparents, cousins, aunts and uncles. It's probably a blessing that I have no siblings to offend. I'm an only child. Only and lonely.

I thrummed my fingers on the table, which irritates him. "But wouldn't they help jog my memory, if I saw them? Even a bad memory would be better than nothing, Giles. That is, if I really am Tennyson."

Giles lifted his imperious eyebrows. "Maybe." His "maybe" gave me a little hope. "You are Tennyson, you know."

"But what if I really am Marissa?" I uttered the last sentence aloud.

"You are Tennyson Claxton! Not this imaginary character. I thought you'd stopped that nonsense." He was definitely annoyed this time. "Tennyson, you must face reality."

"Please, Giles! I am desperate to see someone. Anyone." Anyone who's not Giles and his tribe of institutional androids.

"Not if they will upset you. You remember the mirror episode?"

"I do remember my family," I protested. At least I remembered their pictures and what I'd been told about them. It felt like I remembered them.

But they might be very different from my sketchy memories, different from their photographs and videos in *The Big Show of*

Tennyson O. Still, it would be nice to be wanted, to be part of a family, to have visitors, someone to talk with other than Giles.

"Do they all hate me?"

"Of course not. They're your family. I think you do remember them. Don't you?"

And even as my Fog seems to be lifting, I find myself saying the things Giles wants to hear. Even as I hear myself say these things, I'm of two different minds. I can prattle back the approved script. I wasn't sure if that was progress or not.

"Of course I remember them," I lied.

Chapter 4

THE NIGHTMARE CAME again last night.

The cast-off thoughts of an incubus haunt me and press me and smother me while I sleep. Recurring and mutating, but always returning to taunt me. It calls me out of the Fog.

In the dream, I am running. It is very dark and the only thing I can see is the dim outline of a house. It resembles the home I lived in growing up. The home of one of me, anyway. It's a little two-story white Victorian cottage with green shutters and trim, only three feet tall. There are lights on inside and the tiny door swings open for me. With every step I take I shrink, until I am almost small enough to fit through the front door. Something is hard upon my heels. Someone calls my name. This time, I can't quite remember if the voice calls for Tennyson or Marissa. I'm almost home, almost up the front steps and through the door. But I never quite make it.

My face was wet with tears when I woke up, my heart beating like a drum in my chest, a sour taste in my mouth. Despite feeling like someone was in the room watching me, I was alone. I was conscious of the ever-present camera, but it was dark. I put my hand on my chest and willed my heart to slow down.

The first time I had the dream, weeks ago now, Giles was there beside me, suddenly turning on the bedside lamp. The glare hurt my eyes. "Tennyson, are you all right?" He reached for my wrist to take my pulse. He wore a T-shirt and silk boxer shorts. "What is it?"

"Nothing. I'm fine." I gathered my wits, wiped my face, cleared my throat. "Why are you here?" The clock said two. I had blotted out the memory of him beside me. Or incorporated him into the nightmare.

"You screamed. You wouldn't want me to ignore that, would you, Tennyson?" His hand lingered on my shoulder and I tried to shrug it off. He hugged me close, then after a moment, took my pulse again.

"Please go away, Giles." Even my dreams weren't safe from him. "You're spying on me."

He smoothed back my hair and smiled. "Tell me about the nightmare. I can take it away."

I didn't want him to do that. It was my nightmare, not his. Mine. I have always found meaning in my dreams. I think I have, anyway.

But that first time, I described the dream and the dollhouse. Now, Giles makes a habit of working late, waiting for my distress, waiting for the nightmares, even after he agreed to leave me alone at night, after I made the sex stop. And now, I cannot sleep at all until I hear his car pull away.

"It was an anxiety dream, Tennyson. After all you've been through, it isn't surprising." He sat on the bed and took my wrist, placing his finger on my pulse. "In the dream, is someone following you?"

There was a feeling of being chased, but no one else was in my dream. Not until Giles mentioned it. Now I questioned myself.

"I don't know." Possibly it was *him.*

"What does the shrinking house look like?"

Like a dollhouse. Any dollhouse. I shielded my eyes with my hand. "It's a toy, Giles. It doesn't mean anything."

"Let me give you something to ease your anxiety. To help you sleep. Don't worry, it's not addictive." He practically purred, using his soothing voice. The hair on the back of my neck stood at attention.

"No." As hard as the dream was, I wanted to will it away naturally. Not with a pill, suppressing it into some dark chamber where it would continue to lie in wait for me. I willed Giles away as well, but I have found that doesn't work.

"When you wake up screaming, it means something. What are you remembering?"

"No meds, Giles!" I needed every ounce of consciousness, particularly now, now that I'm free from the big slumber, the coma, the medicated Fog where I was little more than a zombie. I tried not to think of him as a pill-pushing thug in a lab coat. Maybe he meant well. I smiled. A small smile was all I could manage. "It's nice of you to offer me something." To drug me insensible so I won't bother you. "But I don't want to wake up feeling groggy." Or to wake up and find you next to me in my bed.

"Just for tonight, take a pill," Giles persisted. "Please. It's very mild stuff. I'm your doctor, you know." He rolled out one small white pill from a prescription bottle.

The only thing worse than my nightmare was Giles's attention to it. I'd say anything to get him to leave me alone.

"Okay, whatever you want."

I swallowed. He was satisfied. The magic trick came in handy. The pill rested first between my fingers, then under my pillow.

"I'll be right back." He patted the queen-size bed. He left, no doubt to make some digital notes about my nightmare.

I reconsidered and took the pill. I decided I'd rather be senseless when Giles returned.

Since the first night terror, I am afraid to write in my journal while he's on the premises. I don't want him to discover me defacing *The Odyssey.*

Giles always checks on me before he leaves the office. He's very late some nights. The click of the doorknob alerts me. If I were more egotistical, I'd assume it was because he was crazy about me. Mad with lust. But he is not in love with me, no matter what he says. Even without a memory, or too many memories, I know these things.

When I hear him leave through the front entrance of his office, I creep quietly to the window to watch his BMW pull away. I see the lights of his car bounce off the trees, down the path to the road. Once the lights are gone and the darkness returns, I can breathe again.

Since the first nightmare, I am learning not to scream. Before I go to sleep, I concentrate on not making a sound. Recently, the warning has come in my dream, while I'm still asleep.

"Not a sound, not a single sound. He'll hear you."

Hid in dry foliage thus Ulysses lies,
Now when I have the nightmare, I don't make any noise.
Till Pallas poured soft slumbers on his eyes;
I have awakened with my hand over my mouth,
And golden dreams (the gift of sweet repose)
Screaming silently until my pulse slows down.
Lull'd all his cares, and banish'd all his woes.
I write in my between-the-lines journal.

I have a recurring nightmare, and I have a recurring question.
If I'm not Marissa, why am I having her dreams?

જ

"What do you remember about the first time you met Dr. Embry?" Dr. Chu asked me this morning. He's one of the psychotherapists on staff. He smiles, trying to put me at ease. His dark almond eyes look kind, but I can never read them. I see him daily during this break in my more intense treatments.

People here have trouble with anger and depression. Not just me, I am told. When you lose pieces of yourself, anger comes with the territory. Anger turned inward becomes depression, they tell me. Depression without release becomes numbness and blankness.

This morning I felt particularly blank. I shook my head.

"Nothing." I didn't mention the nightmare, not wanting to hear the questions I could script myself: What do you think it means? Where does the dollhouse come from? Who or what is chasing you? Why do you think you are *shrinking*?

I usually see Dr. Chu in the morning after Giles arrives for the day. The doctors believe I'm fresher in the morning after a good night's sleep. If they only knew what I battle during the small dark hours.

"Take your time. Deep breaths." First, we practice relaxation exercises. Dr. Chu says it is especially hard to remember things when you're under stress. How would he know? If he's stressed, he hides it well. He has a round, guileless face, seemingly as blank as the sun. He dresses in dark slacks and pale shirts and matching ties. His blue lab coat hangs on the back of his office door.

Dr. Chu has a soothing presence. He is always calm. A picture on his desk shows a happy young couple. Dr. and Mrs. Chu on their wedding day. He has a life outside the Campus, with a smiling wife, who is pretty and petite with shiny black hair. He never discusses his outside life, but I imagine it is happy. He's unfailingly in a good mood.

"How is your tea?" he inquired.

"Tasty. I like cinnamon." During my sessions, we always drink herbal tea with a bit of honey. I wonder if he has to drink tea with everyone he talks with, or just me. Because that could get old for him, I think. Nevertheless, I appreciate the effort.

"How is the arm coming along?"

"Aches a bit." I stretched my fingers and bent my wrist as far as it would go to feel the twinge. I have physical therapy for my left arm and wrist three times a week, followed by a workout in the fitness room to work on regaining my core strength. There is no pool, which is a shame. I would love to swim. Swimming would help my arm. And my head.

I'm slowly regaining my full range of motion in my left arm, or so the physical therapists say. It doesn't work that well yet, but at least it's still attached. That's what I say.

The compound fracture is another souvenir of my reckless night wrecking my Porsche. It was a bad break and it still aches, particularly if it's going to rain. Giles tells me how lucky I am that I didn't break my right arm, being right-handed. I'm so lucky I should buy a lottery ticket. Most of the time I'm glad I don't remember the accident or anything about that night.

Dr. Chu took my arm and turned it over, gently running his finger over the thin red scars on either side where the surgeons braced it with titanium and pieced it back together.

"It looks good. Keep working on it."

I nod. He checks his notes. After my talk with Dr. Chu, I will be escorted to the glass-and-steel building behind the stable's false front. I will take lots of tests. Today the tests are to see if my short-term memory is working.

The Phoenix Phase lab assistants try to figure out how they might fiddle around to plug up the holes in my long-term memory. The doctors talk about fugue states, and why I might want to block my memories. Whether I'm Tennyson or Marissa, I want my memories back. I don't want to share them with the world.

The most interesting tests involve the brain scans, where I can see different parts of my brain light up like a pinball game depending on the thoughts I think, the tasks I perform, the images I'm shown. My brain is an explosion of lights and color. The only thing that's missing is a score card—one that I can see, anyway. Although someone is probably busy keying away, sending the results to Giles.

"What's the point of all this?" I asked Giles one time, Giles who knows all and sees all.

"In layman's terms, we want to see if memories can travel to other regions in the brain," he said. "If you damage a part of the brain that holds a specific memory, can you learn to remember that same thing in another part of the brain?"

"And the verdict?"

"Jury's still out. But we're seeing some promising developments. For example...."

"Promising" is pretty much the last word I remember from this speech, before he started talking about algorithms and logarithms.

I got music, I got rhythm. Who taught me that song?

Once a week, I meet with my entire treatment team, the various doctors and assistants, including Dr. Chu, Giles, his research assistants, the physical therapists, the fitness director, and a few others. And just to kick it up a notch, there's always a nurse or a doctor from some other team at the Campus, someone who might notice something about me from an outsider's point of view. It's exhausting.

If I have any strength left, there are arts-and-crafts busy-work activities in the dayroom or on my own, but in my free time, I prefer to return to my rooms to read or sleep.

"Better now?" Dr. Chu interrupted my thoughts. "The first night you met Dr. Embry?"

"Right. It was in the spring. Two years ago. At night, when the magnolias were in bloom. The scent of flowers was heavy. It was just before a rainstorm." I can imagine the scene, because Giles has described it to me. But imagining it is not the same as really remembering it. Is it real life, or a movie I've watched a hundred times?

"What color are your eyes?" Dr. Chu likes to throw that one in.

I hesitate less and less. "They are—brown."

"That's fine. Work hard, Tennyson," Dr. Chu said. "After all, what are we without our memories? An empty box."

"Maybe Tennyson Claxton is an empty box," I said. "Once you get past the pretty wrapping paper."

"Nobody is an empty box," he assured me. "Try to relax. Do something you enjoy. What do you enjoy?"

I have no idea. "I like to read," I said. I didn't mention that I also like to write between the lines.

Oh indolent! to waste thy hours away!
Of course I'm indolent. I'm a pampered prisoner.
And sleep'st thou careless of the bridal day?
Bridal day? With Giles? Never!
Thy spousal ornament neglected lies;
"Spousal ornament"? His ring? Or his lies?
Arise, prepare the bridal train, arise!
Any train but that one.

This passage summed up everything I was trying to avoid.

Chapter 5

"I HAVE A surprise for you, Tennyson."

Giles blocked the afternoon sun, throwing a long shadow over the carpet and the Charlotte Brontë tale I was reading.

"Did you hear me, Tennyson?"

Tennyson, Tennyson, Tennyson! Please call me something, anything else! He stood in the doorway until I acknowledged him. I'm not deaf. I was only trying to ignore him.

"Yes, Giles, I heard you, Giles." Blocking the sun with my hands, I looked up.

The thought struck me again that if I really were his fiancée, if we were really engaged to be married, wouldn't he have some term of endearment for me? "Honey" or "dear" or "darling" or "sweetheart"? Or even "Tenn" or "brown eyes" or "hey baby"? No, certainly not something like "baby." He's not that kind of guy. But no, I am always Tennyson, sometimes Tennyson Olivia, or even Tennyson Olivia Claxton, as if I'm in trouble with the principal.

Perhaps Giles is incapable of giving anyone a pet name. He is not a Southerner. He comes from Ohio, he says, near the icy waters of Lake Erie.

I imagine the kind of nickname a neuroscientist would embrace. Something like "my sweet synapse" or "my little gamma ray." Giles lacks that kind of imagination. I mentally begged him to go back to work.

I returned to my *Jane Eyre*. I knew the plucky orphan and governess would eventually conquer her problems and deal with the madwoman in the attic. I was less sure about me. Perhaps I was the madwoman in the attic.

"Don't you want to know what it is, Tennyson?" Giles took the novel out of my hands. I glared up at him.

"A set of keys?"

I've been wondering about my keys. Door keys, house keys, car keys, gym locker keys. I must have had a set of keys. Where were they? Were they lost in the accident? What would they unlock?

Suddenly and fiercely I wanted my own set of keys, as if they would unlock my memory. But if I had the keys, where they would take me? Could I manage on my own? I would need money, a bank account, a place to stay, a job. A map, a plan, an identity. Keys! I would not need Giles.

"I'm serious, Tennyson." He waited. An expert at waiting. I gave him that.

"Tell me when I can have my keys. And for that matter, my driver's license, my Social Security number, my credit cards, my passport, my ID." Wait, I would have to settle on an identity in order to have an identification! I felt myself deflating.

"Your dollhouse is here." Giles looked pleased. He took my hand and pulled me to my feet.

"Dollhouse? My dollhouse? Does it have a key?"

I shook my hand loose from his. He looked puzzled.

"Perhaps a key to your dreams. Or your nightmares."

Giles insisted on taking things so literally. He made me feel so silly, so small, so like a mouse, like a doll in a dollhouse. I wish he'd never found out about the nightmares. I wish he'd never been in my bed and witnessed my vulnerability.

"I don't have a dollhouse." I wanted to wipe the know-it-all expression off his face. "You bought me a dollhouse?"

"It's your old dollhouse. I didn't think it was possible that it was still around, but I asked and there it was, in storage in your grandparents' attic."

"My grandparents?" For a moment my heart fluttered. I gazed out the window. "Are they here?"

"No. The dollhouse is here."

Hopes defeated. "If they live nearby, why don't they come visit me, Giles?"

"They will. Eventually." When I've learned the right things, say the right things, and jump through Giles's Pavlovian hoops. "Tennyson, for now, it's important to keep your focus here, not to worry about relatives with whom you don't get along."

"Yes. Interfering with this interminable boredom would be a real waste of time." He acted as if he hadn't heard me. Sarcasm isn't Giles's forte.

"Octavia kept it for you all these years, hoping to give it to her grandchildren someday. Our children."

I almost gagged. He didn't notice. "My dollhouse?"

"She sent it over, and I've had it set up in the conservatory."

"Octavia?"

"Your grandmother, you remember, Tennyson. Octavia Marie Standish Claxton."

"Yes. Octavia." I tried to picture the woman. I was sure I'd seen hundreds of pictures of her. But why should I try to see her if she wouldn't come to see me? "Do I call her Grandma? Or Grandmother, or Nana?"

"No. You had some rather unflattering names for her. Come along."

Giles took my hand again, leading me out the door, along the gravel path, and through the side door of the spacious, circular, glass-topped conservatory attached to the rear of the great house. Leafy plants and trees paraded around the circumference of the room. In the middle of the room, perched on a round mahogany table, was the thing Giles called a "dollhouse."

It was immense. The tiny dollhouse of my nightmares was a birdhouse, a garden shed, an outbuilding, compared to this grand architectural monument. The two had nothing in common.

"It's a castle," I said, feeling stupid. It looked like Cinderella's palace, or maybe more appropriately, Mad Ludwig's Castle, full of turrets and swirls and Bavarian excess. It was hardly a plaything. "It belongs in a museum. It's as big as a museum."

"Octavia said it's based on one in a museum in Chicago," he said proudly.

"Colleen Moore's dollhouse." I stared at the thing. Who was Colleen Moore? I wondered. An early twentieth-century actress. I gave myself a gold star.

"Yes, that's right." He was pleased. I had answered correctly. "Though it's not quite as big as the original."

It must have taken hours, if not days, to move it and set the thing up here. It probably was shipped over in an armored truck.

"I've seen it." Of course I meant at the Museum of Science and Industry, behind the protective velvet ropes. With my mother. But when was I in Chicago? How old could I have been?

"That's right." He smiled at me. "Your grandparents commissioned this especially for you when you were a little girl. I'm delighted you remember it."

He didn't see the incredulous face I made, because he turned away and pressed a button on the base of the platform. A motor whirred. The front wall opened to reveal the rooms inside. Each room with its precise tiny furnishings was decorated with scenes from a different fairy tale, with princesses and glass slippers and dwarfs and evil queens.

"What kind of child would have a thing like this?"

"A Claxton, of course," he answered. "Tennyson Claxton."

"An heiress?"

"That's right," Giles agreed. Only an heiress would have a doll castle suitable for a princess, not a mere dollhouse. I looked for the dolls that lived in the castle, the mother, the father, the children. But all I found were Goldilocks and the Three Bears, Snow White and the Seven Dwarfs, and Sleeping Beauty and her Prince. Each figure was an impeccably crafted miniature work of art. I must have frowned as I tried to remember the dolls that were in the little dollhouse in my nightmare.

"What's wrong?" Giles was fiddling with the switches, turning lights on and off.

"There's no family of dolls," I said. "There usually are."

"Don't be so prosaic, Tennyson." He stopped fiddling with switches and stared at me. "These are princesses. Suitable for you. A princess in your own right."

"Ridiculous. Insanely extravagant. This could not be meant for a child."

He put his arm around me. Ownership, not affection.

"Nothing but the best for Tennyson Olivia."

Giles pressed another button and another dollhouse wall slid smoothly aside. He was rapt with fascination.

Outside the conservatory window something moved and my shoulder twitched. I lost interest in my grandmother's miniature marvel. Giles's lackey, Roy Barnaker the Barnacle, was out there.

"Who is Roy Barnaker, Giles? Exactly who?" I pointed to the man in the bushes.

"Roy?" Giles tore himself away from the dollhouse. "You know. Roy is one of my assistants. He's a valued employee."

"Like Jordana Morgan?" Jordana was the research assistant who flirted with Giles when she didn't think I was paying attention.

Giles straightened up and looked at me. "Not at all. They have very different duties."

"I don't like him." Roy stared at us as if he knew he was being discussed. His eyes never blinked. He reminded me of a lizard, darting out from under a bush when you least expect it. "He's always there, gawking at me."

"He's keeping an eye on you for me. He's one small part of your support system. I trust Roy with your life."

"Is he a doctor?" Doctor Death, I wanted to say, but didn't.

"No." Giles didn't elaborate. He nodded to Roy through the window, exchanging some silent communication.

"I'm not asking for his whole résumé, Giles, I just want to know why that barnacle is always lurking around."

"And I have told you." He left my side and picked up a miniature troll from the Three Billy Goats Gruff room. I took the small figure from him.

"Why do I need him? What do you think I'm going to do, Giles? Run away? I have no place to go and no way of getting there."

"You must have confidence in Roy. And me, Tennyson." Giles moved closer and lowered his voice. "Always trust me."

I dodged away from his embrace. How soon could I escape the Campus and Giles Embry and the cameras and Creepy Roy Barnaker? Did I have a cell phone? Someone I could call for help? One friend in the entire world? A wave of despair nearly bowled me over.

"A bodyguard is a reality for people like you, Tennyson. Consider him part of your security team."

"I don't feel secure, and I'll never trust him." Or you, I added silently.

Giles attempted an approximation of human empathy and pulled me close. I had gotten used to him doing that. I didn't object.

"You have me, Tennyson. There is nothing to worry about. And you're making progress, real progress. You will be able to leave the Campus someday."

"When?"

"In the meantime, please put up with Roy, to humor me."

Giles patted me on the back and returned to the improbable dollhouse. I couldn't blame him. It was far more amusing than I was. Roy was still outside, hovering. Every time I walked across the grass, his shadow darkened my path. Often, he'd be sneaking a cigarette. He'd offered me one yesterday as I walked by.

"I don't smoke." I loathe the smell of it, the stupidity of it, the expense of it. "Did Tennyson smoke?" I asked him.

"Maybe you just don't remember, Ms. Claxton. Maybe you smoked once." He was as good as Giles at not saying things.

I examined my fingers. No telltale nicotine stains lingered from the past, from before the accident. "I've never smoked."

"Maybe you quit," he said, squinting through the toxic smoke.

It's hard enough having Giles know things about me I don't remember, but unthinkable that Creepy Roy also knows. Things he hasn't read in the tabloids. Something awful.

"Did you know me before I came to the Campus, Roy?"

"Unlikely we would run in the same circles, don't you think?"

"How long have you worked with Giles?"

"A while." He inhaled deeply. "A good while."

"Where did you work before?"

"Around." He exhaled. "Here and there."

"Did you know me before?" I repeated. "Before the accident?"

"I heard about you. I read about you." He looked at me for a few seconds, before tossing the cigarette. He ground the butt into the grass. "You're famous."

"How'd you meet Giles?"

"Don't recall. You'd have to ask him…"

I blinked at this remembered conversation. Roy was still outside, waiting for an order from Giles.

"I know you must remember your amazing dollhouse, Tennyson." Giles turned me back to the castle. "No little girl could forget this. Why did it frighten you?"

That thing wasn't my dollhouse. It didn't figure in my nightmares. It frightened me because it had nothing to do with me. And yet somehow it did.

"It's not a dollhouse." I smiled. "It's a palace for a princess. I'm not a little girl and I'm no princess."

"Sure you are." He pulled a picture from an envelope, an eight-by-ten color photograph. "Maybe you remember this."

It was a picture of me as a little girl, one that wasn't in *The Big Show of Tennyson O.* I was seven or eight, dressed in pink ruffles and surrounded by a gaggle of girls just like me. I held the tiny princess dolls in both hands, a victorious grin on my face. Looming over me was the miniature castle, the capital city of my little world, the world I ruled. I stared hard. The picture clearly showed my eyes were brown.

"Well?" Giles persisted.

The photograph wasn't familiar, but I could certainly imagine the scene, the dress, the ice cream and cake. It came to life.

"Maybe. Maybe I do. Yes."

ଔ

When I went to bed that night, I found the possibility of that grandiose toy castle with its dragons and moats haunting my dreams, more frightening than the shadowy dollhouse, the one I could never quite reach. I didn't relish the thought of a tiny troll running after me. Trying to remember more about the castle and the birthday party in the picture kept me awake half the night, as did the light that leaked from the other side of the duplex.

Giles finally left and started his BMW. I slipped into the gap between my bed and the wall and began to write again between the lines.

> **Amid these joys, why seeks thy mind to know**
> If I don't know who I am, I'm no one.
> **The unhappy series of a wanderer's woe?**
> I'd trade this prisoner's woe for a wanderer's.
> **Remembrance sad, whose image to review,**
> Am I the brown-eyed girl in that old photograph?
> **Alas! must open all my wounds anew!**
> I seem to remember her. And then I don't.
> **And oh, what first, what last, shall I relate,**
> Every day and night another nightmare.
> **Of woes unnumber'd sent by Heaven and Fate?**
> I wonder. Is this my fate, or my own fault?

After all my agonizing, I had no dreams. I'd worried myself out.

Chapter 6

"TENNYSON, WHY AREN'T you wearing your ring?"

It was Giles the Interrogator, always looking so bright and cheery in the morning, filling his cup with inky coffee. He never battled sleep demons. I had deep shadows beneath my eyes. I hoped my glare in his direction was as dark as those shadows.

I was sick of staying in my suite, sick of therapies and tests, and I was itching for freedom. I settled for visiting the dining room before the rest of my day began and pouring a cup of coffee for myself at the sideboard. I was followed inevitably by Creepy Roy. I wondered if he ever took time off. Did he ever go home? Sleep? There were others who always seemed to be wherever I was, but he bothered me the most. He was the one I remembered.

The dining room was an elegant remnant of the original estate, with polished wood floors and generous bay windows beneath mullioned windows. Tables and chairs were set up in geometric order. It may have been a ballroom when the house was private. Unfortunately, it wasn't large enough to escape Giles.

The nicest thing about the community dining room was that so few of the residents recalled the notorious Tennyson Claxton, because of their own memory disorders. Only the staff knew. Giles, digital toys in hand, motioned for me to join him. I took my time adding cream and sugar to my cup before trudging over to his table. Ringless.

"The ring, Tennyson?" He lifted my bare hand and let it drop.

The ring, always the ring. The giant pink gumball of a ring I was not wearing was supposed to signify my engagement to him. If it was real, which I can hardly believe, I don't want to know how much it cost. No, wait, I do. It looked like something a child picked out of a gumball machine. The central rose-colored diamond was at least five carats and quite absurdly gaudy, surrounded by white diamonds. It flashed like a mirror ball in a disco. The ring was on my hand when I woke up this morning. It startled me and I took it off and tucked it away in the underwear drawer. Did I really pick out this preposterous ring? Could I ever possibly have wanted such an engagement token?

"It doesn't look good on me." Mine were not elegant hands, not the hands of a pampered princess. My nails were jagged, my fingers had writing calluses, and my cuticles were dry and cracked. The gaudy jewel didn't go with my everyday outfit of pants and polo shirts. It didn't go with me, period.

Giles picked up my hand and examined it again.

"We'll have to do something about that," he said. "I want you to wear the ring, Tennyson. Our ring. You wouldn't want to lose it."

Not true. I would like to lose it, along with all my other baggage, like Dr. Giles Embry.

"I'll wear it when I remember you." I smiled and Giles glared back. He was about to say something, but he didn't.

Giles is a puzzle to solve. I have started studying him the way he studies me. I toyed with the idea of following him with an actual notepad in my hands and jotting down my observations. If I could find an actual notepad in this digital fortress. He wouldn't appreciate the irony. Giles is not good with irony. He might suspect, however, if he was very attentive, that I was mocking him.

I've been increasingly curious about what I could have seen in Dr. Embry. Beyond his conventional good looks, his brilliant reputation, and his well-placed social connections. In theory, he was quite a catch. In practice, he was— What was he? The catcher. I'm starting to think I'm the catch.

It bothers me that Giles knows so much more about me than I do myself. What if I am crazy, and I don't have a life to go back to? What if I never truly remember who I am? What if I never leave the Campus? My fears mount like unpaid bills. But my worst fear comes in the middle of the night before I surrender to sleep, and my nightmares.

My fear is that I might never know who the right me is: Tennyson or Marissa? Or someone else entirely?

"Tennyson, you've progressed a great deal. I think it's time we go away for the weekend and get to know each other again." Giles again, staring at me over his coffee. "You'll wear the ring. For me. Won't you?"

Go away? It was all I wanted. With Giles? Unthinkable.

I picked up my cup and wandered over to the window, staring through the diamond-shaped panes. It was raining, a soft rain on a gray day, making the spring leaves even brighter and greener in contrast, and more welcoming. I wanted to go outside and get soaked to the skin. I wanted to wash away the Campus, and Giles. He followed me.

"About the weekend," he said again into my ear.

Leaving for the weekend and not coming back was my recurring fantasy. I just didn't want to leave with my jailor.

Giles, of course, was talking about sex, which I was now denying him. Sex in the Blue Ridge Mountains, all alone with Giles. My nightmares would be complete.

"I don't want to sleep with you," I said very slowly. I sipped my coffee.

"That's a ridiculous thing to say." He turned me around to look at him.

"Isn't that what you mean? Isn't that what you want from me?"

He reached out and rubbed my shoulder. "It is only natural for us to sleep together. We've been a couple for years now. We are engaged, Tennyson."

"Not if I don't remember it."

I watched his eyes. Giles may have been made of ice, but I could see his patience was running short.

"Who knows what memories it would bring back? You want that, don't you?" Giles dropped his voice and actually sounded wistful. Or an artful semblance of wistful. "We used to have so much fun together, Tennyson."

"Did we?" I almost believed him. "Are you in love with me, Giles?" I wanted to say, Are you in love with Tennyson?

"That's a silly question." The curtain that seemed to open for just a moment closed again. He was suddenly interested in his bleeping iPhone.

"Maybe so, but you're not answering my question. If everything I say is silly, why on earth would you want me? It's obvious that I annoy you."

"Yes, Tennyson. We are in love. You don't annoy me." He said it to the phone, not to me. He might have been in love with his phone for all I knew. "You're just confused," he added, another mantra of his.

"I'm confused again?" See how he turned that one around? It's always the woman's fault, isn't it? Always my fault.

"We must get back to normalcy in our relationship, Tennyson. It will be good for you, for both of us. This is one way of doing it."

"Normalcy, Giles? How dare you." I paused and took a breath, gathering steam, letting it build. *Let it blow*, I thought. Why the hell not?

"I'm living in your laboratory like a lab animal! I don't remember knowing you or having a relationship with you. I can't remember my recent life. My family hates me. I have no friends. The rest of it is smoke. What memories I do have are of two people. Two different women. Both of them me. Not you. And my eyes have changed color. I'm probably insane. How's that for normalcy?"

He rocked back on his heels. "Your eyes— Your eyes have always been brown. You are one woman, with some false memories. You're— You're upset."

"And the point goes to Dr. Giles Embry. Yes, I'm upset! Damn you and damn this place, and damn my missing memories. To hell with all of you!"

He smiled. Oddly, he seemed pleased.

"Now that sounds like the old Tennyson. You want to get well, and I want to help." He reached for my shoulders again and I moved away. "Let me help you. You never were cold, Tennyson. Not to me."

"First I'm confused. Now I'm cold? For withholding sex from a stranger? Another complaint. Let me notify my complaint department."

He leaned in close, brushing his lips against my hair. He didn't worry about the residents seeing us. Most of them would never remember.

"What memories we could summon. Together. Away from here. There is something to muscle memory, after all." I guess this passed for sexy talk with Giles. I had the feeling I've heard a lot of crazy lines in my time. No proof, of course. He tried his dazzling smile on me too, a rare event.

"Why do you bother with me, Giles?"

"We're engaged," he explained for the hundredth time, as if I were again the dim student somehow wrongly admitted into an advanced course of study, Engagement 401.

"Why did you fall in love with me?" I really did want to know.

A sort of grin played around his mouth. "So many reasons."

"Was it the money?"

The heiress label was at odds with my perception of myself, yet it seemed to have an effect on everyone else. I don't feel connected to money, but money is the prime motivator, the love of which is the root of all evil, and money seems to be connected to me.

"Aside from the money, Tennyson," Giles said, at least admitting money was part of the equation. "There was always something about you I found attractive, compelling. We understood each other."

"We don't understand each other now."

"More than you think. We go back a long way."

I snorted. Great. He loves me because we're old pals and I'm a rich girl. Not even the quest for sex could pry an earnest endearment from Giles Embry's lips. Not "Tennyson, my love," "my life," or "my dearest," or even "sugar." But to be honest, sugar would never describe me.

He tried again. "I thought you wanted to get on with your life."

"It's all I want."

"Our relationship is central to your life, Tennyson. My life. We are going to be married. People who are going to be married are intimate. They have sex. They sleep together." Straightforward. Clinical. That's Giles.

Trapped. That's me. I did not want to think of Giles and sex together in the same sentence, let alone the same bed. It depressed me. I didn't love this man, but I hoped that I had loved *someone*, sometime, somewhere, deeply, wildly, passionately. Recklessly. I wish I could remember who he was. It makes me sad that whoever he was, he wasn't around to save me from Giles Embry. And worse, that I couldn't save myself.

"When can I leave the Campus?"

"This weekend. With me."

"On my own. Forever." I'd give him the pink gumball ring as a memento.

"When you can function in the outside world."

"But there must be some other place I can go. Away from this rarefied bubble. This dollhouse."

"Your family wants you here."

"Locked up? Like a prisoner? I don't even believe I have a family. Convince me! If I really have a family, they can't stand to even visit me. I realize the accident was reckless and stupid and my own fault. I've been kicked out of schools, hooked on drugs, dragged through the media. Apparently I'm so terrible that my family prefers to have me jailed inside these locked gates than unleashed upon the streets."

He was silent for a moment.

"Perhaps we could arrange a visit from one of them," he said.

He tapped something into his phone, a note that might have had nothing to do with me. It could have been to remind himself to send his shirts to the laundry. A note to order supplies for the lab. Or a text to someone. And then another one.

I refused to look at him anymore. I stared through the raindrops spotting the window. Jordana Morgan, Giles's assistant and chief sycophant, sprinted up the walk without an umbrella, holding her tablet to her chest, taking care that it wouldn't get wet. She glanced up at the window and saw me, or perhaps she saw Giles. He was the one on whom her gaze always landed. She dismissed me with a look. Her focus remained on him.

Jordana had perfected the haughty librarian look some men find so attractive. Her dark silky hair was pulled into a tight ponytail and her mocha-brown eyes were serious behind the ugly black-framed glasses, which counterbalanced her fine even features. She was tall and slender, and I've seen Giles smile at her. A warm inviting smile, unlike all the cool, gratuitous smiles he throws my way.

He waved her in, happy for a distraction. I couldn't gracefully leave, however, before Jordana said hello. She nodded to me and sat down at the nearest table. Giles took the chair next to her while I remained standing. I didn't care for the way the two of them silently conferred, heads nodding toward each other, appraising me in unison. This bug was under the microscope again.

"I'm leaving so you two can conspire," I announced.

"You don't have to go, Tennyson. I just have reports for Dr. Embry," she said.

"Thank you, Ms. Morgan." He reached for the tablet she offered. "I'm sure this can wait."

I wondered why they tried so hard to make me think they had a formal last-name-only relationship.

"Now, what are you two up to?" Jordana asked, oh so casually.

I heard a thousand questions every day. I was learning to answer only the ones I wanted to answer. I ignored her, but Giles was happy to oblige.

"We're discussing our plans to go away together for the weekend." He smiled again. For whose benefit, I didn't know.

"Oh. How nice," Jordana managed to say. Did she bristle? Flash an annoyed grimace at Giles? That was interesting. My memory may have been shot to ribbons, but my female radar was working.

"We're not going away," I said. "I'm not ready."

"You're not wearing your ring." Jordana stared at my hands. Her nails were perfectly groomed, with a coat of pale lavender polish to match her lavender lab coat. My ridiculous ring would look better on her finger than mine. But why was she so interested in my ring anyway?

"No, I'm not." I tucked my hands behind me.

"She will wear it," Giles said. "When we go away."

"You know, Giles, ring or no ring, other men might ask for a date before presuming further intimacies." I slammed my cup down on the table.

"Tennyson," Giles began, then stopped, frozen by the look on my face. "Do you mean you *want* to go on a date?"

This man was supposed to be a genius. "Even that would be torture," I said.

Giles doesn't behave at all like a man in love or lust, not even a cold fish of a scientist. Even if he and I had advanced to the stage where we took each other for granted, he could have pretended a show of seduction for a woman who didn't remember.

At the same time, I wondered why I was so hung up on this. There was abundant evidence of my promiscuity: the infamous sex tape, the unwise dalliances that provided tabloid entertainment for the masses, the endless stream of men I'd been linked with. Why did it all feel so foreign to me?

"I'm sure you have some fascinating lab reports to discuss."

Giles nodded absently and turned back to Jordana. They looked very natural together, with their dark hair and glasses and handsome features, both in their crisp lab coats, his blue, hers lavender. Like an ad for the joys of science. Lab geeks in love. I headed toward the door.

The rain was abating and the sun would soon be out. I was thinking about taking a walk before my first appointment when I caught sight of Creepy Roy, standing underneath the magnolia tree. Bad weather never seemed to bother Roy. Rain or shine, he was on the job. He sucked on an ever-present cigarette.

I decided to stay inside.

Chapter 7

TO AVOID ROY, I detoured to the small library on the second floor of the main house.

The reading room was one of my few refuges. It had racks of current magazines and bookcases filled with books, many of them in large print for the older residents. But those who chose to sit in the soothing green room seldom read the words. They preferred looking at pictures.

There was a big old beige computer in the back corner. But like the books, I never saw anyone using it. I'd never even thought to try it before, when I was in the Fog. I walked over and hit the keys automatically. Nothing happened. It was plugged in, but it wouldn't power on. I turned my attention elsewhere.

The place was pleasant and airy. I claimed the wing chair by the window where I could see the top of a glass building that clashed with the green fields and white fences. A matching chintz sofa was positioned near it, in front of the fireplace, my favorite place in the library. But today someone else was sitting there. Her pale green lab coat gave her away as staff, her name embroidered in dark script: Hailey Croft, RN.

Friend or foe? I wondered. Giles was right about one thing: I was suspicious of everyone. Had he sent her to spy on me?

Her lab coat covered khaki slacks and a knit top. She didn't wear those pastel hospital scrubs that resembled pajamas, for which I was grateful. It was bad enough being locked in here, without everyone dressing like we were attending a giant sleepover. I suppose Giles Embry could be thanked for the modicum of formality. Ms. Croft was leafing through a *Vogue*. I had seen her on the grounds but had never spoken to her. Her large green eyes and friendly face were topped with masses of curly light brown hair that had become more unruly in the rain. She ran her hands through it in an attempt to comb it, then gave up and gathered it into a ponytail and wrapped it with a green band.

I must have been staring. That's how I am when someone new enters my limited universe. Hailey looked up and offered the magazine to me. Did she think I'd have a tantrum if she didn't?

Many people treat me that way. In addition to forgetting whole years here and there, I guess I've forgotten how to behave. I was embarrassed.

"No, thank you. You're on your break," I said, putting up my hands. "I have all the time in the world to figure out what they're wearing this season. Not that it matters here."

"Thanks," she said, looking at me with curiosity, but not as if I were some kind of faulty microbe. "You're Tennyson Claxton."

"That's what they tell me." I smoothed my hair back and wondered if it was long enough for a ponytail.

"You're not as stuck-up as I expected," she said.

I laughed. She wasn't what I expected either. "It's pointless being stuck-up when there's no one to notice, don't you think? Or maybe I forgot how. It would nice to think I'd forgotten a few bad habits as well as—other things."

"Maybe." She grinned, showing even teeth. "Of course, we don't get to read much anymore about the madcap Claxton heiress."

"Well, *Vogue* is not exactly a tabloid, and I'm on sabbatical from the *National Enquirer*." It was nice to get my miserable reputation out of the way early.

"Me too. I'm Hailey." She extended her hand. "Nice to meet you."

She was about my age. Mid-twenties. The age my friends would be, if I had any. "Where do you work?"

"Meds Three."

"That's got to be depressing."

I probably shouldn't have blurted that out. Meds Three: the medical floor for residents with terminal illnesses, in addition to the holes in their minds. It was locked because of the "floaters," the people who, if they weren't watched, would simply walk away, not knowing where they were or where they were going. Like dandelion fluff, they would float away with the wind. And they didn't know how to float their way back. They were following some light of their own.

Residents on the other floors are not locked up all the time, although everyone is carefully watched. Most of them are allowed in the day room and in the inner gardens, where they sit like flowers, turning their faces to the sun, smiling blankly. I can tell when they don't recognize their families, because someone leaves crying.

"Meds Three makes you happy you've got all your marbles,

that's for sure," Hailey said. "It's not so bad if you got a sweet patient, like mine. I'm one of Miss Jasmine Lee's nurses."

Miss Jasmine Lee! Close to ninety years old, Miss Jasmine—everyone called her that—was a Campus celebrity, one of the very first residents. She'd been there for three or four years and couldn't remember much of anything anymore, but she always smiled. Her fortune kept her well-tended by private nurses who worked in shifts. I had seen her on the grounds, her wheelchair pushed by an RN or an orderly. Miss Jasmine wasn't a floater, she was beyond floating away, and she hadn't the strength to roll away on her own. She looked ancient, with blue-veined skin stretched over her delicate bones. She was always immaculately dressed in pale nightgowns with matching sweaters and slippers, her two long white braids carefully tied with matching satin bows.

She had no family. It was common knowledge that her money would go to the Campus when Miss Jasmine went to God.

Giles always stopped to talk to Miss Jasmine, taking her hands and bowing to her. It surprised me how gentle he could be with the frailest patients. Even his voice became softer around them. I liked to watch him with Miss Jasmine. He was a completely different man, and I wondered why he couldn't treat me with the same courtesy. I guess I'm no Miss Jasmine.

"She's a dainty old thing. Bless her wicked old heart, as we say." Hailey grinned and wrinkled her freckled nose. "She's let go of so many things. Still, Miss Jasmine has her wants. She is very specific about the color of the nightgown she wears every day. It's usually a pink day, a blue day, or a yellow day. Sometimes lavender, rarely green. Simply everything must match. Or she throws her brush at me. Good thing we have multiples of everything, because sometimes she wants nothing but pink for a week. I suspect there is more going on in her brain than everyone thinks."

"Really? Why?"

"She has this look, a light in her eyes, as if she's the only one in on some private joke. She loves making us do her bidding. Every once in a while, her mind is clear as a bell, for a whole minute, then it fades."

Miss Jasmine reminded me of an old, old baby, her every need satisfied, her tantrums always coddled. "Does she recognize you?"

"Me? No. Not as myself, that is. There are days when I'm her sister, or her mother, which I find alarming, or her best friend—and we are headed off to a cotillion. It's sweet. She tells me about all her beaus. I gather there were many. She could never decide on just one."

"She likes you."

"Maybe because I'm from Richmond too. She hears those old familiar Richmond tones in my voice."

"Your accent isn't that strong," I said.

"It comes and goes. It might be a tad stronger when I'm around Miss Jasmine. It's comforting for her. And Lord knows, after a day with those old ladies, I sound like I'm a hundred."

"Rumor says she won't last much longer." Everyone knew Miss Jasmine had cancer and a host of other ills, as well as Alzheimer's.

Hailey stopped flipping the magazine. "That's what people say, but it's so hard to tell. Cancer grows slowly in very old people. You would think it would take them quickly, but it doesn't. Often it lingers, just like they do. Miss Jasmine may be here a while longer or she could go tomorrow."

Hailey tossed the magazine on the mahogany coffee table, then stood and stretched. "I'm finished with *Vogue*, it's all yours."

"The magazine for me should be called *Fugue*."

"Would that be the 'Toccata and Fugue in D Minor'? Or the other kind?"

"The other kind. Dr. Embry says I could be experiencing a sort of a slow-motion fugue state."

"Fugues are all the rage this year, Tennyson. But it wouldn't go with last year's wardrobe."

"I don't know," I said. "If you don't remember your clothes, they'd all be new to you. I could wear pink every day, like Miss Jasmine, and I'd never care." I stared at my baggy khakis and blue knit polo shirt. I never questioned where they came from. They simply appeared in the closet of my suite each week, the shirts embroidered with the Campus logo. If I'd ever cared about clothing, that care had disappeared with my green eyes.

"According to those grocery store rags, Tennyson Claxton's never worn anything twice."

"Then I must not be her." I fingered the Campus logo. I was a walking, talking advertisement for the Campus.

The sun was out now and mist was steaming off the red brick walkway. The room was getting warm.

"What do you do for fun, Hailey? When you're not at Miss

Jasmine's beck and call?" I longed to hear about normal things.

"Me? Friends, movies, dinner. The occasional beau, though no one right now. I'm taking a break. Typical things. Things that would bore Miss Tennyson Claxton."

"You'd be surprised. I haven't been to a movie in— Of course I can't remember. Seems like forever though."

Hailey's phone dinged to alert her to a text. She read it and shrugged.

"That's one of them now. Nothing urgent. I'll call her later."

I felt a twinge of envy. She had people who cared about her and she had a phone to keep in touch with them.

"Tell me about your friends."

"There's Heather. That was her just now. And Mercy. The three of us met at G.W. University. Pre-law. We all hated it. I mean really, does the world need more lawyers? Now, I love what I do, but Mercy has the most interesting career. The most dangerous, too."

"Dangerous? What does she do?"

"Oh, she doesn't really talk about it much. And she says it's not really dangerous. She calls herself a problem solver."

"Is that a fancy name for an insurance adjuster or something?"

Hailey shook her head.

"More like an investigator. It sounds like a job you'd make up, but she fixes people's, um, difficulties for them. Except of course for difficulties like my hair. Even Mercy Underhill, problem solver extraordinaire, can't figure that one out. This weather makes this nest of snakes on my head even wilder." She released the ponytail and gave it another go.

"It suits you," I said. "Like a water nymph. A naiad."

She laughed. Her laugh winkled her freckled nose and widened her bright blue eyes. The sunlight created a halo around her light brown hair.

"That's me all right, a naiad. My hair is naiad hair."

"What kind of problems does your friend Mercy solve?"

"The kind that people have when they can afford her services. People with money. People who get into terrible trouble and can't get themselves out. They need someone with common sense and connections."

"Mercy went to law school?"

"She lasted longer than I did, but she didn't finish. She's a special type of private investigator, but she doesn't like that term.

She just takes care of issues quietly, without newspapers nosing around, or paparazzi. You know."

"So they tell me. I probably need a problem solver. She sounds like a good friend to have."

"I'm sure your friends are pretty interesting, Tennyson," she said. "Or at least notorious."

I leaned back and closed my eyes. "I don't think I have any friends."

"Don't be absurd, Ms. Tennyson. Rich people always have friends."

"As many as they can pay for? Working for Miss Jasmine has made you cynical, Hailey."

"Sorry. My mother always says I blurt before I think."

"Blurt on. Please. I appreciate it. Anyway, I must be proof it isn't true. The friends part. I'm such a charmer, no one's ever visited me here."

"No one? No friends? No family?" Hailey stared at me. "Nobody?"

I made a zero with my fingers.

"Dr. Embry doesn't think it would be a good idea. Maybe he knows I don't have any friends."

"No visitors." Her eyebrows lifted slightly. "That's odd."

"Why? Tell me, Hailey. It certainly feels odd to me. Even murderers in prison get visitors."

I saw people come to the Campus on visiting days. I was more and more aware that I wasn't like the other residents.

"I'm not a doctor, and the therapies here are supposedly cutting-edge. All those protocols Dr. Embry has put together. Phoenix, Pegasus, Prometheus, Icarus." She smoothed her naiad hair again. "I shouldn't presume."

"Presume away, please." I was desperate for an answer that didn't come from Dr. Embry or his crew. "You don't work for him, do you? For Giles, I mean." I jumped up in a panic.

She looked me in the eyes. "Everybody here works for Dr. Embry, in one way or another. But not directly, no. Our paths hardly cross. I'm just a nurse. I have my one special patient to take care of, that's all I do here."

I sat down on the edge of my chair. "Whatever you tell me, Hailey, I'd never tell anyone, certainly not him. Believe me."

She took a moment before answering.

"From what I gather, you are missing time, even years, and you don't believe, or want to believe, that you're actually Tennyson Claxton."

"No secret is safe here, I guess."

"Scuttlebutt. People talk. I shouldn't say anything. I could lose my job."

"You're the first person who's talked to me like I'm not brain-damaged."

Hailey adjusted her lab coat. "With memory loss like yours, I'd expect they'd want you to be surrounded by familiar things, music, photos, friends, family. Familiar context always aids recall."

"I am surrounded by context! Videos, slide shows, virtual reality immersion, talk therapy, drugs, *The Big Show of Tennyson O*. Dr. Embry says I should be remembering everyone I ever met, from his treatment protocol. I'm in the Phoenix program. But—"

"Dr. Embry? You don't call your fiancé by his first name?"

"We're a little more formal than you might think."

"He does seem like a formal kind of guy." Hailey checked her watch. "Break's over. Gotta go. Nice to talk to you, Tennyson. See you around?"

"I'd like that."

Hailey Croft was like fresh air for me. A human being, not one of Giles's robots. I hoped. She smiled and ducked out the door.

Chapter 8

WITH HAILEY CROFT gone, the room seemed emptier than before. For a minute.

Miriam the Screamer entered. That's what the staff call her. She's one of the Meds Two residents, in the middle stages of Alzheimer's disease. She sat down determinedly with a large book on her lap, trying to read words she didn't understand anymore. She wore her silver hair in a French twist, but the strands came loose and fell around her shoulders. Her lovely pink cardigan was buttoned wrong. Her dirty glasses hung forgotten on a cord around her neck.

According to Campus rumor, Miriam was once a brilliant woman who tried very hard to retain the last of her intelligence before the inevitable dimming of the light.

"Hello, Miriam, how are you today?"

She eyed me suspiciously. "I don't know you. Who are you?"

"I'm Tennyson. Do you remember me?" I should have known better.

"Remember you?!" She shrieked at me. "I speak five languages! How can you expect me to remember you? Five languages! I speak English and Spanish and French and— I don't want to remember you!"

"I'm sorry."

I backed toward the door. Miriam kept screaming, five languages forgotten. An orderly nearly Miriam's age rushed past me to calm her down.

"Don't fret about that, Ms. Tennyson. When I piss off Ms. Miriam, she cusses me out in some foreign language. Course she might be talking in Pig Latin for all I know."

"Pig Latin would be better."

"Doesn't take much to light her fire. The closer she gets to when the light goes out, the more scared she is. I feel for her. Folks here are deeply scared. And angry."

Miriam's anger was something I understood too well. She would never leave the Campus. Her world would continue to shrink, like the forgotten words of five languages.

I desperately hoped my world would expand, rather than

diminish, like so many of those at the Campus.

I backed out of the room and fled down the stairs through the front door. I was due at the memory lab for more tests, more electricity lighting up my brain. I ran down the path through the garden, sun streaming through the wet trees.

Before I reached my destination, the strangest thing happened.

Jonathan VanCamp knew who I was.

It doesn't sound like anything at all, yet it was monumental. Jonathan's one of the residents at the Campus. He was leaving the memory lab as I entered. Despite the déjà vu of our weeks of daily introductions, he had never recalled my name. I grew tired of his blank, searching stare and the lack of recognition, even though he was always good natured about it, as if he were meeting me for the first time. It was frustrating, more for me than for him. I know it sounds cruel, but it hurts to be invisible, unknown, unremembered, more than to float in the downy fog of amnesia. I am the invisible woman, not just to Jonathan VanCamp, but to my family as well. To the world.

Jonathan suffered severe brain trauma in a skiing accident. He was just twenty-nine when it happened. He still looks like a boy athlete. His eyes are guileless and friendly. I've been here for months. He's been here for years. Seeing Jonathan always reminded me that not everyone at the Campus is old. Besides me, that is.

"Tennyson," he called to me and waved. "Hey, Tennyson, how are you doing?"

"Jonathan?" I stopped short. He was clear, not confused, which astonished me.

"And just look who came to see me. Veronica, my darling wife." He held her hand. "Isn't that great? Do you two know each other?"

Before today, Jonathan did not recognize his spouse, a dark-haired Madonna who came faithfully to see him, three times a week. For the past three years, they tell me. She usually left weeping. Veronica leaned her head on his shoulder, tears running down her face. But this time her tears were jubilant. She nodded to me happily. She was too emotional to speak.

Now, unbelievably, he recognized me, looking at me directly, without the puzzlement and blank expression. He reached out and took my hands.

"The black cloud is gone. Dr. Embry says I've had a remarkable breakthrough. That's what he called it. A remarkable breakthrough."

"How wonderful, Jonathan."

His cloud was gone? My Fog was lifting too, but I was still lost. I could hardly speak. I blinked away my tears before they could fall. Is there a chance that someday I won't feel like a complete stranger in this world?

"Dr. Embry says I'll be able to go home soon," he said. Veronica nodded in agreement.

"Home?" I hardly knew what that meant. It filled me with longing for something I couldn't place. "You're going home?"

"Not just yet, Jonathan." Giles materialized behind him, a dark space in the afternoon light. "Don't outpace yourself. This is indeed a remarkable breakthrough, but there's more work for us to do. Much more work. It will be a little time before you go home."

I refused to look at Giles. "You really know me, Jonathan?"

"Hard to believe, I know." Jonathan laughed and tapped his head. "There are still shadows up here. But things are becoming clearer, falling into place. Like wearing a pair of magic spectacles."

He turned to Veronica and they laughed together. I was happy for them. Sad for me, but now possibly with a speck of hope. Giles seemed jubilant in a way I'd never witnessed before. He actually laughed and hugged me.

"It works, Tennyson. Memories can travel through the brain. They can be reactivated, moved, reinstalled, revived. It will work for you too. I know it will."

Veronica broke her hold on Jonathan for a moment to throw her arms around Giles. "It's a miracle, Dr. Embry. You brought Jonathan back to me."

Giles accepted her joy as his due. As we watched them walk away arm in arm, Giles took my elbow.

"You're due at the lab."

He escorted me personally into the lab. It was always cold in there. I could see him through the glass of the control room, still beaming.

I didn't perform well. Not even the number sequences. All I could think about was Jonathan moving from the darkness into the light. Maybe Giles was right. Maybe I should trust him.

As soon as I could, I slipped back to my suite and sought my journal. Ulysses had his troubles. I had mine. But sometimes those troubles were the same. I circled these lines.

They eat, they drink, and nature gives the feast:
The trees around them all their food produce:
Lotus the name: divine, nectareous juice!
(Thence call'd Lotophagi); which whoso tastes,
Insatiate riots in the sweet repasts,
Nor other home, nor other care intends,
But quits his house, his country, and his friends.

That's me all over. No house, no country, no friends. Had I eaten the lotus plant? Perhaps Giles's magic pills were made of lotus blossoms.

Chapter 9

GILES IS ALWAYS hovering over my shoulder when I want him elsewhere.

Doesn't he have a job to do? Pursuing his noble quest to restore personal histories to other trauma victims? Easing the pain of souls suffering from Alzheimer's disease? Impressing key politicians or rich benefactors? Preening in front of the ladies?

If Jonathan is really recovering his memory, and if Giles has found the key, I need the same key. Unfortunately, then I need Giles. This fills me with both hope and despair. I'll have to dance to Giles's tune if I ever expect to leave this picture-pretty but soul-stifling place. I don't think I'm terribly good at other people's games. Nevertheless, I've resolved to try a little honey to catch the fly.

I lifted the pink-and-white diamond ring out of its black velvet box this morning. I slipped it on the appropriate finger and stared at it. It fit perfectly, but it didn't go with the khaki slacks that hung on me, or today's dull tan polo shirt. Since I have been lodged at the Campus and my eyes turned brown, my daily attire is as dull as I am.

When I had green eyes, I must have worn makeup that enhanced them and dressed in colors that deepened them. Without my green eyes, I no longer have any interest in what I wear, and I haven't bothered to ask where my own clothes might be. Though I've seen endless videos of myself at fashion shows and galas, wearing Dior this and Gucci that, I don't remember them, or the feel of wearing them. It's tricky putting on clothes when you don't want to look into mirrors. I didn't dwell on whether the muddy tan shirt flattered me or not. Now that I think about it, probably not. Clothes simply appeared in the closet, were taken out, worn, discarded, and came back freshly laundered. Occasionally, I would find a blue or pink oxford cloth button-down shirt for variety, but still with the Campus logo. When I was in the Fog, I only cared that I was clean. But now the Fog was lifting, and I knew that the ring looked silly on me.

Giles opened my suite door like the king of the castle and presented himself. Why weren't there trumpets? It was a special day.

"Good morning, Tennyson."

"Don't you look spiffy," I said, and he smiled. He enjoys

compliments, though he doesn't give them. Giles had changed from his casually stiff everyday look into a severe dark gray suit, softened by a crisp sky-blue shirt and matching tie, which made his eyes shine like frosty blue diamonds. If only they held some warmth for me, I might have been moved.

"I'm testifying before the Senate today, Tennyson. You haven't forgotten, have you?" He seemed tense. Perhaps a trip to Capitol Hill could do that to a person. I knew my grandfather Abercrombie Foxhall Claxton had been a senator, but the Senate held no tense memories for me.

"How could I forget, Giles? Everyone's talking about it. Everyone with a working short-term memory. You'll wow them on C-SPAN."

Even the residents who didn't quite understand what C-SPAN was, or the U.S. Senate either, had caught the excitement in the air. The hearing would be televised. A giant television screen was set up in the dining room where all could delight in Dr. Embry's big moment. His big moment was the Campus's big moment. I pulled myself up out of the chair, relieved that he'd be away most of the day. It was a rare occurrence.

"I'll be interested in what you have to say about my testimony."

His testimony or his performance? "Me? Why would you care about my opinion?"

"Why wouldn't I?" He turned the cool blue gaze on me. "You're quite intelligent, Tennyson. And since coming to the Campus, you've shown a more serious side than I've seen before. We know some brain injuries can effect changes in personality. Yours has been profound."

"I don't have a personality," I said. He laughed without warmth.

"Nonsense." He picked up my left hand and held it for a long moment. He graced me with a rare smile. "You're wearing your engagement ring, Tennyson. That's good."

I retrieved my hand. The pink stone sparkled in the light, surrounded by its henchmen, a row of substantial white marquise-cut diamonds. They could be rhinestones, for all I knew. I waggled my unsightly nails.

"It doesn't belong on these hands. I don't even have a nail file."

Someone at the Campus was afraid I'd try to file myself to death, or stab myself with the pointy end.

"A manicure. That can probably be arranged." He straightened his tie, which didn't need straightening. "You're remembering more, you're making strides. You're improving every day."

Perhaps I was only testing well. "How do you know I'm better? Tennyson Claxton could be a false memory. Like Marissa."

The truth was that I didn't feel like either of them. Perhaps I was really someone else entirely. Someone without a name.

"I'm the doctor here." That was something he'd never let me forget. "And I know who you are."

I glimpsed brown eyes and shaggy brown hair in the corner of a mirror and turned away.

"Giles, who did this to me? If I have implanted memories, who engineered them? Where did I pick them up?"

"It doesn't matter. We need to move forward, Tennyson, not backwards. Together we will vanquish your Marissa. She's nothing but a phantom."

Giles made himself comfortable on the camel-colored sofa and picked up his tablet. He tapped and scrolled, scowling. I assumed he was going over his oral statement to Congress. He slipped on his reading glasses and ignored me. Classic Giles I'm-finished-with-you-don't-bother-me behavior.

"It does matter. Until I find out who did this to me, and why, I won't stop asking."

He glowered at me over his glasses. "What brought this on today? Did you have another nightmare?"

"No. Why do I have someone else's memories?"

"You made them up." He looked smug.

"I did what?!" Oh, at last, a *scientific* explanation. "So they aren't actually another person's? They're from my own imagination?" From an earlier nightmare, I pictured the lifeless woman on the table, the one who resembled me. Her unseeing eyes were brown. Did I make her up as well? "That's ridiculous. Why on earth would I do that?"

"Why is the hard question. Everything else is explainable." He moved from the sofa and took the wing chair opposite me. "There was someone you used to see before the accident, a therapist. You went through a lot of therapists."

"Sounds like me, I suppose."

"The last one had an unhealthy attachment to you. He had his own hidden agenda. I believe your false memories happened as a result of your therapy with him last year." Giles stared through me.

"You started to believe you had other memories."

I felt my mouth drop open. "Before the accident?"

He nodded. I blinked. Did Giles Embry really just answer a question with a fact, not an evasion?

"Tell me."

"It is difficult to say exactly how it began with you." He put the tablet aside. "But the process is well known. A false memory can start with a suggestion, a word, an idea from an authoritative source when you're in an unstable, suggestible state. This fact seems meaningful or attractive to you in some way. You try to place it within your own life narrative to make sense of it. It becomes embedded as a memory, or what feels like a memory. You begin to think this story happened to you. Other people, with good intentions or bad, tell you it did happen to you. There have been experiments on this effect. Someone, call him Jensen, insists you were at a picnic, for example. You weren't there, but he describes it so thoroughly you think you must have forgotten that picnic. Your mind knits together what you've been told into a seamless narrative. Then Jensen says, for example, Do you remember having a big fight with your best friend at the picnic? You respond, Yes, I remember now, she tried to move in on my boyfriend! The false memory now has explanatory power, and you elaborate the memory to serve your own needs. The impostor memory takes hold."

Was it that simple? I tried to fight the wave of emotions threatening to break over me.

"These are classic experiments. Sometimes the suggested memory becomes stronger than a real memory," he continued. "Your mind needs it to be true to explain something, so you add details, colors, characters, dialogue, consequences. You would swear you remember what you wore, what you said, what was playing on the radio. It's called fabulation. Some subjects believe in their own fabulations more strongly than their real memories."

"I was an experiment?"

"No, Tennyson, you were looking for a way out of your troubles. It's like these phenomena that come in waves."

"What phenomena?"

"False memories. A sort of psychological epidemic. Witchcraft in the basement. Alien abductions. Things that never happened."

"What about Marissa? Where did I even get that name?"

"I have no idea." He laughed. "This phantom Marissa is such a prude, don't you think? The Tennyson I know would have insisted we have sex to relax me before my big day."

The sex thing! He wouldn't leave it alone! At least he hadn't mentioned taking me away for the weekend again. What would Tennyson say?

"And you would have told me no, because you were busy and didn't want to wrinkle your spiffy suit." I took in the starch in his shirt, not to mention his soul, and decided I'd nailed it. "You have to keep your mind on your testimony."

"Exactly so. But you would have tried. At least once."

"Back to Marissa."

He shrugged. "Something happened. Rehab was stressful for you. You were suggestible."

"Rehab?" I must have missed that edition of *The Enquirer*. Along with the sex tape episode.

"You've lived a wild life, Tennyson."

"One I obviously wanted to forget."

He captured both my hands in his. "Exactly. But listen to me, Tennyson Olivia, you were effervescent, alive, wild, experimental."

"I was trouble."

"Yes, and troubled, but finally growing up. You were tired of disappointing the family and you decided you wanted a simpler life."

"I sure as hell would like one now."

"So you invented Marissa, with the help of your last quack shrink. You created her, dwelled on her, obsessed over her. Somehow those false hopes took hold as a false history, a made-up memory that never happened. Fiction, Tennyson."

"All this happened in therapy? What's the name of this therapist? Why didn't he tell me these memories weren't true?"

"He had his own agenda, Tennyson, to make you dependent on him. Do you have any idea how many charlatans try to defraud rich girls?"

"I was used?"

"Too often. As I said, you went through therapists like Kleenex. Another hobby of yours. You stopped seeing Jensen before the accident. He's another thing you forgot."

"Jensen." I latched onto the name like a life preserver. Someone who knew me before the accident. Someone who wasn't Giles or Creepy Roy or a robot lab assistant. "What's his first name? If he has a clue to where Marissa came from—"

Giles scowled, clearly annoyed that he'd let that much slip.

"This obsession with Marissa must stop. Now that you know how it might have happened, more or less, you can sort through the fakery and dismiss it."

He took my hand and touched the ring as if to shine it.

"No. I have to know all of it." I jumped up and pulled my hand away.

His jaw worked. "You don't want to know. Jensen was into some very questionable stuff. Pseudoscience, feel-good therapy. He was practically a one-man cult."

"I liked him, didn't I?"

I immediately pictured some guru from California, long blond hair and Hawaiian shirt. He must have been more fun than Giles. I needed to find him.

"He harmed you, Tennyson. When you realized it, you stopped seeing him. We made sure he wouldn't come near you again."

We? "Where is he now?" The only link to my past. The genie was out of the bottle. I wasn't going to let Giles put the stopper in it.

"He's gone."

"Where?" How could I get to the bottom of this mess I'd made of my life? Where could I find this Jensen guy and make him talk to me?

"This is upsetting you." Giles stood in my path and stopped me. He put his hands on my shoulders. "While I'm delighted you no longer want to rely on medication, you should take something for this anxiety. I'll give you something. Just a little white pill."

"Why, my dear doctor, with my well-known history of drug abuse, would you push drugs on me?"

He sighed. "I am more than aware of your history, Tennyson. You are agitated. Take a breath and realize what he's done to you. You're being irrational."

He spoke calmly, but veins on his neck stood out in relief. I was jumping out of my skin, but so was Giles. Talk of Marissa always set him off. Talking with him sets me off. I fought the urge to needle him further to see whether he'd explode like a Tasmanian devil.

"I'm not irrational."

Giles took a deep breath. "What would you call it when you've invented another identity for yourself, someone innocent, naïve, less worldly?"

"Instead of a shallow, slutty, self-absorbed, drug-addled, train wreck of a parasitic socialite? I can't imagine. Who wouldn't want to be me?"

"I don't like to hear you denigrate yourself. When people seize onto another persona, they sometimes call it 'delusions of grandeur,' but in your case, Tennyson, it may be delusions of squalor."

That was almost a joke, and I almost laughed. But Giles never joked.

"What happened to Jensen?"

"You don't have to worry, Tennyson. He'll never harm you again. There was an injunction. Are we finished?"

I wanted Giles gone as much as he wanted to go. But finished with Marissa? Not by a long shot.

"Yes. The U.S. Senate calls." I picked up the tablet with his notes and handed it to him. "Good luck."

"I'll see you later." He gave me a peck on the forehead and left. I thought he seemed relieved. I was.

It was clear that Giles had carefully edited the life he wanted me to recall. I was drained from the encounter, but I had a name: Jensen. I would find this Jensen and make him tell me how Tennyson Claxton and Marissa Brookshire intersected, what he knew about the accident, and how I really wound up at the Campus. The computer in the reading room was a start. If I could remember how to use one and figure out how to get it working.

These days, I could barely manage a blow dryer.

Chapter 10

THE DINING ROOM was humming. Residents and staff filled rows of chairs, waiting to watch Dr. Embry on the television. Even those who couldn't remember who he was. Any excuse for a party. Even I was interested in seeing Giles in action before the Senate panel.

"He's my brother." One of the old men on Meds Two pointed to Giles on the big TV.

"He works down at the bank," another said. "It's old what's-his-name."

The television was tuned to C-SPAN. The screen showed a Senate hearing room on Capitol Hill, decorated in royal blue and eagle gold. The hearing was promoted as "A Crisis of the Mind, the Challenge of Managing Diminishing Mental Capacity," or something like that. Watching Giles on camera would reassure me that he wasn't, at that very moment, watching me.

But he didn't have to. Creepy Roy sidled into the crowded dining room. No one spoke to him. His presence was barely acknowledged. People always gave Roy Barnaker space. Part of it was the reek of cigarettes that surrounded him like a toxic cloud. The entire campus was supposed to be a non-smoking environment. I assume Giles gave him a license to pollute. Roy leaned against the far wall to get a good view of the screen, and of me.

I moved a few seats further away from him, grabbing a chair next to Paul, another one of Giles's forgetful floaters. White-haired Paul wanders the halls and whistles old-fashioned tunes I've never heard, or perhaps I've forgotten them. He always wears a jaunty checkered vest over his shirt, no matter how warm the weather. He stared at me with that peculiar blank stare of unrecognition, so prevalent among residents at the Campus.

"I'm saving this chair for my Jenny." Paul patted the seat I wanted. "Have you seen her? Never mind, you can sit there, Missy, until she comes." His Jenny has been dead for years. I thanked him and sat down. He promptly forgot me.

The noise level in the room dropped dramatically as the on-screen chairman banged the gavel to commence the hearing. People blinked at the sound and turned around to watch. The screen offered several different views of the room, including the committee members, the press, and those testifying.

There he was. My so-called fiancé, impeccably turned out, his blue tie matching his eyes, and looking deadly serious. He was seated at the witness table, flexing his mental muscles, and for once with paper in hand, riffling for show through the printed pages of his testimony. He would not need to refer to his notes, he would have it all memorized. Memory was Giles's specialty.

I was curious to see how Giles behaved with normal people. Or if politicians weren't normal, at least other people, people outside the cloistered realm of the Campus.

The camera pulled back from the table to cover the hearing room audience. My breath caught. There in the background behind Giles was my grandfather, Abercrombie Foxhall Claxton. I knew him from *The Big Show of Tennyson O.* He was still introduced as "Senator Claxton" or simply "the Senator," a courtesy title, since he'd retired from the Senate. He was all steel-gray hair and gravitas, with a hawk-like visage. His shirt was as starched as his hair, his tie a red regimental stripe. He looked like a senator straight from Central Casting.

Giles had neglected to tell me that "the Senator" would be there at the hearing. I didn't know I would even care, but I was suddenly riveted by this scene and the easy camaraderie between Giles and my grandfather. Giles was good enough for his company, but I was not. It stung.

I had learned that in his political circles the Senator was affectionately—or sometimes not—known as "Fox," or "the Fox." The newscaster told us Senator Foxhall Claxton was expected to be called to answer questions by the committee.

Giles started to speak and the camera focused on him. I'd like to say a hush fell over the crowd in the dining room at the Campus, but it didn't. The room was full of random chatter. Most of those present had already forgotten what they were doing there.

"Memory loss is the cruelest kind of thief, because it steals the soul," Giles began. "It happens in all kinds of families, no matter their social standing, their wealth, or lack of it. It can happen to you. It happened to me. My own mother died of complications from early-onset Alzheimer's disease. Her dementia started with the mildest confusion over small things when I was in high school. It ended with bewilderment, tears, anger, and finally, silence. I was a stranger to her. She died recognizing no one."

I was stunned. This was a Giles I'd never seen, exposing a part of his life he'd kept hidden from me, his painful, vulnerable past. Or perhaps he had told me all about his mother at some point, before the accident. Perhaps I had loved this vulnerability, this sensitivity. Why couldn't I remember those things?

"If my mother were alive today, we could begin to treat her. We might be able to retard the disease and extend her life," Giles continued. "We are hopeful of a cure at the C&B Institute's Hunt Country Campus Memory Project. But there are other afflictions we treat at the Campus. They are all part of the puzzle of memory. Each mystery requires a slightly different approach..."

This kinder, gentler Giles baffled me. The Dr. Embry that he showed to the aged residents, to Jonathan, to other people. The brilliant, compassionate, blue-eyed scientist, driven by his personal connection to his work. It was a powerful image, but was it true? The sand shifted beneath my feet. There was more to this man than I'd given him credit for. Why wouldn't he reveal that Giles to me? The Giles Embry who might make me care?

"The other side of the coin is that sometimes our memories are too terrible to live with," Giles continued. "The rape and abuse survivor, the soldier who has seen the horrors of war. They suffer the post-traumatic stress, the agony, the flashbacks. But even with them, we are seeing breakthroughs at the Campus. There are experimental drugs that promise to block the traumatic memories that prevent them from living their lives to the fullest, if we were allowed to begin a phase-one study. The most promising experimental drug we've developed is one we're calling Hypnopolethe."

I'd heard that name at the Campus. It wasn't part of my treatment protocol. I was there to *remember*, not forget. The drug's name seemed to be a mashup of names from Greek mythology: Hypnos, the god of sleep, and Lethe, the river of forgetting that the dead drink from. I'd already fallen into the river of forgetting, and I was desperately paddling for the shore.

Hypnopolethe was one of the drugs that, so far, had been tested only on rats. I wondered about the men who resided on the other side of the Campus, in the steel-and-glass buildings where they screamed in the night because they had seen and done terrible things. Did they want to forget?

Giles went on, delving into the facts and figures of the Campus's daily business, the role of the C&B Corporation, the C&B Foundation, the C&B Institute, the difficulty of raising money for long-term memory research, the need for additional funding. He referred obliquely to Jonathan VanCamp and to me, in his testimony about promising memory-loss research subjects, but not by name. I was grateful. I wanted nobody's sympathy or compassion.

I was riveted again when Senator Abercrombie Foxhall Claxton was asked whether it would be better to conduct such delicate research in a government facility, perhaps at the National Institutes for Health, or the National Institute for Mental Health. He faced his former cronies with a hard face and direct gaze.

"Senators, you know I have always believed the private sector can better find solutions to our nation's problems than a bureaucracy-chained government. I'm not about to change my mind now. The C&B Memory Project Campus is just one example of how this works in reality. Nevertheless, a generous government grant, provided without regulatory handcuffs, would go a far way toward realizing our goals."

The chairman raised his florid face, glaring at my grandfather.

"Senator Claxton, we know you have your own personal bureaucracy at the C&B Corporation, with its tentacle organizations reaching into any number of areas," said Senator William Widen, from the hardscrabble mining region of Pennsylvania, Fox's key antagonist on the committee. As old and distinguished-looking as Fox, Widen was equally scrappy, equally severe. "And now you say you want public funds too. You want to feed at the public trough as well. You want to have it both ways, Fox."

"Well, Willie— Pardon me, the gentleman from Pennsylvania has just heard that our research at the Campus is unraveling the mysteries of memory. Our work there might even assist some members of this august body to remember that they are here to serve the people, and not the other way around," Fox replied. Laughter rippled through the hearing room.

"That so, Fox? I understand you, tragically, have personal knowledge of this. Your injured granddaughter is still in residence there as a patient, is she not, after her terrible crack-up back in January. For which I'm sure we all extend our sympathy."

I was glued to my seat, aware of Campus staff faces beginning to turn in my direction. My cheeks were hot with embarrassment.

"You are aware, Senator Widen, that I do not draw my family into the spotlight of public scrutiny, if I can possibly help it," Fox said.

"True. I have heard she is quite capable of doing that herself," Senator Widen cracked. There was a small but audible gasp from the hearing room crowd at this less-than-senatorial jab. "Perhaps not anymore, as it seems she is now incapacitated. She is little more than a vegetable, as I understand it. My sincere condolences, Senator."

I'm a vegetable? That's what the media said?

"The gentleman from Pennsylvania is sadly misinformed." Senator Abercrombie Foxhall Claxton seemed to grow taller in his seat. His glare frightened even me, right through the TV screen. "All you need to know, Willie, is that my granddaughter Tennyson is doing remarkably well, entirely because of Dr. Giles Embry and the dedicated staff at the Campus. She is making strides in her recovery we would never see at any other facility in this country. I daresay our researchers could even address the failing capabilities of your dear wife, Mrs. Widen, who I am informed, sometimes forgets herself and her circumstances and must be driven home by her chauffeur, who also acts as her caretaker. My sincere condolences, Senator. Now, gentlemen, are there any other well-meaning questions?"

Everyone in the dining room was looking at me now. I felt as I'd been stripped naked. I fled from the room. Hailey Croft followed me into the hall.

"Tennyson, are you okay? Can I help?"

"I'm okay. At least that wasn't on the nightly news." My blood was pulsing fast through my veins. "But I suppose it will be. Any minute now."

"I'm so sorry. I'm guessing that's one Yankee politician who won't be invited to supper at the Claxton manor anytime soon. Must have been rough, listening to that senatorial smackdown."

"I suppose I ought to be used to being a public spectacle by now." I sagged against the wall and tried to smile. I don't think it was working.

"Not if you don't remember anything about it." She seemed puzzled. "You really don't remember that life, do you? Being a celebrity? Being all over the news?"

"Not that part of it." I peered down the empty hall. I hoped Creepy Roy was still in the dining room, glued to the image of Giles, his hero. "Maybe I didn't want to remember that life. Maybe I made up a new one. Dr. Embry can tell you about it. Anyway, Hailey, I just had to get out of there."

"Understood. I couldn't stand to listen to that old gasbag talk about me for another minute."

"Which old gasbag?" We both laughed.

"The one who is not your grandfather," she clarified. "On the other hand, I'd say your granddaddy is his own kind of scary." I silently agreed. "You going to be okay?"

"Sure. Heading to the library. Pick up something vacuous and glossy to read."

"That reminds me, Tenn. I'm gonna call you Tenn, okay? Your very formal fiancé, the good doctor, cornered me for a little tête-a-tête after our chat in the reading room. Seems our Mr. Barnaker is telling tales on you."

Oh God. Creepy Roy saw us together? My pulse started to race again. "Giles cornered you? What did you tell him?"

"Heck, I just went on and on about us looking at the pictures in *Vogue* together and all the latest fashions you're crazy about."

"That's it? Really?"

"That's all we talked about, right? You remember." She winked. "Girl talk. I chattered on about clothes, clothes, clothes. And shoes! Till Dr. Embry's eyes glazed right over. It's a particular talent of mine. When he came out of his coma, he told me it would good for you to have a friend. Someone you could talk about clothes with."

"Oh, Hailey. Thank you. And he bought it? So it's officially all right for you to talk to me? For us to talk?" My mood turned. "Wait. I get it. He wants you to spy on me."

"I believe he does. But I'm no tattletale, Tennyson. Every last person in this world is entitled to a private thought and someone to talk to. Without surveillance. You, me, everyone."

"I hope so."

She nodded firmly and turned to go back into the dining room. "You take care, Tenn. I've got to stay tuned in here. Good gossip."

"Yeah," I smiled. "Let me know if anything juicy happens. Or if they mention poor Tennyson the vegetable again."

"You got it." She saluted and was gone.

I tried to put the hearing out of my mind. I had things to do before Giles returned, heady with the triumph of his—and the Fox's—Capitol Hill moment.

Chapter 11

A NEW CAMERA perched over the doorway, peering into the reading room.

I stopped dead and glared at it. It was probably wired for sound as well. But would it reach the entire room and the computer? Who knew? Giles was a complete bastard. First he tried to enlist Nurse Croft as a spy and then he stepped up the surveillance in the library.

At least Hailey had given me a heads-up that he was aware of our conversation. I wasn't sure whether I could trust her or not. I would have to trust someone. I wanted to cry. But I had other things to do.

Creepy Roy was nowhere to be seen, but I knew he wouldn't be far away. He rarely entered the little library, though. Perhaps he had some kind of book allergy, due to raging illiteracy. Usually he was content with lounging on the lawn, smoking, within view of the windows or outside the door.

I needed to find somebody named "Jensen." Giles clearly regretted mentioning him. Therefore, I reasoned, I was on the right track.

Two ancient ladies sat on the faded flowered sofa, a pair of white-haired bookends. They held books in their hands, but they seemed to have forgotten why. They didn't turn the pages. Occasionally they giggled and whispered to each other. I relaxed. They smiled sweetly at me. I waved back, careful not to say anything that might set them off, like Miriam the Screamer. I grabbed a magazine for the benefit of the camera, then I walked to the little desk in the back corner.

The old dead computer was gone, replaced by a shiny new one with a large screen. It gleamed, fresh out of the box. A new computer and new spy camera? Was this another trap? Or was I so self-involved that's all I could think about?

I had to take a chance. I sat down at the new keyboard and tapped a key at random. The screen sprang to life. And so did I. It was as if my fingers knew what my memory didn't. I typed more random characters. They appeared magically in a search box. I looked around. The sofa ladies were paying no attention to me. I thought there was no way the camera at the door could see what I was typing, the angle was wrong, but I had no idea what kind of spyware this thing might contain.

The moment I touched the keyboard I was typing fast, by touch. Simple screen skills and search functions came back to me. I felt like a genius just for getting into the Web and finding an e-mail program, but specifics eluded me. I couldn't remember any e-mail account I might have had. Not an address, not a password, nothing. I knew I must have had one. Everyone has e-mail.

I searched on my name to see what would happen. Information overload is what happened. Thousands of hits and several hundred news accounts of the infamous car accident popped up:

TENNYSON CLAXTON IN CAR CRASH—NOT EXPECTED TO LIVE

Not expected to live?

ONCE A PARTY GIRL, NOW A VEGETABLE

Ugh. There were quite a few of those. Further down, a few years ago:

SENATOR'S GRANDDAUGHTER'S HOMEMADE SEX TAPE GOES VIRAL

Oh God. I didn't read beyond the headlines. I searched for Marissa Brookshire. No luck. She didn't seem to exist on the Internet. A wave of disappointment nearly flattened me. Maybe I did invent her. At the moment that didn't matter. I had to focus on my mission or I would be caught up in the sheer mass of redundant information.

Jensen. Sorting through thousands of Jensens was hopeless, but the words *therapist* and *psychologist* and *Virginia* narrowed it down. I finally found a practice listed for a David Jensen in Northern Virginia and a phone number, which I committed to memory. I wanted an e-mail address or street address to go with his phone number, but before I could explore any further, the atmosphere changed. I looked up to see Creepy Roy sidling into the room. I barely had time to erase my search history and close the browser.

"What are you doing?" He was much closer than I liked. He smelled of tobacco.

"What does it look like, Roy?"

"No need to take that tone. Just asking." He was always weirdly placid, as if he were on one of Giles's wonder drugs.

"I don't like being followed."

"You should be used to it by now, considering all the people who try to follow you. Giles keeps them away from you. I keep them away from you. I mean no one no harm."

I stopped myself from correcting his grammar. "So now you're protecting me?" I kept up the conversation while repeating Jensen's phone number in my head, tapping the numbers on my fingers.

One of the ancient flowered-sofa ladies turned around at the sound of our voices.

"Is he your boyfriend?" she asked, with eyes wide and a big grin on her face.

"No, he's not," I said.

"Big sisters are such a pain," she said to her friend. "She's my big sister. She keeps secrets."

"I'll tell you later, sis," I said to her.

"Do you promise?" She looked doubtful. I nodded and handed her a picture book. She started flipping the pages, forgetting me.

"I watch out for you, Tennyson." Roy's voice was plaintive. "Until Giles says you're ready to go back out in the world. Giles wants you to have a wonderful life."

"Our definitions of wonderful life are two entirely different concepts."

"What are you looking for in here?"

"I'm playing solitaire. Alone." I picked up a magazine, still concentrating on the phone number. Roy didn't move. I tossed the magazine back on the coffee table and stormed past him.

I stalked back to my rooms with Roy in pursuit, slammed the door, and shut the blinds. Peeking through the slats, I watched until he showed up at his favorite bench beneath the trees, where he could keep an eye on the door to my suite.

What was I thinking? Why had I risked using the reading room computer with Giles's cameras everywhere and Roy shadowing me? It was almost certainly a trap. Giles orchestrated and watched my every move. I was isolated. Cut off from the outside world.

If I wanted anything beyond food and clean clothes, I was expected to beg for it. Following the accident, when I was in the pharmaceutical Fog, I didn't care. I hadn't even been aware of the days of the week. But now my mind is clear, today is Wednesday, and I'm never going to forget what day it is again.

I peeked through the slats of the blinds.

Roy the Barnacle was still outside, smoking, leaning against a tree. It was after lunchtime. I watched until he got bored and headed back to the dining room. Even Roy had to eat. But he wouldn't be gone long. If luck was with me, I'd have ten minutes before he returned with a sandwich to resume his vigil.

The door to Giles's office was unlocked. I had never gone in there without asking before. I'd never even thought about it. Once I woke up from the Fog I tried my very best to stay out of Giles's space. Now I slipped through the door, afraid of hidden cameras watching my every move. I didn't know if he kept his own office under surveillance as well. However, he kept so many things about his life private, I was willing to bet he didn't want cameras watching him in his own private spaces. It was a chance I had to take.

There was an office phone on Giles's desk. It had an intimidating number of buttons and lights, but I bucked up my courage, peered closely at every tiny label, and found an outside line. I punched in David Jensen's number. My hands were shaking.

A receptionist answered, took my name, and put me on hold while I watched the clock and estimated how many minutes I had till Creepy Roy, or Giles, came back. A man's voice came on the phone, a friendly voice, sounding very surprised.

"Tennyson, is that really you?"

"Are you David Jensen?"

He laughed. "Of course it's me. I heard you were recuperating at the Campus, but I had no idea you'd progressed so far. I'm sure good old Giles has never left your side. How are you, Tennyson?"

He sounded happy to hear from me. Shouldn't he hate me for getting him in trouble?

"I don't remember you, Mr. Jensen." I felt like crying. "After the accident— I'm empty. My memory. So many things are gone."

"You don't remember me? Tennyson, is this a joke?"

I choked back a sob. "Not you, not therapy. Whole years of my life. Vanished."

The voice sounded puzzled. "If you don't remember me, then why are you calling? How do you know my name? You must remember something about—"

"Giles let it slip. This morning."

There was a pause. "Ah. I see. He was accusing me of fraud and charlatanism, no doubt. We've been around that block before. And Tennyson, it's not Mr. Jensen, it's David. Please. We're old friends."

Old friends? "He mentioned that I had been seeing you and— I need to know a few things. About myself. He won't let me talk to anybody. He tells me things. Lies, I think. I'm sorry for disturbing you, Mr. Jensen. David. I'm sorry, this is coming out all wrong."

"It's all right. You can depend on me, you know that." Another pause. "Maybe you don't know that. You sound different, Tennyson. Listen, I have a patient waiting. But I do want to talk to you. Please make an appointment with Bev. As soon as you can."

"Bev?"

"My receptionist. You don't remember Bev, either?"

David Jensen had a nice voice, even if it seemed perplexed. I held onto the tiniest hope he was a part of my jigsaw: the solution. Someone who had known me in my pre-accident life.

"I don't know where you are, and I don't know Bev, and I don't have any way to get there, David. I'm so sorry." I sounded lame. Everything seemed stupid and impossible. Especially me.

"Don't worry, Tennyson, we'll find a time to get together. And you're apologizing? Twice now?" He sounded gently amused. "This is new behavior."

"Dr. Embry—Giles—doesn't let me leave the Campus. He doesn't want me to talk to you."

"Golden Boy never did. Do I detect some reality breaking into this infatuation?"

I wanted to ask so much more, but time was running out.

"Maybe you could visit me here at the Campus?" I could have visitors, couldn't I, even if Giles kept my family away from me?

Giles never went anywhere without an electronic device, an iPhone, a BlackBerry, a tablet, something with his schedule and his clinical notes. But I knew he also kept a written copy of his schedule in a black leather-bound appointment book on his desk. That was his master schedule, and he synced all his appointments to that book. I'd watched him do it. It was open to today. I flipped through the book and found an out-of-office block of time two days from now.

"Friday looks good," I said. "At ten?"

He took a moment to check his own schedule.

"My morning is booked that day. But I'll move things around. I'm curious. I haven't seen the mysterious C&B Campus, it's a nice drive, and I'd love to see you. To help you. Friday at ten it is."

"Giles won't be here and I'll make it worth your while. I don't have any access to money right now, but as soon as I get out," I promised him. "You can charge me double. And double mileage. It's very important for me to see you, David. Please."

"First you're sorry, and now you say 'please,' and you even know about charging for mileage?" David said. "You didn't forget you're loaded, did you?"

'Loaded' was a word I could relate to, unlike heiress.

"Completely. I worry about money all the time."

"Well, stop worrying. By the way, I like the new Tennyson. I don't think I've ever heard you say please before. Not complaining, just saying."

"Giles says your personality can change after certain types of injury. The accident—"

"Giles says a lot. Stop already. I'm teasing you. Of course I'll rearrange my schedule. I'd do it just to see the new Tennyson."

I exhaled with incredible relief. "You'll never know what this means to me. I'd like to talk about some memories, ones that may not be real."

I heard another voice in the background on his end of the phone, probably the Bev I didn't remember.

"Friday, Tennyson. I've got to run."

I hung up. My hand was shaking. I quickly wiped the phone off with my shirt tail to erase any telltale smudges. Better safe and paranoid than sorry. Through the window, I could see Roy slogging back to his post, his lunch in a brown paper bag. After a quick glance to make sure I hadn't disturbed Giles's desk or left anything behind, I slipped quietly through the adjoining door. Then I bolted back through it to fix Giles's appointment book.

I lay down when I got back to my rooms. My heart was pumping furiously. I wouldn't make a good spy, I didn't have the nerves for it.

On Friday, Roy would no doubt squeal to Giles about David Jensen's visit. After I find some answers. And only after that will I worry about Giles Embry's reaction.

I tried to concentrate on David Jensen's voice. It was warm, open, sympathetic, welcoming. I didn't know if he was tall or short, old or young, fat or fit, bearded or clean shaven. I couldn't conjure any image of him at all. I had to assume he would recognize me, brown eyes and all. I hoped someone would recognize me. I certainly didn't.

I pulled out *The Odyssey* and read before I started writing.

A port there is, inclosed on either side,
Where ships may rest, unanchor'd and untied;
Till the glad mariners incline to sail,
And the sea whitens with the rising gale.

David Jensen would be my next port of call in this gale. I hoped he would be a safe harbor.

Chapter 12

I WAS EDGY but exhausted.

I tried to take a nap. I could not sleep. The familiar uncomfortable feeling that I didn't fit in my skin seized hold of me again. Whatever my true place in the world might be, it wasn't at the Campus.

I had a clear goal in mind for my near future. David Jensen would help bring back to me who I really was and help me find a way to leave the Campus. Perhaps I would soon meet whatever family I had left, including the not-quite fire-breathing ex-senator, the famous Fox.

Giles returned just in time to pretend he was having dinner with me. Two meals were delivered to the suite: Southern fried chicken, potatoes, gravy, carrots. Overcooked comfort food, a Campus specialty.

He showed up with his tie loosened, his jacket off. He was relaxed for a change, relieved the tussle with the Senate was over. I wondered whether he'd even had a glass of wine or two with a senator. I'm not complaining. Giles can wine and dine whomever he wants. He was away for hours and it felt like I had made a breakthrough.

"Hello, Tennyson." Not, "hello, sweetheart," as someone in love might say. "Did you watch the hearing?" Ever so pleased with himself.

I nodded slightly. He would no doubt be briefed on my day, if he hadn't already been. Giles didn't mention it. He couldn't know that I had contacted David "New Age" Jensen.

"What did you think?" Giles asked, meaning the hearing.

"You were brilliant. As usual." I stopped myself from rolling my eyes. "However, I was startled to learn that I am— How did Senator Widen put it? 'Little more than a vegetable'? Artichoke? Green bean? Cauliflower? What kind of vegetable would you say I most resemble?"

He snorted. "Widen is a jerk. He was just trying to needle Fox."

"By needling me?"

"He's a politician, he'll use anything he can." Giles was

annoyed. He wanted to talk about himself, not me. "I'm sorry if it upset you."

"Perhaps next time you could trot me out like a prize lab monkey, to show I can walk and talk and feed myself."

"Are you really that upset?"

I don't think the part of the brain that recognizes sarcasm is fully functional in Giles. "I saw you cozy up to your buddy, Senator Abercrombie Foxhall Claxton. You neglected to tell me my grandfather would be there."

"I didn't tell you? I'm sure I did."

"Slip your mind, Giles? Or is it my mind that's slipping? That must be it. Or maybe you didn't think it was important enough to tell me, or I was important enough to know." I narrowed my eyes. "How stupid do you think I am? How long are you going to feed me information with an eyedropper?"

"Two things." He held up two fingers like a college professor. "First, I didn't know Senator Widen would question your grandfather. Second, you haven't been curious about these things. Not until now, anyway."

He busied himself with some chicken and gravy.

"Not curious? All I do here day to day is try to remember who I am and what my life is all about! You didn't think I'd be interested in seeing my own grandfather?"

"You haven't been before. You had issues with him."

"I'm interested now. It's time you started sharing some information with me. For starters, where do I live? How long have I lived there? Do I like it? Do I have roommates? Friends? Exes? What do I like to do? Where is my family? Have I been disowned? Do they think I'm a vegetable too?"

He put down his fork. "Where is this coming from?" He lifted an eyebrow.

I wanted to throw my food at him. "From me! Where the hell do you think it's coming from? I'm human, Giles! You treat me like a lab rat, a science project, a thing, certainly not like a woman you allegedly love."

"Tennyson Olivia, I have not been treating you like a 'thing.' You are my most valued—" He hunted for a word. 'Possession' was the word I heard in my head. "You are the most precious thing in the world to me."

"Wow. That was almost personal." The way he looked at me

was unsettling, distant. "I want to meet my family. Even my grand-father, the old Fox. Do you hear me, Giles?"

After I spoke up, relief hit me like a wave, tension draining from my limbs. As fatigued as I felt, at that moment I felt strong enough to defy Giles.

He sat back in his chair, keeping his gaze on me. "You have a townhouse in Georgetown. It's just as you left it. I'll take you there someday."

"I have a home?" *I existed.*

"You look like the old Tennyson when you smile like that." He reached for me. Maybe he wouldn't be surprised or angry about David Jensen after all.

"And my family?"

"I'll see what I can do to arrange a visit with someone. It will be a test, Tennyson. For them, as well as for you. Do you understand? We'll see how you react to each other."

I was willing to agree to practically anything at that point.

"I understand."

"By the way, what else did you do today?"

He lifted an eyebrow. I wondered if he knew. But that was impossible.

"I watched the testimony. It was riveting. Tell me about your mother, Giles. I never heard, or else I didn't remember, that she'd been ill with Alzheimer's. And tell me about Hypnopolethe. You wouldn't really use it on those poor guys in the screaming ward, would you?"

He turned his attention to his dinner. I learned nothing more. Giles didn't tell me anything that hadn't been said at the hearing.

ೞ

When I was finally alone in my suite for the night, Ulysses was making all the wrong moves too. I wondered whose Odyssey was going down the tubes faster.

My soul foreboded I should find the bower
Of some fell monster, fierce with barbarous power;
Some rustic wretch, who lived in Heaven's despite,
Contemning laws, and trampling on the right.

The nightmare was waiting for me when I fell asleep. I entered it halfway through, as if I'd walked in on a movie in progress. I was almost at the steps to the dollhouse's front door. It opened slowly, flooding light into the darkness. A figure was silhouetted in the light, but I couldn't see who was standing there. I was afraid it might be the dead woman who kept flashing across my memory.

I stopped short of the threshold and woke up.

Chapter 13

TOMORROW I'LL MEET David Jensen. Today I had a visitor. An older woman who looked vaguely familiar entered the living room of my suite without knocking. If she did knock I didn't hear, lost in thought. She slipped in quietly and stood in the open door, regarding me. I tried not to look as surprised as I was. I didn't want her to think I was one of those blank-eyed, open-mouthed inmates of the Campus who gape in confusion at every face.

"I'm your grandmother, Tennyson."

Octavia Claxton. It took me a moment to recognize her from the pictures and videos in Tennyson's *Big Show*. Giles had finally listened. I wanted to meet my family and here was an emissary. Oddly, I felt nothing except curiosity. No urge to jump up and embrace her and yell, "Hello, Grandmother! Here at last!" Nothing like that.

"Hi." I sat still.

"You really don't know me, do you?" She circled me. "I did wonder if this memory problem of yours was one of your little performances. Though they were never actually little."

That didn't sound too friendly. "I don't know about my performances, but they tell me I have been in a fugue state. Or something like that. I keep expecting to hear music, but alas, I do not."

"Still a smart aleck, I see, Tennyson." Her tones were flavored with a hint of a Virginia lilt.

I stood up and examined Octavia Claxton. She was trim and tall and athletic. If she was my grandmother, I knew she must be in her late sixties or early seventies, but she was a marvelously well-preserved woman. With her buttery tan and silver-blonde hair, she could pass for forty-five in dim light.

I could imagine her in a navy-trimmed white sweater and tennis skirt, with a wicked overhand serve. But maybe I was just recalling one of the photos or videos I'd seen. Now that she was standing here in the flesh, I didn't know what to do.

My grandmother wore camel-colored slacks, a matching sweater, and an ivory silk shell, paired with a double strand of pearls and pearl earrings. On her perfectly manicured left hand she wore what looked like a three-carat diamond in a platinum band. Her watch was deceptively plain, with a slim black leather band. Wealthy but not ostentatious. Old money. I seem to have a good eye for that kind of detail. Tennyson Claxton would, wouldn't she?

I was suddenly self-conscious. I folded my fingers, conscious of their grubby appearance and the lumpy pink ring I despised on my left hand, which I was wearing to please Giles. Aware of looking unkempt next to this elegant creature, I hastily unclenched my hands and ran my fingers through my hair in an attempt to comb it.

She wasn't a thing like the grandmother I thought I remembered or imagined. I don't know where that thought came from, but my grandmother would never look like this. I smiled and shook my head. I was afraid I might blurt out something horrible like, *You're not my grandmother!* So I said nothing.

"Hello, Octavia." Giles sailed through the door. "I'm so glad you could make it. I saw your car." He kissed her on the cheek and put his hands on my shoulders to steady me. I worked hard not to jerk away. "You remember your grandmother Octavia, Tennyson." He frowned and switched on the digital display on the wall for my grandmother's benefit. "She does, of course, Octavia. She's seen all your stills and film clips. Thanks for lending us your archive, by the way."

"Oh, yes. *The Big Show of Tennyson Olivia Claxton,*" I finally said.

Giles ignored me, eyeing the screen. News clippings of the Claxtons, social notes, a wedding announcement for Tennyson's parents, a glamorous photo of Tennyson's blue-eyed mother, a home movie of Tennyson on a pony, a news bite of Tennyson smiling at some charity ball, they all flashed by. Who was that woman who looked so much like me?

"Don't torture the girl, Giles." Octavia stepped closer to me. "If she doesn't remember, she doesn't remember." She tapped the screen to freeze the distracting montage.

"She is remembering more and more, Octavia," Giles cut in. "However, you must realize this is very stressful for Tennyson, as I warned you it would be."

"Tennyson is still in the room," I reminded him. "And she's not deaf or dumb, even if she is somewhat memory-impaired."

"Still spirited too, Tennyson," she said with a sly smile, and they both looked at me.

She was stately, this Octavia Claxton, and she knew how to put Giles in his place. I appreciated her for that. I wasn't so sure I cared for that clear-eyed stare when she turned it on me.

"The fact remains, I am your grandmother and you are my only grandchild."

Did she say it with a hint of despair? I was weary of the Tennyson-as-family-disappointment scenario. Perhaps the Claxtons had hung too many dreams on the only grandchild. Too many expectations for one person to bear.

"You could tell me about my 'little performances.' Maybe I'd remember something," I replied. "I'm told I can be very memorable."

"Don't be impertinent, dear." Octavia squared her shoulders. "We will begin again."

"Good idea." I tried to remember my manners. "Welcome to my cell. Won't you sit down?"

Octavia crossed the room to the window and selected a comfortable chair. She watched me like a hawk, very much resembling her fierce husband, the Fox. My grandparents: The Hawk and the Fox. And me, the Lab Rat. I sat down across from her. Giles leaned against the door, casually blocking my escape, ready to grade my performance, always the cool observer.

Giles won't always be there, I promised myself. Although he treated me as if I were some kind of rare, expensive jewel—possibly a radioactive one—there were still no warm feelings from him. He valued me. There was a difference. Soon, I will leave and make it clear we are not a couple and never will be. I will tell Giles that I am grateful for his tender loving care and his efforts toward my recovery, but that's it. Done, over, and out.

All this went through my mind as we looked at each other. This odd situation did not seem to faze Octavia Marie Standish Claxton. The woman must have a steel-belted spine. She had impressive posture.

"We almost lost you, Tennyson." She added, "You almost killed yourself, you know."

Making it my fault, of course.

"I've been here for months, and this the first time you've come to see me."

"That's not true at all." She turned her stare on Giles. "What have you been telling her?"

He flinched ever so slightly. "She doesn't remember," he answered. My fault again.

"We all came to see you after the accident, Tennyson. Your grandfather and I, your father, the rest of the family. Even your mother."

"My mother?" It had been so long since I had a mother. It was years and years since she died. But wait: That must be Marissa. It was Marissa who didn't have a mother. I recalled that Tennyson's mother was a spend-happy divorcée who collected men the way she collected jewels. She'd been out of my life for years. So perhaps the feeling was the same, either way.

"You were unconscious for so long. When we first visited, you were still in the coma. When you woke up, you didn't know anyone," Octavia said. "Under the circumstances, we deferred to your doctors. To Giles." She continued to gaze pointedly at him, but I couldn't read her intent. "To give you time to recover and—collect yourself."

Collect myself. I liked that. It sounded so genteel. Just calmly picking up the pieces, like a jigsaw puzzle that would fit neatly back together.

"She is coming along, Octavia," Giles said on cue. "She was fascinated by the dollhouse, weren't you, Tennyson?" He crossed the room and stood behind my chair. "We'll hang on to it for a while, if you don't mind." His hand was heavy on my shoulder again.

"As long as you need it." She turned toward me. "Giles said you have nightmares about the dollhouse. Do you remember it?"

Not that dollhouse. Another dollhouse. "The doll castle you gave me? No, that dollhouse is perfectly astonishing, and beautiful." I wanted to turn the subject away from my nightmares. They weren't public property. "I can't believe anyone would give that to a child. It's so extravagant."

"Frankly, I thought so too. But you loved it, and your grandfather could never deny you a thing, even something as foolish as that. 'Granddaddy, can I have a dress, Granddaddy, can I have a pony, Granddaddy, can I have a castle?' And there he would be, saying, 'Yes, Princess, I'll give you a dress, a horse, a castle.' Your every wish."

"Senator Fox?"

"Yes, Senator Fox."

"Children can be such self-centered little monsters." I laughed from pure nerves. Had I ever felt so out of place? Surely this woman could see I wasn't Tennyson Olivia Claxton, I wasn't her grand-daughter, I was some kind of defective facsimile, an impostor? Perhaps she would acknowledge it, if we could just get out of this room and away from Giles. I was anxious to leave the room. It was so empty of me. Whoever I was. I stood up.

"The flowers are lovely in the gardens here, Octavia. The wisterias are beginning to bloom a little early this year, I think. Would you like to take a walk? Just the two of us?"

Octavia's expression softened slightly. "My dear. You loved wisteria when you were little. Anything purple. You would gather bouquets of it in your arms, leaving lavender blossoms everywhere."

It was a beautiful picture. Then suddenly I remembered being a little girl, arms full of lavender flowers, running in a fantastic garden. No, the blossoms were lilacs, not wisteria. Weren't they? Or was it just a movie I'd seen? But now I had a visitor, a real visitor, and I wasn't willing to share her.

"Too bad you have a meeting," I reminded Giles. "And you must have some reports to go over. So I guess it's just us girls."

"My meeting?" He was sideswiped. "Maybe I could join you after—"

"No, no, no, I'm sure you have to answer all those follow-up questions from the Senate committee on your research and supply all those impressive facts about C&B and the Campus's good work."

Octavia also stood. "Go along, Dr. Giles. I'm sure your little meeting is very important. My granddaughter and I want to get reacquainted, and you've kept me from her long enough. Besides, it's much too beautiful a day for us to be sitting here inside. Goodbye."

She left him standing there struck dumb, and she took my arm and escorted me into the gardens. As soon as the door closed behind us and we were out of earshot, I had to speak up.

"I'm very sorry, Octavia. Before we go any further, I couldn't possibly be your granddaughter."

Octavia nodded. "He told me you would say that."

Giles was waiting for me around every corner, before I got there. I cursed him for it. Why couldn't he just let fate take its course?

"He says it's part of my memory problems? Because of the accident?"

She shook her head. "You've said it before, for many years, in many variations, when you did have your memory. 'I hate you, I'm not your granddaughter, I'm not part of this family.' You've said it in anger for some perceived slight or another, or on the very rare occasion I said 'no' to you. Everyone has feelings of displacement at some time or another, Tennyson. We all say it: I'm not yours, you're not mine, I hate you, I love you, I just don't know about you. It's human nature." She smiled at me, as if indulging a rebellious youngster. She had lovely teeth.

"But you don't have those feelings," I said to Mrs. Calm, Cool, and Collected.

"I know my place in this world. I am Octavia Standish Claxton."

I admired her certainty. "I wish I knew my place."

Octavia brushed my hair out of my face. "For good or ill, you are my granddaughter."

"What was she like?" I asked. "Tennyson, I mean."

"There'll be none of this third-person nonsense, Tennyson."

It was a command and I didn't want to antagonize a potential ally. "What was I like?" I amended.

Octavia headed down the path. She seemed to know where she was going. "You have always been high-spirited and attention-grabbing, and always in trouble. You have the annoying habit of speaking without thinking and acting without considering the consequences. At top speed."

"So it seems." I assumed we were both thinking of the accident, and the ill-advised sex tape, among other things.

"You can be exasperating. Aggravating. Even infuriating."

"I'm paying for it now." I was grateful she skipped the specifics. "So why on earth would I want to be Tennyson Claxton?"

"Because it's who you are! Because you've always had every possible advantage, as well as beauty and brains, though so far you've squandered them. Yet I was always fond of you. I still am." She paused at the large sundial and checked her watch against it. "We understood each other, you and I."

"What about the accident? It was my fault, wasn't it?" I felt deeply ashamed, even more so with her beside me.

"Yes, it was your fault. It's a hard lesson, Tennyson Olivia. Taking responsibility is a big step. A first step for you."

We ambled past the boxwood hedge, through an ornamental

gate opening into the English garden with its geometric pattern of brick walkways, through the bushes and flowers. The shrubs were greening and plants budding. The lavender wisteria drooped lower over the high stone wall, and purple and pink irises bloomed along the paths. It was a pretty place, the garden of my prison. I tried to imagine myself elsewhere: in an office, at a job, at a desk, on the go, working hard, meeting friends the way Hailey Croft did, so effortlessly.

We sat on a bench and watched squirrels racing back and forth from tree to tree, hunting for nuts.

"You really must not be feeling yourself these days, Tennyson. I hardly recognize you," Octavia said at last. The sunlight lit her hair like a soft cloud.

"Really?" It made me hopeful. Maybe I wasn't Tennyson and she could finally see it.

"Don't get excited. You know what I mean." I didn't, until she pointed at my clothes. "You might do something with yourself. Those clothes! Where on earth did they come from? You might as well be wearing sackcloth and ashes."

I looked down at my boxy polo shirt with the Campus logo, my baggy khaki slacks, my plain white tennis shoes. Where did they come from? Other than the closet, I had no idea.

"I don't know. They were here. They keep bringing more just like them. They're always clean," I added hopefully.

She sniffed grandly. "A better wardrobe is in order. Honestly, what is Giles thinking? Keeping you in those rags? You look like you should be tending the gardens here, not strolling in them. And your hair!" She ruffled it with her fingers and pushed it off my face.

"I'm growing it out." It reaches my shoulders now. It seems to grow fast. I pulled at it.

"It needs a trim. And really, my dear granddaughter, a bit of makeup, a spot of blush perhaps? It wouldn't hurt. You're so pale. You look about twelve years old." She shook her head, remembering something, a smile tugging at her lips. "At that age, you painted yourself up like a dark clown. You said you were 'Goth, but pretty Goth.' I had no idea what you were talking about. You've always had pretty eyes, but you painted them up like Cleopatra."

"I don't have any makeup."

"No?" Her eyebrows lifted.

I turned my face away. I didn't want her to look in my eyes.

How could I tell her they were the wrong color? "I have nothing to dress up for anyway."

"Not Giles?" I said nothing. "A phase, I suppose. You were forever trying to change yourself, all your life, when you were in fact just fine the way you were. I didn't understand it at all when you decided to change your nose. Really, Tennyson, it was only the tiniest bump. The Claxton family nose, we call it. Very distinctive, rather like your grandfather's, in miniature."

"My nose?" My hands reflexively reached for my face and a wave of horror washed over me. "I had plastic surgery? A nose job?" I shook my head. I would have to find a mirror and force myself to look into it. "No! I didn't! I would never!"

She was studying me again, and I willed her to see me for who I was: a stranger. I was someone else. She removed my finger from my nose.

"I have to admit it. You were right," she said. "Now that all the swelling has gone down, it suits you perfectly. We should have known Giles would select just the right surgeon."

"Giles thought I should change my nose? How utterly perfect! How completely Giles!" Has he always been trying to change me?

"I don't know whose idea it was. You never liked the bump, but he supported you completely. The change is very subtle and you still look like you, my dear. For the most part," she breezed on. "But what is the point, when you present yourself like this? With a little color on your lips and cheeks, you wouldn't look so pale and wan, so lifeless. A change of clothes and you won't look like the gardener."

I was still reeling. "How could I be Tennyson?" I whispered to myself. Octavia didn't hear me.

"You're not nearly as talkative as you used to be, Magpie." She smiled again, showing off those bright, exquisite teeth. Porcelains, I assumed. Old money and great dentistry.

"Magpie? Is that my nickname?"

"A perfect name for a chatterer like you. Perhaps now it's merely ironic."

At least it sounded friendly. "I prefer Magpie to Tennyson. Who named me Magpie anyway?"

"Your grandfather, I think. You hated it when you were a child."

"I can imagine. How far do you live from here?"

She looked crestfallen. "I assumed if you remembered anything, you would remember the Farm. Foxgrove Manor. We're just down the road a piece, on the other side of Middleburg. Your grandfather still travels a good deal, but he finds the old place a respite from his duties at C&B."

"Middleburg. Horse country." Something about Jacqueline Kennedy and foxhunting came to mind. The vision of it in my head was quaint, picturesque, moneyed.

"Blacksburg Downs is waiting there for you." Octavia looked at me as if I knew what that meant. Was that a place? The name of the estate? I had nothing. "Blacksburg Downs, Magpie. Your horse."

"My horse. That's my horse's name?" I should have remembered that from the video deluge.

"You named him yourself. After your favorite place to ride when you were little. Your grandfather indulged you, as usual."

"I'm sorry, Octavia, but I am hopelessly confused." I stood up.

"Blacksburg Downs was your first pony. Your favorite pony."

"There were multiple ponies? And how many ponies and castles can one little princess have?" I remembered wearing a little red-velvet-collared coat and funny velvet britches. "I've been told things, shown images, memorized names and dates, but I don't want you to think I actually remember—my horse."

I stifled an inappropriate giggle. Who else had I forgotten? My personal stylist? My chauffeur, my butler, my ladies in waiting, my ten lords a-leaping?

"You stayed with us in the summers, nearly every year, and it made more sense for us to board Blacksburg for you. With the other horses." She snapped off a fading flower from the stem. "Your parents always moved around so much, together and separately, and then of course there was the divorce. You always loved the Farm." A few more floral imperfections were plucked and tossed as she spoke.

No, I wanted to say, that wasn't me, in the summers I waded for clams, at the edge of the ocean. *Don't go out too far. Stay with your grandfather.* Dirty bare feet, squishing my toes deep into the wet sand and mud, a blue bucket full of clams in my grimy, yet successful, little hands. Sand caked around the nails. The picture came over me like a wave on the beach. Marissa's memory. A false memory.

I had to sit down again. I closed my eyes, willing the memory to stay, to expand.

"Tennyson, are you all right?"

The moment evaporated. I straightened up and realized I had an appetite.

"I'm a little hungry."

"Then we must feed you. You are too thin, even for you. And the Duchess of Windsor was wrong. You *can* be too thin."

I noticed she didn't say you could be too *rich*. Octavia looked at her watch.

"You're not going?" I was disappointed.

"I'm not supposed to tire you out."

"Orders from Giles?"

"He's a brilliant man and he loves you."

"As much as I can be loved."

"I assume he knows what course of treatment is best."

"So I'm told. Constantly." I looked at the engagement ring and twisted it around.

"Giles cares for you. And, Magpie, I do believe it is not simply the money. Of course, the money is there, no use denying it when you are a Claxton. That's why love is so difficult for people like us. It's always complicated. But he has deep feelings. Anyone can see that."

The money. The way they all talk, there must be a lot of money. Octavia looked like money. When I think about money, I think about making my lunch every day to save a few lousy dollars.

But if there's money? I'll need some to get away, to put together a plan to leave the Campus. Would it be all right if I borrowed cash from Tennyson? Just until I escape and get back on my feet again? Crazy thoughts.

"The money?" I must have looked as puzzled as I felt.

"I swear, Tennyson. Did you take a dull pill today, or is what I say to you so unfathomable?"

"I don't think a lot about money," I lied. I constantly worry about what things cost.

"Typical. The economy has been no friend to us, but I dare say we're all still quite solvent. Comfortable."

Comfortable. Deliberately vague. I knew it would be gauche to ask about Tennyson's—or my—checking account or credit cards. Was there enough to leave, to go to Europe, or South America, or anywhere without Giles? Enough to start a new life? Enough to hide forever?

Still, how much would I really need? If I'd had a dollar and the key to the gates I'd have started walking that very minute. But I didn't have either one.

"Who is paying my bills? I can't imagine insurance covering this place."

Octavia threw me an exasperated look, which I took to mean it was all being taken care of.

"By the way, your father is flying in from Hong Kong this week. He wants to see you. Now that Giles has relented enough for you to have visitors."

"I don't have a father." I didn't say it bitterly. It was simply clear to me. Marissa wondered who her father was. And Tennyson hated hers. I couldn't recall knowing either one, though I'd seen pictures of one of them.

"Tennyson, I have put up with a lot from you, but this estrangement from your father is over." Octavia's steel spine was showing.

"I'm sorry. I mean, I don't remember my father."

"Well. That may be for the best. You two can start over. Porter wants to see you. In a few days. Give him a chance. For me."

Porter Quantrell Claxton was reputed to be one tough bastard in business, and in marriage, and a well-known playboy. He headed one or more of C&B's many foreign enterprises. He was featured in Tennyson's memory books. A picture of him was coming back to me. So I have a father after all, I mused.

"For heaven's sake, Tennyson, you're his only child!"

"He's a man, isn't he? He could have more children. He might have already, from what I hear."

"No, Magpie. As much as your grandfather and I might hope for more grandchildren, there will be no others. Your father can't have any more children."

How Octavia knew such sensitive information, I didn't know. Did he have a vasectomy after I came along? I would think that no more grandchildren would be a relief. Why should my dodgy DNA be replicated?

"So you see, Magpie, you're all he has left." Octavia sighed deeply. She stood to examine some emerging rose blossoms. "I realize Porter always expected more from you than you wanted to give. I know how badly you were hurt by the divorce. It's time to heal the rift. The perfect time."

"And my mother?" I tried to conjure up her face. Long gone,

long dead. She blended in my mind into something like a movie star crossed with a troubled saint. I still missed her. And Octavia was telling me I had a mother, alive and kicking? It was unsettling, to say the least.

"She was here after the crash. Flew up from South America. Stayed a whole *week*." Octavia's tone made it clear that this was slacker behavior and not up to Claxton standards. "At present, she's in Argentina with her current polo player. I don't think we'll be seeing her again any time soon."

"Oh." It felt like the moment when you wake from a wonderful dream and reality sets in. It had been so long since I'd had a mother. It would be nice to pretend.

"You haven't been on good terms with her for some time. I suppose she loves you, you always love your family. You have no choice in the matter."

"Really?'

"Love is in your blood. Love doesn't always involve liking."

"I disappoint everybody, don't I?" So much information. Giles hadn't prepped me for these complications in *The Big Show of Tennyson O*.

"Not all the time," she chuckled. "We haven't gotten in a screaming fight today, have we?"

"Screaming fight? Doesn't anyone like me?"

"Giles does," she said, teasing me. She picked up her small expensive-looking clutch and smoothed her clothes.

"Please don't go, Octavia. Grandmother. I never have visitors. And I'm so—lonely."

I barely got the words out and had to blink to keep the tears away. This woman might or might not be my grandmother, and her personality was starched, but I liked her. She said we'd always understood each other. I reached out my hand and she took it.

"Why Magpie, I had no idea."

"It would mean so much to me if you could stay just a little while longer."

"There is Giles to deal with," she pointed out.

"You don't seem to have any problem with him."

"No, I don't. You could take a few lessons. However, when it comes to the health of my family—"

"My health is fine. And I need you."

Those were the words she needed to hear. She agreed to stay a while longer if I agreed to eat something. She made a call and a picnic was brought to the gardens. We sat on the bench and ate and talked about nothing and everything until the sun sank low in the sky.

Sated with good sandwiches and sweet iced tea, and finally some bad coffee, there was a lull in the conversation and I rushed to fill it. I was happy to converse with someone, and glad for the practice, in anticipation of David Jensen's visit the next day.

"Octavia, my feelings for Giles have changed." Actually, as far as I could remember, they hadn't changed at all. He made me frightened and uncomfortable. On a good day. Try as I might, I couldn't summon up any feelings for him, not even friendship, let alone love. But if I am Tennyson, and Tennyson once loved him, then yes, those feelings have changed.

"Have they?" She didn't seem surprised. "It seems like a lot of things have changed with you, Tennyson. Even your manner of speech. You almost sound like a Yankee."

We stared at each other. This was yet another difference between me and Tennyson. "And you still believe I'm your granddaughter?"

"To be sure. There is no denying you have changed and ultimately that may be for the better. But you are mine, Magpie, for good or ill. Forever."

"I have to get out of this place, Octavia. Away from the Campus. I can't breathe. And Giles— Well, it's all so confining."

"Now that sounds more like the restless girl I know. However, Dr. Giles says you're not ready to be out on your own. We have always relied on him to take care of you."

"Giles says so many things. To everyone but me." I was irritated. They must have had quite a few conversations about poor memory-impaired Tennyson, poor not-quite-a-vegetable Tennyson.

"Don't give me that look, Missy. It's only natural we'd converse about your progress."

"I hate that everyone talks about me behind my back." My coffee had gone cold.

"My dear girl, you are a Claxton. People will always talk."

Was it any wonder I wanted to invent a new life? "Next you'll be quoting Oscar Wilde! 'The only thing worse than being talked about is *not* being talked about.' "

"Ah, you do remember some of the things you say you can't

remember." She lifted her cold coffee in a toast, sipped, and made a face. "This is dreck. I'll have some real coffee beans sent over. Now, as I said, Giles is insistent that you should stay here for a while longer. It's not forever, my girl. He said the concentrated therapy is working, it's bringing you back to us. I know you're in a break in your therapy right now. It must be boring for you, but he says he has a new protocol to start you on very soon and—"

"I need to leave this place. As soon as possible. Believe me, Octavia. Maybe I could stay with friends?" I stopped. It was a stupid thing to say. I don't remember having any friends. But I must escape before Giles puts me back into the Fog.

She cocked her head. "Wouldn't you rather stay with us?"

"I'd jump at the chance." I looked toward the road. "I'd leave today."

"Would you really, Tennyson?"

"In a heartbeat."

Octavia lifted one eyebrow. Her face took on a calculating expression that I couldn't quite read. I waited, breathless. She looked behind me, at a shadow crossing the lawn.

Giles, of course. We couldn't think of anything more to say.

೮೩

In last night's nightmare saga of the dollhouse, I almost made it through the door. My grandmother was inside. Not Octavia, my other grandmother. I could see her painting. I wanted to reach her. I had something important to tell her. Outside, the walls of the dollhouse began to drip blood. Inside the dream I was screaming, but I woke up holding my hand over my mouth.

At least Giles wasn't there to attempt, in his awkward and overbearing way, to comfort me.

I slipped into the gap next to the bed and reached for my pen and my book. I opened it to a random page and read the first lines that my eyes fell upon.

With heavy hearts we labour through the tide
To coasts unknown, and oceans yet untried.

Chapter 14

I THOUGHT FRIDAY would never come.

David Jensen was due in a few hours. I couldn't wait to see him, but I dreaded the unknown.

Still smarting from Octavia's criticism of my appearance, I tried to take some care, but I didn't have many tools at hand. I searched all the drawers in my suite, looking in vain for makeup or a curling iron. Nothing. Most of the drawers were empty. I settled for a crisp white shirt with the ever-present Campus logo and black slacks, and wetting and combing my hair. I pinched my cheeks for a blush. I'd done what I could. I settled down to a cup of coffee and tried to calm my nerves. It wasn't working.

The connecting door to the office opened and slammed shut. I jumped at the sound.

Giles wore smugness as easily as he did his tailored suit. I briefly wondered why he wanted me to look so drab when he was such a peacock. The way he stared at me unleashed a dread that began to creep up my spine. I told myself it was too late for Giles to prevent Jensen's visit. But the closer Giles came, the faster my heart beat.

He leaned over me, brushed my hair with a kiss, and casually dropped the local morning newspaper into my lap. He had thoughtfully opened it and folded it into a square, revealing a small story under a News Briefs column. I'd never seen him with a newspaper before.

"I'm sorry, Tennyson. This kind of news is never easy. Perhaps you should have consulted me before you called David Jensen."

Giles indicated the paper. He had circled a headline.

PROMINENT LOCAL PSYCHOLOGIST FOUND DEAD

David Jensen, a respected Loudoun County psychologist, was found Thursday night in his car, dead of an apparently self-inflicted gunshot wound. According to police, Jensen had been seen at a local bar earlier in the evening. An autopsy will be conducted, police sources said. His colleagues expressed shock at his death....

There was more, but the paper dropped from my hands.

"He's dead?" I blinked. It couldn't be true.

"Your friend Jensen killed himself. Suicide. I always suspected he was unstable."

I gagged into my napkin. I couldn't hate Giles any more than I did at that moment.

"What did you do?" I demanded.

"Me? What do you think I did? This has nothing to do with me. Jumping to rather paranoid conclusions, aren't you? I know you wanted to see Jensen and pump him for information. False information, I'm afraid. Unfortunately, that won't be possible now. He couldn't help you. He led you to believe in myths about an imaginary person. He would only have told you more lies. His death is a tragic and unforeseen development, but—"

"I don't think so."

"You don't think it's tragic?"

"I don't think it's unforeseen."

He considered that, or seemed to. "Perhaps you're right. Perhaps it was something about meeting with you that he feared. Feared so much that he had to— Well, it doesn't matter now."

"My fault? Is that what you want me to think? That I somehow caused this?"

It was a horrible thought, yet the moment he said it, it seized me. Was this my fault? I looked at Giles. His eyes glittered like a snake. Or the snake charmer.

"I never blamed you, Tennyson. Why don't you trust me?"

"You spied on me, Giles. You're always spying on me. No one else could have known I called David Jensen."

Was it the computer, or the cameras, or his phone? It didn't matter. He set a trap and I fell into it. Jensen was going to talk to me. Giles stopped him. Simple as that. I was certain of it.

"Tennyson, don't you see how damaging he was? Rest assured, he can't harm you anymore." Giles looked unbearably satisfied with himself. "He can't harm either one of us now."

"Shut up, Giles. Just shut up!" I fled from him, shrinking as far away from him as I could get, backing into the far corner. "David Jensen could have told me about Marissa and where she came from. He could have helped me understand who I am." The words caught raggedly in my throat. "Why did that mean he had to die?"

Giles cornered me. I braced myself against the wall, but I

couldn't get away from him. He leaned against me and trapped me with his arms. His voice purred like a tiger.

"Tennyson, he would have spun you tales of orphanages and fairies and ogres. Lost princesses saved by white knights. Sometimes the therapist uses his patient to seek his own cure. He was using you."

"No! I don't believe it. I don't believe you. Marissa is real—"

He slammed me hard against the wall. "Stop! This obsession with Marissa must stop. Now." The muscles in his jaw worked and tightened. "I will protect you, I promise. Jensen is dead and no one will connect you to his death. You have nothing to worry about. But this mania will stop. We will go back to our lives the way they were before the accident, and we will be married. Very soon, I think, don't you? We don't really need a big wedding, do we?"

With one hand around my throat, he held my face still and kissed me hard. With the other he embraced me tight. Controlled me. Perhaps he thought I would respond this time, submit, surrender. I bit his lip and struggled to turn my head, gulping for air.

"No!" I jerked away from his grasp. "This won't end, Giles. And marrying you is the last thing on earth I will do. Do you hear me?"

He narrowed his eyes. He wasn't handsome anymore.

"Name the date, Tennyson."

"Never. That's the date. If you think I'm marrying a stranger, a killer, you're insane."

He grabbed my shoulders, slamming me against the wall again. Then he took a step back. Just a step. I was still cornered.

"All right, Tennyson. I'm going to have to tell you some things. Some ugly truths."

"About Marissa?"

"About you."

"Which me?" I leaned against the wall to keep from falling.

"The real you. It won't be pleasant and I had hoped you wouldn't insist. I didn't want to do this, because I care for you too much."

"Stop lying, Giles. Tell me the truth for once."

"We're going for a ride."

He pulled out his phone, never far from his fingertips. "Fern, cancel all my morning appointments."

I'd never seen him cancel his plans before. Not for me.

"What are you doing? Where are you taking me?"

He seemed to be calculating some invisible equation. His voice dropped into that purr again.

"Maybe you really do need to know what happened that night."

"What night?"

"The night of the accident, of course. That's where this all began, and ended." He folded his arms and stared at me. "I did everything in my power to protect you. I always have. But now you insist on the truth, and I'll tell you. Remember one thing, Tennyson: I care about you. You were told it was a one-car accident? That's not the case. There was another car involved. The night of the accident, Marissa Brookshire was in the other one."

Heat flooded my body. He had never before acknowledged that Marissa was anything but an illusion. Was she the lifeless woman haunting me? The woman on the table?

"What happened to her?"

"Marissa Brookshire is dead," Giles said. "Tennyson, you killed her."

What he was saying couldn't be true. The room spun and the walls went away. I felt as if the earth cracked open beneath my feet.

You killed her.

Chapter 15

THE NEXT THING I was aware of was being in Giles's car. It was the first time I'd been allowed in his precious silver-blue BMW coupe. We were driving down a narrow road between endless white picket fences. The sun was in my eyes. I squinted. Giles was wearing sunglasses.

"All better?" he asked. "Awake now?"

I nodded, but I refused to look at him. I felt like vomiting, but I couldn't move. I was Tennyson. I wasn't Marissa. She was dead. David Jensen was dead. Giles was in control. I was helpless.

"Where are we going?"

We had left the Campus. After being isolated there for so long, I felt exposed, and I wondered vaguely why I wasn't wearing sunglasses, or carrying a purse. I thought about taking someone's life. If I had killed someone and Giles had too, it made us the same, somehow, didn't it?

"There's a place I want you to see." Giles pointed to the road ahead. I saw nothing but white fences and grassy meadows. I leaned my head back and watched the pickets click by.

"Why?"

"Because you asked for it." That sounded threatening. "Apparently you had to find out this way, Tennyson. I didn't want you to find out at all." I could feel his gaze on me. "Perhaps it's for the best if you see for yourself. I didn't realize to what extent you were affected by the accident. How deeply your memory was compromised, twisted. I, of all people, should have known there would be more than simple memory loss. There are times when the brain steps in to protect you. The mind can blot out terrible memories. And create them."

"Does it act like the drug you described to the Senate? Hypnopolethe?"

Maybe I should take that drug. I didn't want to be Marissa or Tennyson. I wanted to be an anonymous woman without a troubled past. I wanted to be no one.

"Sometimes," Giles said. "But now you need to know. You must understand who you are, who we are."

I closed my eyes. I didn't know where he was taking me. I didn't really care. I fell into the Fog again.

ꕥ

When I woke up, we were standing in the Union Cemetery in Leesburg, Virginia, in the newer section of the graveyard. I didn't see a sign, so Giles must have told me where we were. The ground before us still bore the slightly raised mound of a recent burial. A flat marker in the earth bore the name MARISSA ALEXANDRA BROOKSHIRE.

I was aware that it was steamy in the sun, and the trees and grass glowed an exaggerated green. Everything took on an unreal brightness, in contrast to the darkness inside me. The recently watered dirt was soft. My feet sank in with every step. Sprinklers turned on in another section next to us. There were few people in the cemetery. If I had screamed and fallen to the ground, no one would have found it unusual. After all, it was a place of mourning.

Marissa was dead and I was a killer. All my fault. How could I bear the guilt? Giles's explanation hadn't clarified anything. None of it felt real. But he made sure he was there to comfort me. He put his arm around me and I let him, without a fight.

"What about her family?" I asked. She must have had family. How many people had I hurt? My grief expanded, filled the day, the sunlight, the whole world. "Where are they?"

"None came forward." Giles said.

"What about friends?"

"That's all I know."

"Did David Jensen have anything to do with Marissa Brookshire?" He was dead and she was dead and neither could defend themselves.

Giles's jaw clenched again. "Jensen was a dangerous lunatic. He convinced you of things that couldn't have happened. And at some point, after the accident, you must have heard Marissa's name, heard that she died at the scene. You incorporated her name into your fictitious history."

"But why? That can't be possible. You told me I had a traumatic brain injury. I was unconscious. How could I have known about her?"

"You were conscious for some time after the accident, before your mind closed down. I didn't know how much you retained. At that moment, as she was dying, you wished to take her place." He followed me, hovered over me. "You wanted Marissa Brookshire to live and Tennyson Claxton to die. To take responsibility, for once in your life. That's what you tried to do, deny who you were and give life to a dead woman. The rest came from your own imagination. And your guilt."

Giles had lied to me before. Which part of which story was true? I shrugged off his arm and staggered away from him, closer to the grave. I didn't trust a word he said. With his cool analytical voice, Giles could make anything sound reasonable. But I could only trust what I could see and all I could see was a fresh grave with Marissa's headstone.

"Is that really what happened?" It was time to remember something. "I saw the photographs. I read the news stories. It was a one-car accident, Giles. No one else. Just me."

I shook my head to clear it. My eyes were wet. He lifted my face and looked into my eyes.

"Yes. You saw photographs of your car. But think. You're a Claxton, Tennyson. There is a thing called Claxton money, and Claxton power. Many things are possible for Claxtons, and for those who protect them. Before the press got hold of the whole story, I was able to make certain information—go away."

I sank to my knees and bowed my head at her gravestone.

"Did I see her dead?" I clearly recalled the woman in my nightmares. I saw her face, so much like mine.

A flash of surprise crossed his face. "Perhaps. Yes. You might have seen her before we could take control of the accident scene. Perhaps that's part of what triggered your breakdown. And Tennyson: Marissa had the green eyes."

"I'm so sorry," I said to Marissa. Green eyes. No wonder she was haunting me, but why did she look so much like me? I made the Sign of the Cross.

"What are you doing?" Giles asked sharply.

"I need to pray." I craved forgiveness and absolution, even though I knew it couldn't be possible. Giles grabbed my arm and jerked me to my feet.

"There is no need to be maudlin. You look ridiculous." He looked around to see who might be watching. No one. His tone gentled into the purr again. "You never believed in God before, Tennyson. It would be ludicrous to start now. This is not an opera!

It's time to move on with our lives. There's nothing you can do for her. Marissa Brookshire is dead. Put her behind you. It's all about us now."

&

The only release I could possibly have was in writing down my story and my sins. As for Ulysses, he too had known death. And given death, and witnessed the raging Cyclops.

He answer'd with his deed: his bloody hand
My hands were on the wheel.
Snatch'd two, unhappy! of my martial band;
Two people dead. Because of me.
And dash'd like dogs against the stony floor:
It was an empty road on a snowy night.
The pavement swims with brains and mingled gore.
Marissa is dead. I saw her face.

Chapter 16

I AM HAUNTED by David Jensen and Marissa Brookshire.

Giles, in his oh-so-solicitous manner, forced me take something to help me sleep. I was out for two days. After that, he kept attempting to ply me with drugs. I refused to take any more. I suspected he was hiding it in my food as if I were a cat. I tried to eat as little as possible. Easy. I had no appetite.

If facing the mirror was hard, facing myself was worse. I barely noticed that Porter Claxton failed to show up for that much-heralded father-daughter reunion, due to "urgent business concerns." I wasn't surprised. I never expected to meet my father. He was still a fiction.

I was soul-sick for a week, guilt-ridden over a crime I couldn't remember and a crime I didn't witness. The burden of two deaths. Writing in my journal was almost a lost cause. I could barely get out of bed.

Giles kept assuring me that Marissa's death had been neatly dealt with and there would be no repercussions for me. He said there was not even a death notice in the newspapers.

"Now that all your secrets are exposed, you can move forward," he said. "We can move forward. Together."

"What does my family think of the great Claxton cover-up?"

"I wouldn't mention it to them. They'll think you're raving."

"Meaning you arranged the cover-up without telling them?"

"I don't bother your grandparents with details they don't need to know. It would only upset them."

There was no question of going to David Jensen's funeral. Giles forbade any talk of it. I managed to find Jensen's obituary in a local newspaper someone left behind in the dining hall. An actual paper newspaper, not just a scanned clipping of a smiling Tennyson Claxton at some ball. It must have belonged to a memory-impaired resident rather than one of the staff members, who were always plugged into technology.

In that newspaper I finally saw a picture of the man I had been desperate to meet. He had been heading into middle age with a receding hairline, a graying beard, and a warm smile. David wasn't what I considered attractive, but he had a face that looked trustworthy, someone in whom I might confide. However, appearances can deceive, as I have learned.

Why would Jensen kill himself immediately after agreeing to see me? When I called him, he could have said he was too busy, he had plans, he wasn't interested. No, he said he wanted to see me. He didn't sound worried or afraid. Certainly not of me.

Jensen's obituary had a puzzled tone. He had no known history of suicide attempts or depression, it said. To all, he seemed to be a happy, upbeat guy. His career was solid and his social calendar was full. He was on good terms with an ex-wife. A dream vacation with a girlfriend was planned.

No one knew where Jensen got the gun. He wasn't known to own a gun. The weapon wasn't registered. And the paper pointed out that David Jensen had always advocated for stronger gun control.

I tried to imagine him sitting alone in his car and deciding to end it. I couldn't.

Who really pulled the trigger? Was it Giles? Or Creepy Roy with his nicotine-stained fingers? His dead-eyed stare came to mind. I hoped Roy wasn't the last thing David Jensen saw in this lifetime.

Since the incident in the cemetery, only one thought has kept me going: fleeing from Giles Embry. I can't do anything about Marissa's lost life. I must do something about mine. As for Giles, he seemed almost alarmed by my deep blue depression. He and my treatment team decided that Pegasus, Phase Two of my treatment protocol, had to start soon. I didn't know what it entailed exactly, only that it promised to be more grueling and invasive, perhaps even surgical, and I didn't want to be subjected to any more of Giles's mind games.

The only friendly face around me was Hailey Croft. She went out of her way to chat with me. She warned me that Giles always wanted her observations after he'd seen us cross paths on the cameras. Hailey made it clear to me that while she was happy to report our frothy conversations about fashion, she was not his puppet or his spy. We were becoming friends, of a sort.

I knew I had to shake off this ennui and call on the kindness of strangers. Or strange relations. I started writing between the lines in my journal again.

We to thy shore the precious freight shall bear,
If home thou send us and vouchsafe to spare.

 C3

Today, the end of May, it was my grandmother who came to my rescue. Not even Giles Embry could defy Octavia Marie Claxton.

Octavia came to see me every day. Some days I could barely speak to her. She would sit and watch me while I slept. She didn't know why I'd sunk into the blues, but that was the great thing about her. She took it in stride. She soldiered on. I insisted that our meetings be private, without Giles. Every time I saw her I campaigned to leave the Campus and run away to her house, if she would have me.

"But what about your therapy?" Octavia asked. "Doctor Giles says your therapy is crucial."

"If I need therapy I can visit the Campus, or I can find new therapists," I insisted. "Physically, I'm fine. My arm is better, my stamina has increased." I looked at the angry inches-long thin scar on my arm. It had faded, but there was some residual puckering. I had other scars, but they were hidden inside me and my soul.

"You like your doctors here," she said, after a pause.

"Some of them."

As much as I liked and respected Dr. Chu, I was tired of endlessly chatting about myself and playing memory and mind games. My brain had been relentlessly scanned and found wanting. I memorized *The Big Show of Tennyson O.* I could name all the famous Claxtons and Standishes going back seven generations. How much more could I take?

It was time to listen to other voices, to meditate instead of talk, and to meet the rest of the infamous family. I didn't want to be Tennyson Claxton, but I was trying to resign myself to her fate.

"Please, Octavia, you can send me back if it doesn't work out," I lied, never intending to return. If she didn't want me, I would find a way to run.

"Well, Magpie," she said carefully, "Fox and I are more than willing to try, though Giles is dead-set against it. I insisted. And when I insist on something, my dear, I get my way."

"You did? Giles backed down? I don't know what to say." Saying I owed her my life would have been too dramatic.

"In any event, he wants you back here at the Campus for an intensive stay. Several weeks of therapy. In a month or so, perhaps."

We'll see about that, I thought.

"It's settled? I really can leave with you?" I was afraid to breathe. Afraid it would dissolve around me.

"You may, sugar. Today is the day. But Doctor Giles will be visiting the Farm daily to keep an eye on you, and your progress."

"I'm free to leave this place? Today? Oh my God, Octavia! Thank you." She wasn't very huggable as grandmothers go, and I was out of practice at hugging people, but I couldn't help hugging her.

"Freedom always comes at a cost, Tennyson," she said softly as we embraced. Uncle Sam had nothing on Octavia Claxton. She lived by a set of iron-clad rules.

She smiled and handed me a package. It had become part of our ritual. Every morning, another little gift. She brought me expensive roasted coffee beans, a silk blouse, some pretty makeup. I had no way to reciprocate.

"I don't have anything for you," I complained.

There was a small store on the grounds where residents could purchase a few items: candy, gum, sodas, magazines. Warm socks were a huge hit with the older residents. There was nothing there to buy for someone like my grandmother.

"Don't you think coming back into our lives is a sufficient gift for your grandfather and me?"

"I haven't exactly been a welcome gift before."

Octavia smiled at that. "But you are a gift, Magpie. And you don't have to open this one now. Why don't you save it for after I leave?"

"I'm not coming with you?" My throat went dry.

"Giles insists you must attend to your session first. He'll see you come home directly afterward. Or I will skin him alive."

At that moment, Giles arrived to end our visit, as cheerful as a thundercloud. As Octavia had predicted, he promised to darken our every day at the Farm with his presence, so I would never rest easy. That's not exactly how he put it.

"You will need these for anxiety, Tennyson." He handed me a hefty vial of pills. "You will be overwhelmed as your world expands. You may have breakdowns. These will help you, until the medical team and I can get to you."

"Thank you, Giles. So thoughtful. So trusting."

I'd find a toilet to flush them down later. Whatever they were, I didn't want them. He took my hand, eyeing the engagement ring on my finger. It still looked preposterous on my hand, but it made him happy. He presented me with a silver cell phone, brand-new, pre-programmed with his and Dr. Chu's and several other Campus doctors' phone numbers. It wasn't romantic, but it was practical. Just like Giles.

Dr. Chu handed me a cup of hot tea. It was our last session before I left the Campus.

"You changed your brand," I commented.

"Yes. Chai makes a nice break, don't you think? There's a bit more body and it goes well with cream." He offered me a small pitcher.

"Chai with real cream. It's just constant stimulus overload around here, Dr. Chu."

He smiled. "Are you afraid to leave?"

"I'm afraid to stay."

"You're better. Your memories are stronger and clearer."

"Yes. I'm working on new memories from here on out."

"That's good. It's positive. Have you promised yourself anything?"

"I'm pretty sure I promised to become a better person." It sounded false even as the words left my mouth. I could just as easily have chirped, *I'm a people person*, or *I want to work for world peace*. Nothing bothered Dr. Chu.

"You've made great progress, Tennyson. I'm very pleased. We're all pleased."

"There are still a few gaps."

"There's always more work to do. We'll still be seeing each other twice a week, you know, so don't be a stranger." He smiled again and I smiled back. I couldn't wait to be a stranger. "You do realize that Dr. Embry believes you'll soon be back here? That the stress of re-entering the world will be too much for you?"

"I'll have to prove him wrong."

Chapter 17

DRIVING PAST THE gates and guards of the Campus that afternoon left me weak.

With relief. And trepidation. Octavia's promise to skin Giles alive must have made an impact. He predictably insisted on delivering me to the Farm in person. He wouldn't dare double-cross Octavia Claxton.

The last of the dogwood blossoms were fading and the trees had taken on a richer, deeper green. Masses of roses bloomed under the turquoise sky. Everything was so beautiful on the outside. I was leaving the Campus. Was it really so simple? Could I fly away and change my life? I sighed.

"Are you sad, Tennyson?" Giles couldn't tell the difference between a sigh of contentment and one of despair. I wasn't going to help him out.

"Not at all. Could we have some music, please?"

One more quiz about my state of mind and what I remembered about the Claxton family estate, the Farm, and I would jump out of the car. Giles located some smooth jazz on the BMW's satellite radio. It set my teeth on edge, as I'm sure he knew it would. I took the controls and found a classical channel. They were playing Ravel's "Pavane for a Dead Princess." I tried not to find random symbolism in it.

"You're very quiet," he said.

"Enjoying the ride." Relishing my departure from the Campus and from Giles. It was almost a fait accompli.

We hadn't discussed Marissa or the accident since that day in the cemetery. He didn't bring it up. I couldn't bear it. I desperately hoped that what he told me about the accident was another tale designed to control me. I planned to find out more as soon as I could manage. I held on tight to the slender fact that I had a friend (Hailey Croft) who had a friend (Mercy Underhill) who was supposed to be a "problem solver."

I wore the pink bazooka ring to please Giles, to make leaving easier without another argument. I had no intention of being tied to him in unholy matrimony. My hands were finally manicured, cuticles no longer ragged, and the nails filed and painted a pale pink. My hair was combed into something like a style. Hailey had supplemented my makeup supplies (courtesy of Octavia) with samples from one of her many friends, one who worked at the Chanel counter at Nordstrom. I applied it fast and with a light hand. Looking in the mirror for any length of time was still painful: My eyes still were brown. Hailey assured me I looked fresh and natural. Even Giles seemed to respond to my improved appearance. But I couldn't tear a compliment from his lips. I realized I didn't want one. Not from him.

My clothes were as woefully prosaic as usual, a pair of jeans that bagged and an oversized yellow polo shirt with the ever-present Campus logo. I was a walking advertisement for the memory—and style—impaired. In the BMW's trunk was one borrowed rolling suitcase, half full of clothes. At the Campus, it seldom occurred to me that I might have, or even need, more possessions somewhere in the world. I hadn't needed much there. My suitcase held khaki slacks, Campus logo shirts, and some utilitarian underwear. I tucked my copy of *The Odyssey* in between layers of khakis.

Perhaps embarrassed about my paltry wardrobe, Giles said, "Don't worry, you have closets full of clothes at the Farm."

"Why didn't you bring my things to the Campus?"

"You didn't need endless distractions about what to wear. Which shoes with which dress. How to wear your hair."

"I worried about those sorts of things?"

"Quite a lot, actually."

I contemplated the simplicity of having one suitcase. I enjoyed the way it offered me mobility and didn't weigh me down. Too bad everything inside it was so ugly.

However, I had something beautiful, too. In my lap, I held something far more important to me than my drab clothes: a new leather Hermès bag, the gift from my grandmother. I unwrapped it the moment I was alone in my room, and I was stunned. It was a handsome purse in a nice rich red, and I knew a little something about Hermes, a.k.a. Mercury, the divine messenger of the Greek gods, who also happened to be Ulysses' helpful great-grandfather in *The Odyssey*.

The purse looked very expensive, just the kind of handbag a Claxton heiress would find essential, and I'm sure Octavia didn't have Greek mythology in mind when she picked it out for me. Inside the matching wallet was $1000 in cash with a note from her: "You might need a little mad money, just until you get settled."

A thousand dollars? Mad money? From the grandmother in my mind—whom I might have made up—that would be about twenty bucks. A windfall of $1000 would be earmarked for the proverbial rainy day, stashed in a savings account after a mad dash to the bank.

Even more critical than the cash were my driver's license, my Social Security card, and a couple of credit cards, American Express and Visa, with my name embossed in raised print. Tennyson Olivia Claxton has credit cards, therefore she exists! I heard the words *credito ergo sum* in my head, and I wondered how on earth I was able to make bad puns in Latin. Blame it on Ulysses.

There was a checkbook in a matching red leather cover. There was nothing in the register, so I had no idea how much was in the account. It didn't matter. These ID cards were my passport back into the world, though I had no idea how I could still have a driver's license after my deadly accident. Maybe it was the Claxton magic. I decided not to question my good fortune.

I studied the documents like they were a Rosetta Stone, hunting for clues about myself. The signatures on the cards: Were they mine? In some of my gentler memory therapy sessions I had been made to practice writing my name, Tennyson Olivia Claxton. It was close to the ones on the cards, though not identical. Handwriting changes over time, Giles had said. No problem. And I'm sure I can learn to form that exuberant T, the extravagant O, and the oversized C. All I need is a few blank checks and charge slips to practice on.

I gazed out the window of Giles's car, which he regarded with far more affection than me. On takeoff he had nonchalantly stroked the leather upholstery, checked the mirrors, donned his sharp Ray-Bans, and pulled on expensive leather driving gloves.

The grass was the color of promise, and the feathered clouds, lit from within, appeared as if they had been painted on an azure canvas. Along the side of the road, I saw an impromptu memorial for someone who died in a car accident. A homemade cross was wound with fading silk flowers.

My mood swung like a pendulum. Had anyone laid flowers at the site of my terrible crash, of Marissa's death?

"Did it happen here?"

"Did what happen?" Giles hadn't seen the memorial flowers.

"The accident. Is that where it happened? Back there, where those flowers were?" We were speeding down a country road, leaving the cross and flowers far behind.

"Don't be morbid, Tennyson." Giles squeezed my hand. "It's not healthy to dwell on it."

Was he serious? He could blithely tell me I killed somebody with my car, and I wasn't supposed to be morbid? Why was it so easy for him to dismiss everything I'd done and experienced?

"I can never make amends for what I did, Giles."

He glanced over at me with a look I hadn't seen before. "You are helping people, Tennyson, more than you'll ever know."

"How am I supposed to be doing that?"

"With your recovery. If you can recapture your memories, your history, it will be a breakthrough in memory research."

"Like Jonathan?"

"Exactly like Jonathan. The same treatments that are working for the two of you can work for others with traumatic brain injuries and severe memory loss. You're showing us the way forward."

I snorted in response. Being a good little lab rat didn't make me a good human being. No matter how important his research was and how much I was helping him, the world would be better if I hadn't caused that accident, if someone hadn't died.

Giles would no doubt write me up as a case history in some medical journal. I would be called Patient A. "Patient A exhibited anger when she was brought to the research institute, empty of her personal history and identity…" Patient A. Is that how you treat someone you love?

He slowed the car as we passed between emerald hills with white-fenced horse pastures and descended into the picture-perfect town of Middleburg, Virginia. Perfect, at least on the surface. We passed several empty storefronts, evidence that the town's economy was not quite as lush as the surrounding countryside. Giles said we were close to the Claxtons' famous Farm, so I paid careful attention to my surroundings for anything familiar. I tried to breathe deeply, as Dr. Chu had recommended, and empty my mind of anxiety so that memories might surface, like koi in a pond. No koi. Just nerves.

Nevertheless, I was charmed by this little place. Middleburg resembled something out of time, a storybook come to life. The town was quaint to excess, and the Hunt Country culture alive. Or perhaps there was some kind of costume event going on. A man and a woman strolled down the street in red riding jackets, white jodhpurs, and riding boots that reached their knees. I wondered if they'd just tied their horses to a parking meter. I wished I had a camera. I didn't think about using my new cell phone. I wasn't up to speed on it yet.

"Don't stare, Tennyson," Giles interrupted my thoughts. "You're gawking like a tourist."

"But everything is so interesting, and I *am* a tourist." I would have taken a picture. Lots of pictures. A short walk, a mug of coffee, that would take my mind off my troubles for a minute, or so I told myself. "Look, there, that sign: A Cuppa Giddy Up. Must be a coffee shop. For horses. Down there, in the basement. Stop the car!"

He pulled over to the curb in front of the shop. "Are you feeling all right, Tennyson?"

"I didn't get my coffee this morning." The truth was I couldn't eat or drink anything. I was angling for more time, even though I was desperate to know where I belonged. "I have butterflies."

"They are your family. There is no reason to worry. And if it's all too much for you, I can take you back."

"No, thanks. You're right, though. This is going to be such a big change for me. Consider my contribution to science," I said. "My amazing brain and all that. My brain needs coffee. Now."

"Very well. If you must have coffee, let's go. I wouldn't want to deny your brain." He opened his car door. I nearly flew out of mine.

"It's such a pretty little village. I'd like to look around."

"It's coming back to you? You practically grew up here in Middleburg."

"Here? In Never-Neverland? Really?" I was charmed because it was so different from any place I remembered, not because it was familiar. "Well, then I'd like to get reacquainted."

The couple in riding clothes was heading to the same coffee shop. And then the worst possible thing happened. The woman turned around, went wide-eyed, and grinned at me. She rushed over and gave me a big hug.

"Why Tennyson Olivia, darlin', is that really you? Up and walkin' around in the land of the living?" She had a Southern accent thicker than Hailey's. "After all the stories we heard! Well, I mean, they made it sound like you'd never see the light of day, ever again. I mean—" She stopped, embarrassed.

I had no idea who she was. I looked at Giles for a clue, but he was looking at her.

"You stuck your foot in it again, Lavinia," her companion said. He shook his head and then turned toward me. "It's wonderful to see you again, Tennyson, you look splendid." He extended his hand to Giles. "Hello, Giles."

"Hudson, Lavinia, good to see you," Giles said, but he didn't seem pleased to see either of them.

The man hugged me in turn and kissed my cheek. I held on hard to every name I heard. Hudson and Lavinia, and they know me well. Was Hudson a first or a last name? Who are these people?

"Hello, Hudson," I said. "So nice to see you two again."

"I, for one, am thrilled to see you looking so well, Tennyson."

Lavinia was one of those aggressive blondes, a combination of girl-next-door and cheerleader vamp. About my age, I guessed, with a sprinkling of freckles across her nose and, I suspected, malice in her heart. Her hair was restrained in a tight little bun at the back of her neck. Her eyes were glittery blue with a hard expression.

"Lavinia. Long time." I figured that was safe to say.

"I must say I hardly recognize you," she continued. "And your hair! Well, you must be workin' on a new style, I guess. Oh, it suits you, it suits you!"

My hair looked like hell. I knew that. "Growing it out," I said. I kept trying to place her, but nothing came. She gave my wardrobe one of those superior up-and-down glances.

"Giles, aren't you taking care of our Tennyson?" She possessively tucked her arm inside his.

"Tennyson is getting the best care possible." Giles removed her arm and placed his hand on my shoulder to show ownership. "She's doing wonderfully."

"Of course she is." She hugged him in a familiar manner, while addressing me. "You will be riding in the hunt with us, won't you, Tennyson?"

I envied her the expert cut, fit, and panache of her riding togs, yet I sincerely hoped she did not mean I would be riding a horse. I had never ridden a horse in my life. At least I didn't think so. That familiar feeling of displacement swept over me and I wanted to escape.

"No riding for me anytime soon, I'm afraid. Still recovering," I managed to say.

Lavinia's face was suddenly all concern. Her eyes narrowed into appraising slits. "You do look a little peaked, at that. A little sunshine and fresh air on horseback, that's what you need. You'll look like your old self in no time."

You look like a bitch, I wanted to say.

"And you are looking ever so *robust*, Lavinia." I cast a knowing look toward her seams. I was gratified when she blanched. I instinctively knew where to land the blow. Yay me. I stopped short of saying, "Bless your heart."

I didn't like Lavinia or her phony concern. I could imagine her sounding the alarm that Tennyson Claxton was on the loose again, and looking *dreadful*.

She spun away from me as I were on fire and gave Giles a look I had seen from other women. I wondered whether they had a past history. "It's wonderful to see you again, Giles," she breathed huskily.

He returned her look with a smile, not caring if her clothes were too tight. Hudson frowned. Aha, they all had a mutual history. I took it all in.

"It'll be a while before Tennyson is up to company," Giles said.

"I prefer a quieter lifestyle these days," I chimed in.

"How lovely. It must be divine to have your very own personal physician." Lavinia winked at Giles. "Nevertheless, dear Tenn, call me the very minute you are up to having lunch and one gigantic gossip session. I want to know simply everything."

"So do I," I agreed.

As soon as they were gone I asked Giles if she and I were close friends.

"No. You hate each other."

"Good. I would hate myself if I liked her."

He actually laughed and allowed me fifteen minutes to sip a latte to go while we took a walk around the historic Red Fox Inn, which was practically knee-deep in Hunt Country paintings.

"You've been here a hundred times. Do you recognize anything?" he asked.

Not a thing. "Sure I do. It's all horses, all the time here, isn't it?"

"Are you finished with that latte yet? We have to get to the Farm." He checked his Rolex and looked pointedly at my unfinished drink. I took his anxiety as a tribute to the awesome power of Octavia.

"Let's go. I promise not to spill any coffee on your precious leather upholstery, Giles. See, it even has a lid."

How satisfying it would be to spill something sticky on his

BMW's seats. But not so close to the hour of my liberation. Nothing was going to stop me now.

He rushed me back to the car and grudgingly allowed me to bring my cup along. Not without a final scowl and a growled, "Be careful with that. You're always so careless with everything."

Sure, we're a loving couple engaged to be married soon. In which circle of Hell?

☙

We traveled the rest of the way in silence, to the top of a hill with a clear view, I was told, of the Blue Ridge Mountains. My anticipation switched to dread as Giles turned down a long narrow road anchored on each side by a heavy stone wall. At the end of this approach, tall iron gates barred the way and a guardhouse was attended by a live guard. In a uniform. The gates creaked open slowly for us. Inside the gates, on the vast front lawn, stood a large and handsome bronze statue of a horse with a bronze plaque I couldn't read. With my Campus-trained surveillance senses, I detected video cameras tucked into the hedges, no doubt recording my—our—every move.

I had come to another fortress.

Above the iron gates, a large wooden sign with gold lettering announced we were entering FOXGROVE MANOR. No street number or road address. Just the name.

"Just how large does a house have to be before you're allowed to name it?" I said aloud as we passed beneath it. "Octavia said it was a farm. This looks like a small nation."

Farm, I was learning, is one of those adaptable words rich people are fond of, like *comfortable*. I'd pictured a farm with a weathered red barn and a windmill and a cow. This was an estate with a name.

"And you thought the Campus was grand."

Giles laughed again. Twice today. It wasn't a sound I was familiar with. He turned on his winning smile, the one that could turn a woman's head. A woman like Lavinia.

By the time we reached the main house and pulled into the immense circle drive, Giles was back to his lectures-and-doom persona. I'm surprised he didn't require Octavia to sign a receipt for the delivery. When we parked, he gave me one more warning before he released the door locks on the BMW.

"Remember, Tennyson, you are doing this against my better judgment."

"I remember." As if I respected his better judgment.

"Do you have your phone?"

"Yes, you just gave it to me."

"I'll be calling to make sure you're settling in all right. I'll call you every day. Do not hesitate to call me for any reason."

I smirked. "This must be evidence of your ardent desire to be close to me."

"Don't lose that phone," he said.

"Is that another flaw of mine, forgetting things like cell phones, in addition to forgetting my history and misplacing my mind?"

Giles ignored me. I vexed him. I enjoyed vexing him.

Once I escaped from the chilly yet stifling air of his BMW, it hit me: We were there. The humble ancestral abode of the Claxton family. Suffice it to say, I had a different image in my mind. I had seen pictures, thousands of them, but they hadn't made the proper impact. This place was so much bigger.

With its circle drive, tall white columns, and manicured lawn stretching away to the distant woods, Foxgrove Manor reminded me of an elegant country club. A big one, surrounded by a big golf course. It felt as if I should pay admission at the door and join the line for the tour. Was there a friendly docent waiting inside to offer the historical perspective and warn me not to touch the furniture, stay outside the velvet ropes, and no flash photography?

"This is the Claxton home?" I was way out of my depth. But it was Foxgrove or the Campus. The devil or the deep blue sea.

"Tennyson." Giles drew me close. "I know you crave your independence, but you must take it in small steps. Just rest this afternoon. Not too much excitement. Remember, I'll always welcome you back at the Campus. You are ready for Phase Two, Pegasus. We can cut short this interim whenever you're ready."

"I'm fine, Giles. I have to leave the nest sometime, right?" I smiled as innocently as I could. I stared at the manor house.

The place was miles of red brick and black and white trim, a blend of Southern Colonial and MGM grandeur. The side wings were attached to the original fieldstone structure built, I had learned in *The Big Show of Tennyson O*, by Claxton ancestors in the early 1700s. Foxgrove Manor was on the National Register of Historic Places, according to the brass plaque by the door. On the columned porch, I gazed up to the overhanging roof, three stories above us. Cameras were mounted at the top of the pillars.

"There's so much security. Like the Campus." I thought I'd left all that behind with Creepy Roy the Barnacle.

"Oh, more than the Campus. You'll be perfectly safe here," Giles said. "I've made sure of it."

"I was afraid of that."

He grabbed my wrist and felt my pulse. "It's racing. This is a bad idea, Tennyson."

Before I could retort that it was simply his company that made my heart race, the great doors finally opened. Octavia, the queen of the castle, deigned to come outside and greet us herself. Several small and noisy beagles trailed her, their paws clattering on the brick walkway. One of the dogs, speckled with light brown splotches, instead of dark ones, and with soft pale brown ears, jumped at my knees.

"Down, Princess. She is so happy to see you, my dear." Octavia leaned down to pet the tan-and-white dog and gently scold her, which the dog took as words of love. "King and Duke here are a little more polite."

They wagged their tails furiously and I laughed. That was their cue to jump up in unison.

"They're wonderful," I said. "Are there more?"

"Not in the house. These rascals are rejects from the hunt, you know. Some puppies just do not make the grade as hunters, so we make them pets. You remember, dear, we've always had beagles. However, these days Fox says I can't have more than three hounds in the house at any one time. Now sit, you scoundrels," she commanded and all three dogs sat. But only for a moment, before they were up and sniffing the new arrivals, begging for love.

I squatted to pet them and they were all over me. Giles remained standing, stiff as ever. I got to my feet, though Princess was still begging for my attention. She whined.

"Stop that now," Octavia said to the dog. Octavia hugged me briefly, then stepped back to cast a critical eye on my clothes. "You're here at last, Magpie. You'll want to freshen up and change into something presentable. Do come in, both of you, we needn't stand here on the porch all day."

As we stepped into the huge front hall I finally got a good look at her clothes. She'd changed from the casual outfit I'd seen her in earlier. Octavia was impeccable in a pale pink tailored blouse and crisp linen slacks, pink bejeweled sandals on her feet. Not a silver hair out of place.

I felt shabby and tugged at my collar. "I'm afraid everything I have looks like this."

"Don't you dare worry. There are fresh clothes in your room. Though I expect you'll want to go shopping soon, those things may be five minutes out of date." I must have looked surprised. "Giles kindly moved some things over from your townhouse yesterday evening."

My townhouse. To which he obviously has the keys. And where he goes through my things without asking me or requesting my input. I wasn't surprised, but I was curious what he picked out.

"Giles is always so helpful," I said, wondering about my townhouse. He'd mentioned it was in Georgetown, but not exactly where. Not that I had the geography of Georgetown in my head. That was all theoretical, while I was at the Campus. I turned toward him. "Why didn't you ask me what I'd like?"

"You bought them. I assume you like them. I didn't want to bother you with the details," he said. "I simply brought a few things I thought would make you feel at home."

"That would be very clever indeed." As if anything could do that.

"It doesn't matter, Magpie. Do you recognize anything?" Octavia led me round the hall. Giles gazed at me, expecting his prize student to respond appropriately, but I was the class dunce.

"It's larger than I—than I remembered," I managed to say, feeling more and more out of my element. I'd seen the Claxton home movies, which certainly showed the size of the place, but I was not prepared for the reality. It was funny how all the facts I had learned slipped away from me at the front door. If by 'funny' I meant terrifying. "And by the way. Thank you so much for the purse, Octavia. I love it."

I clutched it as if robbers were lurking. Did I think someone was going to take it away from me? Yes, I did.

"I'm so glad. You needed something with a little style after being fashion-deprived for so long." She threw an unhappy look toward Giles, who departed to extract my suitcase from the trunk.

When he returned I reached for it, but Octavia shook her head. "Oh, no, dear, that's not necessary. Hector will get your bags for you. Where's the rest of them?" A sturdy, dark-haired man emerged silently from one of the side rooms, nodded at her and at me, and hefted my single piece of luggage. It was light as a feather in his hands. "Is that all she has?" Octavia glared at Giles, which cheered me. "You mean to tell me my granddaughter has been there for months with nothing to wear? We entrusted Tennyson to you, Giles Embry. Just how have you been taking care of her?"

I giggled. Yeah, take that, Giles.

"She didn't need the distractions of fashion," he answered defensively. "She needed to recover. Besides, Tennyson never even asked about those things."

"That is true," I said. "Clothes were the last thing on my mind."

"Well," Octavia said, shaking her head, "I imagine that will change soon. Now that you are home. I expect you're hungry. Graciela will set out lunch in the gazebo. It's such a lovely day."

Graciela and Hector were staff, I supposed. "Yes, thank you. I haven't eaten anything today. All I had was a latte."

Again, Octavia's glare was directed at Giles. Octavia was at that age and station of life where women, certain women, are afraid of nothing. Not even Dr. Giles Embry. I liked her quite a lot.

"I tried to get her to eat," Giles said. "No appetite. She was too distracted."

"You just told me you were keeping her from distractions," Octavia pointed out icily.

"But now I'm hungry," I said. "Starved, actually."

"You'll be joining us for lunch, Giles? If you must?" Octavia inquired. "Of course you're welcome to stay." Her glare said just the opposite.

"Ah. No. Sorry, Octavia. I'd love to. But I have so much going on at the Campus. Though I suppose I could cancel a meeting or two." He checked his watch.

"Don't stay on my account," I said. "I'm with my family now."

I opened the front door myself, not waiting for a servant, and practically shoved him through it. I smiled as brightly as I could, imagining him far away. Giles stood on the porch indecisively for a moment, but he looked relieved. Maybe he didn't want to explain why he'd been keeping me in rags. He seemed positively intimidated by Octavia. I resolved to study her and learn how it was done.

"I've got to get back," he said to Octavia, not to me. "The C&B board meeting is tomorrow and I have a lot to do. But I'll be here for dinner this evening, if I may. You'll call me if there are any problems?"

Octavia lifted one eyebrow. What kind of problems did he expect? That I was going to make a run for the electrified fence? Or vault over the stone wall past the guardhouse? Surely not on my first day. I'd have to save some exciting activities for tomorrow. Besides, I wanted to get a look at that closet full of my long-lost clothes. Maybe they would provide some clue to my personality.

"We'll expect you this evening, then," Octavia said without a hint of welcome. "Cocktails at six-thirty, dinner at seven."

"I wouldn't miss it," he replied.

Giles kissed my cheek and squeezed my hand meaningfully, a clear warning not to misbehave and blurt out something inappropriate, say about Marissa.

He needn't worry. Her name still stuck in my throat. I couldn't have said her name without risking tears. I watched Giles put the silver BMW in drive and recede down the long drive to the gates. I was so relieved to see him go I could have somersaulted across the lawn for pure joy.

And yet, at the same time, I felt lost, like I was jumping off the high dive into unknown depths.

Chapter 18

GILES'S BMW VANISHED from sight.

Octavia informed me that Graciela had made my favorite for lunch.

"Really?" I wondered what on earth that could be. "That's not necessary."

She put her arm around my shoulder. "Dr. Embry explained to me that sometimes a person's tastes and preferences can change after—after an experience like yours, even your personality. But come now, everyone loves escargot and caviar, don't they?"

I couldn't stop my nose from wrinkling. "Fish eggs and snails? That's my favorite?"

Octavia laughed, a clear crystal sound. "Only kidding, Magpie! You've always hated both of them. You always complained how snails squiggled down your throat and caviar was too salty."

"You had me going, Octavia."

"You always preferred a hamburger to a snail. But it's not hamburgers, not today. Come along." The dogs thought she meant them and trailed us happily.

I took in the beautiful surroundings and glanced back at the climbing roses around the front door. "I don't know this place, Octavia. I don't remember it. I don't even know what I should call you."

She made a wry face. "I suppose 'Grand-mère' would be out of the question. You used to call me Nana when you were little. But when you got older, you started calling me Tavia."

"Tavia. I like that. Tavia it is, then."

I followed her deeper into the house, past a grand curved stairway that paused at a landing and disappeared high above me. A huge Palladian window above the front doors spilled light the length of the entrance hall, and I examined the wallpaper murals of Williamsburg's colonial history above the velvet loveseats for some hint of familiarity. They were pretty, but they were not the murals I remembered. Octavia nudged me.

"Does the old place meet with your approval?"

"It's gorgeous. Hard to imagine anyone actually living here."

I stopped short of saying it looked like a museum, or that I was afraid to touch the furniture. I wondered if alarms would ring if I stepped too close to the paintings.

"It's not so grand as all that. I'll show you around after lunch."

Octavia strolled on and I followed the leader. Behind the house, awning-covered walkways led into a series of gardens. Roses in pink and white and yellow climbed everywhere, on fences and fence posts, fragrant and lovely. Even the air felt expensive.

"Fox! Magpie's home," Octavia called to someone in the side garden.

The tall man whose white hair and craggy face I had seen on TV stepped forward into the sunlight. Senator Abercrombie Foxhall Claxton, in the flesh. My grandfather. He lifted an eyebrow as he watched me approach. I'm sure I did the same thing.

Much of what I knew about my grandfather was courtesy of *Sixty Minutes* clips in *The Big Show of Tennyson O*. He was even taller than he looked on television, about six-three, physically fit, sharp-eyed and alert. He certainly appeared senatorial, but I hadn't forgiven him for not visiting me while I was at the Campus.

"Senator." I put my hand out. He pulled me into a hug.

"Senator?" He laughed in deep and oratorical tones. "If that's how you're going to greet your old granddad these days, I like it." He looked at his wife. "She can stay, Octavia."

"Just try and get rid of her," my grandmother shot back.

Should I have felt something, some recognition? "You never visited me."

"I did see you, but you didn't see me. Sometimes it's hard to follow doctor's orders, Magpie. But we thought it was for the best. Giles was most emphatic that we shouldn't confuse you too soon."

"Now there's all the time in the world for more confusion," I said. "And Giles does not always know best."

"Sounds like a lovers' spat to me," Foxhall said. "Your fiancé is a world-class leader in memory research. That's why we trusted him with you. He is a most valuable contributor to the success of C&B. And we approved when you became engaged."

"I do not remember being engaged." I twisted the silly pink ring around my finger. "And that's something—"

"It must have been hard for a person like you to be sequestered at the Campus, but that's over, for now. You're home, Tennyson. Welcome home."

Home? This plantation, or mansion, or estate, or whatever it was? It wasn't my home. It was more like a luxury resort hotel. "I don't really recall this place either."

"Nothing to worry about. I expect it'll start to come back to you, now that you're here. Later on, you can see Blacksburg Downs. That ought to cheer you up."

But would it cheer up the horse? He would certainly know if I was an impostor, wouldn't he? What if he tried to bite me? What if I was expected to saddle him up and ride like Calamity Jane? That would end badly for both of us. I was saved from more fearful thoughts by Octavia, who hustled us along to our lunch. The dogs attempted to follow along, until Graciela called them back to the house.

It was a perfect day to dine outside. Lunch was set up in an iron-and-stone gazebo overlooking a small pond. A round table was set for three with pink linens and white china. Graciela had prepared artichoke quiche, tomato and avocado salad, fresh-squeezed lime coolers, and chocolate mousse for dessert. I don't know if they were my favorites, but they were tasty and I was starved. Without Giles hovering over me to witness every bite, my appetite was much improved.

To avoid the subject of *me* again, I asked the Senator about the C&B Institute, the mysterious benefactor of the memory institute.

"Why Magpie, you've never cared about business."

"I'm turning over a new leaf. Many new leaves. Giles says you practically *are* C&B. Meaning 'checks and balances,' right?"

He eagle-eyed me. Uncertain that I could be interested in things that weren't fluff? We all knew I hadn't even finished my fluffy degree in art history at Georgetown. Or uncertain he could trust me?

"Quite right. And C&B is a vast organization with far-reaching goals. We've got our fingers in quite a few pies, you might say."

"The short version, Fox, for pity's sake," Octavia cut in.

"What kind of organization?" I asked. "Political, philanthropic, scientific?"

"All of the above. C&B is also a think tank, one that also takes action, but not the way you probably expect. It's not Democrat or Republican, right or left. This country is on the verge of terrible times, Tennyson. It's a very dangerous world, and we're in for more economic unrest, perhaps even a depression, more terrorism, more refugees, global political chaos. C&B is trying to prepare, and to explore ways of dealing with the future. Some of us have come to realize that our American system, our checks and balances, is out of balance."

"What if all your doom and gloom never happen?"

He smiled. "Then we will have done our job."

"Where does memory research fit in?" And why did I become part of it, I wanted to say.

"One of our many interests. A vital one. Many minds, great minds, have been trapped by dementia, Alzheimer's, brain injuries, post-traumatic stress disorder. I've always been interested in this issue. I've seen brilliant men and women lose themselves in a tangle of broken connections in their brains. I'm even more interested now, because of your situation."

"It was a terrible twist of fate that you were in that accident," Octavia said.

"I caused that accident," I said, ashamed.

"Yes." Foxhall took a moment to study me. "I'm glad to hear you take responsibility, even if it makes you sad, which I see it does. But that's all in the past. If Giles's work can bring you back to us, Magpie, who knows what we can do with other minds trapped by illness, accidents, and disease? Can you see the possibilities?"

"I see Giles is a little too thrilled to use me as a prize test case."

"Giles's memory research is vital, but it's only a small part of the overall picture. C&B's big tent can effect change, put the right people into places at the top, position our political allies to do the most good, and maybe even prevent the fall of our form of government. So much of our way of life has already been chipped away. We have a lot of work to do."

Foxhall was serious, dead serious. I was being blessed with a one-on-one campaign speech, and he clearly believed in his cause. He could also be scary, intense. I knew I was widely considered a careless airhead party girl. Maybe I could use some of the Fox's intensity.

But his intensity didn't bother me nearly as much as his absolute faith in Giles. Whose side would he choose when it came down to it?

ॐ

After lunch, Foxhall headed back to his office and Octavia and I resumed my tour. We wandered through the reception hall and up and down the grand staircase, through the front parlor and living room, and past an immense room that looked like a ballroom, all in varying shades of white, gold, and pale blue. There was a wonderful library, two stories tall with a galleried atrium and rolling ladders, which I planned to explore later. We peeked into the media room, more parlors and sitting rooms, and a large room below garden level that she told me had once been the bowling alley. My extravagant doll castle had been shipped back from the Campus and now filled one end of it. She pointed out the formal dining room with its hand-painted silk wallpaper, a background of pale green with jewel-colored birds and exotic flowers. That reminded me of something, but I couldn't remember what. We continued into the breakfast room, the kitchen, and the butler's pantry. The pantry was bigger than my suite at the Campus.

We took a breather in the solarium at the back of the house. It was filled with purple and white orchids. Rare and delicate flowers were a special interest of Octavia's. The structure was similar to the one at the Campus, although more ornate. The wooden frames around the glass were old, but the triple-pane glass with solar coating was completely up to date.

"I enjoy tea here in the afternoons, when I'm home." Octavia indicated a grouping of wicker furniture with floral-covered cushions in the center of the solarium.

"This is really your domain, isn't it?"

She laughed. "The entire house is my domain and I love every inch of it. Foxhall bows to my decorating sense. Yet this room has extra-special memories for me. This is where your grandfather proposed to me, amidst a bank of orchids and roses. He was no fool and he was very handsome."

"Foxhall set the scene?" I wondered how Giles had proposed to me. Probably in a text message, between meetings.

"And delivered it on a silver platter. Come along, there's more. Much more."

I was astonished by the wine cellar, built cave-like into the bedrock beneath the cellar. It was stocked with thousands of bottles of wine, a good share of them from the Virginia winery in which my grandparents were partners. They would never run out during parties. Then we were on to the second and third floors. For exercise, all I needed to do was run from room to room. It would be a marathon.

There were two separate wings of bedrooms on each floor,

divided by a central upper hall at the top of the stairs. Down one wing, Octavia showed me the master suite, hers and Foxhall's, decorated in shades of pale green and rose, with silken drapes and bedding and hand-painted antique furniture. A floral damask sofa was positioned in front of the fireplace. On the same wing was the bedroom my father occupied when he was a boy. When he stayed at the Farm these days, he preferred one of the cottages on the property, Octavia explained.

I expressed the appropriate compliments on the décor and we headed to the other side of that hall. I was running out of superlatives. I seemed to be saying "wow" at every turn.

She brought me to an eye-popping yellow bedroom at the end of the opposite wing.

"We know you don't want to feel too hemmed in by the rest of us. You need your privacy, am I right?"

I stopped at the door. If the rest of the house was harmonious, this was a sour note. It was filled with sleek modern furniture and abstract art on the walls. I tried not to shudder at the clear Lucite chairs and table that took the place of a desk. After seeing the other rooms, this one was a shock. I took a step back. The room was too bright. I stayed in the doorway.

"This is your room," she said.

"My room?"

"Giles was in early this morning to set things up for you. It's been a busy day for us all."

"He was here?" Alarm bells clanged in my head.

"And one of his assistants, a Ray or Roy, something or other. Unpleasant-looking man."

"Set up what things?"

"I wasn't paying much attention, there was so much to do. Giles said it was important to place things just so. He said you are easily agitated and he knows how you like things. For instance, he changed the position of all the furniture."

I was instantly on alert. Video cameras to spy on me? Microphones to listen to me wake from my nightmares? Is that why he let me leave the Campus? Because he assumed he could go on monitoring my every move? Perhaps even more efficiently, because I would be off guard. Was Octavia in on it too?

"Giles overestimates my fragility, and he has no idea at all about my taste." Nor did I, for that matter, but I was learning quickly. I didn't like anything about this room. There was a painting of a woman with dislocated Cubist features. "Is that a Picasso? That print over the bed?"

"Oh yes, your little Picasso. Well, no, it's not a *print*, dear."

Honest to God, a real Picasso over my bed? I hated it. It looked too much like the way I felt.

"You decorated this room yourself, you know." She looked at me quizzically. "You don't remember? It was always a bit avant-garde for my taste. I suppose that was the point. Don't you like it? Don't you want to come in?"

"The color is just—too much. The furniture. Everything. I'm sure everyone has gone to a lot of trouble, but—"

"Magpie, sugar. Why would you care about that?"

"Why wouldn't I?"

She seemed amused. Better than offended, I decided.

"Perhaps one of the other rooms would be more to your liking?"

"I can stay somewhere else? Some other room?" A reprieve.

"You're home, Tennyson. Of course you can stay in another room. It's not like we don't have the space. I keep all of my rooms in a state of readiness for guests."

"Like Martha Washington."

"Where did you hear that?"

"Not sure. Mount Vernon, I suppose. Martha was very particular about her hams, too. Virginia ham."

"Good hams were the sign of a proper Virginia homemaker."

Octavia led on. There were three other large bedroom suites on this wing. One was outfitted in handsome earth tones, with no-nonsense boxy furniture, definitely intended for a masculine guest. Another was frilly and elegant in whisper-pink silks with silkscreened paper on the walls. Very Marie Antoinette. I was beginning to feel like Goldilocks, looking for the room that was just right.

Finally, we stepped into the third suite. It was painted a pale blue with white moldings and wainscoting, and I could breathe again. A large four-poster bed was decadently swathed in lush silk-embroidered blue coverlets and pillows. Matching drapes dressed the windows and the window seat, overlooking the garden. There was a small fireplace with a white marble mantle, in front of which was a delicate blue-and-white toile-covered wing chair and ottoman. Full bookshelves were stationed on either side of it. The bathroom featured a claw-foot tub and a small adjacent dressing room. Unlike the hyper-yellow Cubist Modern room, this one felt safe. It felt like me. A very strange sensation.

"This is lovely," I told her. "It's not the largest, but it's the prettiest, I think."

"I've always thought so," Octavia agreed. "This must be your room then. See that sweet little writing desk there? It belonged to Martha Jefferson, Thomas Jefferson's wife. It was given to me by my mother. You know, I stayed in this room the night before I married your grandfather. We had a lovely garden wedding, right out there." She went to the window and indicated the spot.

"Not a church wedding?"

"There was a minister, of course, but I always thought the garden was prettier than any church."

Someone like Octavia would think so—she in her immaculate silk blouse and pressed trousers. She might be a fading rose, but still a rose. Yet she still had her thorns. Bringing me here over Giles's objections proved it. Looking at my grandmother's perfect grooming and bearing, I felt self-conscious.

"Giles said there would be other clothes for me?"

"Yes, in the other room."

She followed me back to the jaundice-yellow room with Picasso's fractured woman on the wall and the transparent furniture. In the closet, itself the size of a small bedroom, were dresses, blouses and slacks, many with the price tags still on them.

"Oh, Tavia! You didn't go to all this trouble for me, did you? Buying all these things?"

I held up a price tag on a preposterous purple lace camisole. Over five hundred dollars. I gasped.

"Oh no. That's all yours, dear. These came from your own closet in Georgetown."

I stared at racks of shoes and boots and shelves of sweaters. It was like a private boutique. I didn't know where to start, but I selected a couple of simple dresses, slacks, and blouses. I set them on the bed and tried on some shoes. They were my size, but they were ridiculous, the toes too pointed, the heels too high.

"Try these," Octavia said. She pointed to a pair of moderately heeled sandals that wouldn't kill me. I slipped them on. Much better.

There were drawers full of lace bras and matching underwear. At the Campus I hadn't been interested in clothes, but my heart took a leap at such pretty things. The top drawer of the vanity was full of makeup and expensive cream-and-gold packaged creams. I smiled at Octavia.

"These can't be for me?"

"I thought you might need a few supplies, something fresh to help you feel attractive again."

But did I need an entire cosmetic counter full of them?

"Thank you. I would like to feel human once more." Yet how could I ever feel like myself without my green eyes? I pushed the thought away. Those green eyes weren't mine. They belonged to a dead woman I'd killed.

I looked around to see if I might need something else. A monster flat-screen TV on the wall caught my eye.

"We'll have the television moved to the other room for you, along with your clothes," Octavia said.

"Oh no. Not the TV," I said. "Why would I want a TV in the bedroom? I'd much rather read on that window seat."

"You have changed, Magpie." I opened my mouth to say something, but she patted my shoulder. "For the better, I'm sure. People change. It's a good thing."

I grabbed an armful of clothes and started back to the blue room. "I'll get the rest of these things later."

"I'll have someone move them for you."

"That's so nice of you, Tavia, but I'm happy to do it." And I wanted to make sure that other things, like tiny cameras and microphones, didn't come along for the ride. Besides, I didn't really want all of those things. They might have been mine once, but some of them could stay in the Yellow Room. Forever, for all I cared. Octavia made herself comfortable in the Blue Room's wing chair while I put the dresses in the closet.

From the window, I could see a poolhouse and the loveliest outdoor pool I'd ever seen, set among the magnolias, with waterfalls cascading over massive rocks. The pool included a lap lane and a diving well. The Blue Ridge Mountains provided the backdrop. Wow, I said to myself.

"Tell me about the pool," I said as I arranged my new closet.

"You like it?" Octavia sounded surprised.

"It's gorgeous. How is the water? Cold?"

"Oh no. It's heated. You understand, we are civilized folk in this neck of the woods. We don't just jump in the old swimming hole anymore."

"Do you use it a lot?" The pool looked pristine, the water crystal-clear.

"Your grandfather and I occasionally take a dip. You always liked to sunbathe by the pool, you would tan as dark as a walnut every summer, but it is so bad for the skin. I used to do it too, you know. Why does something that feels so good have to be so bad for you?"

"Tanning? Me?" It didn't strike me as a good idea either. Still, I couldn't wait to dive into that clear water and swim out all my worries. Octavia turned her evaluating eye on me.

"You're as pale as I've ever seen you."

I looked down at my arms. My scar seemed to glow in the room's soft light. It could be worse. "I'll need a swimsuit."

"There should be some around. We keep extras in the poolhouse for friends. They're brand-new. Graciela picks up a fresh batch every spring, in a range of sizes. But I imagine they're too modest for you, Magpie."

"Modest? What do you mean?"

"They're mostly one-piece."

"Perfect. The only kind, if you're serious about swimming."

Octavia gave me a funny look, but said nothing.

How long had it been since I'd been in the water? A year, or even two? It was so tiring trying to remember, and then recalling too much or too little. But I knew I was a swimmer, since I was a child. And my grandmother had told me to make myself at home. In a home with a great big swimming pool.

I finished the closet, and Octavia kissed my brow and left me alone to rest. I couldn't get the water out of my mind. I slipped outside and found my way to the poolhouse, where I considered the batch of Jantzen swimsuits I found there. All one-piece. I picked one that fit me in a vivid grass green, still trying to match my memory of my lost eye color. The suit was a dead ringer for the one I wore on my swim team. Wait: swim team? I was on a swim team? A definite maybe.

A lineup of high school girls in green suits and white rubber caps came to me. I willed the memory to come closer, but it wavered like a heat mirage on the edge of my mind. That would have to be enough for now.

I skipped the bathing cap and pulled my hair back into a skimpy ponytail, grabbed a fluffy towel, and ran outside. Having eluded

Octavia and most of the rascal beagle pack, Princess was waiting for me, wagging her tail. She settled down at the side of the pool to watch.

The air was warm and the late afternoon sun danced on the water. I dove into the deep end and swam toward the shallows. Despite being a heated pool, the water felt cool and delicious on my skin. I turned and swam another lap. It was wonderful.

When I came up for air, I heard Octavia screaming. She looked scared to death.

"Tennyson, what are you doing? Get out right now!"

What? Why? Was there something wrong with the pool? Cleaning chemicals? I detected just a faint whiff of chlorine. I swam toward her end. "What's wrong?"

"You can't swim!" She sat down carefully on a lounge chair. Her face was white. "You've never swum in your life. You've always been deathly afraid of the water."

"Me? Apparently not. I love the water." I was breathing hard, it had been a long time since my last swim, but I felt better. I tried to hoist myself out of the pool, but my arms felt weak, especially the one I'd broken. I swam over to the steps. My grandmother looked away as I climbed out. I had frightened her, and I was sorry.

"Octavia, look at me. I love to swim. I'm at home in the water. You can see I'm not Tennyson, can't you? I cannot be her." Even as I said it, I seemed to remember parties here on the lawn at the Farm. Music from bands, tables heaped with food, and people dancing.

"Don't say that." She walked over to me and held my face in her hands. "I look at you and I can see who you are. Your eyes, your face, the way you say things. Even the way you walk, graceful as a gazelle. You are my granddaughter. And I am not going to lose you again, Tennyson Olivia."

"I can swim, Octavia. I am a swimmer."

"There is some explanation, some logical reason for this," she insisted.

"Don't tell Giles." He would spout some convoluted neurological nonsense about how Tennyson the Infamous Hydrophobe could now swim like a dolphin because of her brain trauma. The neurons that relayed her fear of the water must have broken and recombined in a new pattern, blah, blah, blah. How did that square with my memory of my meet-winning freestyle? My high school swim team?

Octavia and I exchanged a look, a moment.

"No, of course not. It's our little secret." She smiled at me, Octavia, never at a loss, like Ulysses, temporizing, rationalizing, making it up on the fly. "You must have taken a swimming class somewhere. Perhaps at school, at Georgetown. It's just like you not to tell anyone in the family about it. Perhaps we should keep it that way. For now."

We hugged, briefly. We had entered into a pact. She would not tell Giles about the swimming pool, and I wouldn't rock the boat. I was grateful, but puzzled. Why was she helping me?

"You're good at this," I said. "And you're very good to me. But Octavia—"

"That's enough, Magpie." She sat down on a beach chair with her lemonade. "If we must, we'll merely explain that you took a few swimming lessons while you were at the university. To surprise us." She lapsed into her own thoughts. "Your grandfather will be so impressed that you took it upon yourself to conquer your fear of the water. He applauds courage. So do I."

It was a plan. She made it seem almost plausible. What I couldn't puzzle out was why Octavia would welcome so obvious an impostor.

We might both have been thinking the same thing: What had become of Tennyson?

The beautiful swimming pool drew me back like a siren's song. I dived in and returned to my laps. I swam till I was spent. Octavia sat quietly watching me.

Chapter 19

OVER COCKTAILS IN the garden that evening, Octavia prepared Foxhall for the news.

While I was given a tall lemonade, they sipped gin and tonics. No one wanted to see Tennyson dog-paddle back into a booze bottle. Including me.

"A drink now and then is fine, but it's never attractive to be too dependent on spirits," Fox opined for my benefit. "Now, Tennyson, what's this I hear? Octavia tells me you swam in the pool today. End to end. She says you looked like a mermaid in the water."

I caught her eye and she gave me a little smile of encouragement. "You have a wonderful pool. I must have taken swimming lessons, but I don't remember where or when." That felt true. I've always known how to swim. I was sure of it.

"Memory is a funny thing." Octavia arched one eyebrow at me.

"Did you visit Blacksburg Downs today?" Fox inquired.

"No, I'm sorry. I was tired after my swim." I'd been avoiding the horse, convinced he would know I was a phony. "Tomorrow," I promised.

It was the Senator's turn to appraise me. "No doubt about it, my dear, you're quieter, more adult than I've ever seen you. A very welcome development. You have pleased me and I didn't expect that. Indeed I didn't. And you're looking so well. That's a pretty frock."

"Thank you." I glanced down at the sleeveless violet "frock." It was the first time I'd worn a dress since I'd left the Campus. It was deceptively simple, nicely fitted with clever seaming and a slightly flared skirt. Not knowing what my style might be, I tried on four or five dresses before settling on this one. I tried a dash more makeup, I wanted to look good for my first evening home, but I'm not sure I achieved the same effect Hailey had. It wasn't easy to do my eyes. I was trying to make myself look in the mirror for longer periods of time without dying inside.

"I'm so happy you're out of those baggy rags that Giles brought you home in," Octavia said. "You look much more like yourself."

Did I? I hoped so. "Where are the dogs?"

"Outside," Foxhall said. "They are not allowed to overrun the dinner hour. Don't worry, they are being spoiled rotten even as we speak. We'll let them join us later."

I was beginning to enjoy myself—when Giles showed up. He was late, not that I cared, and to make it up to me, he brought me a large bouquet of yellow roses. At least two dozen.

"These are the first flowers you've given me," I said. "That I remember, I mean."

"They're your favorites," he said.

"Really? They're beautiful." I would have been delighted with a handful of dandelions, if they were from the right man. But these were from Giles, which meant they had an ulterior motive. To impress me? Or to impress my grandparents? Graciela appeared at my side and put them in a vase.

It was disconcerting to have someone always nearby to help me out. It reminded me of my deficiencies. And what kind of crazy hours did Graciela work? I hoped she got overtime.

The reunion began well. It might have been pleasant. Until suddenly it wasn't. When Giles found out from Octavia that I'd rejected the yellow bedroom, he was livid.

"That room is yours! Your grandmother and I went to a lot of trouble making that room ready for you. I cannot believe you found it lacking," Giles complained bitterly. "It is perfect for you. It is your own room, the one you decorated yourself."

"Like a kindergartener on acid," I shot back. "My tastes have changed. It might interest you that I don't care for screaming yellow walls and squat uncomfortable furniture. Maybe I did once, but I don't anymore."

I didn't mention the biggest reason I hated it: my conviction that he had hidden cameras and microphones there. No need to open a public conversation about my paranoia.

"It's not about you all the time, Tennyson. You could try thinking of someone else once in a while," he growled.

I do. I think of Marissa Brookshire and David Jensen quite often.

"And what on earth does this have to do with you? Giles, I'm not comfortable in that garish room. I'm in another one that I like much better. One that doesn't need to be changed, or inspected, or approved by you. It's. Not. Your. Room."

"Don't argue, you two," Octavia cut in. "Tennyson can stay

wherever she wants. You know that, Giles. Our home is her home. When she was a teenager, I swear she changed rooms once a month, just for a different view."

"Thank you, Octavia. I might do that." I winked at her. "I might choose a different room every night." How then would Giles hide his spy cameras?

Octavia clapped her hands in delight. "This gives me a chance to redecorate that room. I never much cared for that particular shade of yellow."

"Now, now, you're supposed to be lovebirds," Foxhall interrupted. "Tennyson is home where she belongs, Giles. Dinner is on the table, and I suggest we go in."

Giles grabbed my left hand. I saw him checking to make sure I was wearing his big pink engagement ring. I was, but I shook him off.

"I can manage by myself, thank you."

"If y'all insist on having a quarrel, take it outside," Foxhall said. "I hate it when the good crystal gets broken." I must have looked shocked. My grandfather gave me a hug. "My apologies, Magpie. Perhaps those days are over."

Dinner was restrained, but delicious: salad, garlic potatoes, filet mignon, and for dessert, strawberries and cream. As my grandfather had promised, after dessert was served the beagles were allowed in for a few minutes of loving and squealing. Giles and I were chilly but civil. No crystal was smashed.

Before he left, Giles ostentatiously pulled Foxhall away for a lengthy and private conversation. I could hear the murmur of their voices from the library.

"Don't worry about them." Octavia and I took our after-dinner coffee to the living room. The north living room, the one nearest the west dining room.

"Men! Are they having brandy and cigars in the boys' club?" I bristled at the thought.

"Foxhall doesn't smoke cigars anymore and I'm sure it's just Foundation business. Bores me to cinders. It was my inspiration, early in our marriage, to make the men leave the ladies' presence after dinner if all they were going to do was yammer about the latest House bill or Senate committee or poll numbers or what have you. It's best to digest your dinner in peace. But if you want to listen to all that political folderol, my dear, by all means, feel free to join them."

She sipped her coffee serenely from a delicate china cup. I followed her example.

"No, Tavia, I don't want to join them. I'd much rather be here with you. It's just that— Do you think they're talking about me?"

"Maybe." She shrugged. "Or possibly Giles's deplorable manners tonight."

"Does the Senator believe everything Giles says?"

"Fox doesn't believe half of what anyone says, except me. He does not let Dr. Giles Embry lead him around by the nose, if that's what you're afraid of."

Exactly what I'm afraid of. "Then what are they talking about?"

"Most likely how to persuade the Senate to agree to provide some serious funding for the Campus. Dealing with that ass Widen. Providing answers for the committee. Answers only the staff will read, I'm sure, as the senators can't be bothered. I don't miss that life, Magpie. Frankly, I can't stand those pompous old blowhards. Except Fox, but that's because he's *my* blowhard. Life is much nicer and quieter far away from Capitol Hill."

Giles finally emerged from the Fox's den. "I have to be going now, Tennyson. I'll call you in the morning. Octavia, always a pleasure. Senator, we'll talk about that little matter tomorrow."

He shook hands very formally with the Senator, pecked Octavia on the cheek, crushed me in an unfriendly hug, and brushed my forehead with his lips. He hustled out the door as if his pants were on fire.

I watched as he jumped into his BMW, and I kept watching until his taillights disappeared around a curve. I turned to my grandmother, still standing in the doorway.

"Please, Octavia, don't let Giles anywhere near my room again."

She laughed. "That's not what you used to say."

"Very funny. I don't want him poking around my room or my things, especially when I'm not here."

"He won't be happy about that."

"No, he won't. Promise me. Please."

"I promise. As long as you're prepared for it, sugar."

Chapter 20

I'M RUNNING TOWARD the dollhouse.

I shrink, smaller and smaller with each step. The door opens and I run inside.

The scene shifts. I'm not in the dollhouse, but in some winding gray corridor with infinite branching hallways. I'm pushed through a doorway into a dark room.

In the center, a single overhead light shines on a woman lying on a table. The closer I come, the more familiar she looks.

I realize it is me and I am dead.

℗

I jerked awake, heart pumping, pulse throbbing.

It was two-thirty in the morning, according to the clock radio at my bedside. I remembered I was in the pretty blue room at Foxgrove Manor, my grandparents' home. The saving grace was that I wasn't at the Campus and Giles wasn't in my bed, or in the next room.

I heard a whimpering at the door and opened it cautiously. Princess, the little beagle with the light brown spots, trotted in and thumped her tail furiously, looking up at me.

"Oh, Princess. Are you lost too? I'm not sure where you're supposed to be," I whispered. Princess jumped up and licked my hands, whining. "I guess you think it's here."

She plopped down on her bottom, the very picture of obedience, and then jumped up on me again. She was an attention hog, but she was sweet and she took my mind off my nightmare.

Once my breathing was under control, I crept to the window and my new friend followed. I opened the heavy brocade drapes, held back the white sheers, and peered out over the rear garden. Everything was silent and peaceful. I wanted to soak up some of that peace. I curled up on the window seat and pulled a soft cotton throw over my legs. Princess jumped up beside me and I petted her velvet fur until we both settled down.

What on earth was I doing here?

I felt strange in my own skin, dislocated, out of sync. Unlike my grandmother, I didn't know my place in the world. The Claxtons seemed to accept that I was Tennyson. Giles insisted on it. Why couldn't I? Only the dog didn't care who I was, and she was a comfort.

The waxing moon was almost full. It shone bright in the country sky, without the city's light pollution to dim it. Shadows fell over the land, leafy black giants.

My eyes became accustomed to the moonlight and I glimpsed something below: a tiny flare of light under a tree. Someone lit a match. I supposed it was for a cigarette. My breath caught in my throat.

Only one person I knew smoked.

I told myself I was wrong. It could have been somebody other than my bête noir. After all, there seemed to a lot of people on the Farm, from security guards to stable hands to the housekeeping help. I was told some of them lived in cottages on the property. I held my breath until he moved across the lawn, his lanky frame silhouetted in shadow, his distinctive lurch betraying him. He turned toward my window.

I leaned back out of sight, but not before I was convinced that my fears had followed me.

Creepy Roy had trailed me here. Princess growled in sympathy. She must have picked up my mood.

I had tried to lull myself into thinking I'd escaped the clutches of the Campus. Was Foxgrove Manor just another prison? I stared until Roy retreated back into the darkness.

I couldn't go back to sleep for quite a while. I was afraid of returning to that dark place with the dead woman who looked like me. Princess, however, had no problem. She was soon fast asleep, her head in my lap.

I reached for my copy of *The Odyssey* to check out what Ulysses was up to. As usual, it wasn't good. Ulysses or Tennyson Claxton, which of us has the worse luck?

Let not Ulysses breathe his native air,
Laertes' son, of Ithaca the fair.
If to review his country be his fate,
Be it through toils and sufferings long and late.

Long and late. That described my first day of so-called freedom.

I picked up my pen and started to write.

ᥴᤰ

My shiny new cell phone rang promptly at eight o'clock in the morning. Princess stood at the door waiting to be let out. I opened it and she bolted. I was groggy from lack of sleep. Denying the impulse to smash the phone on the floor and stomp on it, I answered.

"Good morning, Tennyson. This is Giles."

As if I didn't know. "Isn't it a little early to be spying?"

"I've warned you about your tendency toward paranoia. Nurturing unfounded suspicions can be dangerous to your mental stability."

My ass. "I'm talking about your man. Roy. Roy Barnaker the Barnacle, Creepy Roy. Creepy, creepy Roy."

"And your point is what, exactly?" Giles sounded bored.

"He was here last night, outside my window, staring at me, watching me."

"Roy's job is to keep you safe," Giles said. "You didn't sleep? You were supposed to take your medication."

"Don't gaslight me, Giles."

"I'm afraid I don't know what you're talking about."

"There is more than enough security here at the Farm without your pet troll lurking around. Enough security for a rich ex-senator. Enough for the president, for that matter."

"Roy is familiar with your special needs."

"My special needs? I am not mentally deficient, Giles."

"Trust me, Tennyson."

How many times had I heard those words?

"I am not a child and you are not my keeper."

I set a photo of Giles face down on the Martha Jefferson writing desk while he talked. I wondered briefly how the picture even got there. I hadn't taken it with me from the yellow bedroom, where it had been set in a place of honor, like a shrine. I picked it up again and this time deposited it in the wastebasket.

"Are you taking your vitamins the way you're supposed to?"

"You bet," I said.

My yummy vitamins, chock-full of mind-numbing dope. Oh yeah, I'm sure those are vitamins. I decided to remove the daily dosage and hide them, just in case Giles comes around to count the pills. But on second thought, maybe I should take them to a pharmacist and find out what they really are.

"You have your session with Dr. Chu the day after tomorrow. I'd rather you saw him sooner, but I'm giving you time to settle in." His cool tone annoyed me.

"I am not going back to the Campus under any circumstances."

There was a long pause on Giles's end. "I see. Then Dr. Chu will see you at Foxgrove at eleven a.m. I'm willing to accommodate your whims until you can gain some perspective, Tennyson." He paused for a moment to let that sink in. "But only so far."

"Don't hold your breath."

"I'll drop by later today. See how you're adjusting to life with your grandparents," Giles said. "It can't be easy for you."

"Easy as pie. I'm adjusting just fine. And I think we should see other people. Go spy on some other woman. If you hadn't noticed, my feelings toward you have changed."

He was silent, so I hung up the phone. It was no use talking to Giles.

I picked up another picture of me, one without my alleged fiancé. It was one of several someone had placed around the room. There was one with me and Octavia and Fox, in a rare moment of peace. All dressed to the nines. It must have been taken before the plastic surgery. I stared at the photo. It was not an unattractive nose, it was distinctive and striking. I wondered why I decided to change it. I ran my finger down my nose and quickly checked my reflection in the mirror. The face was my own. The brown eyes, however, were still alien.

Another stylish photograph made Tennyson look like a runway model. I couldn't decide whether she was petulant, dissatisfied, or merely aggravated by the photographer. Poor little rich girl. Still a mystery, but no one cared. The world thought I was dead, or a vegetable? Fine.

It was time to dress, but I had some trouble deciding what to wear. At the Campus I was so used to grabbing the first thing I saw in the closet, a freshly washed rerun of what I had worn the day before. Here there were so many choices. I finally set aside a pale blue cotton skirt, a sleeveless white blouse, and sandals.

The adjoining bathroom was well stocked with soaps and cosmetics and fresh razors. That alone felt like a luxury. I shaved my legs. I couldn't remember the last time. Not shaving my legs? For months? What a fog I must have been in! I indulged in creams and oils. A dash of makeup kept me from looking pale and ill. I combed through my hair and decided if I didn't have blond hair anymore, I should at least try some highlights. Shopping. I would have to go shopping.

My stomach grumbled. I followed my apparently new nose in search of breakfast and some of Octavia's bracing and delicious coffee.

My grandfather was rambling around the enormous kitchen all by himself, managing to look like a senator even at home. He wore tan slacks and a pale blue shirt, looking pressed and groomed. I could smell his aftershave.

"I like my privacy in the mornings, Magpie. And my coffee strong and black," Fox said. "Once I'm up, I kick everyone out until lunch time."

"Then I'll leave." I started to back out.

"No, no. Not you. Doesn't apply to family, Tennyson. I mean the staff. I don't want them underfoot in the mornings." He hugged me and grinned.

"Where is Octavia?"

"She was up and out hours ago. Your grandmother is an early riser, but you always took a little more after me."

"It's only eight-thirty." Did sleeping till eight really mark me as a lazy slugabed?

"Day's half gone."

I watched as he made coffee, pressing a few buttons on an automatic coffee maker built into the wall. I was fascinated by the thing, which he said was always set up the night before for his convenience. Colombia special dark roast. The aroma was intoxicating.

"Now, where are the cream and sugar? I don't know what happens to it. Graciela never puts it back in the same place twice, I swear." He began opening and shutting cupboards.

Grumbling about the cream and sugar was no doubt part of his daily routine. I found the sugar bowl on the counter and the creamer in the refrigerator and handed them to him. He poured me a large mug. Fox was right about his brew. It opened my eyes.

"That does the trick," I said.

"All those years of having to listen to crashing bores and looking polite," Foxhall explained. "A man needs his coffee. These beans were invaluable on the Hill."

"Would it be all right if I had something to eat?"

A curious expression crossed his face.

"You're home, Tennyson. Help yourself to anything you want. If you and I had risen earlier, we could have asked Graciela to cook something. I'm not quite certified on all the equipment, except for the coffeemaker. But I can pour myself a mean bowl of cornflakes."

"Heavens, I'm capable of making myself some breakfast. I'll see what you've got."

I found some oatmeal and the breakfast stoneware. I popped the bowl of oats in the microwave for a minute, then added some nuts, sliced bananas, milk, brown sugar, and a dash of cinnamon. My grandfather watched me like the proverbial fox.

"I've never before seen you lift a finger in the kitchen," the Fox observed. "Where on earth did you learn that?"

"It's only oatmeal. And I did go to college. For a while." I wanted to say I had a degree, but that apparently wasn't true. Wasn't I working on my master's degree? I suppose that was a nice fantasy, something I'd made up. "I'd like to go back to college, Senator."

"Would you, Magpie?" He seemed surprised and pleased. "I'm sure it could be arranged."

"I don't know if Georgetown would let me back in." Oh God, the tuition would be sky-high at Georgetown, so many steps above a state university. But it had such pretty grounds, perched on the hill above the Potomac, with views of the river and D.C.

"Oh, I think they'd take you back. You're really quite bright, my dear, or you wouldn't have gotten in, in the first place. And I've found the right donation usually greases the right wheels. Of course you might be on probation at first."

"Oh my God, really? Georgetown University?" I could feel tears sting my eyes. Why did I feel so grateful?

He watched me with interest. "There is no problem that cannot be solved. Anything else on your mind, Magpie?"

"Yes, Senator. There was a man here last night. He was outside my window, watching me."

"Giles said something about that before he left last night. He thought it was necessary, so I didn't object."

"He told you he put Creepy Roy outside to spy on me?"

"That's what you call him? Is that a nice name for Giles's assistant? Our Dr. Giles is most concerned about you, and your safety. And I know for a fact he wants to resume your—" He paused, hunting for the right word. "Romance. Which seems to have fallen on hard times."

"There is no romance to resume. Giles Embry may be some kind of genius, but he needs a course in remedial courtship." I stabbed my oatmeal to keep my hands busy. "Why all this security? I'm not going to run away, if that's what everyone is afraid of. I begged to be allowed to come here."

I had to admit to myself, however, running away had crossed my mind. Until I saw the gates, the fences, the guardhouse.

"You think you could run away from us?" Foxhall's laugh was deep and it startled me. "Most unlikely. No, we don't intend to lose track of you again, Magpie, honey. I don't believe you'd run away anymore. You're much more mature now. Giles is simply concerned about outside threats."

Foxhall took my cup and refilled it. He motioned for me to follow him with my oatmeal into the bright breakfast room with its many-paned windows. I admired the chandelier with its amusing fruit-shaped crystals and the copper-topped table.

"This is real cozy, sharing coffee with your old granddad. You look a mite worn out this morning. Didn't you sleep well, Tennyson? Is the room not to your liking?"

"I love the room and I feel very comfortable there. It's the most beautiful place I've ever slept. It's just a new place to me. I simply can't sleep with Creepy Roy stalking me. But I had some company. Princess."

"Aha. Those hounds think they own the place. Put her out if she gets in your way. About the other thing, Magpie. I know how hard it is to feel like you're on public display. It's the life I chose, but my family didn't. Let me talk to Giles. Perhaps we can come to some happier solution. After all, you need your beauty sleep."

It was going to be another gorgeous day. I heard barking outside the window. Octavia strolled across the lawn with her three adoring beagles at her heels, Princess having abandoned me for the moment. She scolded them, and they paid no attention. Princess rolled on her back for a tummy rub. Octavia sat down on a bench in the garden to play with the dogs. My grandfather thumbed through a stack of newspapers on the table. I picked up one he discarded.

"I like to have this quiet time before I head off to my office," he said. "A chance to catch up on some of the daily news, slanted though it may be."

Foxhall's offices were out back, Octavia had told me, in a separate building down a sloping hill. He also had an office in Fairfax County. As CEO and ringleader-in-chief of Checks & Balances, Abercrombie Foxhall Claxton could work anywhere he liked. And he preferred the Hunt Country of Virginia to anywhere else on earth.

"Please, Senator, have Giles call off his guard dog."

He set the newspapers aside and put his hand on mine.

"Do you remember when someone kidnapped you when you were a child?"

I felt my eyes pop open. "I was kidnapped? I don't believe it!"

"I'm glad you don't remember." He returned to his paper.

"Oh no. You can't just open with a statement like that and not follow up." This episode hadn't been covered in *The Big Show of Tennyson O.* "What happened?"

"I shouldn't have mentioned it." Foxhall leaned back in his chair, stretching his long frame. "It was a very traumatic and trying time for all of us. May have set into motion many things that happened in your life, Tennyson. The public's fascination with the Claxton heiress, the money, the politics, the various family tragedies. It might have been different if there were more grandchildren. The attention would have been spread out. Might have spared you some of it."

"The money or the fascination?"

"Both. But that wasn't to be. You are the last Claxton, the last of my line." He stared out the window and then back at me. "That is why we, the family, try so hard to protect you."

"What happened? I have a right to know."

His fingers thrummed on the table. "Two men abducted you from your school playground. They jumped out of a black car and dragged you away. You screamed bloody murder. Bless you, you were a screamer, even then. You were seven."

"That wasn't in *The Big Show of Tennyson O.*" He looked blank. "That's what I called my video scrapbook. At the Campus."

"Ah. I suppose it wouldn't have been. Do you remember anything about the incident?"

I flashed back to something from my childhood, the memory of hiding from somebody, of being afraid, and my grandmother comforting me. Not Octavia. My other grandmother, Anne. The fictitious grandmother. It felt like a real memory. Could it have been a game? I upset my cup and spilled coffee on the table. I grabbed a napkin to wipe it up.

"I remember hiding and being afraid."

"Do you, Tennyson? You were apparently unharmed. At first we didn't think it had affected you at all, but for weeks afterward your parents found you playing hide-and-go-seek. With your dolls. Always hiding from the bad men in the black car."

The "bad men" struck a chord. But not quite the way he described it. An elusive memory, hiding and editing itself.

"What happened to them?"

"The police and the FBI caught up with them about forty-eight hours later. It seemed you slept through a lot of it. The FBI thought you'd been drugged. Ten million dollars is all they demanded. But even when a ransom is paid, there's no guarantee that a kidnapping victim will be found alive. We would never pay a ransom. We would never bow to blackmail. Not this family."

"Not even for me?"

"Bowing to scum like that, paying them off? It would have opened the floodgates. There would have many more attempts."

It's easy to say that in retrospect. "What if they'd sent my ear back in a box?" I stared into my coffee.

"Happily, they did not."

"Did the incident involve my dollhouse?"

Foxhall looked pleased and patted my shoulder. "In a way, it did. Not long after the incident, I bought you the most ridiculous dollhouse in the world for your birthday. Something your grandmother has never let me forget. It goes without saying that I'm much happier that you remember that fantasy castle and not the ugly details of the kidnapping."

"You said it happened on the playground. At school?" I kept trying to remember something that was knocking around in my head.

"A man in a black limousine stepped out of his car to grab you, while his accomplice stayed in the car with the engine running."

"I don't remember it that way."

I smiled at him and conjured up a memory. Real or false, I didn't know. I was about seven or eight. I was being quiet as a mouse. "We won't let you let them take you," my imaginary grandmother was saying. "Those bad men will never take you away from us." Grandma Anne wiped my tears. "There now. You are my big, brave girl, aren't you?" That was all I could remember.

"Was I a brave little girl?" I asked.

"You were always fearless on horseback."

"My parents were still together then?"

"Yes. They didn't divorce until you were fourteen. Unfortunately, your home was a war zone for years before that."

I seemed to remember fourteen as a momentous year. Perhaps it was because of the divorce.

"Are there any news clippings about the kidnapping?"

"They are archived in my offices. Why would you want to relive all that?"

"I want to know all of it, Senator. I don't care if some of it isn't pleasant."

He rubbed his forehead. "It's all there. Once the police and FBI became involved, everything became public information. Potentially damaging to my political career. And potentially dangerous to your safety, of course." Another reason the Claxtons locked me away at the Campus? I'd be bad for business? "It can be arranged for you to see all of that, though it may take some time."

Perhaps the actual news clips, words in black and white, would jog some tiny sliver of truth out of my fragmented memory. "Thank you, Senator."

Foxhall shook his head. "Where on earth did this polite granddaughter come from?"

"Who knows?" I had to take one more stab at getting Creepy Roy off my back, or at least out of my shadows. "Tennyson Claxton is forgotten now. Most of the world thinks she died in that car crash in January or else she's a brain-dead vegetable, like Senator Widen said. If I'm forgotten, I don't need a bodyguard."

He shook his head. "You are the heir to the Claxton empire. It makes you a tantalizing target, my dear."

Empire? How much is an empire worth, I wanted to ask, but didn't. And how much is enough to put a target on your back?

"Then let me choose my own security," I pleaded. "I will keep a low profile, believe me. I don't want anyone to find me here."

Of course that last bit was a lie. I just didn't want Giles to find me. The Fox's manner changed subtly. My cozy breakfast with old Grandad was over.

"I shall take it under advisement, my dear. And now I need to get to my office." He gathered his papers and left.

Chapter 21

I SIPPED MY coffee. Foxhall's information was intriguing but puzzling.

I didn't quite remember being abducted from a playground and being held by kidnappers for two days, and yet it sounded vaguely familiar. I remembered being afraid, of my grandmother comforting me, of being warned about "bad men." Every little girl is warned about them, or should be. My memory of that moment was vivid. Yet utterly uninformative.

The more I dwelled on that moment, the more I feared it would become just another memory, floating, unprovable. Could I be so easily fooled into building brand-new memories that were false?

The car accident, Marissa's death, and now Foxhall's story, it all came at me in waves of emotion. I wanted information from an unbiased source.

Could a freelance "problem solver" be an unbiased source? Mercy Underhill's phone number was branded in my brain. I wasn't about to use the silver cell phone Giles gave me so he could track me. I had seen a phone in the poolhouse that he might not know about. For his every measure, there must be a countermeasure, I decided.

Octavia caught up with me before I reached my destination.

"When are you going to the stables, Magpie? You haven't even visited Blacksburg Downs yet."

Great. The amazing wonder horse. Another test to see if my memory would magically bubble up to the surface.

"Honestly, Octavia, I don't remember that horse."

"There's no time like the present." She squeezed my hand and pulled me along. "You'll never know until you see him. He misses you, you know."

It was hard to say no to the woman who was giving me shelter from the storm my life had become. In the paddock a groom was tending to a group of eight streamlined-looking horses, prancing about, running this way and that. Octavia stopped to say hello. The beagles followed us, circling our legs, jumping up now and again.

"Come along, Princess, Duke, King."

Princess sat down next to me, thumping her tail and turning liquid brown eyes on Octavia.

"She stayed in my room last night," I said.

"I thought as much. She's taken a shine to you."

"I like her too." I bent down and hugged the dog.

"She's a naughty nuisance." Octavia leaned down and scratched various furry chins. "You behave yourself, Princess." The dog slid down all the way on her belly and rested her head on her front paws, eyes pleading. "I'm not fooled a bit, Missy."

"She's good company." I petted the dog and her companions.

"You know your fiancé doesn't care for dogs underfoot."

"I didn't know that. Then I shall have lots of dogs. Good Princess." A man headed our way and Octavia stood to greet him.

"Good morning, Ethan," she said. "How are our beauties today?"

"Morning, ma'am. They's doing just fine."

His accent was molasses thick. He came from someplace further south than Virginia. Ethan was of medium height but a muscular build. He wore cutoff shorts, cowboy boots, and a denim shirt with sleeves roughly sheared off at the shoulders. Curly salt-and-pepper hair trailed out in a ponytail under his battered straw cowboy hat. His face was dark from the sun. Octavia introduced me to this man I must have known before.

"Hello, Ethan," I said.

He tipped his hat to me. "These are our latest polo ponies up from Miami, Ms. Tennyson. Good to see you back on your feet."

"I'm thrilled to be back home, but I have some—difficulty with my memory," I explained.

"No kidding? Well, don't you worry, Ms. T, I'm the head trainer and I'm taking care of these ponies right now. They come here once a year to rest."

He must be kidding. I grinned. "Do horses really need a vacation?"

"Oh yes, ma'am, it's terrible hot in Miami in the summer. These ponies, once they reach Virginia, they like to have died and gone to heaven! In the mornings, they get that nice wet dew in the grass to sink their hooves into. Oh yes indeed, they do love Virginia. It's a real vacation for them. I gets 'em ready to go back and play polo all winter."

"See how happy they are," Octavia said.

"Polo ponies on summer break. I learn something new every day." My comment was punctuated by one of the horses whinnying.

We moved on to another fenced-in field where a newborn foal vocalized at the fence and Octavia stroked his mane. The baby was chestnut brown with a white star pattern on his head and his chest.

"Isn't he a beauty?"

"Gorgeous," I agreed. "What's his name?"

"Pirate's Booty." I looked at her. She gave me a little smile and said, "Your grandfather named him. Pirate Red is his daddy and Booty here was something of a surprise. This baby is only two weeks old, but I can tell he's got a champion's bones. Blood always tells in a thoroughbred."

The foal whinnied loudly, lost and afraid, and his mother answered with a neigh of her own, as if to say, "I'm right here, silly." He turned and trotted over to the mare to nurse. We laughed at the scene.

"Who is his mother?"

"Gypsy Queen. You see, Magpie, Pirate's Booty knows right where he belongs." Octavia gestured me inside. "Come now, it's time for Miss Tennyson Claxton to get back on her horse."

The very prospect of riding a horse made me dizzy.

"How about a few remedial riding lessons?"

"I grant you, that could be a good idea. You do seem a little overwhelmed today, Magpie." She patted my shoulder. "But a Claxton never stays overwhelmed. Remember that. Now, let's get reacquainted with your pet pony."

She must have been as curious as I whether Tennyson's horse would know me.

On the outside, the stable's architecture had touches of the main house. The brick and the trim were the same. Inside, natural wood stalls gleamed as if polished daily. The building was clean and bright and climate-controlled. The high windows under cathedral ceilings made it light and airy.

We passed a room with saddles, bridles, ropes, and other equipment hung on the wood-paneled walls. I must have looked puzzled. Octavia said, "That's our tack room."

I poked my head inside. It had the feel of a club lounge, complete with bar seating and a marble-topped counter and sink. The floor was hardwood and an iron chandelier lit the room. I would have lingered, but Octavia pointed the way back to the stalls. Each was roomy and furnished with fresh hay and sweet-smelling cedar chips. These horses lived better than some people I must have known.

"It's sumptuous." I tried not to trip over the excited beagles that sniffed at every stall.

"We're putting on our best face for the stable tour this weekend."

I stopped. "Stable tour?"

"The Hunt Country Stable Tour, to be exact. Been going on for nigh on sixty years. Our stables here are not quite the largest in the county, but far and away the nicest, in my opinion."

"And people buy tickets for this?"

"For charity. Some towns have home tours, others have garden tours. We have our stable tour. Don't tell me you wouldn't pay money to see these beautiful places."

Sure, if I had the money. "Do you meet the people who come by?"

"Oh no." Her hand fluttered at the very thought. "Ethan is in charge of all that. I leave the Farm for the event. It's much too busy. So many people take the tour."

I recognized Blacksburg Downs. He was the tall dark horse with a white stripe down his chestnut face and friendly eyes. I'd seen many pictures of him as he grew from a foal to a yearling to a prize-winning racehorse. His racing days were over and he was content to live out his days on the Farm. He stared at me, flapped his ears, and flared his nostrils. He nuzzled my hand, as if he knew this was part of the game. Octavia fed him an apple and scratched behind his ears. He neighed softly. I could tell they were old friends.

"He's always been our most gentle horse."

"I hope so."

"Tennyson has come home, Blacksburg." His ears twitched and he turned his head to stare at me. He seemed willing to go along with her. "She's forgotten everything. Even you. But she'll learn again."

The horse shook his head, then neighed and rubbed my shoulder with his nose.

"Hello, Blacksburg," I said. We eyed each other and I decided he would keep my secret, at least until I got in the saddle. "I don't recall anything about English riding," I told Octavia. "Throw me on a Western saddle and maybe I can hang on like a kid at camp."

I had the distinct feeling that's all I knew of horses, a few trail rides at camp. But where?

"Tennyson Claxton may be many things, my dear, but a Girl Scout was never one of them. And a Western saddle is like sitting on a sofa. Why, that takes no skill at all."

"Exactly."

She handed me an apple to feed my horse, who kept nudging me as if he expected something more. He lifted his head and stared at me, eyes opening wider. He cocked his head and sniffed me again suspiciously. But he was silent as to his opinion.

"He wants you to take him out for a ride," Octavia said. "Just a gentle ride, Tennyson. You don't have to jump."

"Jump? We used to jump? Together?"

"He won't throw you."

I felt the panic rise and a pain shot up my left arm, as sharp as a warning. "Maybe later," I appealed to Octavia. "Please."

"Very well. One more day, sugar."

"I will gird my loins."

I knew I had to ride Blacksburg Downs soon. His neigh mocked me as I left.

After her plans to get me back in the saddle fizzled, Octavia left me to my own devices. I headed back to the poolhouse to find the phone and prayed it would be safe. My last phone call, to David Jensen— I couldn't think about that.

I dialed the number I'd memorized. Mercy Underhill answered the phone herself on the first ring. Hailey Croft had already told her about me. Mercy suggested we meet to discuss my problem. Either in Middleburg or in Leesburg, at her office, would be fine. I said I'd get back to her.

That was so easy, I wasn't ready for the next step. I hadn't figured out how to slip away from Foxgrove Manor.

I needed a car. Perhaps I could borrow a car from my grandparents? There seemed to be a lot of vehicles around. I had no idea if I'd be entrusted with one. Based on my driving record, I wouldn't trust me. Out of ideas for the moment, I stepped back outside. Octavia was waiting there.

"I swear, Magpie," Octavia said, "out here at the poolhouse again? You've turned into some kind of a fish."

"Mermaid. Mermaids have green eyes," I said without thinking. I looked away from her. "Tavia, I was wondering if I might borrow a car."

"Don't you like it here at the Farm?"

"Oh, yes, it's beautiful. I love it. But I would like to go out. Just to a coffee shop, or something. I haven't been off the leash for such a long time. Simply getting coffee on my own would be a big adventure."

She smiled and gave me a hug. "Is that all, just coffee?"

"Pretty much."

"Nothing harder than coffee?"

"What you must think of me." I was momentarily crestfallen. My reputation preceded me wherever I went. Drugs, alcohol, scandals, notorious homemade sex videos. "Maybe to a drugstore for a magazine? I'd have to borrow a car. I'd be very careful, I promise."

"I can't believe it took this long for you to ask. Fox and I were taking bets. I lost."

"Oh." It was all I could think of to say at the moment.

"You're not in a prison here, Magpie. This is your home too."

"Giles led me to think it was more like house arrest."

She made a face. "I will have to have a word with that man."

"Don't, Tavia. And please, if you don't mind, don't mention this conversation to him."

"Very well. It will be our secret. For now."

"And a car?"

"Let me talk to Fox. I'm heading to Leesburg tomorrow for my hair appointment. If you like, you could drive me."

Leesburg! One of my targets. "Drive your car?"

"Yes, the Mercedes. You could visit a coffee shop or a boutique, stock up on whatever you need, while I enjoy my spa day. Or maybe you'd like to join me? They could probably do something with your hair."

My hands flew to my head. "It's that bad?"

"No, no, no! Of course not," she fibbed. "However, you used to change it rather often. Maybe you'd like a new look?"

"Maybe I would."

I was elated. Someone who seemed to like me was going to let me drive her Mercedes, and I had someone to see, someone new. I had a red Hermès purse with a thousand dollars in it and a driver's license.

Road trip!

Chapter 22

"WELL, WELL, WELL, Tennyson Claxton, as I live and breathe. What are you doing here?"

After refusing to ride my horse, I took refuge in the far gazebo near the tree line surrounding the property. The gazebo was festooned in purple blossoms and I was snuggled into a cushioned chair after my morning swim, perfectly positioned to take advantage of the morning sun and the garden in all its spring glory. I was perfectly happy to be alone with a wisteria curtain all around me.

I blinked at the man who addressed me from his horse and wondered if horses were allowed on the lawn. Apparently they were.

"What gives, Claxton? I thought you were done forever with us simple country folk."

The rider diverted me from *A Tale of Two Cities*. I'd lifted it from the bookshelf in my room. No doubt the man on the horse, whoever he was, thought I was dead, or close to it. Everyone else did.

"Who are you?" I lifted my sunglasses and sat up straight to get a better look at him. I put the Dickens down. I knew how it ended. The impostor died.

"Oh, is that how it is?" He dismounted gracefully and tied his horse to one of the iron posts. "I'm not a fan of the Claxtons' Evil Empire so I'm persona non grata? Or am I just the boy next door, kicked to the curb for more sophisticated company?"

Next door? Where would that be? All I could see were trees and fields and the faraway buildings of Foxgrove Manor. This guy must know me. His words had a playful feel, as if he'd said them before. To me, or someone like me.

"I don't see any curbs." It really was too early in the day for puzzles, especially when they were the old Tennyson's leftover puzzles.

"Alas, you've forgotten me, but certainly you didn't forget old Boomerang here." He patted the horse's nose. "Boomer for short."

This stranger was pleasant to look at. He had longish sun-kissed brown hair, bright with gold streaks. His eyes were deep and hazel, shaded by his hat, and he had the easy stance of man who was secure in the world. His jeans and boots were well worn and fit him well. He waved his hand in front of my face.

"You paying attention, Claxton?"

"Trying. What are you doing here, whoever you are?"

"Riding. Even though I oppose his politics, your grandfather—you remember him? with his crazy empire-building plan to take over the world?—still lets me gallop across his land occasionally. It's the neighborly thing to do." He smiled at us, me and his horse, as if he'd said something charming. He had a nice smile and beautiful teeth. I was still puzzled.

If this handsome stranger was just going to be rude, or witty in a way I didn't understand, I didn't know what to say.

"Sorry, I'm not up on the Senator's grand plans. I'm a bit out of the loop, newspaper-wise."

"Is that really you, Tenn, or have aliens taken your brain to a faraway planet, a quieter one? The Tennyson I know doesn't read the newspapers anyway, unless her name is splashed across the front page."

I stood up. Now he was annoying me. "If you must know, you have the advantage over me. I don't even remember the last few years of my life. Make that many years. There was an accident and—At any rate, I don't remember you. Or your name. Or the horse you rode in on."

"I don't believe it. You and I go way back beyond the last few years of your life, Tennyson Claxton. You're telling me you've come down with a case of amnesia? Must be convenient for a person with your colorful history." He rubbed the horse's nose and sat down on the chair next to mine.

"Maybe I've just blocked *you* out."

He found that hilarious. It didn't look like I was going to be able to shake him very easily. I sat down again and rubbed my head where it was beginning to hurt.

"Like to see you try."

"You don't believe me?"

"I do recall something about your Porsche kissing a tree on some country road around here. You always did like speed. You're a fast girl." He smirked.

"Hmph. If you could tell me more about what you know about me, it might be educational. And you might tell me your name before I walk away."

He acted as if I were playing some kind of joke. Nevertheless, he offered his hand for me to shake.

"Brendan. Brendan Troy, Ms. Claxton. I haven't changed all that much. Maybe handsomer, if that's possible."

"We were friends?"

I don't see how I could have forgotten this man.

"We've known each other forever, our families being neighbors and all." He lowered his voice conspiratorially. "To tell the truth, we've always hated each other."

"Hate is a strong word." So I hated him? I hated Lavinia, too. Did I hate everybody?

"Maybe we just aggravated each other. Growing up together the way we did. Do you mind?" He helped himself to a cup of strawberry lemonade from the pitcher Graciela had set out on the table. "Believe me, we know each other pretty well."

So let me get this straight: I hated Brendan, but I loved Giles? I really was on the wrong planet.

"We haven't shared any communicable diseases, I hope." I hoped I sounded wry.

"No communicable ones, no." He took a swig of the lemonade and regarded me with a laser stare. "You really don't remember?" His eyes seemed to change colors in the morning light—hazel, green, gold.

"No, but I can imagine. You were probably the class clown. And class hell-raiser?"

His voice dropped to a seductive growl. "Oh, so you do know me, Ms. Claxton. Course while you lost your memory, I changed my ways."

"Don't you be bothering my granddaughter, Brendan Troy. She prefers more polite society than the likes of you. These days, anyway." It was Foxhall, astride his favorite horse, Pirate Red. Apparently everyone rides all over the lawn here.

"If she only prefers polite society, Fox, then why did she pick me for her escort at her debutante ball? There are pictures to prove it." Brendan grinned at me.

Foxhall leaned forward over his mount. "Magpie, this ill-bred scoundrel is Brendan Montague Troy the Third. Your former escort."

"I never use the Montague," the interloper said. "Thinking about changing it to Mike."

"Mike Troy sounds like a barkeep at an Irish pub," I said.

"Aye, colleen, that would be Mister Brendan Michael Troy, himself, at your service," he said with a broad Irish brogue, and he made me laugh again.

"Whatever he calls himself, he's lived on the next farm over for most of his life," Foxhall put in.

"Not nearly as big as Foxgrove Manor," Brendan offered. "Just as pretty, though."

"I doubt we can get rid of him now," Fox said. "Rides all over the property like he owns it. Even if he has curious ideas about life and politics."

"Curious?" I asked.

"Curious," Brendan agreed. "Why don't we go get Blacksburg Downs out of his stable? We can go for a ride and I can tell you all about myself."

"Tennyson has forgotten a few things," the Senator said.

Brendan faced me. "You could not have forgotten your own horse."

"Don't worry, she's going to get back on that horse," Foxhall said.

"Someday. Tomorrow. I might not have the strength today."

I offered my scarred arm as proof. Brendan took it and gently ran his finger up and down the puckered skin.

"Looks like you had a nasty break. But you can't expect to get your strength back if you don't use it. No time like the present, right?" He took my other arm and I pulled away. "See, lots of strength there. Besides, that horse is as gentle as a lamb with you."

"Magpie," Fox interrupted, "this is my doing, I'm sorry to say. I told this ne'er-do-well he could earn the privilege of crossing my land if he agreed to help my granddaughter remember how to ride."

I glared at the two of them. Four, if you counted the horses.

"Sounds like collusion. And coercion." I was trapped like the proverbial lab rat.

"Collusion, and the pleasure it would give me to teach you something, for a change." Brendan took both my hands in his. "Course I don't believe any of this for a second. Tennyson Claxton practically grew up on a horse."

My heart sank. Why couldn't I take riding lessons from a stranger? Someone who didn't have a history with me, the "expert horsewoman" who had never ridden a horse, except maybe at camp—if I went to camp—so far as she could remember?

"I'm tired from my swim," I said.

"You can't swim!" Brendan's eyebrows rose a foot. "You're scared to death of the water."

"Only half a mile this morning, but I'm out of practice. Felt great, though."

"Seems she learned how to swim. In college," Foxhall said.

Brendan's brows climbed even higher. They exchanged looks, looks I translated as *What the hell?* and *Search me!*

"Well then, a little ride should be nothing for you." Brendan wasn't going anywhere. "Appears to me that if you conquered your pathological fear of water, riding Blacksburg should be a snap. You may have forgotten him, but he hasn't forgotten you. Go on, put on your jeans and grab your boots."

"Fine! Maybe if I fall off and break my neck it will make both of you happy!"

Brendan Troy had the nerve to chuckle as I stormed off. My grandfather and Pirate Red took off at a brisk trot.

Brendan was in the same place when I came back in jeans and boots. He heard me stomping across the gravel walk. He'd polished off the lemonade and was leaning against the gazebo. Tipped over his face, his hat revealed only his grin. I glared at him.

"Come on, it's not as bad as all that." He gave me a tap on the shoulder. Just a simple touch. Like an old friend. Not at all like Giles, with his cold, possessive pawing. I stopped and stared at Brendan, wondering if I remembered him. My debutante ball? No, he reminded me of someone I'd known, a boy who went into the service. But no, that boy never came home to me. They couldn't be the same guy.

"You thought of something," Brendan said.

"I wondered if you reminded me of somebody. That's all."

"Well, Magpie, no doubt I remind you of myself. I'm pretty hard to forget."

"You think pretty highly of yourself, Mr. Troy."

"I took lessons from you, Ms. Claxton."

"I guess turnabout is fair play then."

The sky was intensely clear, there was a cool breeze blowing, and the rose bushes were in full mad blossom in a riot of colors, pinks and whites, reds, yellows and purples. I felt light-headed. Maybe it was the company.

Or the prospect of being killed by a bucking bronco.

"You are not going to die," he assured me as we walked toward the stables, his horse following behind.

"You say that now. Be sure to remind me as I'm flying through the air."

He escorted me to the stall where my horse, Blacksburg Downs, was lazily munching on something.

"Confidence is the most important thing when you ride a horse," Brendan told me.

"You certainly don't lack any," I countered.

Blacksburg Downs looked smug, if that was possible, as if he knew all along I would return. He rewarded me with a loud neigh. Brendan lifted the saddle from its place on the wall. I stepped up on a block to swing my leg over the horse.

"What the hell do you think you're doing, Troy?"

Giles appeared out of nowhere, furious and out of place in his tassel loafers and navy blazer.

In contrast, Brendan Troy seemed right at home around the hay and horses, and he had a vibrancy that sparked the air. He'd insulted me, in a semi-sweet way, but he hadn't treated me like I was damaged goods or an invalid.

"We're going to take a riding lesson, Embry. Refresher course for Tennyson here. Says she doesn't remember ever riding this horse. Can you believe it? Me helping her out with a riding lesson was the Senator's idea, and for once I think he had a good one." Brendan turned back to me and Blacksburg, but Giles blocked him.

"Tennyson is my patient. Her physical and mental condition is not stable. She is subject to blackouts and fugue states, and she could fall off that horse at any time and reverse all of our progress. You have no idea how much danger you're placing her in."

"She's not as fragile as you think," Brendan snapped.

"*She* is right here in the room," I said, even though it was the stable. "Have the courtesy to talk *to* me and not *over* me. Both of you."

Giles raised his eyebrow and smiled: I must have sounded like the old me. He pulled me down off the block and put his arm around me, territorially, for Brendan's benefit. I shook him off.

"I'm sorry, Tennyson." Giles clearly wasn't sorry at all. "This is a terrible idea."

"I need to do this."

"Perhaps, but not yet. The thing is, you don't even remember having these episodes." His voice softened, surprising me. "Your health is delicate and very important to me. Do you even remember riding your horse?"

"I remember the photographs."

Brendan moved in close behind me. "It'll come back to her, Embry. Like riding a bicycle. We'll take it easy. Of course it's up to you, Tennyson."

"She won't be able to—" Giles began.

I broke free of both men. I hadn't wanted to ride that horse, but if Giles was against it, I was going to do it. Right now.

"I need to start doing all the things I used to do, Giles. Don't I? Unless of course I'm not really Tennyson—"

"Not Tennyson?" Brendan looked baffled.

"Pay no attention to her!" Giles ordered him. "It's part of her illness. A phantom. Of her memory disorder."

I stepped in between them. "If I really am Tennyson, riding a horse should come back to me. Right, Giles? Right?"

He stood still, seething over being outmaneuvered.

"Did you forget our lunch date?" he finally spat out.

"We don't have a date. You said you were coming over later this afternoon. We didn't mention lunch."

"I was able to get away early," Giles said. "Just in time to save you, it seems."

"Bad timing, Embry." Brendan pushed between us. He was slightly bigger than Giles and much fitter. "The lady has a riding lesson. Right now."

It's now or never, I thought.

"Let's ride," I said, as I stepped up and swung my leg over the horse's back. Blacksburg whinnied eagerly and stamped his hooves. Giles fell back, eyes wide, looking gut-punched. It was worth it just for that moment.

"I'll have a word with the Senator!" He stormed out of the stable.

Brendan mounted Boomerang and led us down the path in a slow walk. Blacksburg Downs followed the other horse's lead, even though I could tell he wanted to run. My horse took pity on me. As promised, he was gentle as a lamb. He didn't run, buck, or throw me off. He whinnied a lot. I talked back to him, but I don't speak horse.

Confidence was the main thing, Brendan said. I was trying to manufacture some of that while concentrating on not falling off. He kept saying things like, "Ease up on the reins, Tennyson. You don't need a death grip. You're tense. Relax. Let the horse do the work. He knows what he's doing—"

One short trip around the paddock took far longer than I expected. By the time the ride was over, my legs ached and my left arm felt weak. I was shaking, but I was alive. And Giles was gone.

Brendan eyed me suspiciously as I dismounted.

"You really can't ride, can you? This isn't an act?"

"What was your first clue? When I told you I couldn't ride? Or when you had to see it with your own eyes?"

"Damnedest thing I ever saw. You can swim, but you can't ride? Tennyson Claxton was born in the saddle. Even if your mind went away, seems like your body should remember."

I thought so too. "Like riding a bike?"

"Exactly. Listen, we'll go riding again, don't worry. You've got the desire, I can see that. You're smart and athletic and you pay attention, and whatever you've forgotten, you're trying pretty hard to bring it back."

"Just trying not to fall off. I'll never be the rider I was."

"Sure you will. Trust me."

He handed me a brush and I took my turn grooming Blacksburg Downs. I was so happy with this horse that I kissed his neck.

"Thank you for not killing me, Blacksburg."

Brendan handled the gear expertly and put my saddle and tack away for me. I wondered where he fit into the picture, aside from the pictures of my debutante ball in *The Big Show of Tennyson O*. He didn't look like a cowboy back then. Was he another spy sent to keep an eye on me, this time by my grandfather? A more pleasant spy to look at than Creepy Roy?

"Brendan, why are you here in the middle of the day?" I asked.

"Riding my fence line, ran into Fox, he said you were back home here, thought I'd like to see you."

"You two are friends?"

"I wouldn't go that far."

"What do you do for a living? Humor me. Pretend we've just met."

He nodded. "Horses, mostly. My horse farming keeps me pretty busy. Family business, started by some distant ancestor." He turned around to face me. "Keep brushing. And I have a little consulting business."

"Consulting?" It sounded to me like being unemployed. "What kind of consulting business?"

"For people with large estates, horse farms, stables. I advise them on security, protecting their property, their livestock. Sometimes on other things."

"What, like background checks and burglar alarms, that sort of stuff?"

"Occasionally. These days, mostly it's how to protect their land from greedy developers."

"And how did you come by this expertise?"

"My, my, Tennyson. Aren't you all twenty questions. I'm in the equine business myself. And in case you don't remember, I was in the service. A short hitch in military intelligence. And no, that's not always an oxymoron."

"Are you working for my grandfather?" I slowed down my brushing.

"Working for him? I have done so, on occasion, despite our differences."

"I mean today."

He shook his head. "Nope. Riding lessons are free."

"Did he hire you to be my bodyguard?" I felt stupid asking.

He snorted. "Don't jump to conclusions, Tenn. You're still very good at that. Foxhall asked me to help get you back on your horse. I'm happy to help, since we're old friends, or whatever we are. And I can see you need lessons. Daily lessons."

"Everything I say, everything I do, will you report it all back to him?"

"It's a riding lesson, Tennyson. That's all. If you remembered me, you'd know I wouldn't tell Senator Foxhall Claxton anything I didn't want to see on the front page of *The Washington Post*." Brendan moved closer and took the brush. "I have to admit I was curious and all. Rumor had it back in January they were going to pull the plug."

They pull the plug when your brain is dead. Sometimes I wished they had unplugged me. Then I wouldn't carry the burden of Marissa's death. Not on this earth, anyway.

I sat on a hay bale, ignoring the little sticks that poked my bottom. "It was that bad?"

"So I heard. Somehow you magically pulled through, with the help of Svengali, the brilliant Dr. Giles Embry."

"Sarcasm?"

"Aw, you noticed."

"And he's kept me locked up ever since."

"There was a time, Tenn, when getting shackled to that jackass seemed to be your main goal in life."

I shuddered and changed the subject. "Does your farm have a name too?"

"Far Meadows Farm. Named by my great-great—I don't know how many greats—grandfather, right after the Civil War. It was a dream of his, after witnessing all that bloodshed, to retire to some place far, far away."

"This is part of that blood-soaked land, isn't it? Still haunted by the ghost of John Mosby?"

"You remember old Colonel Mosby and his Rangers but you don't remember me? I'm hurt." He laughed. He didn't seem hurt at all. "Never mind, you're right, Mosby rode all over this land. But that was long ago."

"How old are you?" These were all things I knew I should have known. He was being very patient with me, not treating me like I was stupid or crazy. He'd been like that on horseback too. I hoped it would last.

"Three years older than you. Give or take."

"I'm twenty-six, so you're twenty-nine?"

"No, I am almost twenty-eight and you are twenty-four, soon to be twenty-five. Not many women would claim to be older than they are. And yet guys do it all the time. Why is that, I wonder?"

That's right, I thought. Marissa must be twenty-six. Not me.

"Maybe I just wish it was two years from now and I would've figured all this out. What did the Senator tell you about me?"

"He told me you've changed a little." Brendan pulled up a hay bale to sit down next to me. "And you've forgotten nearly all your bad personality traits. He's very proud of you."

"He said that?" It was my turn to raise an eyebrow. "And 'nearly' all?"

"You're still pretty darned stubborn. Thought for a minute there I'd have to use a crane to get you up on that horse. But then you just turned on a dime, grabbed the reins, and went for it. That's you all over."

"What do you think, Brendan? After all, you're supposed to have known me all these years. Am I Tennyson?"

"Who else would you be? There's only one Tennyson Claxton. One's enough, right?"

"You say that now," I said.

"What does that mean?"

"I don't know."

I rose from the hay bale and started brushing straw off my jeans. I wobbled. I had no idea that riding a horse required a pair of sea legs. Brendan steadied me, and I regained my balance as we were leaving the stable.

Until I spotted Creepy Roy outside the barn.

Chapter 23

ROY WAS EVERYWHERE, like a spore. He was lurking in the shade of a large magnolia tree across the paddock, partly hidden within its overhanging branches and white blossoms.

He was watching me, as usual, and taking particular note of my company. I had no idea how long he'd been there, but I was pretty sure he was collecting a lot of overtime. Enough to keep him in cigarettes.

I stumbled again and Brendan grabbed my elbow to keep me from falling. He followed my glance.

"Who is that guy?"

"His name is Roy Barnaker. Creepy Roy, I call him. He spies on me for Giles."

"He's stalking you? The old Tennyson would just throw a fit, slap him in the face, and sue him for harassment."

Was he was mocking me again, trying to get a rise out of me? "I'm sorry the old Tennyson isn't around to do that. But since it's only me—"

"Hey, where are you going?" Brendan asked.

I marched toward Roy's magnolia tree. "To settle a score. Wait around if you want."

Creepy Roy's cigarette dangled from his fingers and fouled the air. I noted with some satisfaction there were purple shadows under his sleepless eyes.

"I want to talk with you," I started.

"I'm not going anywhere." He took a drag off the cigarette and blew a smoke ring.

"Why are you here again? Why are you always lurking around me? Why are you the one Giles picked to spy on me?"

"I don't spy. I'm here to protect you."

"I asked you a question, Roy." I folded my arms and planted my boots in front of him. "Why you? Why would Giles pick someone who makes me so uncomfortable? To keep me off balance?"

"I make you uncomfortable?" He scratched the side of his face. "News to me. Giles trusts me."

"Don't you hate it? Following me around all day and all night, living under bushes, scurrying back to Giles to squeal on me, like a trained monkey?" Brendan stood by, watching. I couldn't read his expression, his hat shadowed his face.

Roy thought about it for a minute. "It's a job," he finally said.

"A job?" And here I thought he simply *enjoyed* the whole silent-menacing thing.

"Just a job. That's it."

"It's a crappy job, Roy! What does Giles have on you to make you do this horrible work?"

"Don't know what you're talking about."

Something clicked into place. Something about his blankness. Had Roy been one of the men who screamed in the night? Who had the nightmares taken from them? Was that why he seemed so vacant?

"Were you a soldier, Roy? In treatment at the Campus? Were you a patient of Giles?"

"A soldier?" He blinked. "Was I? Maybe. Once, I think. Why would you care anyway?" His eyes looked haunted. "I don't remember. Maybe I don't want to remember everything."

"Are you like me, Roy? Big holes in your memory? Big empty hole in your life? What about the men who scream in the night? Were you one of them?"

He tossed the cigarette to the ground and stomped on it. On top of everything else I had against him, he was a polluter and a litterer.

"A man's gotta have a job."

"Why doesn't Giles hire a spare monkey, just to give you a day off?" Roy was proving to be hard to bait, but I kept trying. This was the longest conversation I'd ever had with him. He stared at the ground.

"He trusts me. More than anyone else."

"Why would he trust you?" He was silent. "How long have you known me, Roy?"

"A while."

"Damn it, Barnaker, talk to me! I don't want to hate you."

For the first time he looked surprised. "You hate me?"

"I guess we're both learning new things. What else do you know about me, Roy? From before the accident?" Roy Barnaker and I must have collided before I was taken to the Campus. Some shard of memory almost surfaced. "What happened to me the night of the accident?"

Roy avoided my eyes. "You crashed your car. Giles told you what happened." He fished out another cigarette from a pack in his shirt pocket. His fingers were trembling, but he managed to light it. "What's it matter? You're rich. Look at everything you got. Tennyson Claxton has a wonderful life, right? What's it matter what I gotta do? You have your wonderful life."

"Pieces of me are missing, Roy. Big black holes of me. Like you. Don't you think I'd rather be normal, have a normal life, have a normal job? You can tell me what Giles won't, what he's keeping from me. Or you can be his tool. Talk to me, Roy."

He leaned against the magnolia and regarded me.

"It's a job. I don't like everything I do, okay? Giles has to tell you this stuff himself. I'm not supposed to. He doesn't want you upset. I'm just here to protect you. That's all."

He blinked and took an extended drag off his cigarette. Roy Barnaker's cool was back, and his face fell into its usual blank expression. His soul, what was left of it, retreated into a dark hole. His visible transformation frightened me and I backed up.

"Tennyson?" Brendan asked. He was right behind me. "You okay?"

"Sure. I'm a brick." He put his arm on my shoulder and steadied me. Brendan had that teasing look in his eyes again.

"You call that score settling? Where was all the screaming, slapping, foot-stomping? Girl, you've got a ways to go before you're filling those high heels of yours. Or your riding boots."

"I'm working on it."

"Another lesson tomorrow," he said.

"Tomorrow I'm having a spa day with my grandmother."

"Well, then, we'll have to start early. Seven a.m. sharp. See you then." He tipped his hat and turned on his heel to climb back up on Boomerang.

It was time for lunch. I was starved, but I was filthy. I smelled as fresh as Blacksburg Downs. Cleanliness and a quick shower won out over hunger. When I was sanitized, I found Graciela still in the kitchen, wiping the counters.

She had worked for the Claxton family for thirty-odd years, I knew, along with her husband Hector, the caretaker and trusted jack of all trades. Graciela was handsome, not pretty, with strong features and lovely dark hair shot through with silver. Petite but sturdy, her arms were sinewy and strong.

The kitchen was her domain, and I'm not sure she wanted me in there. She must know lots of secrets, I thought, all the dry bones cluttering up the family's closets. If I could get her to warm up to me, Graciela could be a great resource. She might be the one person who could see me for who I am.

I asked if I could make a sandwich.

"You? Make a sandwich? What kind of sandwich?" The look on her face was priceless. "You're going to make it? All by yourself?"

"Peanut butter and jelly." I laughed at the thought. "Or anything you have on hand. And I'll make a salad too, if you have the ingredients."

"You? A salad?"

Graciela stared at me openmouthed. Apparently she found this so extraordinary, she let me take over her kitchen, just to witness the miracle. I found everything I needed, and more, in the refrigerator and the pantry.

"Where did you learn to make a sandwich, Tennyson?"

I washed my hands at the sink. "From my mother, I guess. Where does anyone learn how to make a sandwich?" I gazed at all the breads: whole grain, artisanal rye, raisin, French, sourdough. I was amazed at the variety of food they keep on hand here. "It's not that difficult, even for a Claxton."

She rolled her eyes. "You never offered to help in the kitchen before."

"Sorry. My recall is shaky. I guess I have a reputation."

"Putting it mildly," she sniffed.

"Shall I make you one too?"

"Why not? This I got to see."

She found me a lot more amusing than I did. I stared at the available offerings: Virginia ham, salami, roast beef, and a dizzying variety of cheeses. I decided on ham and brie on sourdough. Graciela deigned to slice some tomatoes and avocados and rinse the lettuce (three kinds). The results were delicious.

Graciela allowed that my sandwich-making skills weren't too bad. I took my lunch and a large iced tea out to the patio, where she joined me. I seemed to be her entertainment for the day.

I spent the rest of the afternoon by myself, lazing around the pool and swimming. Swimming is something I *know* how to do. On the poolhouse phone, I called Mercy Underhill to arrange a meeting tomorrow in Leesburg.

I hoped to God this would turn out better than my last appointment.

Before dinner, I returned to my bedroom and pulled out my journal. I had Giles. Ulysses had his Cyclops.

Joy touch'd my secret soul and conscious heart,
Pleased with the effect of conduct and of art.
Meantime the Cyclop, raging with his wound
Spreads his wide arms, and searches round and round.

I fell asleep and dreamed of Giles, who had one big eye like a Cyclops and was eating a gigantic sandwich the size of a ram. Ham on sourdough.

When I awoke it was time to dress for dinner, and I chose a pretty apricot-colored dress. It was just like playing dress-up.

Chapter 24

I PRETENDED I was on some kind of vacation.

Someplace far, far away. I was in some kind of velvet bubble, floating on air, yet afraid it would pop sooner or later, leaving me flat on a gravel road in the middle of nowhere.

After a pleasant dinner without Giles, during which neither Giles Embry nor Brendan Troy were mentioned, I hid away in the library. It was my favorite room in the house so far (I'm not sure I'd seen them all yet), with hunter green walls, plaid flannel upholstery on the chairs, a huge leather chesterfield sofa, and wonderful old volumes in the sturdy bookcases. The paintings were all horse country foxhunting scenes, but the inevitable Claxton family photos crowded the mantelpiece. I saw my brown eyes everywhere. At least the books were familiar.

I found the old vinyl record albums, hundreds of them, vintage vinyl full of big band music and swing and jazz and blues, neatly shelved next to an expensive-looking stereo system with a genuine turntable. Apparently my grandparents enjoyed their music in its purest form, with the original pops and scratches. I took out a Benny Goodman album, placed it carefully on the turntable, switched it on, and watched the needle drop. I was conscious of not playing it too loudly. As the King of Swing swung into "Stompin' at the Savoy," I snuggled sideways into one of the oversized wing chairs, my legs slung over the arm, my feet air-dancing to the music.

I stared up at the painting over the fireplace, a standout amid the other horsey decor. A comely maid atop her horse led the riders on a fox hunt. Her fiery red hair streamed over her navy coat. She was trailed by men wearing red and black jackets, mounted on horses of every color, hounds close on their heels. I had to search for a moment before I found the fox, peeking out of a hollow log in the corner of the picture.

My grandfather, the Fox, strolled into the room and paused at the door. I struggled to sit up straight.

"As you were, young lady. This is your home too. If you want to sprawl on the furniture like a cat and play my old music, feel free. Long as you don't scratch my records."

"I was very careful."

"I'm sure you were." He sat in the matching wing chair. "You're comfortable here, aren't you?"

"In this room? So comfortable I can hardly keep my eyes open."

He turned in the direction of my gaze. "Do you remember that painting, Magpie?"

"I don't, but it's lovely."

"It should be. You made me buy it when you were eight years old, because of the pretty lady. You always thought a woman should be out in front of the pack, leading the hunt. You told me so."

"I must have been pretty smart at eight." I wished I were that smart now.

"Expensive tastes, too. That painting cost me forty-eight thousand dollars."

I gasped and sat up straight. "You spent that kind of money on an eight-year-old? You are kidding me!" It was a nice painting, but seriously, I could buy a car with that kind of money. Two really nice cars.

"A famous artist, too." Foxhall Claxton found me very amusing. "Hell, it was a good investment, its value has only risen since you were eight. So you were a smart art collector even then. I've become quite fond of our pretty rider over our fireplace. She will be yours one day."

"No," I said automatically. "Besides, that will be a long time from now."

"Yes, many years from now. I intend to live to at least a hundred. Just to spite my enemies. In the meantime, you'll have all the time in the world to get to know your family again."

I stood to get a closer look at the expensive painting. How many other treasures were casually gracing their walls? There was an ugly Picasso in "my" yellow bedroom. Did they buy that on one of Tennyson's whims too? Again, I had that unreal feeling of not belonging. I hated myself for adding up every penny, measuring out the cost of everything, always feeling so broke, when there was obviously no reason for it. These people were *stinking rich*.

"This is a beautiful library," I said, just to change the mood.

"It's beautiful in every season, Magpie. We will have many more seasons."

I imagined fires in the fireplace and wondered where I would be when the winter came, when snow would blanket the landscape. I gazed out the French doors leading to the patio, and the darkening Blue Ridge on the horizon.

Benny Goodman started playing the slower-paced "Moonglow." Foxhall held out his hand.

"Would you care to dance, my dear? This is one of my favorites."

"Love to." I didn't have to remember the steps. I simply knew them.

We spun around the room in a slow foxtrot until the song ended. Foxhall grinned and applauded softly—whether for me or Benny Goodman, I couldn't tell.

"Now where did you learn to dance like that?" he asked.

"From my grandfather," I said without thinking. I executed a spin.

He beamed. "That's right, Magpie. You learned from your old granddad."

I wanted to say, "My other grandfather." But the Senator seemed so happy, why ruin the moment? I was quite certain I was taught to dance in just this way, in somebody's living room, listening to old records. Another foxtrot came on and we began to dance again, until Foxhall stopped short, as the music played on.

"Ah, there you are," he said to someone behind me. "Come on in and get reacquainted with your daughter."

I didn't know what he could be talking about.

Someone stepped into the library behind me and I turned to see who it was. A man stood quietly watching me. Octavia brought up the rear. I was supposed to know him. I knew that much.

"Tennyson?" was all he said.

His presence didn't set off any bells, whistles, or memories, but I recognized him from the videos and memory books.

"You're Porter Claxton," I said.

My alleged father. The playboy son of Foxhall and Octavia, currently between marriages. I recollected that he served on several C&B boards, supposedly the reason for his recent visit to Hong Kong and his no-show at our non-reunion at the Campus. I was sure Hong Kong was just an excuse. Now here he was, smiling at me.

"Come here. Let me look at you." He was used to issuing orders. I did as he asked, curious. Unlike the Senator, he didn't offer me a hug. He took my hands in his. "You've made an amazing recovery."

"She even dances," Foxhall said. "Beautifully."

"Physically, I'm doing pretty well," I answered. "But my memory—"

"Giles told me about your, um, condition," Porter said. "But he has great hopes for you."

"So I've been told."

He squinted at me and examined me from all sides. "You don't know me?"

"I've seen your pictures. You seem to be one of the people I've blocked. Completely."

How could I be this man's daughter?

He managed a wry smile. "We've never had what you could call an easy relationship."

I nodded noncommittally. Porter Claxton resembled Foxhall, but he was less sharp-featured. He must have been close to fifty, but which side of it, I couldn't remember, and he had Octavia's brown eyes, darker than the brown eyes I saw in my mirror.

The younger Claxton was casually dressed, like his father, in khakis and a light blue oxford cloth shirt, tassel loafers without socks, and tortoiseshell glasses. He added a patterned ascot at the neck. His dark hair was sprinkled with gray, and I could see why so many women had thrown themselves at him, besides the money. He was old-movie-star handsome.

I didn't know what to say to him. I felt nothing. Well, perhaps a little annoyed at having our dance interrupted. I had no touching father-daughter memories.

"I really don't know you," I finally said.

"That could have its advantages," Foxhall said, ever the diplomat. "No messy history to deal with."

"And you seem quieter than you used to be, Tennyson," Porter said. "However, I'm sure we'll get reacquainted soon."

"What am I supposed to call you?" I asked.

"Magpie calls me Senator," Foxhall put in, to the visible annoyance of my father.

I couldn't call him "Dad" or "Father," it would be too strange. "Sir" would make me feel like I was back in school.

"And she calls me Tavia, just like old times," my grandmother added. "She could call you Porter, for now."

I shot her a look of relief, and she smiled at me.

"Porter will be fine. For now." Porter Claxton stared at me for a long time. I stared back. He shook his head. "God, you really don't know me, do you?"

"Do you know me?" I was unmoored. Lost. At sea. My skin didn't fit me.

"Of course I do." He reached out a hand, but stopped short of touching me again. "Giles told me that sometimes you don't think you're really Tennyson."

"That was just a phase," Octavia broke in. "A phase in her recovery. That's over."

She must be right. Who else could I be, since Marissa was dead?

"A phase?" Porter repeated. He looked like a man who wouldn't approve of people having phases.

"I'm sure Giles explained it all to you," I said, thankful that Giles wasn't there to explain. "His explanations are so smooth, so practiced, so neurologically correct. He makes you believe what he wants you to believe about me. He doesn't let you see who I am. Whoever that is. No doubt he'll expect you to report back to him, so he can make another evaluation and adjust my medication. He'll be grateful. Do tell me what the right answers are, Porter, the ones that will make Giles happy. I'll be happy to parrot them back to you. The answers that will win me my freedom."

"That's quite a speech, Magpie," Foxhall interrupted. "You have a gift for it. You just need a little seasoning as a public speaker. And perhaps a little diplomacy."

"No need to get huffy, Tennyson," Porter said. "Everyone is simply trying to help you. Giles warned me that after this kind of injury your personality can change."

"For the moment, let's leave Giles Embry out of it," Fox said.

"I'd love to," I said.

"Why?" Porter asked. "What's going on? Is the bloom off that particular romance?"

"There is no romance," I said for the thousandth time.

"That's not what Giles says. He also said you're risking great injury by trying to ride that horse of yours again, so soon after the accident."

"I am not exactly 'riding,' Porter. I'm taking a few lessons. Giles doesn't know me."

"But Giles Embry is our most brilliant researcher at the Campus, he's making incredible strides…"

I couldn't listen anymore. I fled, out through the French doors onto the lawn, away from the house lights. It was dark by then and the Pleiades, all seven sisters, were high in the sky. I kicked off my sandals and spun around barefoot on the cool grass until I located the Big Dipper, pointing my way to the star I sought.

My grandfather followed me out and watched me looking at the stars. I didn't mind his company. He was a good dancer, and dancing had brought us a little closer together. He let me watch the stars alone for a moment before he spoke.

"What are you doing out here, Magpie?"

"I'm looking for the North Star. I want to find True North, so I'll know where I am."

 cs

When I finally escaped the Claxtons to my blue bedroom, Ulysses was waiting there for me. As alone as I was.

Why sits Ulysses silent and apart,
Some hoard of grief close harbour'd at his heart?

Why indeed. It looked like Ulysses was faring no better than I. I started to write down more of my story. Whoever I am.

Chapter 25

"NOW YOU HAVE your freedom for the day," Octavia told me.

I dropped her off at the spa in Leesburg in the morning. I stepped out of the idling Mercedes to give her a hug, and she gave me a peck on the cheek.

"I'll be ready by about three," she added. "But if you like, you could come back here a little early. Perhaps you'd want them to do something with your hair? It always used to cheer you up to put a blue or purple streak in it. Anything to shock your grandmother."

"I'm sure that was charming of me." I touched the ends of my hair, self-consciously. Still the brown color I was so unused to, it was barely past my shoulders. "Is it that bland and boring?"

"Your hair is perfectly fine, Magpie. It's much longer than you used to wear it, and it's nice and shiny. But if you'd like to have a mini makeover, now's your chance. And look at you today, you're so dressed up. Just for coffee and shopping?"

"Am I?" I glanced down at myself. I had pulled a deceptively simple sleeveless blue linen dress from the closet, along with purple low-heeled sandals and a sky-blue pashmina. "There are so many clothes in that closet, I feel like I'm shopping at Neiman-Marcus every time I open the door." I touched the green malachite necklace that I'd put on. "Is it too much?"

"You look very sweet, my dear."

I don't think *sweet* was what I was aiming for, but it was too late to change.

"You'll really be here till three?"

"I have a massage scheduled, a facial, and hair and nails."

"The works?" I felt the surprise on my face.

"It's a spa, my dear. And I do love my spas. They keep me young."

"It must be true," I grinned. "It's working."

"Let them do something crazy with your hair. My treat."

I said I would see how my morning went. I would have at least a couple of hours to myself, even if I took her up on the makeover. Octavia would be tucked away safely at her spa, leaving me with her big black Mercedes and no bodyguards or shadows in sight. Either my grandparents had called off Giles's snoops or they were getting better at blending into the scenery. I was trying to let go of the tension in my neck. It was difficult.

At first I'd been afraid to take the wheel of the big car. But Octavia trusted me. That boosted my confidence, and it didn't take me long to get used to the feel of it. I was extra-cautious heading to the coffee shop in downtown Leesburg, following the directions I'd memorized. Leesburg was about twenty miles northeast of Middleburg, and considerably larger, but not so big, I hoped, that I could get lost.

I found Shoe's Cup and Cork on North King Street, across from the courthouse, right where it was supposed to be. I ordered an iced chai latte, tall and cold. Right behind me, a man came in and ordered black coffee. He was unremarkable, sandy-haired and pudgy around the middle, wearing a suit. I briefly wondered if Giles had sent him. The pudgy guy flirted with the counter girl and ignored me completely.

Then I spotted a woman sitting in a corner reading a newspaper, with a view of the entire cafe. She *was* watching me. She gave a barely perceptible nod of her head and I approached.

"Mercy Underhill?" I asked, very softly.

"Yes. You must be Tennyson Claxton."

"So they tell me." We shook hands. It had already been quite an adventure for me, on my own out in the real world, and I realized I was a little shaky. I took a seat.

"Let me guess. This is the first time you've hired someone like me," she said.

"As far as I know." Mercy Underhill looked like— Well, like nobody in particular. I assumed that was deliberate. In her plain white shirt and black slacks, she might be mistaken for a waiter, or a teacher, or that nice teller at the bank. A gray jacket hung over the back of her chair. She had dark chestnut hair and pale skin. She wasn't remarkable looking, until you looked closer.

Behind her dark-framed glasses, she carefully downplayed her good looks. She had creamy skin and large eyes, and when she was inclined to smile, she looked completely different. Stunning.

"Mercy is a pretty name," I said.

"I was named after a seventeen-year-old girl who lies in a cemetery in New England. Part of the ancient Underhill clan, most of them now under the ground. That Mercy was all things good and sweet. I am nothing like her." She smiled.

I laughed. "And I am nothing like the Tennyson Claxton you might have heard about."

"Fair enough."

"Thank you for meeting with me."

"My pleasure. It's what I do."

"Hailey says you solve problems for people."

"When I can, and when a client can pay for my services. I'm not inexpensive. But I'm worth it."

"Is a check okay?" I had my checkbook, but no idea how much was in my account. I—or Tennyson—had neglected to even write down the current balance. The account might be empty, or closed. I would have to find out.

"A check is fine. Later. For what it's worth, Hailey says you're not crazy, and she should know. I told her I'd reserve judgment." Mercy glanced around. There were a handful of people in the shop, but they were all out of earshot. "If it gets any more crowded, we'll slip out and continue this conversation at my office. I assume you have a serious problem. What do I need to know to help you?"

"More than one problem, I'm afraid. First, you should know I have severe memory impairment, and I may be paranoid. And delusional. Giles says it's one of my issues."

"Giles being—"

"Dr. Giles Embry."

"Aha. Isn't Dr. Embry your fiancé?" She lifted her cup and sipped, all the while watching me.

"So he says. I don't even remember knowing him, before—the accident. I won't marry him. It's going to be tricky to untangle the situation."

"He still wants to marry you, I take it?"

"Yes, even though he doesn't love me. He doesn't even like me. At least that part is mutual. For him, it must be the money. Or something. And the funny thing is, I don't even know how much money we're talking about."

"You have forgotten a lot." She paused to jot down a note. "Go on."

"There were surveillance cameras everywhere at the Campus, the research institute where I was being held—treated—after my accident. Hailey's probably told you about that. Now I'm at my grandparents' place, and Giles is still spying on me. He calls it security, for my protection. But it's more than that. I don't need special security at Foxgrove Manor, the place is a fortress. Walls, gatekeepers, guards, alarms, the whole works."

"Do you have a for-instance?"

"There is a man who follows me. His name is Roy Barnaker. He reports to Giles."

She gazed casually around the cafe. "Is he here?"

"I haven't spotted him today, but then he didn't expect me to be leaving the Farm today, and I don't think he'd expect me to be out and about. My grandmother let me drive her car and drop her off at the spa. If you smell cigarettes, that's probably Roy."

"Description?"

"Looks like a skinny ex-con or ex-druggie. Maybe ex-military. My guess is a combat vet. PTSD. Shaggy gray crew cut, like an iron gray halo. Chain-smoker."

"Charming. Anything else?"

"Is it possible to bug a cell phone?"

"It's very possible, and a cell phone can be used to track your movements. You believe your fiancé has bugged your phone? Has he had it under his control?"

I studied my chai and collected my thoughts, trying not to seem like the brain-damaged invalid Giles liked to paint me. I knew I sounded disjointed.

"When I left the Campus, he handed me a new smartphone."

"Nothing says 'I love you' like the gift of invasive tracking technology," she said. I reached into my bag and retrieved Giles's gift. She lowered her voice to a near whisper. "May I?" I handed it to her. "Have you been using it?" She examined it carefully, without pressing any buttons.

"I'm afraid to," I whispered back. "Giles calls me on it."

"Do you keep it with you?"

"Mostly I leave it in my room, in a drawer. I brought it today in case my grandmother needs to reach me. And to show it to you."

"What did you use to call me?"

"A wall phone in the poolhouse. I was afraid he might have had someone tamper with the phones inside the house, at least the ones he thought I might use. But I'm supposed to be terrified of the water, so I figured he wouldn't bother bugging a phone out by the pool. I hope I was right."

"Are you terrified of the water?"

"Not at all. I love to swim. It appears I am not the person I was before the car accident."

"You must have known how to swim. It doesn't just descend on you like a gift from above." She tossed the phone from hand to hand. "Did you use it to navigate your way here this morning?" I shook my head no. "If you haven't been using it, it shouldn't be this warm. This kind of phone can be turned on and off remotely. So, if I turn it off, completely off, and it turns back on by itself, someone is playing with it from a distance."

She turned it off. We looked at each other. It was like waiting for a bomb.

"That seems really far-fetched. Even for Giles."

"I know." She smiled. "But it's not. You're not the first woman who's come to me with a controlling man. Or a stalker."

It only took a few moments before the smartphone on the table lit up and jangled. It displayed a number I knew well. We both stared at it.

"Answer it," Mercy said. "It's not a snake."

"No, but he is." I picked it up and put it on speaker. We were in the back of the coffee shop, no one else could overhear. "Hello, Giles."

"Tennyson, where are you?" His consonants were extra clipped.

"Why?"

"I tried the house. You weren't there." That was a lie. He would have tried me on the cell first. If he called the house during the day, he'd have to go through Graciela. I wouldn't have presumed to pick up a ringing phone at Foxgrove. "And Roy doesn't know where you are."

"Really? Too bad." That, at least, was a victory. "You should fire him."

"Where are you?" I looked at Mercy. She nodded.

"I'm in Leesburg."

"What on earth are you doing there?"

"Having a latte. It's a spa day. Octavia's having a massage." No need to lie, particularly if he was tracking me.

"You didn't consult me!"

"So what? I'm having a day with my grandmother. You think she's going to kidnap me? I don't recall you informing me of your schedule either."

"Tennyson." His voice dropped, tightly controlled. "I only have your best interests at heart. You must rest, take care of yourself. And take your meds. If you don't, you're apt to become—confused."

"Stop treating me as if I were some kind of invalid." I wished I could cut him off as easily as turning off a phone. "Rest assured, I'm quite safe, Giles."

"I'll be the judge of that. Call me the minute you get home. I'll be speaking to Octavia and Foxhall as well."

"I am not a child, Giles." I slammed the phone down on the table.

Mercy reached over and turned the phone off. "We'll see how long it takes for him to turn it back on. When he does, wrap it up so it's muffled."

"Why?"

"These are clever little gadgets. On this particular phone the battery can't be removed, so it's hard to fully disable it, and the microphone can be turned on remotely, if you know how, so that someone, like your Dr. Giles Embry, could listen in on your conversations. I could disable it, but that would tip him off that you have help. He might try other measures."

"He already has."

Mercy lifted her eyebrows, ever so slightly. "Besides the security guards? Go on."

"When he let me out of the Campus, I went to stay with my grandparents. Octavia, my grandmother, took me to a room that she said was mine when I was living there before, a room she said I decorated myself. I hated it on sight. Bright, garish, modern, uncomfortable. Not me at all, whoever I am." I shook my head at the memory. "She was very gracious about giving me another room."

"I imagine there are a few extra rooms at Foxgrove Manor."

"Like a resort hotel. When Giles found out I'd switched rooms, he went ballistic, said he'd prepared that room especially for me, it was my room and I was going to love it, by God. So I suspect he planted something in there."

Mercy smiled. "We'll run a sweep. I'm taking the case, by the way."

"You believe me?" I felt like I'd swum a mile.

"Let's say I'm intrigued. And this might be fun."

"For you, maybe," I said.

The phone turned on. It lit up, but did not ring. I jumped a little, but I picked it up anyway, wrapped it up tight in my pashmina and shoved it down to the bottom of my Hermès purse. Mercy nodded her approval.

"That ought to do it. Now, Tennyson, tell you what. Go buy yourself another cell phone. One that Dr. Embry doesn't know about." Mercy handed me a business card. "They're just down the street. Tell them I sent you and you want their best prepaid phone package, they'll know what you need. Don't use your name or a credit card or a check. Pay in cash. Do you have enough cash on you?" I nodded, but I wasn't sure. "Bring your new burner phone and we'll continue this conversation in my office in a half hour or so. It's around the corner. We'll leave here separately. You can use the back entrance of my building to get in."

"Is that necessary?"

"I don't see your shadow or smell smoke, but you're frightened and I'm careful. And you do want to feel like you're getting your money's worth, right?"

She picked up her cup and her newspaper and left.

Chapter 26

I WAITED TEN minutes, sipping my iced chai. Then I walked to the phone store and told them, "Mercy Underhill sent me."

They went right to work. They set me up with a brand-new black smartphone, with lots of prepaid minutes and a new phone number. It seemed like such a good idea I bought a second one in white, with yet a different number. It might come in handy.

Minutes later, I was sitting in Mercy's office. Before we exchanged a word, she checked over my new phones. She seemed pleased, and a little amused, that I'd bought two of them. She tapped both numbers into her own phone, along with the number of my smartphone from Giles. When we unwrapped that one from my pashmina, it was hot to the touch. She put her finger to her lips again for silence. She quietly pulled a roll of duct tape from her desk and stuck a small strip over the microphone. Then she pulled a phone-sized silver pouch from another drawer, put the evil phone inside and sealed the flap. She handed it to me.

"The little pouch blocks microwaves," she whispered, "so that phone is now off the network. But keep it wrapped anyway. If you-know-who has a hard time reaching you, I have a feeling it won't break your heart. Use one of your new burner phones to contact me. Now let's check on you. Just pretend we're at the airport. Without the groping."

She pulled from a cabinet a long black electronic wand, with a cable snaking into a flat black box with a display. It blinked and beeped when she switched it on. She had me stand so she could wand me gently, without touching me, and then she scanned my shoes and my red Hermès purse. The box blinked but didn't beep. She gave me a thumbs-up.

"You thought I might have been bugged too?"

"Here in the Washington, D.C., area we have more spies per square mile than anywhere else in the world. Everybody wants to know what everybody else is doing. You'd be surprised what people can do."

"You don't think I'm being paranoid, then?"

"I wouldn't hold it against you."

Now that we could talk, she showed around me her cozy offices. The bronze plate on the door said Windswept Consulting. Mercy told me she was one of four "problem-solving" specialists there, a registered private investigator in the Dominion of Virginia with credentials in several nearby states. Her specialty, she said, was problem-solving for a variety of wealthy clients, and her special gift was doing it efficiently and quietly. As she explained it, her firm did whatever it took, short of breaking the law, to deal with their clients' "challenges," and to keep their dirty laundry out of the public eye.

The offices were calming and comfortable, with a touch of Hunt Country decor about them, in shades of pale blue and cream. The furniture wasn't showy, but it looked pricey. A small reception area led to four private offices. Mercy's had a window that opened above the street, letting in a breeze.

"Okay, your first problem. Possible bugs in your house and phones. If security is so tight at Foxgrove Manor, how do we get me into your rooms to conduct an electronics sweep?"

Mercy leaned back behind her desk. I'd thought about this on the drive over.

"Have you heard of the stable tour?"

"The Hunt Country Stable Tour? Oh yes." She leaned forward. "That's promising."

"It's this Saturday. Foxgrove Manor is on the tour again this year. Octavia said the staff runs the tour and the family always clears out for the day to avoid the crowds. But I could stick around, saying I want to see what all the fuss is about. I do, actually, because I don't remember ever seeing it before. You show up for the tour, and if anyone asks, I say you're an old friend of mine. What do you think? You'll need to buy a ticket."

"If you don't remember anything, how would you remember me?"

"How about this? Maybe you could get Hailey to come with you? I know her from the Campus, and she could 'introduce' us. I could meet you at the stables, then bring you two up to the house for some refreshments and show you around."

"Could work. Hailey loves new experiences. Unfortunately, she'll want to tour each and every stable and tack room and pet all the dogs and ponies. But a job's a job."

"Our stables are very nice. Those horses live better than many people do."

"One thing, Tennyson. Certain people in your family's social circle might know who I am, but they would be most reluctant to give me away. Just something to be aware of."

Panic shot through me. "Have you ever worked for my family? Or Giles?"

"No, nor has anyone in my firm. I checked before I met you today. We try to avoid any conflicts of interest. I assume friends of your grandparents won't visit them this Saturday, because they won't be there, and they've probably already seen your stables."

"Sounds like we have a plan." My heart was racing.

"See you on Saturday then. Hailey and I will be at Foxgrove, most likely after we've tramped through numerous other stables and horse stalls." She leaned back in her chair. "I won't call you unless I can't find you, and if I do call, I'll use your new number, the black one. Anything else I can do for you?"

"I have a laundry list." From my purse, I produced two small envelopes, each with several strands of hair I'd stolen from Octavia's brush and Foxhall's comb. I carefully pulled out a few of my own. "For DNA. I need to see if I'm related to someone."

"You couldn't just ask them? I mean, for starters."

"It's complicated."

"Whose hair is this?" Mercy asked, holding the envelopes to the light.

"That one is my grandmother's. Octavia Claxton. The other one is Foxhall Claxton, my grandfather."

Mercy set the envelopes down and fished out a fresh one from her desk for my hair. She sealed it and jotted notes on each envelope.

"Are you telling me you have serious doubts that you're Tennyson Claxton? Hailey didn't mention that. You want to tell me what this is all about? Every once in a while I like to get a handle on what I'm doing, especially when millions of dollars' worth of trouble walks in the door."

"Is that what I am?"

"Possibly. Best to be prepared."

"I have to be sure of your discretion."

"I couldn't do this job without total discretion. And please don't hold anything back. Believe me, I've heard it all."

I kind of doubted that. "I was in a bad car accident." I rubbed the scar on my arm.

"A terrible thing to do to a Porsche. I read about it."

"I don't remember it. I suffered a traumatic brain injury, they say. And broke my arm."

"And you drove your grandmother here today? I'm a little surprised you didn't lose your license along with your memory. But then, you're a Claxton."

"All I know is that she gave me Tennyson Claxton's driver's license and credit cards. They seem to be mine. Don't worry, Mercy, I have a check book. Current balance unknown, but I hope you can help me with that too."

"Will do. Why don't you think you're a Claxton? You can tell me. I don't make a living by spilling secrets."

I took a deep breath.

"I have two sets of memories. Partial, fragmentary, confusing, very messed-up memories. Sometimes I remember being Tennyson Claxton, and sometimes—someone else called Marissa. Huge parts of each life I can't remember at all, and some pieces are all mixed up." I had her complete attention. "Maybe I didn't want to be a Claxton, so I fabricated a half-assed set of false memories and the accident put my brain through a blender. That's Giles's theory."

"Your stalker. But not *your* theory. Not many people come to my door looking to turn down a fortune. I'm guessing the chances are ninety-nine point ninety-nine percent that you really are Tennyson Claxton. Rich, famous, and beautiful. Damaged, but recovering. Would that be so bad?"

"Yes." There, I said it. No going back now. "Giles kept me in a bubble. I found out the name of one of my old therapists. One of many, I gather, one that Giles hated. Giles let his name slip one day. Jensen. David Jensen. I thought this Jensen guy might be able to help me remember something about myself, things Giles wouldn't tell me. I used a library computer at the Campus to find him and I called him on Giles's office phone. It was stupid of me, incredibly stupid, and I'm sure now it was a trap. Giles let me find him and the night before I was supposed to meet him— Jensen killed himself. Allegedly. My gut says Giles killed him, or had him killed, just so he couldn't talk to me. I got this man murdered. It was my fault."

Mercy's turn to take a deep breath. She swiveled in her chair and opened a handsome dark wood cabinet, revealing a mini refrigerator full of sodas and frosty glasses. She pulled out two bottles of root beer and two glasses.

"Sorry this isn't a Humphrey Bogart movie," she said. "This

would be a bottle of pretty good rye whiskey."

"But it isn't, and I'm not drinking anymore. I'd love a root beer, thanks."

She handed me a glass, opened the bottles, and poured.

"For some reason," Mercy said, "root beer always reminds me of summers when I was a kid. Too young to drive. Hot summer nights, nothing to do, just dying to grow up and leave that little town. There was one cool place for kids to go in the summer, and that was the A&W drive-in. My big brothers would let me tag along sometimes when they made a root beer run. Not very often. I guess that's why A&W Root Beer always tastes a little bit like freedom to me."

I needed more of that taste too. It was delicious. I couldn't remember the last time I'd had a root beer.

"You don't think my story is bizarre?" I said.

"It's very bizarre."

"You don't seem surprised."

"It's one of my talents, listening to bizarre tales and going, 'Yes, I see, and then what happened?' Plus I said I'd reserve judgment about whether you're crazy. They did let you leave the Campus."

"It's not supposed to be a place for crazy people. I'm not crazy, officially, just—memory impaired."

"That's something, anyway."

I traced my finger in the frosty mug. "I left against Giles's wishes. He was furious. I played the family card. My grandmother made him back down. She likes me, and nobody crosses her."

"Good to have someone on your side. Were you having sex with him? I have to ask."

"Let's say this is one memory I don't want to recover. I've blocked it out. He was having sex. At least, he was always in my bed with me. I was on heavy meds. I call it the Fog. After I started palming my meds and came out of it, I kicked him out of my bed."

Mercy frowned. "Did you consent to sex with him?"

"No! Not knowingly. I never would, not with Giles. But we were supposedly engaged, I guess he assumed—"

She shook her head.

"He can't, Tennyson. For a doctor to have sex with someone under his care and control is wildly unethical. And in your condition, on those meds, you couldn't give informed consent to sex, no matter what you said or didn't say. That makes it rape."

"But it's just my word against his. I can't think about this right now. What if I'm not even Tennyson?"

"Things get even more complicated. More criminal. You'll need a legal team."

"First I need to know things. I need to know who I really am. And one more thing." I wrote down a name on one of her cards: Marissa Alexandra Brookshire. "I want to know anything you can find out about her."

"Who is she?"

"A dead woman. Buried in a cemetery near here. I may have killed her in that accident."

Mercy sat up straight in her seat. So she hadn't heard it all.

"I read that it was a one-car accident. You think it wasn't?"

"Giles says I killed her. He says he suppressed all the evidence. He thinks the shock and guilt contributed to my breakdown and my memory problems."

"Giles has a lot of theories." She sipped her A&W.

"He told me she died that night and it was my fault." I'd never said it out loud before.

"And he says a lot of things. If you're involved in anything illegal, like say vehicular homicide, I would have to disclose that to the authorities, at some point."

"I know. Would that also include fraud?"

"You mean if you turn out not to be Tennyson Claxton?"

"Everyone insists I am."

"Then you're acting in good faith. You don't know you're not Tennyson Claxton. Let's see what happens with the DNA."

"Would this be a good time for me to write you that check?" I pulled my checkbook from my new red purse.

"May I look at your checkbook?" I handed it over and she flipped through it. It looked crisp and new in its red leather cover, matching the purse. The check register was blank, not a mark on it, and it was a new pad of checks. None were missing. She handed it back.

"Tear one from the middle, Tennyson, not the top or the bottom. I won't cash it till I check out the account. I'll let you know."

My pen was poised. "How much?"

"Let's call it a thousand for now."

"A thousand? That can't be nearly enough. For the DNA and everything?"

"For starters." She smiled at me. "We'll call this a retainer."

I wrote the check. I hoped my signature would pass at the bank. And if it didn't— What would that tell me?

"Thank you, Tennyson. Now you're my client. Our first problem is your Dr. Embry. I'm interested in his unhealthy fascination with your every move. And I'll get started on your other concerns. Those names again?" She pulled out a legal pad.

"My shadow? Roy Barnaker." I spelled Barnaker for her. "I call him Creepy Roy. I don't know where he's from. The therapist was Dr. David Jensen, of Fairfax. The woman in the accident was Marissa Alexandra Brookshire. She was twenty-six years old. She had blond hair and green eyes."

ဢ

A few minutes later, I was in the Union Cemetery, staring at Marissa's gravestone. Once again the cemetery was silent. Marissa Brookshire was beginning to feel unreal to me.

"Are you there, Marissa? Can you ever forgive me?"

A small Catholic church stood on the other side of the cemetery, the Chapel of the Immaculate Conception. I walked between gravestones and stepped inside. It was a simple white gothic structure with brown timbers outlining the arched ceiling, beautiful in its simplicity. I dipped my fingers into the holy water and made the Sign of the Cross, genuflected at a pew in the back, and knelt to pray. I begged for clarity, and an end to this nightmare. I tried to let my mind go still in the hush of the empty chapel.

I doubted very much if the Claxtons were Catholic, despite the fact I'd gone to Georgetown University, a Catholic university. The family's religious affiliation, if any, was another subject not covered in *The Big Show of Tennyson O*. I'd have to ask.

Before I left, I lit three candles, one for Marissa Brookshire, one for David Jensen, and one for me. I watched them glow for a moment and then I lit one more, for Mercy Underhill. I left a twenty-dollar bill in the offering box. It felt like a lot of money.

I headed back to the spa, wondering if there was time to do something with my hair, and what that could possibly be. Once upon a time, I reflected, what to do with my hair might have been the biggest problem I ever faced.

Chapter 27

WHEN I ARRIVED at the spa, Octavia was still a work in progress behind a private door.

To my surprise, one of the stylists was waiting for me. "Octavia said you'd be back." She waved me behind the lacquered screen to her station.

An hour and a half later, with a subtly terrific trim and blond highlights framing my face, I looked like a different woman. My new waves were flattering, and I couldn't stop running my fingers through them.

There was nothing I could do about the color of my eyes, of course, and I wasn't about to try to explain to this woman why that was a problem, but a makeup lesson taught me how to work with my new combination of brown eyes and blond hair. My eyes really did look bigger and brighter, before I had to look away.

Octavia was waiting for me in the lobby when I emerged from the laboratory of beauty.

"Magpie! Of all the things I imagined you might do, blond was not one of them. But I like it. It suits you." She fingered a lock of my hair.

"You really do like it?" I don't know why her approval meant so much to me.

"I do." She graced me with her full smile, almost as if she was seeing me for the first time. "Didn't I tell you they're wizards here? Now, let's go home. Giles will be joining us for dinner and you'll want to look pretty for him."

Looking pretty for Giles was the last thing I cared about. This makeover was for *me*. I wanted to look more like *myself*. Even better, I could go about my business without people assuming I was the notorious Claxton heiress.

Back at Foxgrove Manor, I reached for a bright green silk dress. It had short transparent sleeves and the skirt fell in waves to my knees. It flattered my figure, and I imagined that in that green dress I could almost see the real color of my eyes, the green behind the brown. I put large pearl studs in my ears.

At the last minute I grabbed the silly, ostentatious engagement ring. There was no sense in starting a fight with Giles at dinner tonight. Plenty of time for that later.

Despite the ring, he wasn't happy when he saw me. I had changed, visibly. And that was not allowed.

"What have you done to your hair, Tennyson?"

Somehow that pleased me. It was the first time I had begun to feel like myself. Whoever I was.

"Don't you like it?" I smiled at him.

"That color looks cheap." His lip curled in a sneer.

"Really? It cost enough, it should look very expensive. Octavia likes it too. The whole makeover was her idea. And a brilliant one."

"I haven't seen that dress before, Magpie," Foxhall said, mock-surprised, as if Tennyson Claxton ever wore something more than once. "Very pretty."

"It's green! You hate green." Giles was determined to be unpleasant, and it was one of his gifts. "You never like the way it makes your skin look. I agree. I don't like it either."

"Too late. You're agreeing with the old me. This, Giles, is the new me. I love green."

He grabbed my hand, eyed the big pink ring, and seemed to relax a bit. He forced a smile past the sneer. I decided to simply ignore him.

Porter was staring at me too. "With your hair that way, you look like your mother," he said.

My mother? "I haven't thought about her in such a long time."

"Not surprising, Magpie," Octavia said. "You two have never gotten along."

But we did get along. I loved my mother, I thought. Yet it was such a long time ago, I wasn't going to argue.

"However in the world did I manage to offend so many people in one family?" I asked.

There was general silence for a long moment.

"Let's go in to dinner." Octavia stood and led the way to the dining room.

I said as little as possible at dinner. I nodded and smiled, even gleefully, at Giles. After dinner, Porter and my grandfather retired to the library, yakking about some obscure political issue. Giles asked me to take a walk outside. Politely, not warmly. I nodded, politely. I stood up and he grabbed my left hand again, to assure himself I hadn't lost the ring during dinner. He guided me to his BMW. He

drew me close, pressed me against the car door, and kissed me. I
didn't respond. He stopped.

"You used to like that."

"I'm different now."

"You loved me once, Tennyson. You will again."

If loving someone were simply a matter of will, things might be
different. Had the old Tennyson loved Giles that way, by sheer
willpower? Simply because he was a great catch, the brilliant young
doctor her family approved of? I couldn't command myself to love
him. Or like him. Or even to lie to him. Silence was the best I could
do. The look in his eyes was hot, intense, and angry. I said nothing,
and he changed the subject.

"You have an appointment with Dr. Chu tomorrow."

"I know. He'll be here at eleven."

"I'd prefer that you return to the Campus for your therapy
sessions, but for now, I'm deferring to your wishes." No, to my
grandparents' wishes, I amended silently. "It's all arranged. I
promise."

Be mindful, goddess! of thy promise made:
Must sad Ulysses ever be delay'd?
Around their lord my sad companions mourn,
Each breast beats homeward, anxious to return.

Chapter 28

GILES LIED TO me again. I don't know why I was surprised. This morning, while I was waiting for Dr. Chu to arrive for our twice-weekly session, Giles pulled his silver BMW into the circle drive, scattering gravel.

I met him at the door. Until he arrived, I'd felt positively cheerful. Things were looking up, after my meeting with Mercy Underhill and my new look, and knowing I was seeing Dr. Chu instead of Giles. I hadn't detected Creepy Roy all day, or smelled the tell-tale cigarette. I'd slept soundly, with no nightmares. I even enjoyed my early-morning riding lesson with Brendan and Blacksburg Downs.

"There's been a change in plans, Tennyson," Giles announced. "Come with me."

"No." I crossed my arms.

"Dr. Chu will have to see you at the Campus today, due to a sudden change in the agenda." Giles looked quite pleased with himself as he made this announcement. My heart sank. So that's what he meant the night before, when he said everything was "arranged."

"I'm not going. I'll just wait until Dr. Chu can come here."

"As your physician, I can't allow that. You're coming with me."

Giles grabbed my arm and steered me to his car roughly, bruising my arm, practically pulling it from the socket.

"You intend to drag me over there against my will?"

"Listen to me, Tennyson," he said tightly. "I know you don't want to go back there. I know what it represents to you. You've made a lot of progress by coming here. But it's vital we do not interrupt your psychotherapy sessions, especially your first week away. Get in the car, please."

"I need my purse." I broke away from him and ran to the house, nearly running down Octavia standing in the doorway.

"We didn't expect you, Giles," she said evenly. "Are you staying for lunch?"

"He wants to take me away!" I sent her a pleading look. Surely she wouldn't let me go.

Giles smiled at her, his most charming smile. "Just for a couple of hours, so she can keep her appointment with Dr. Chu." He shrugged. "I'm so sorry, Octavia. Chu simply couldn't get away."

"That does sound reasonable, Tennyson." She gave me a small hug and winked. "Run along with Giles. You need to get out and about."

"The Campus is not out and about," I protested. "It's down the rabbit hole. A prison for people who are too damaged to know they're prisoners."

Giles stepped in between us and put his hand on my arm, giving it a little proprietary squeeze. "I'll have her back by two at the latest."

Damn. That meant he intended to have lunch with me. Octavia nodded her assent, and Giles won the point. Graciela appeared at the door and handed me my red purse.

"You promise to bring me back here by two? Octavia will be expecting me." I tried to catch her eye and plead for backup, but she was looking at Giles, not me. He was wearing a navy blazer, white shirt, and slacks. No tie, which was unusual for him. I was wearing another bright outfit from the bottomless closet, a short coral skirt and a black and coral blouse. I held on tight to my purse, which held my new black cell phone, the one he knew nothing about, and my precious ID cards.

Giles kissed my forehead ostentatiously. "I promise. And after your session, why don't I take you out to lunch, to a little Italian place we used to go?"

"A lunch date? Why, that sounds very nice, Giles," Octavia said. "You two have fun."

I glared. She didn't need to be quite so helpful to him. I'd rather muck out the horse barn than have lunch with Giles.

"Dr. Chu apologizes for the inconvenience, Tennyson, and so do I. You look lovely today."

All this smooth talk was for the benefit of Octavia and Graciela, not me.

Giles half-dragged me back to his car and shoved me into it. He turned silent, now that we were speeding away from his more sympathetic listeners, and I was too angry to speak. If I spoke, I knew I would end up screaming. He turned the car onto Snickersville Turnpike, back to the place I feared. As we passed through the gates of the Campus, he broke the silence.

"I know coming back here might feel like you're slipping backwards. Share your feelings with Dr. Chu. I'm sure you have a lot to tell him."

"Not really." As much as I like Dr. Chu, I couldn't tell him anything. Whatever I said would go directly to Giles. "I hate it here."

"Have you been remembering more?" Giles prodded. "Since you returned to your grandparents' house?"

"Oh yes, I'm recovering so many golden memories. Lots of things are coming back to me." That was only half a lie.

"Our memories become entangled with our dreams and our hopes," Giles blathered on. "At the bottom of it all, there is a memory that is true."

"Do you believe that?"

"Yes, I do." He parked in the staff lot behind the main house. His arm firmly in mine, he escorted me to Chu's office. "I'll meet you later. My office." He nodded to Chu and departed.

I drank spiced tea with Dr. Chu, who said he was pleased I was there and that I seemed to be continuing my progress. Chu was almost someone I could confide in. He said he was sorry about not being able to drive to my grandparents' house. His schedule had been rearranged by Giles.

"I understand," I said.

"What are you thinking about these days?"

Which dilemma to choose? "My grandfather told me somebody kidnapped Tennyson when she was seven years old."

"I see. Are you speaking in the third person because it's less frightening for you to distance yourself from that event, or do you really think it happened to somebody else?" he asked. It was a friendly warning.

"Sorry. It was very frightening. My grandfather told me someone kidnapped *me* when I was seven and held me for ransom." I told Chu I remembered hiding from some bad men, but I couldn't be sure if what I remembered was a dream or not. Maybe I'd turned a real event into a game.

"It really happened and you do remember." He smiled wide. "Very good, Tennyson."

"And turning it into a game?"

"Your way of coping with the trauma."

"Is that wrong?"

"No, it was simply your way of protecting yourself. Making a game of it so it wasn't threatening. Very natural for a child that age."

I contemplated my tea. "Is that why I was such a brat?"

He surprised me by laughing. "You're not a brat anymore. You're much more your own person than you were when you first came here."

If only that were true.

"Giles doesn't think so."

"Between you and me," Chu said, "there are personal feelings at play with both of you. It colors things."

"He's controlling."

"I can't comment on that."

The conversation turned to safer subjects. My daily routine, my schedule, my horse, how I was getting along at the Farm. I surprised myself by saying I wanted to start exploring my life more. I was curious about the townhouse that Giles said I owned in Georgetown. I didn't mention that part.

"I will come to your grandparents' place next time. Unless you want to come here," Chu said, clicking off his tablet to close the session.

"Definitely not here. Please come to the Farm, just you, and I can show you around. It's very pretty and you can meet my horse, Blacksburg Downs." For some reason I was proud of owning him, though I still couldn't imagine taking him out for a run alone, just me and my horse.

I was allowed to make my way to Giles's office by myself, a sign that Dr. Chu trusted me. He could have escorted me. But I knew if I strayed from the path, the cameras would alert Security and I'd be in Meds Three lockdown in no time. Walking down the halls and through the gardens felt far too much like old times on the Campus and made me very uneasy.

My feeling of dread grew the closer I got to my old cottage. I knocked on Giles's office door and entered.

"I'm on a conference call, Tennyson," Giles said, putting his hand over the mouthpiece. "Please, just wait for me in your suite next door."

"It's not my suite. I'll wait outside in the garden." My old rooms were too close to my idea of being in prison.

Giles spread one hand, gesturing for me to give him five minutes. "Go on inside, Tennyson. It's broiling out there. You'll be more comfortable in your suite."

He had a point. The sun was hot and the humidity was rising. My sessions with Dr. Chu, kind and bland as he was, always wore me out. I shrugged and turned the doorknob to my old room. As I stepped inside a terrible smell hit me like a tidal wave and nearly knocked me down.

I screamed and my stomach roiled. I doubled over and put my hand over my mouth, trying not to scream again.

Chapter 29

ROY BARNAKER WAS sprawled across the sofa. Sightless blue eyes stared at me, a film beginning to form over them. Dried blood had poured out of his nose, and there was bloody foam caked around his mouth and on his chin. I gagged, but I couldn't turn away. His face was ashen, his lips bluish-white. He looked disappointed.

Creepy Roy was dead.

His right sleeve was rolled up, a necktie tight around his bicep. A syringe was sticking out of his arm. What looked to me like drug paraphernalia—a spoon, a lighter, a plastic bag of white powder—was spread out on the coffee table.

Roy was even more repulsive dead than he was in life. The smell of death mingled with the stale mustiness of the air conditioning and the reek of tobacco.

The other day I thought I'd glimpsed a crack in his armor. I told him I hated him. I wanted to find out what he knew. I thought of David Jensen and everything lost with his death. Now Roy was taking other secrets with him: what he knew about Tennyson and what really happened the night of the accident. I leaned against the wall, trying not to slide down to the floor. Trying not to throw up.

Something about the remorseful expression on Roy's face— But the more I tried to remember, the more it faded.

It was only a moment before Giles burst through the connecting door to the suite, though it felt like he'd left me alone with the dead man for a very long time. He stopped short, taking in Roy and the syringe. It seemed unnecessary, but Giles leaned down and felt for a pulse. He glanced at his watch. He straightened up and shook his head. Then he gathered me in his arms.

"Tennyson, I'm so sorry. I had no idea Roy was using again. Here, of all places. Are you all right?"

"Using? He was an addict?" Giles thought a former drug addict was the proper bodyguard to protect me? What would the Senator say about that?

"Heroin. He'd been clean for years." Giles sighed dramatically. "I'd better make some calls and clean this mess up."

"Is that all Roy was to you? A mess to clean up?"

"Come into my office, Tennyson. You don't need to see this."

"Yet I did see it. And you sent me in here."

He checked his watch again. "I'm afraid our lunch will have to wait."

Giles always was a man with a head for details.

I slipped out of his arms and took one last look at Roy. I wondered where the tie came from. Roy never wore a tie. This one was blue silk, with a small diamond pattern, a tie like one Giles would wear. It matched his eyes. And Giles wasn't wearing a tie. He took my hand and guided me out, taking care to wipe the door and doorknob with his handkerchief. I stared at him.

"What are you doing?"

"I'm not subjecting you to a police interrogation. Not that there's any question of your involvement, Roy's obviously been dead for a while. But you don't want any more trouble, Tennyson. The police don't need to know you were in this room. The end result will still be the same: Roy Barnaker died of an overdose. I'll deal with the police."

"Like you did with my car accident?"

He didn't respond. He steered me into his office and pushed me into one of the leather chairs. "Stay here."

"I thought Roy was your friend."

"A sort of a friend. I gave him a job and he was a loyal employee."

"You don't seem upset."

"I feel his death, yes, but I'm a doctor. I'm dealing with the situation at hand. And my main concern right now is you, Tennyson. If I'd known Roy was in there, I never would have sent you through that door."

Really? He'd been adamant about me waiting in the suite. Did he intend for me to find Roy? Did he want me to fall apart? Or try to blame his death on me? Or both?

"I'm fine, Giles. It's simply hard to stop thinking about how he looked."

"I can give you something for that," he said soothingly. "To calm you down."

"I don't need drugs. I'm shocked, but I am not in shock."

"You're handling this better than I thought you would."

Giles took my hand—and felt my wrist for my pulse. Always

the contained researcher, not the concerned fiancé. He made a call to Campus Security, explaining there was a "situation" that needed attention. That's all Roy Barnaker was to Giles: A situation. I also heard him say, "No, he's deceased. No rush."

He turned back to me. "You're upset. That's natural. A man is dead."

Giles reached into his top desk drawer and retrieved a bottle of pills. He took one out and handed it to me.

"Is there something to drink? Or do you want me to swallow it dry?"

He reached over to the credenza behind him for a bottle of water. I palmed the pill and dropped it into my pocket. I swallowed a lot of water. I guessed the drug, whatever it was, would take effect in just a few minutes, and acting sedated would work better than throwing a fit.

What an accomplished actress I was becoming. I sat down and tried to slow my breathing. Giles watched me for a moment and seemed satisfied with my performance. Reaching into a desk drawer, he pulled out a lavender tie. He slipped it under his collar, checking his reflection in a mirror on the back of his closet door, and tied a perfect Windsor knot.

Outside, two vehicles were charging up the road through the Campus. I saw them through the office window. Their lights were flashing, but I didn't hear sirens. I felt Giles's heavy hand on my shoulder.

"I'm only thinking of your health and well-being, Tennyson. In light of these circumstances, I think it best that you stay here at the Campus for a couple of days."

Oh. My. God. That's what he wanted all along. Stay calm, keep breathing slowly, there's a way out, I will find it, I won't be trapped here again.

"I'm perfectly fine, Giles."

"That's how you feel now. The meds are working. But when Roy's death hits you, it will have negative emotional effects that will damage your memory. I promise you."

"You want me to stay here? Where Roy died?" I was livid, and scared, but I didn't show it. I kept my voice level. I could feel the blood drain from my face.

"I'll get you a room in the new wing. It's very private."

The lockdown wing where the soldiers screamed? The wing that produced Roy Barnaker? My memory was one thing. My life was another.

"Nothing doing, Giles."

"I'm going to have to insist."

Two men in uniforms arrived at the door, a Campus security officer and a Loudoun County sheriff's deputy. Giles ushered them into my old suite to show them Roy's death scene. As one of the men closed the connecting door, I was already pulling my secret phone from my purse and dialing the Farm.

"Graciela? It's Tennyson. Please send someone to pick me up at the Campus and take me home. Yes, right now, it's an emergency. No, I can't explain, but believe me, it's life and death. Please, please, please—"

The connecting door opened and I stuffed my phone back in my bag. A freckle-faced guy with a shock of red hair approached me.

"Ms. Claxton? You found the deceased?" I nodded. "I'll need your statement, ma'am." He was the Loudoun County deputy. He showed me his badge: Dave Connors. Giles was right behind him, talking fast.

"Ms. Claxton is not up to making a statement, deputy, she's been sedated for the shock, she's under my personal care, I'll make sure you get a statement tomorrow—"

"I want to do it right now, Deputy Connors," I said, standing up. "I'm not sedated, I'm not his patient, and I'll be happy to answer all your questions." Giles took my shoulder and tried to spin me away. "And does he have to hover like a giant bird of prey?"

"No, ma'am, these interviews definitely should be separate." Deputy Dave was as by-the-book as I hoped. "Please make your statement to my partner from your security team, Dr. Embry, I'll interview Ms. Claxton right here."

"Tennyson, wait, you've just had a traumatic experience," Giles pleaded, "and for the sake of your therapy—" The Campus security guy escorted Giles out the office door and shut it behind them.

I sat down on Giles's leather sofa. Officer Connors sat in the chair opposite.

"I'm not fragile, officer, no matter what he told you."

He nodded, taking out a notepad. "Yes, ma'am. But you are a patient here?"

"No. Former resident. I am no longer in residence. I was visiting today to meet with my therapist, Dr. Chu. I live with my family near

Middleburg. After my session, Giles was supposed to take me to lunch, but he was on the phone and he insisted I wait for him in the suite next door." I gestured to the room where Roy still lay. "I opened the door and found Roy Barnaker."

"Did you notice anything out of place?"

"Besides the dead body on the sofa? The drugs all over the coffee table?"

"Yes, ma'am." I saw a tiny tug of amusement at the corners of his mouth.

"I never saw Roy take drugs, though he chain-smoked, one after another. One thing: The blue tie wrapped around his arm was very strange."

"In what way?"

"Roy never wore a tie. It looked expensive, like one of Dr. Embry's ties. Roy was a jeans and lab coat kind of guy. If he was going to shoot up, wouldn't he use something else?"

Connors jotted down a note. "Why did he choose this place to do drugs, do you suppose? Right next to the doctor's office? Doesn't seem very private."

"The suite was empty. I moved back home a few days ago."

"Are you all right now, ma'am?"

"I'm fine. Thanks for asking."

He nodded once and wrote something down. "Maybe it had something to do with you. Maybe he was obsessed with you or something."

I shuddered. "Roy had no feelings for me. Nothing personal, at any rate. He was an employee here. One of Dr. Embry's personal assistants."

"I see. Just a suggestion, ma'am."

I was convinced Giles had manipulated Roy into the room, in order for me to find him. Giles wanted me to relapse. Did Giles stick the syringe in Roy's arm, or had Roy done that on his own? Did Roy intend to overdose? Or had Giles killed him too? I didn't offer any of those thoughts to the freckle-faced Deputy Dave Connors. Giles would soon counter that I was paranoid, delusional, memory-impaired, subject to random breakdowns. When he was through, the cops might not think I was such a reliable witness.

"You knew him well?"

I shook my head. "No. He was my bodyguard, according to Dr. Embry. He's been following me around for months."

"He was dead when you got there?"

"He looked dead to me. I didn't touch him. I screamed. Giles— Dr. Embry—came in and said he was dead."

"Anything else you'd like to add?"

"Maybe you should find out where that fancy blue necktie came from." I didn't mention that a couple of other people might be dead because of me. Or because of Giles.

"Thank you, ma'am, you've been very helpful. That'll be all, Ms. Claxton."

Deputy Dave closed his notebook. The Campus security guard returned and they retreated to the scene of Roy's death to await the paramedics.

I was free to go. I went outside to the garden for a gulp of steamy air. A headache was beginning to form at my temples. I was about to reach for my phone again when Giles appeared at my side. His interview was over too. He put his arms around me and put on quite a show of sympathy for poor me. He was hugging me too tightly for my comfort level.

"I'll get you settled in, Tennyson. Don't worry, it will just be for a couple of days. A precaution against a relapse. I have the admittance papers."

I bet he had them prepared the day I went back to the Farm. "You can't keep me here against my will."

"You are not legally competent. You are not in a rational state of mind. You may be a danger to yourself and others." His hand tightened around my arm.

I pulled my arm away. If I'd swallowed the pill he'd given me, I'd be drowsy and pliable by now. Lost in the Fog. He must know by now that I'd palmed his meds. His other hand went to my throat. He was trying to pull me off my feet when a big black Lincoln screeched into the staff parking lot across the garden. The Senator himself got out.

"What in the ever-loving name of the devil is going on here, Giles?"

Giles froze.

"He's trying to hold me here! Against my will. For no reason." I broke away and ran to my grandfather's side. He put his arm around my shoulder.

"Giles. An explanation, please," the Fox demanded. He looked like a vengeful hawk. "I understand that man Barnaker is dead?"

Giles looked like he'd been hit by a baseball bat, but he recovered his cool quickly. "A terrible thing, Foxhall. Barnaker killed himself. A drug overdose. Tennyson found him. A horrible shock to her. It's my medical opinion as her doctor that she should stay here for observation. You know as well as I do that a trauma like this can affect the memory, she could easily relapse and undo everything we've worked so hard to—"

"I'm not staying here. I'm coming home," I said to my grandfather, very calmly. Our eyes locked together. "With you. I want to be with you and Octavia. I'm fine. My mind is unimpaired. I'm not in shock. Keeping me here would only hurt me. And the family."

Giles took a step toward me, his arms outstretched. I cringed and took a step backwards. Foxhall pushed me behind him protectively.

"Hold on, Giles. Tennyson looks strong enough to me. Why, we just got her back. It's obvious staying here frightens her. We're not about to lose her again. Not even to you. And now that I see the sort of things that can happen here? I'm concerned. Disappointed."

Giles stood still as a statue. His nostrils flared, his jaw clamped shut, a vein pulsed in his forehead.

"Senator. You can't do this to—to Tennyson. I won't be held responsible for her health if you countermand my medical judgment. I was against letting her go home in the first place. She's had a terrible shock. She belongs at the Campus, under my personal care, where we can do whatever it takes—"

"I'm never staying here again, Giles. I'm going back to the Farm with my grandfather."

"Your concerns have been heard, Giles, and duly noted," Foxhall said. "However, I am taking responsibility for my granddaughter, and I'm taking her home, where we don't have any dead bodies. You already have a complicated situation here to deal with, do you not?"

Giles took a step back. "How did you find out about this?" he asked Foxhall.

"Never you mind, Embry. Tennyson and I are going home now," Foxhall said. "And you are acceding to my wishes graciously, aren't you? I wouldn't want to be forced to make this situation even more complicated for you." I looked at my grandfather in admiration. I liked his way with an artfully veiled threat.

"Really, Senator? I think our situation here at the Campus is getting much simpler." His eyes blazed with suppressed rage. "Now that it looks like we'll be approved for our government grant package, we'll be much less dependent on private funding, foundations, big donors like—"

"Like me? And the C&B Institute? Weigh your words carefully, Giles. I wouldn't want this to become a divisive issue between us. Not after everything we've achieved together. After all, I could make—a single phone call."

Giles Embry ran out of words. He spun on his heels and stalked back to his office.

As Foxhall and I climbed into his black Lincoln, two paramedics trundled Roy Barnaker's corpse, neatly zipped up in a body bag, out of my old suite and into a waiting ambulance. There would be an investigation and an autopsy. No one would suspect it wasn't a suicide or an accidental overdose. Whatever role Giles had played in his death would be covered up.

I knew that better than I knew my own name.

𝕮𝖘

"For me? Now, what is that for?" Graciela spread out the new shawl in her hands.

I kissed her cheek, to her great surprise. "It's a small thank-you. Do you like the color?"

One little shawl was hardly enough thanks for saving my life, but I wanted her to know how very grateful I was that she had listened to me and taken me seriously. She'd sounded the alarm and sent Foxhall to save me. The cashmere pashmina I'd bought her was a rich crimson red, bordered with ornate gold embroidery. I hoped she would like it.

She flipped it over her shoulders and looked at herself in the big mirror in the front hall. She smiled at her reflection. Graciela was trying to be cool, but she seemed touched.

"It's pretty. You shouldn't have."

I spied the shawl in a Middleburg boutique after my late lunch with Foxhall at the Red Fox Inn. He had insisted on buying me lunch, in exchange for a briefing on the day's events.

"It must have been a shock for you, Magpie," he'd said after we ordered. "Seeing that unsavory man in that condition."

We were seated in the cozy dining room at garden level on Washington Street, the town's main drag. I leaned back against the wooden bench and gazed at the lovely well-aged paintings of fox and hound scenes on the wall. Hunt Country décor reached its apex at the Red Fox Inn, from the painted iron jockeys outside to the thick fieldstone walls, the hand-hewed ceiling beams, and the ever-present equine theme. It was cool, calm, and soothing.

"It could have been worse. The smell was bad." I tried to shake off the memory, but it hung in there. "Giles ordered me to wait for him in the suite. Senator, he *wanted* me to see Roy dead. He knew the body was in there waiting for me."

"That's a terrible accusation," he said, though he didn't seem shocked.

"It's true."

"You can't be sure of that."

"I can be pretty sure the tie around Roy's arm was not his. It looked like one of Giles's ties."

"If that's true, Barnaker could have stolen it from Giles," he said.

"It's possible. But why?"

The more I thought about it, the more I was sure the tie was there on purpose. Giles intended me to know he was instrumental in the demise of Creepy Roy. It was a warning. There was no way I could prove he'd done it.

The server brought our first course: peanut soup. I sipped a spoonful of the tasty broth.

"I always come here for the peanut soup." Foxhall inhaled the aroma. "You could hardly get a better taste of real Virginia cuisine. Well, except for Virginia ham. I also like the navy bean soup in the Senate dining room, but all in all, I prefer the Red Fox's peanut."

"You won't make me go back to the Campus?"

He stared at me for a long moment. "No, Tennyson. You won't have to go back."

"Promise?"

I suspected I had an ally in Graciela. I didn't know what to think of my father. I wanted to trust my grandparents. But I needed to nail this promise down right now, while the memory of Foxhall's showdown with Giles was fresh. He lifted his eyes from his soup and smiled at me.

"You always insisted on that as a child. Do you know that? Yes, I promise. You will never go back to the Campus against your will."

"Even though Giles thinks I should be in his Phase Two therapy protocol? Pegasus or Prometheus or Tyrannosaurus or whatever he calls it?"

"I would never send you anywhere against your will. I promise, Magpie. You're doing remarkably well with us at the Farm. I can't imagine what good more of Giles's total immersion therapy would do. He's simply upset because your relationship is over."

The rest of our lunch arrived and I realized I was hungry.

"Thanks, Senator. You don't know how happy I was to see you today. And after lunch, would you mind if we stopped by that little shop across the way? I need to buy a thank-you gift for Graciela. And maybe something for you."

"My dear granddaughter. Having peanut soup with you at the Red Fox Inn is thanks enough."

○჻

Grateful to be free, happy to be alive, terrified of Giles's next move, I retreated to my room after we returned to the Farm. Everyone agreed I could use a nap. I retrieved *The Odyssey* from its hiding place in my closet. The book fit perfectly alongside the other ancient leather-bound tomes in my bookshelf.

Hidden in plain sight.

Then from their anchors all our ships unbind,
And mount the decks and call the willing wind.
Now, ranged in order on our banks we sweep
With hasty strokes the hoarse-resounding deep;
Blind to the future, pensive with our fears.
Glad for the living, for the dead in tears.

Glad for the living, for the dead in tears. If I died, I wondered if anyone would ever discover my story, hidden in this old book, between the lines.

Chapter 30

THE WRITING DESK belonged to Martha Jefferson. I thanked her silently for the use of it.

Late in the afternoon, in the quiet of my blue room, I found some Claxton monogrammed stationery in a drawer of Martha's desk. It was delightfully retro. I practiced the ornate T, O, and C of my signature. Aside from the check I'd written for Mercy, I hadn't signed anything real for months.

My signature looked close enough to the one on my driver's license, though my heart beat faster when I actually contemplated going into the world as her. As me. As Tennyson Claxton. I had a driver's license, credit cards, and a checkbook, but a clean, blank register. I called the bank and they talked me patiently through the online account setup process on my new private smartphone. I changed every password and security question. I discovered I had an absurdly high checking account balance. The linked savings account had many more zeroes.

All those zeroes. It was beginning to dawn on me, all the things I could buy.

What I wanted to buy right now would have wiped out the meager savings of a Marissa Brookshire and probably her entire family. I caught a sob in my throat and covered it with a cough. Even if she was dead and buried, she was still with me.

I hoped Mercy Underhill would have some answers for me soon, the truth instead of lies. And I had to warn her that having anything to do with me could be dangerous, even deadly.

That evening, I took a casual stroll far out on the west lawn, past the gazebo, and found a stand of magnolias that concealed me from the manor house. I called her but it went to her voice mail, so I left a brief message: "Roy is dead."

I mentally tallied up a few of the lies that Giles had told me in the last twenty-four hours alone. That he loved me. That Dr. Chu would come to me. That I would not be forced to return to the Campus. That he was unaware Roy Barnaker was lying dead in the suite next door. That everything he did was in my best interests. How many other lies had he told me, and how many had I believed?

 og

The next day I broached with Octavia the subject of buying—
something. I stopped myself from saying, "my own car." We were
sitting at the breakfast table in the bay window overlooking the
flowers. Princess and the other beagles sprawled at our feet. Octavia
looked perfect, as usual, in her signature linen slacks and crisply
tailored blouse, today in a light blue. She looked years younger than
other women her age, but there were worry lines at her eyes and
mouth.

"You had a terrible fright yesterday, sugar. Are you up for
shopping?"

"I might be stronger than anyone thinks."

"You might be at that. You're a Claxton."

"I thought I'd go shopping for—a car."

"Oh? There are cars here at the Farm you can use. You did
beautifully with my big Mercedes."

"I don't want to have to rely on your cars, Tavia. I don't want to
be a nuisance."

"Don't be silly. However, I suppose you do need a car of your
own, and shopping always was a kind of therapy for you. For me too.
What did you have in mind? Another Porsche? BMW? Lexus?"

"No. Something with a strong safety record, good mileage,
reliable, not a car theft magnet. A Subaru or a Volvo wagon, maybe
a few years old."

She set down her coffee. "You want to drive a *used station
wagon*?!"

I couldn't have shocked her more if I'd said I was going to drive
it around the world naked.

"I don't need anything fancy. Just reliable transportation. And a
new car loses so much value the minute you drive it off—"

"Where did you come up with all of this arcane automobile
knowledge?" she asked, quite as if I had suddenly started speaking
Sanskrit.

"Online. *Consumer Reports*. Places like that." Where on earth
had I done this online research? I don't even have a computer.

"That is all well and good and I applaud your intrepid spirit, my
dear, but you are not going to be seen rattling around Loudoun and
Fauquier counties in some shabby old wreck, or even a slightly used
car, unless it was lovingly used by Foxhall or myself. Good heavens,

Magpie! What would people think of us? That we'd cut off your allowance? Turned you into Cinderella?"

Marissa's Grandpa Tom used to tease her that a car was no good until it proved it could go at least ten years and 200,000 miles. By then, he said, if it was still on the road, you'd have driven all the bugs out of it. It was his way of saying they could never afford a new car fresh off the lot. And Grandma Anne would say a good car would last forever if you just kept replacing all the moving parts.

A memory! Grandpa Tom and Grandma Anne. Was it mine? Did I know Marissa? Had we shared stories, memories that I'd made mine? I didn't know. It was gone.

"So you think I should buy a brand-new car?"

"We have standards to maintain in this family." She spilled her coffee in exasperation. "Where on earth did you get this attack of the frugals, Tennyson?"

In Maine, I wanted to say, though I don't know why Maine occurred to me. I'd never been to Maine. I poured myself another cup of coffee.

"Just buy it? A new car? Just like that?"

"Just like that. Now, what kind of car?"

"I don't want another sports car."

My last car was a red Porsche Carrera, the one I drove the night I killed Marissa Brookshire. I knew it wasn't the Porsche's fault, but I couldn't trust myself.

Octavia leaned over and touched my cheek.

"Of course not."

⋄

It was easier than I thought. After breakfast, Graciela drove me to the dealership in her giant Dodge Ram truck.

"I'm very grateful to you," I said. "For everything."

She glanced over at me. "You're different from the girl I remember, Tennyson."

"That's a good thing, isn't it? Did we get along? Before?"

"Never. You were a mean thing. Not just to me."

"I'm sorry to hear that. Not surprised, but sorry. What do you think of Dr. Embry?"

"Haven't you heard? If you don't have something nice to say, don't say it."

I laughed. She was a pretty good judge of character. We

discussed the pros and cons of different cars. She suggested I get a truck.

"What if you want to pull a horse trailer? What if you want to take the beagles out for a day of beagling? Can't beat a big four-wheel-drive pickup."

Graciela was invaluable at the car dealership. A little major-general. No wonder Foxgrove was run so well. The salesman was clearly afraid of her, but he was as nice as pie—because I was Tennyson Claxton, checkbook in hand. Graciela made many demands for options I wouldn't have considered. Finally, she approved and the deal was struck. I wrote a check.

I followed her back to Foxgrove Manor in a brand-spanking-new blue Volvo AWD wagon. Top of the line, loaded, with great safety and reliability ratings. Still, it seemed to me like an awful lot of money. It had better last a decade and 200,000 miles.

My hand was shaking a little when I first put the key in the ignition, checked my mirrors, and strapped on the safety belt. I said a prayer, released the brake, and put it in drive. When I arrived back at the Farm, Foxhall checked it out and insisted we take a spin, with him at the wheel.

"It's not a Lincoln," he said. "But it's pretty nice. Lots of room in back. You could haul a pack of beagles back there."

I was delighted with the Volvo. In general, I didn't believe that you could run away from your problems. But now, at least I could drive away from Giles. And perhaps behind the wheel I could seek my fortune and my fate.

Far other journey first demands our cares;
To tread the uncomfortable paths beneath,
The dreary realms of darkness and of death;
To seek Tiresias' awful shade below,
And thence our fortunes and our fates to know.

Chapter 31

SATURDAY MORNING BROUGHT perfect weather and masses of curious people.

Foxgrove Manor had been manicured to a fare-thee-well for the Hunt Country Stable Tour. Climbing roses tumbled over fences, and the spray from the fountain in the pond sparkled as the sun played hide-and-seek with the clouds.

The stable was camera-ready as well. The brick floor and wooden stalls had been scrubbed and freshened with new cedar chips. The horses were brushed, braided, and frisky. The polo ponies played in the field while the other horses grazed. The morning dew that sprinkled the grass was evaporating in the sun. It was going to be a steamy day.

Ethan wiped his hand across his forehead and replaced his ball cap, pulling his ponytail out of his shirt collar. He and the other staff were wearing jeans and matching green polo shirts sporting the Foxgrove Manor Farms emblem, which I hadn't seen before. Or maybe I had.

"You look very nice," I said to Ethan.

"We like to put the spit and polish on for this event, Ms. Tennyson." He indicated his shirt. "Wore my best shirt. Besides, with these on, our guests know who to go to for information."

I hoped it wasn't going to be too hot for jeans as the day wore on. I had picked a pair of dark skinny jeans tucked into tall riding boots, a tailored green blouse, and a broad-brimmed straw hat. I wore a turquoise and silver bracelet from who knows where and I left that embarrassing engagement ring from Giles in my dresser drawer with his silver phone. Giles had stayed away all day Friday. He left me terse, barely civil phone messages. I didn't reply.

Visitors walked past us, in and out of the barn, men in ball caps and women in sun hats, quiet and courteous.

"They're a very polite crowd," I commented.

"The stable tour doesn't attract what you might call the rowdies." Ethan smiled at an elderly white-haired couple.

"How are the ponies today?" I inquired. "I hope they're not feeling rowdy."

"They's just happy to be alive, Miss. That's for sure. I imagine these boys'll be kicking up the turf a bit, what with so many regular folks to admire them. They like to think they's a game of polo afoot."

"Is it a lot of extra work?"

"Some. Telling you the truth now, not everybody likes it. Makes some of the animals nervous, all these strangers about."

"What about you?"

"Me? I enjoy the chance to show off our beautiful stables for folks once a year. Why not let 'em see a few acres of God's glory? Makes me proud as a polo pony. You need anything, Ms. Tennyson, you just holler, you hear?" He turned to more visitors with a friendly greeting.

I strolled into the barn. Blacksburg Downs was in his stall, beautiful and imperious. He dipped his head, acknowledging me. Brendan Troy had insisted on dragging me out for a lesson even earlier than usual, so we could finish well ahead of the tour.

After my early lesson, Brendan made himself scarce. His stables weren't on the tour this year, but he was helping friends at another farm show off their thoroughbreds. Octavia and Fox had fled the scene too, for a friend's barbecue at a farm near The Plains. They offered to take me with them, but I promised to behave, and I insisted I wanted to see what the famous stable tour was really like. It was old hat to them, but everything was new to me.

I could tell Blacksburg wanted another run. He pawed the ground. I petted him and promised him more later, and I offered him an apple. He accepted it and neighed softly.

My horse seemed to know there was something different about me. Did he think I was just a new version of his Tennyson, or an interloper? He sniffed at me and seemed puzzled, but he agreed to put up with me. He was a patient horse.

"Thank you for keeping my secret, Blacksburg."

He raised his head and flicked his tail, as if to say, "Who would I tell? Do I look like a talking horse to you?"

From behind me, a voice said, "You're a horse whisperer now?" Mercy had arrived, with Hailey in tow.

"I wish. I'd love to know what he could tell me." I brushed my hands on my jeans.

Hailey hugged me. "Hey Tenn! Good to see you, girl. New hair color? You look great."

"Thanks. And thanks for coming."

"Our pleasure," she said. "Your place is so pretty. And the horses. And the men! My, my, don't they look healthy."

Hailey wore dark blue walking shorts and a lighter knit top, her hair an unrestrained mass of naiad curls. Mercy looked sleek in a crisp white shirt, collar turned up, and her jeans cuffs rolled above loafers without socks. Her hair was pulled back in a ponytail. They both wore sunglasses and carried tote bags.

"Have you been to any of the other stables?"

"Oh, yes," Mercy said, with mock weariness. "Quite a few."

"Only two," Hailey interjected. "Rokeby Stables rocked. All those darling beagles."

The famous Rokeby Farm down the road was owned by the Mellon family. Not only were there horses, they featured demonstrations of the sport of beagling: the hunting of hares on foot, in the traditional dark green jackets, while following a baying pack of beagles, all of it coordinated by musical blasts on a hunting horn.

"We had to pet each and every beagle," Mercy said, rolling her eyes at Hailey. "Hundreds of them."

"Only every other beagle! Only thirty or forty of them. All gorgeous."

"We have quite a few beagles here as well," I pointed out.

"Glad we could mix business with pleasure today, Tennyson." Mercy seemed amused. "So many dogs for Hailey to pet, so little time."

"And I love to see how the other half—of one-tenth of one percent—live." Hailey grinned, but then she grew serious. "How are you really, Tennyson? I heard you found Roy Barnaker in your old rooms. With the needle and all. Not pretty. I am so sorry."

"It was a rough day. I'm glad to be back home in one piece."

"Overdose, I heard." She lifted one eyebrow.

"So that's the official story?"

"It's all anybody over there is talking about. Well, those who can remember anything. I guess that means the staff. I never expected you'd return to the Campus."

"Nor did I." A picture of Roy came unbidden to mind, dead on that sofa, the dried blood caked around his nose and mouth.

Mercy intervened. "We will talk about that soon, ladies, but not here. Let's tour."

No one was paying any attention to us. For once people were

more interested in the horses than in Tennyson Claxton. Hailey strolled over to my horse.

"Is this big handsome fellow yours?"

"This is Blacksburg Downs." I petted his nose and he snorted. "I promise we'll ride later, Blacksburg. Smile for the nice people."

He shook his head and neighed loudly in reply. They laughed. I pulled another apple from a box outside the stall. He munched the apple and ignored me.

"I want to see the little foal outside before we go," Hailey said. "He's a darling."

"They're all darling, darling," Mercy said.

I led them to the paddock where Pirate's Booty had collected quite a crowd. He pranced around, showing us what a big boy he was, then he scampered back to his mama to nurse. Mercy caught my eye and looked meaningfully toward the main house, which was partially hidden by a thicket of magnolias and oak trees. Time to go to work.

I cleared my throat. "Ahem. I'm sure you two would like to see the house?"

"Thought you'd never ask," Mercy said.

We took off through the trees, following a winding brick path through the gardens, leaving the rest of the spectators behind. Graciela met us at the front door with an inquisitive expression.

"These are my friends," I said.

"Friends?"

She frowned. Clearly she wasn't buying that. Octavia's beagles, Duke and King and Princess, came running up, much to the delight of Hailey, who squatted down and tried to gather them all up in her arms at once, giggling. The dogs squirmed and whined for pure joy.

"This is my friend, Hailey Croft. She works at the Campus."

"Like Dr. Giles?"

"I hope not, Graciela! These are nice people. This is my old friend, Mercy Underhill. I'm just going to show them around."

She shrugged. "Okay, then. Welcome. You want lemonade in the far gazebo? I know you like that one."

"Wonderful. In a half hour or so? And we'll come down and get it ourselves," I offered. The gazebo out at the end of the garden was far enough away for privacy.

She looked at me like I had two heads. "I'll be happy to serve you lemonade in the gazebo myself, Tennyson. I don't need you underfoot in my kitchen today, of all days."

Graciela had prepared a huge feast for the staff and volunteers working the stable tour. They ate in shifts throughout the day.

"That will be perfect," I said.

"You get hungry, lunch is on the patio, under the awning. Buffet style, help yourselves."

"You're a doll, Graciela."

She shooed me away, wiped her hands on her apron, and headed back to her kitchen.

"Is she going to be a problem for us?" Mercy asked, when we were out of earshot.

"No, she's just very protective of the family, and her turf. She's been very good to me, in her adorably brusque way."

I led them up the grand stairs, followed by three whining beagles begging for attention. We turned down the hall and peered into the yellow bedroom, the one that made me so uncomfortable. The beagles decided to trot off the other way.

"It's very bright." Hailey's eyes opened wide. "Cheerful."

"Like being run over by a big yellow school bus," I said.

Mercy took the electronic wand and its control box out of her tote bag. I started to say something, but she put a finger to her lips. She swept the room and its furnishings methodically, and she soon found a bug in the phone and a tiny listening device the size of a fingernail hidden behind an abstract painting. Not the Picasso. Another just like it was in the bathroom, in the light fixture above the mirror. More troubling, there were two small hidden cameras, one with a view of the shower, the other of the bed. She pulled them loose just enough to show me the wires and then tucked them back out of sight.

She motioned for us to leave the room. I shut the door softly as we moved into the hall.

"Tenn, you don't think Dr. Embry planted those bugs?" Hailey whispered. "Here?"

"We don't know who installed them yet," Mercy said. "But someone is way too curious. Now let's visit your new digs, Tennyson."

Mercy swept my blue bedroom with her bug detector. She lifted lamps, peeked behind pictures, and felt around the windows for wires. She even peered deep into the furnace registers with a flashlight. Finally she shook her head.

"It's clean now. Has anyone been in here, other than you?"

"The housekeeper. My grandmother. And Princess, the beagle." Hailey made herself comfortable on the window seat. "Why would Dr. Embry do such a thing? He's supposed to love you."

"Not me. My money. And I'm afraid my memory problems make me Giles's perfect lab rat."

"You're going to marry him." Hailey looked at me. "Aren't you?"

"No. I'm not. He just doesn't know it yet." I rubbed my bare finger. "Even though I keep telling him."

"About that lemonade?" Mercy asked. "Outside in the gazebo?"

I peered out my bedroom window over Hailey's shoulder. Graciela was already toting a tray in that direction. Apparently she approved of my new friends.

We trooped down to the gazebo to find iced lemonade, muffins, and fruit laid out on the table. Before we said a word, Mercy took out her magic bug-detecting wand and checked the entire structure and about fifty feet out in the gardens in every direction. The gazebo was clean.

"Okay. What can you tell me about the man who died at the Campus?" she asked, as I poured lemonade for the three of us.

"I found his body in the suite where I was lodged. I don't know anything about him for certain. Hailey, do you know if Roy was ever a patient at the Campus? In the modern wing, with the 'screamers'? I think he might have been a soldier."

"The PTSD guys." She nodded. "Was Roy one of them? I don't know. He was already working for Giles when I arrived a couple years ago."

"He was blank," I said. "He told me he didn't want to remember things. But he knew something about me from before. I confronted him here at the Farm, the day before he died. He was almost ready to tell me something."

"Now he's dead," Mercy said.

"Giles said it was a drug overdose. After my appointment with Dr. Chu, my psychotherapist, I went back to meet Giles. He was on the phone, and he insisted that I wait for him in the suite where I used to stay. He practically forced me. That's when I saw Roy."

"You poor thing," Hailey said.

"Giles knew Roy was dead. He wanted me to find him."

"To freak you out?" Mercy asked. "Or to warn you?"

"Trauma induces amnesia in some people," Hailey said. "But that's just the opposite of what you're trying to achieve, right?"

"I'm making it a practice to remember everything now," I said. "I'm writing everything down, so I cannot forget, ever again."

"What else do you remember?" Mercy asked.

"There was an expensive silk necktie tight around Roy's arm, as if he'd tied off with it to shoot up. But Roy never wore neckties. It looked like one of Giles's ties. Roy's not the first one to die either." I related briefly what little I knew about David Jensen's death for Hailey's benefit. "Both men were just about to tell me something about myself, about Tennyson Claxton. Something that wasn't spoon fed to me by Dr. Embry. Their deaths can't be a coincidence."

Hailey set down her muffin, half eaten.

"Something your mind, Hailey?" Mercy asked.

"This is just between us, right? I've been uneasy for some time at the Campus. My patient, Miss Jasmine Lee? She's not long for this world. I love her, but the rest of it? Not so much. I guess what I'm saying is, I'm looking for another job. With Roy Barnaker's unnatural death, I'm kicking up the search a notch."

"The place is a trap, Hailey," I said. "Get out of there as soon as you can."

"In the meantime, keep your eyes open," Mercy said.

"And my mouth shut? Seems I've heard that before," Hailey said with a grin.

"Always good advice." Mercy smiled back. "I didn't even have to say it. Just let me add, be careful."

"Stay away from Giles Embry," I added.

"I mostly do. Strange bird. Though a lot of the nurses wouldn't mind warming his bed," Hailey said. "He still asks me about you."

"Do you ever report to him directly?" Mercy asked.

"No. Thank God. Still, I must say it's wonderful what he's done for Jonathan VanCamp. A little unsettling, at the same time."

"But Jonathan's left the Campus, or he's leaving soon," I said. "Right?"

She shook her head. "Dr. Embry believes it's too soon."

"He won't release him? Giles is keeping him as another prize guinea pig?"

"I probably wouldn't have heard about it, but his wife made quite a scene in public the other day. And I shouldn't mention it."

"Go ahead," Mercy said. "We forgive you."

"Suddenly, there seems to be a lot of red tape with his release," she said, keeping her voice low. "Dr. Embry needs Jonathan's amazing memory recovery as a showpiece, to demonstrate to the world that he's done it, at least this once. He's grown recaptured memories. Restored a whole identity. Rewired this poor man's brain, somehow. But now he's warning that Jonathan could suffer a relapse. I don't know when the poor guy will get released at this rate."

"A relapse? Giles's favorite threat. He wanted me to relapse so I'd be back under his thumb," I said. "I had the Senator on my side. Jonathan only had his wife. I got lucky."

"Speaking of getting lucky, Tennyson." Mercy popped a grape into her mouth. "The DNA results came in."

"That was fast!"

"I have friends in useful places. There'll be a rush charge from the lab. And I have good news and bad news."

"Bad news first."

"It's a match. You're a Claxton. Octavia Claxton is your grandmother. At least she's a direct female ancestor. And Foxhall Claxton is your grandfather."

My heart sank. "What's the good news?"

"You're worth millions." I couldn't think of anything to say. "You don't seem happy, Tennyson."

"I guess I'm surprised." Stunned was more like it. I studied the glass of lemonade in my hands.

"DNA matches are pretty conclusive. The lab report always includes a probability. This one is billions to one." Mercy let me ponder that while she reached into her tote and retrieved a file folder with the lab report. She shared a look with Hailey, who stood up to give us some privacy.

"You don't have to go, Hailey," I said. After refilling our glasses, Hailey sat down again.

"Now that the matter of your bloodline is out of the way. You asked me to look into another matter," Mercy said.

"Marissa Brookshire."

"I found out a little, not a lot. She didn't live in the public eye like Tennyson Claxton." Mercy opened the file. "She moved to Northern Virginia from North Carolina. A teacher at a private school in Falls Church, going to grad school at night for her master's degree in Education Leadership at George Mason U."

My scalp tingled. I *knew* all that.

"How did she manage grad school on a teacher's salary?"

"She had a scholarship where she agreed to work for an under-privileged school district for a couple of years after she graduated. A lot of her tuition was covered that way. And a couple of times she participated in research projects at the National Institutes of Health for some cash. Not sure what the studies were, participants are guaranteed confidentiality. Probably routine stuff."

NIH. That sounded familiar. Marissa always needed money for school.

"A teacher going to night school. She was a hard worker, then."

"So it seems. Marissa was well-liked. Everyone at her school was shocked when she died. Everyone always says that. No obituary, just a death notice. Grew up in Maine, family later moved to North Carolina, no living family that I've found so far. There was a quiet funeral attended by a few people from her school. I'll try and get hold of birth and death certificates, but that takes time without a family connection."

"Did she have a boyfriend?" I was sure she had someone she cared about. Once. I just couldn't quite see his face.

"Maybe someone before she moved here. Marissa Brookshire died in a one-car accident outside of Leesburg. Skidded on ice, rolled her car down an embankment, drugs and alcohol involved. Hours after your accident, and miles away," Mercy said. "You didn't kill her, Tennyson."

"I didn't?" My eyes grew watery and I exhaled the longest breath since I had awakened at the Campus. Mercy handed me a tissue from her bag. Her clients must cry all the time, I thought.

"Tennyson." Hailey hugged me. "Why on earth would you think such a thing?"

"My memories—" I started to say. "And Giles. Giles told me I killed her. In the accident. He said he covered it all up to protect me. Mercy, are you absolutely sure?"

"I'm sure. It's odd, don't you think? The two of you were both in one-car accidents the same night? Yours just hours before hers?"

"Coincidence?"

She grunted. "I don't like coincidences. And there's no evidence Dr. Embry fixed anything with the Leesburg police or the Loudoun County sheriff's department. I have copies of the accident reports. Witnesses saw your car skid at a curve in the road and slam head-on into a tree at high speed. Before that, other witnesses at the restaurant heard a screaming fight between you and Embry before you took off in your Porsche."

She handed the copies to me, but I couldn't focus through my tears.

"Most country cops out here would be mighty offended at the thought they could be bought by one Dr. Giles Embry," she went on. "He's an outsider. They might leave out a detail or two for some local good old boy they've known all their lives, but I have the police accident photos." She pulled photographs from the file and set them on the table. I barely glanced at the wrecked Porsche, the tree, and the snow-covered road. But there were other pictures of a different car, utterly demolished, a little economy car of some kind, a covered body on the ground next to it.

"I didn't kill anybody?"

I needed to say it again. I could feel my face flush red. I nearly tumbled out of the chair. Hailey put out an arm to catch me.

"Oh, girl, what has he been feeding you all these months?"

"I'd like to know that myself."

"This file is yours, Tennyson," Mercy said. "Put it in a very safe place."

"Maybe you could keep it for me until I get a safety deposit box."

"My, what a fast learner you are."

"What happened to Marissa?"

"Her car was found down a slope outside of Leesburg about four a.m. It was very icy that night in January. The car rolled several times. Injuries were consistent with a bad car accident. Her blood alcohol level was twice the legal limit and it appeared she'd been using cocaine."

"That's impossible." I was convinced I was the drunken screw-up, not Marissa.

"She was dead when the car was discovered. And I'll say this, though it may have no bearing on the case. Her body was autopsied by a medical examiner who retired shortly afterward. His name is in there. He's been implicated in some very sloppy work. Not that that's unusual."

"She's buried in Leesburg." I remembered the simple stone, flat against the earth.

Mercy flipped through the pages of her report. "I tried to track what remained of the cars to see whether there were identifiable mechanical failures. Unfortunately, they both went to the crusher. Not enough left for parts. You drove a brand-new red Porsche. She had a little blue Toyota, about ten years old."

"You don't think someone—" Hailey started, but she stopped, lost in her thoughts.

Mercy handed me another photo from the file. "You might want to see this."

I gasped. It was an eight-by-ten color glossy with a blue-gray background. The teachers, like the children, had school photos taken once a year. Across the bottom in black type it read, "Ms. Brookshire, the Quartermaine Academy."

I stared at the photo for a long time. Marissa's hair was long and blonde, darker at the roots. She probably lightened it to match the color it was when she was a child. She looked a lot like me, but I couldn't remember the last time I'd smiled that wide or looked that happy. Marissa wore a bright green blouse that picked up the color of her eyes and made them look like emeralds.

"Her eyes are green."

Hailey leaned over my shoulder. "Oh my God, Tenn, you could be twins." She held the picture up to my face.

"Very curious," Mercy agreed. "The DNA says you're a Claxton. The school sent me this picture the same day. There's no denying that, save for the eye color, Marissa Brookshire was a dead ringer for you. Pardon the expression. Especially now that you've changed your hair."

"And my nose," I added.

"Excuse me?" Mercy said.

"They tell me I had a rhinoplasty a year ago. My idea, though I have no memory of this. Giles supported my decision to change it, according to my grandmother. There was a tiny bump. You can see it in some of my old photos."

"Maybe Embry convinced you it was necessary," Mercy said. "Playing Pygmalion."

"Making me his creature?" I rubbed my nose. "Wouldn't I know if I had changed it?"

"Maybe." A delicate lift of Mercy's shoulders.

"The big difference is the eye color," Hailey said. "Hers were green. Yours are brown."

"You told me you felt as if they had been green," Mercy said. "But that's impossible."

"New nose and brown eyes? Maybe I shouldn't bring this up—" Hailey interrupted.

"Bring it up," Mercy said. We looked at Hailey expectantly.

"There are drugs that can change the color of your eyes. For instance, some meds for glaucoma. Even some treatments to grow longer eyelashes can do it. Not in every case. But green eyes or blue eyes, if they have hidden brown pigment, they can turn brown. The change is supposed to be permanent, I'm afraid."

I sank back into the chair. The DNA evidence, and my eyes, said I was a Claxton. I was almost a twin for Marissa, and a year before the accident, plastic surgery made me look even more like her. Why? All I could think of was that my eyes—my green, green eyes—would never be green again. Could never be green again. But no, I am Tennyson! So they were never green, they were always brown—

"Tennyson." Mercy interrupted my jumbled thoughts. "Was your father married before?"

"My father?" I must have looked blank.

"You remember. Porter Q. Claxton."

"Oh, yes. Him." I shook my head to clear it and focus on a man I barely knew, even though he'd been a subject well covered in *The Big Show of Tennyson O.* "Not before my mother. Several times since. He's between wives right now. Why?"

"I haven't researched him yet. He could have had another child, right? Or maybe a brother who had children?"

I recalled my family history like a good student. "He had a big brother who died of leukemia when he was a child. No other siblings. So, that's a no. What are you thinking?"

"You're the only heir to the Claxton Empire. It's a very, very big pile of money," Mercy said quietly.

"I suppose I am." I didn't know the exact amount. I was afraid to ask.

"Another heir popping up unexpectedly might pose a big problem."

"Not for me! And wouldn't the family be thrilled to find they had some long-lost daughter? My grandfather just about said as much the other night. Did you find anything else out about Marissa? You mentioned North Carolina? And she was how old?"

"Twenty-six. And you are—"

"Twenty-four, according to my driver's license."

Hailey touched my arm. "Tenn, don't jump to conclusions. That's my job. To tell you the truth, I'm not sure what any of this means. What I've heard goes no further."

"It wouldn't make sense anyway."

"Consider me still under retainer," Mercy said. "I'll text you."

"Please," I said. "Look into Giles's history too, if you would. As deep as you can dive."

"A pleasure." Mercy had a lovely smile.

Hailey's phone buzzed. She checked her texts, then she looked up and far away.

"What is it?" I asked.

"Oh my. Miss Jasmine just died. In her sleep." She gazed at me. "I'm supposed to report to Dr. Embry on Monday for a new assignment."

"Don't do it," I urged Hailey. "Quit now! You do not want to work with him."

"If I turn this opportunity down—" Hailey looked troubled. "I don't know if I can just quit, Tenn. Not before I find another job. Without a good reference from him— Oh, poor Miss Jasmine Lee."

"How old was Miss Jasmine?" Mercy asked.

"Very old. This was expected, but today? Unexpected. You don't think Dr. Embry—? No, that's absurd. What am I saying?"

"She was old," I said. "They say she left all her money to the Campus."

"It's true. She did." Hailey stood up and put on her perky Southern girl smile. "Now I have to go back there and act like I 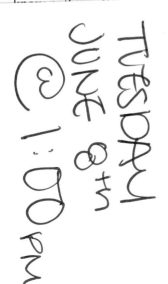 be completely true at this point."

. Don't trust Embry," Mercy said.

. "But as long as I'm there I can be useful. e agent for you guys."

' Mercy said, grabbing her tote bag full of ésumé and get out of there ASAP! In the ay. And Tennyson, that goes for you too. ler Code Red."

y had turned red. And my eyes would be

Chapter 32

THE STABLE TOUR crowds were flooding the grounds of the Farm. This day was the perfect chance for me to skip out of Foxgrove Manor. No one was watching over me, so far as Mercy or I knew, though there was the odd moment where I turned to see if Roy, or his ghost, was stalking me. Or haunting me.

I told Graciela I was going to Middleburg to get coffee and she waved me away. I left the phone Giles had given me in my dresser drawer, still in its security pouch. I deliberately neglected to inform him about my new car and I hoped no one else had either. It was time to travel.

The personal effects that came with me from the Campus contained a key ring. On it were the keys to a townhouse in the Georgetown neighborhood of Washington, D.C. My house. From Octavia, I learned it had been in the family for a hundred and fifty years, and various members of the family had occupied it before I inherited it. I'd found it handy to move there, she said, when I was a (lackluster) student at Georgetown University.

Giles had mentioned it was a nice place and he wouldn't mind living there after we were married, though he also planned to keep his own apartment somewhere in Northern Virginia. He hadn't been very clear on where. Nor had I been curious. Someday, he said, he'd like to show me around my townhouse—as if it were his to show, not mine.

The address was on my driver's license and my new Volvo had GPS. Just getting on Route 50 eastbound heading for Washington was exciting. I wasn't going shopping, I wasn't housebound, I was house *bound*.

Route 50 took me to 66, and 66 to Rosslyn. It was Saturday and the traffic wasn't too bad. The Key Bridge carried me across the Potomac into the District onto M Street, and after a few roundabout turns, Wisconsin Avenue took me up the hill into my neighborhood, just east of the Georgetown University campus. I knew the way—it was an odd sensation.

I passed by the address on P Street, looking for a parking place, navigating the Volvo carefully over the ancient trolley tracks. The streetscape was full of immense old trees, arching tall and green over stately townhouses. I had no idea whether mine had a garage. I managed to park around the block.

On foot, I recognized the house instantly. I'd seen many pictures of the place, tucked away in the lovely blocks of townhouses between Wisconsin and the university. Mine was on a corner facing west, giving it more windows and more light than most. A turret on that corner, capped with a peaked roof, climbed three stories above the street. Dark green ivy crawled over cream-painted brick walls, and vines looped over the windows and door, with hunter green shutters and trim to match the lush foliage. The uneven brick sidewalk was dangerous, but no doubt historically significant.

The whole area was both familiar and unfamiliar. The air was so still, I could hear the birds chatter. I felt the pulse beating in my neck.

Some student housing, I thought. And I didn't even have the grace to graduate. Still feeling like an intruder, I turned the keys over in my hands. It took two of the keys, one for the main door lock and one for the deadbolt.

"Anybody home?" I yelled to make sure I was alone. No answer. I locked the door behind me and gazed at the formal entryway. To my right was the living room.

The place had an air of settled dust, yet it had been occupied recently. Last Sunday's *New York Times* was in a rack by a large leather chair in the spacious living room. A pale pink marble surround and mantle crowned the large fireplace. Above it I was not surprised to find a painting of a horse that looked a lot like Blacksburg Downs. That made me laugh.

At least it wasn't a portrait of Giles Embry.

The décor was white on white with additional touches of pink marble on the coffee table. Antiques mixed with modern. Was it my taste, or a decorator's? No idea. Certainly it was more to my taste than that screaming yellow bedroom at Foxgrove.

A chandeliered dining room came next, with white walls and white upholstered chairs around a glossy black table, followed by a butler's pantry and an updated kitchen with stainless steel appliances and an acre of granite. A powder room off the large hallway was tucked neatly under the stairs. I opened the back door to find a stone terrace and steps to the petite but lushly landscaped backyard. Climbing rosebushes with pink blooms hugged a stone wall. A complete outdoor kitchen was tucked into a protected nook. It was all quite lovely. It looked just like the pictures I'd memorized.

I wandered upstairs over a deep red-patterned runner to the second-floor hall. I peeked in the closets, nooks, and crannies and arrived at the master bedroom, which overlooked the street. Again this room was white, but with deep blue bed linens and pillows. A huge abstract painting in sapphire was hung over the bed. On the dresser, there was a picture of Giles and me in evening clothes at a party. I turned it face down. I had no desire to look at those stiffly grinning faces.

There were men's clothes on one side of the walk-in closet. Women's things were shoved to the other side. I inspected a shirt hung on the door hook. The cuff was embroidered with the initials G.E. Giles Embry marked everything he owned.

The adjoining master bath had obviously been renovated and enlarged for the separate marble-walled shower and tub. Judging by the shampoo, conditioner, shaving cream, and other toiletries, it was stocked for both men and women. The towels were still damp, which surprised me.

Giles must be living here, at least part of the time. Another little something he'd neglected to tell me. And why was he here? The prestige of the Georgetown address, I'm sure. It was at least an hour's drive from his office, out in Northern Virginia, and in weekday traffic it might take two. I backed out of the bedroom, heading down the hall, when I heard voices below, on the sidewalk.

A key jiggled in the front door. It had to be Giles. I wasn't exactly breaking and entering, but I didn't want to be on the same planet as Giles, much less trapped in the same house.

I tiptoed as fast as I could up to the third floor, which seemed unused. I was careful not to disturb the dust on the railing. I slipped into the smaller room above the master bedroom. The bookshelves and the large wooden desk by the window said this was a home office. I didn't see a computer—maybe in a drawer somewhere. Opposite the desk was a sofa covered in a soft cranberry-colored fabric, possibly cashmere. As inviting as that looked, I couldn't risk being out in the open. I slipped off my shoes and crept into the rectangular closet, closed the door behind me, and sank to the floor. I could crawl farther back if necessary and hide behind the rolling suitcases and heavy winter coats, thick with the aroma of mothballs.

There were two voices and they sounded close now. I opened

the closet door a crack. The old-fashioned heat register next to the closet door was carrying voices up from the bedroom below me. I recognized Giles's voice, but not the woman's. They seemed to know each other awfully well. His voice was the smooth and seductive Giles I knew well. She was laughing. I lay down on the closet floor to get as close to their voices as I could. I had a right to eavesdrop. It was my house.

"We don't have much time, Jordana," Giles was saying.

Jordana Morgan? I shouldn't have been surprised. His research assistant was one of the many people at the Campus who believed Giles walked on water. I remembered her as a brainy girl with glasses, gazing adoringly at her brilliant boss. I had wished many times she would take his mind off me. But here?

"You never have enough time for me," she was complaining.

"I'm a busy man. Busy men have urgent needs."

"Then strip, Dr. Embry. Now." Her voice was sultrier than I remembered it. "I'm an impatient woman."

"I like that about you."

Her laugh was like a low growl. "You're in a very vulnerable position, Doctor."

I was horrified and embarrassed, and in a pretty vulnerable position myself. Yet fascinated. I knew Giles liked sex. I wasn't sure he was capable of making love. He sounded enthusiastic, though. Their chatter was intimate, even warm. So he could get excited about being with a woman. As long as she wasn't me.

Surprised, curious, and furious, I didn't know what to do, except wait for it to be over. Was this affair the reason I never felt any heat from him? *Cad. Louse. Rat.* I tried to find an appropriate word for him, in addition to *bastard.*

"Why do you keep saying you're going to marry her?" Jordana asked, while I leaned closer to the vent to hear. "Tennyson doesn't even like you. Not the way I do."

I heard sounds that I guessed were clothes coming off, shoes hitting the floor, the bed bouncing.

"She did before and she will again," Giles replied. "When she remembers me."

"You don't even like her. It's her money, isn't it?"

Another shoe fell.

"Never, ever discount the allure of money, Jordana. But more important than that, Tennyson's big memory breakthroughs are so close. It's already begun. It happened with Jonathan VanCamp, and it will happen with Tennyson. I merely need more time with her. More privacy. More control."

"Jonathan is really more of a miracle, don't you think?"

"I don't believe in miracles. I believe in my research. But research takes money. There are no bounds to what I could accomplish with Tennyson's money."

She laughed again. "It's *her* money. She might object."

"She has no idea what to do with her money. Why does she deserve it? She doesn't even know how much she has. I do. I can use it to benefit the most people."

"Shut up, Giles. If you're so concerned with public service, service me." *Service me?* Jordana had unsuspected appetites. He groaned suddenly. I assumed it was with pleasure. "You want my body and me, Giles. You only want her money," Jordana went on, a little breathlessly. "Say it. Say you want me more than her."

"I do want you, Jordana. And I want her mind and her memories. There is no one else on earth quite like her."

"Dr. Embry, you are a prick! Never, ever say something like that about another woman when you're in bed with me!"

More laughter, followed by more grunting and panting. *In my bed.*

How on earth did I come to be lying on a closet floor, inadvertently spying on people who were busy betraying me? Still, it was a relief to know where he stood. Or in this case, lay. Someday far in the future I could use this as cocktail party chatter: "And there I was, belly to the floor, ear to the register, listening to the big ox and his little vixen rutting away…"

They weren't talking anymore, but they were still going at it. They said they were in a hurry! Why didn't they leave? I checked my watch. Get on with it, I silently urged them, while I sat up and examined the closet. It might once have been part of a nursery, a baby's room next to the nanny's. I silently opened the closet door wider and crawled into the room.

Soft light filtered through a high round window. I saw I was next to a bookcase full of popular fiction, mostly mystery and romance. It was a sure bet these books weren't Giles's. They must be mine. I recognized most of the titles, but I stopped at a large leather-bound book. It was out of place. Like the volume I used as my journal, it was big and thick, with gold embossing on the spine.

It wasn't *The Odyssey*. This was *The History of the Decline and Fall of the Roman Empire* by Edward Gibbon. I picked it up. It couldn't truly be my kind of book, unless— I flipped the pages open and soon came to a place with tiny writing scribbled between the lines.

The engraved bookplate said FOXGROVE MANOR and I found my name on the flyleaf: TENNYSON CLAXTON. It was my diary. Who else would write between the lines? Why did I feel I had to hide it from everyone? In my own home? I tucked the book into my tote bag.

I blinked my eyes and crawled back to the furnace vent. They were talking again. Was the sex part of the afternoon's entertainment over, or was this just a break?

"Listen to me, Jordana. I mean it. You're going to have to move out," Giles said.

Move out? I pressed my lips together to keep from yelling. Jordana was living in *my house*?

"What? Why?" I heard the pout in her voice.

"Tennyson will be moving back in soon."

"But I like this place! I like this address," she protested. "It's classy. It's saving me rent. It's like I'm house sitting. You said—"

"Doesn't matter what I said." Giles's voice turned darker and colder. I recognized that tone too. "Things have changed. I need to get her away from her grandparents and back under my control. And back on her meds. When I implement her Pegasus protocol, Tennyson and I will finally be living together, so she can reintegrate into her old life. I need you to start moving your things out. Tomorrow."

"Why should I bother? If Tennyson doesn't remember anything, how would she even know what's hers or not? So she wears a few of my things, I've worn hers too."

She did *what*? But I had to give Jordana credit. I didn't think she was capable of sarcasm.

"Jordana, *darling*, for one thing, she's not nearly as well-endowed as you are. There could be big questions." He paused. "There is a way you might be able to stay on, though," he said slowly, as if an idea was just coming to him. "Tennyson needs the illusion of freedom, but—"

"Uh-huh. You want to keep track of her and you need a research assistant?" Her tone was icy.

"Exactly. Tennyson needs a companion who could record her movements and activities."

"Not on your life, Giles! You want me to stay here and spy on her while you sleep with her? While you're sleeping with *both* of us? You might not be sleeping with me anymore."

She sounded upset. I felt pretty sick about the idea myself. I must have jerked my arm, and my tote bag fell on the floor with a soft thud. I froze. They went right on talking.

"What I do with Tennyson is none of your business. Anyway, think about becoming her companion. Her personal nanny. I'm having the place wired for surveillance next week. You could stay right upstairs and watch and listen. I'm sure you'd find it interesting. And after she's asleep every night, with a little pharmaceutical assistance, I could come upstairs and visit *you*."

"Sometimes you really are vile, Giles."

I agreed with Jordana on that point.

"I know," he said. "Now turn over." She groaned.

Ewww! I was wrong, the sex part wasn't over. It sounded like Giles was having a lot more fun with this part than Jordana was. If possible, I now hated Giles Embry more than I had before.

Eventually, they stopped. They caught their breath and their voices softened. I heard chatter about where to go for drinks. I waited patiently for Giles and Miss Accommodating Morgan to shower and leave.

They left the bathroom, then the bedroom. Getting dressed. Footsteps going down the stairs. A few moments later I heard the front door slam. I tiptoed to the window in the upstairs office, and from behind the blinds I observed them walking down the street, not touching. Neither one looked back or at each other. For all the world, they looked like business associates. She was in slacks and a sweater. He wore slacks and a navy blazer with a red tie. Even on a Saturday afternoon, having a sleazy sex rendezvous, this man couldn't unwind.

I was incapable of moving downstairs for at least ten minutes, I was so afraid Giles would come back and discover me. When I found my feet, I checked the closet and the desk drawers: no laptop, no iPad, nothing digital at all. I gave up looking for a computer and returned to the master bedroom where Giles had "cheated" on me. Not that I was jealous. Jordana could have him. I was just furious at all the lies I'd been told. Not to mention the disrespect, the humiliation. Someone had remade the bed neatly, as if nothing had happened there. Another lie.

I took a closer look at this room, a large comfortable bedroom with a king-sized bed. A custom-made sofa fit neatly into the bay window. I went through the dresser. One drawer was full of lingerie, larger than my size. All the other drawers were full of Giles's clothes. Giles had taken over. There was no sign of me.

I inspected the women's clothes in the closet. They were not mine. Mostly, they were corporate work clothes in shades of brown and gray and black, as well as multiple lavender Campus lab coats with her name embroidered on them. Jordana Morgan had made herself at home too.

Just for fun, I moved things out of place. I figured that would drive Giles crazy. I scooped up all of her cheap earrings and tossed them under the bed. I found a silk handkerchief monogrammed with his G.E. and threw it in the trash. I rearranged his suits and shirts. I scattered all the toiletries around the bathroom.

At the front door, I checked to make sure *The Decline and Fall of the Roman Empire* was in my possession.

Before I am finished with him, I swear, there will be a companion volume, leather-bound and twice as thick: *The Decline and Fall of Giles Embry*.

Chapter 33

I WAS TOO shaky to drive straight back to the Farm.
I walked around a few blocks in Georgetown, looking for anything familiar, and found Saxby's Coffee Shop at 35th and O Streets. It was tucked into a Victorian house on a corner close to the university. I took a breath and opened the door.

Georgetown students had their noses quietly stuck in their laptops, like study hall. I loved how it felt familiar, the way all coffee shops did, without slapping me in the face with some unwanted memory from my past, any past.

"I need something to keep me awake for the next five hours," the student in front of me pled to the barista.

Why the next five hours? I wondered. It kept me from thinking about Giles sleeping with Jordana in what was supposed to be my townhouse. The student and the barista settled on something tall and chocolate with extra shots of espresso and whipped cream.

I yearned to ask for something that would wake me up from this nightmare. I requested the same drink without the extra caffeine and took a seat with a view of the comings and goings on two streets. I was afraid Giles might pop up in front of me at any moment, like a nightmarish Jack-in-the-Box.

I knew he was in love with the money, not me, but I hadn't realized how cynical he was. And yet he also thought he was saving the world: the ego that ate the Campus. I felt for the book in my bag to make sure it was real. I called Mercy Underhill and began without preamble.

"In addition to spying on me, he's cheating on me."

"Hi, Tennyson. Hang on, I'm getting a root beer." I could hear her opening and closing her refrigerator door. "Are you sure?"

"I couldn't be more sure," I said. "I decided to use the keys on my key ring and check on the townhouse in Georgetown."

"Did you interrupt something?"

"No. They interrupted my house tour. I ran upstairs and hid in a closet while they went to bed. I heard everything though a heat vent."

"You've been busy since this morning. You have a knack for

this kind of thing. The surveillance thing," she clarified. "The rest of the story, please."

I filled her in on the details. "I'm ruining your Saturday."

"I live for this stuff. Let's rendezvous someplace Dr. Embry wouldn't dare show up."

⍧

We met an hour later at a high-end women's boutique in Middleburg. Shopping was reported to be something I liked to do in moments of stress.

"Upstairs in a closet and heard everything?" Mercy was examining the quality of a heather green cashmere jacket with suede patches on the elbows and right shoulder, suitable for hunting. "What are the odds?"

"It was more informative than I expected."

"That is a good thing, Tennyson, even if it's painful. Knowledge is power. You're sure they didn't know you were there?"

"They were pretty busy. I dropped my tote bag at one point and they didn't notice."

Mercy had a wry smile on her face, which made her look friendlier and less formidable.

"You should have let me know where you were going. For backup."

"I didn't know I was going there until I did. It was a sudden urge. I suppose I could have met him at the door when I heard the key." That's what the rightful homeowner in her own home ought to do. The truth was I had felt like an intruder, a trespasser, in my own house.

"You wouldn't have learned anything valuable. Tipped your hand too soon. Who knows what he would have done?" Mercy handed the green jacket to me. "Screwing his assistant: Tawdry but typical. I'll ask Hailey if she's heard any gossip on that topic."

The store's air conditioning made it feel like a fall day. I slipped the green jacket on and studied myself in the mirror. I liked the way it looked and felt and fit. There was a great deal of difference between the elegant jacket and the clothes I'd worn for the past months. The difference that money made. A saleswoman asked if she could help. I promised to call her when I was ready.

"You're going to want photos," Mercy said.

"That seems so—sordid."

"Tennyson, you have to play hardball with Giles. He is an abuser. A rapist. Probably a psychopath. Possibly a killer. He will never leave you alone if you don't have something over him." I was quiet and she put her hand on my arm. "Because of your medical history, your documented memory losses, you have to prove what you discover. Hard evidence, or it's just a case of he said, she said, overheard through a heat vent. He'll accuse you of being delusional."

"Do you believe me, Mercy?"

"Almost one hundred percent. The first rule in my job is never get personally involved. The second rule is never believe anyone one hundred percent." She shrugged. "But I believe you enough to want to take the good doctor out of action. Not just for you, but let's say, for women everywhere. I'm worried about Hailey being at the Campus too. She's entirely too trusting, too good a soul."

"You're right." I nodded. "Anything else?"

"You should buy the jacket."

I looked at the price tag and blanched. "It's six hundred and fifty dollars! There are people in the world who don't have cashmere jackets, you know."

"You act a lot more like a kid who grew up in Maine than Middleburg. You may turn out to be Tennyson's doppelgänger for all I know, her good twin, but you still have to play the part until we figure everything out."

Mercy and I might have been friends in another life. Maybe we would be friends in this life too. The saleswoman stayed out of earshot, but she was watching, ready to be at my beck and call. I stared at my reflection.

"He's playing you, Tennyson or Marissa, or whoever you are," Mercy said. "He's living in your house, sleeping in your bed, screwing his research slut."

"I should have the locks changed."

"Not just yet. Not before we catch him in the act." She dropped something in my hand that looked like a fancy phone. "Just leave it out of sight where you think it might be most helpful. We'll listen in on him for a change."

"Is it legal?"

She raised an eyebrow. "We're not in a court of law. And he's done it to you."

"Show me how."

 C3

Octavia loved my new heather green jacket. It wasn't at all like the things I normally bought. After show-and-tell, I excused myself, citing exhaustion from my big afternoon of shopping. I shut myself up in the bedroom with the book I'd taken from the townhouse, the other between-the-lines journal. I stared at it. I hefted its weight. I touched the embossed leather cover. Even though I longed to know what I had written in it, I couldn't bring myself to read it. Not yet. First I had to get through dinner.

Downstairs, the Senator and my father were sipping bourbon on the rocks. I had lemonade, as did Octavia, who claimed she couldn't stand the taste of bourbon unless it was hidden in a mint julep.

Unfortunately, Giles was expected for dinner. When he arrived, he was in a jolly mood, apparently energized by his clandestine encounter with Jordana and a drink. He still found time to complain that I hadn't answered my phone all day. I was about to tell him where he could stick his phone when Foxhall intervened, and we got through the rest of our dinner with a minimum of shouting. Giles failed to bring up the idea of moving me to the townhouse. I wondered what that meant. Had Jordana refused to play along?

The moment Graciela cleared away the dessert plates, I excused myself, saying I needed to retire early, the stable tour and shopping had worn me out. Giles didn't say good-night or even glance up to see me go.

Before dinner, I had placed my new spy phone in the library where Giles had his usual after-dinner chats with Foxhall. I tucked it away behind the sofa, on the second bookshelf from the bottom, among the classics, where it was dark and the books were old and dusty. I was reasonably sure no one at the Farm would go hunting for a leather-bound volume of Chaucer anytime soon.

Rather than heading for my room, I settled in on the cushions of a chair in the sunroom. The azure sky deepened to sapphire in the twilight. I turned the spy phone on remotely with my black phone, as Mercy had shown me how to do.

I did have a knack for this surveillance stuff. Maybe I'd learned something from Giles after all.

Chapter 34

AT FIRST, ALL I heard was paper shuffling. Then a voice. Then four voices.

Giles, my father, my grandfather, and my grandmother.

This time, however, I wasn't going to remain in the dark. Thanks to Mercy, I had an ear at this meeting, and so did she. Everything I was hearing was being recorded remotely at her office.

"That was quite a stunt you pulled with Barnaker." It was Porter. He sounded angry.

"A stunt? Roy Barnaker died from a drug overdose," Giles responded. "He had a history of addiction. I thought that was all in his past. He fooled everyone at the Campus."

"According to Tennyson, you wanted her to see his corpse." This time it was Foxhall.

"And you believed her," Giles responded. "Isn't it obvious? This is one of her paranoid delusions."

"And yet it sounds like something of which you are capable," my grandfather went on. "To examine the effect a shock like that would have on her fragile memory."

"I had nothing to do with Barnaker's death." Giles again. "He was an addict, and he had a relapse. As for Tennyson, she's not ready to be out in the world. She's doing well, yes, but we can't let her float adrift."

"She's not adrift, she's with us," Octavia protested.

"You knew how potentially traumatic finding his body would be for her," Porter said. My father might be more astute than I thought.

"You say she's adrift? And yet, this girl fooled you, Giles," Foxhall said. "She's stronger than you expected."

"But less able to cope than you think," Giles shot back. "Her corpus of memory is still fluid, still being formed and shaped. Her emotional attachments are still stunted. Bringing her here to Foxgrove was premature. Tennyson should be at the Campus, where I can make sure her progress continues. I know she's not taking her medications here, and that's essential: She should be suggestible, open to emerging memory and recovering connections. She should not be wasting her time riding horses, for example. She needs intensive therapy and medication."

"Indoctrination, you mean. The fact is she's a very different young woman than before," Octavia said.

"What about the other memories?" Porter cut in. "Marissa's memories?"

"Fading," Giles said. "With more intensive intervention, they'll soon disappear."

"She hasn't mentioned Marissa since she's been here," Octavia said.

"How on earth did she ever hear the name Marissa Brookshire in the first place?" Porter prodded. The room was silent for a moment.

Marissa! They all knew about Marissa! All of them. Had Giles sold them the fiction that I'd killed her? That I'd somehow created a constellation of false memories around her? Did he hold that over their heads, as well as mine?

"We can't be sure, can we?" Giles finally responded. "In any case, if she's still in the grip of these false memories, I'm concerned that Tennyson is vulnerable to another breakdown, and then she'll be in a far more grave situation than when she arrived at the Campus. Confused, emotionally broken, lost."

"Is that a threat, Giles?" Octavia asked.

"Simply a prediction, Octavia. If that happens, we're back to square one. But memories are plastic. With my techniques, I can take them away and I can put them back. If the worst happens, if she does have a crisis, as a last resort there's Hypnopolethe. It can erase the confusion, and I can begin again to re-implant and reconsolidate her memories. I'll start with a blank canvas."

Everyone exclaimed at once. "That is absurd," I heard my grandmother say in the midst of it.

Hypnopolethe: The more I heard about it, the more I hated it. The unapproved witch's brew that supposedly wiped the brain clean of memories, good and bad. Some hoped it could be the "nuclear option" in treating the horrors of PTSD and memories too awful to live with. According to Giles, it had never been used on humans, just on lab mice. Was he lying to me? Why wouldn't he?

I wondered about the soldiers who screamed in the night. About the late Roy Barnaker.

It will never be used on me! I don't want to block my memories,

I want to recover them, even if some of them belong to a dead woman. Even if some of them are too awful to live with.

"You are entirely too taken with your own theories, Giles. Must I remind you there haven't been any human test subjects yet," Foxhall said. "There's no way you'll get approval to use that drug."

"It's too dangerous, too horrible," Octavia said.

"Not at all." Giles was as smooth as a snake, and he had every ear. "I know how to handle it. It would solve the problem of her false memories, once and for all."

I was frozen in place.

"Absolutely not! She's our granddaughter. Let her be the Tennyson she wants to be," Octavia said. "The new Tennyson is a vast improvement over the old one. This one has a chance to live a long and happy life."

"Don't forget where your real funding comes from," Foxhall said. "You are not to play games with my granddaughter's mind. Any more than you already have."

"I can't promise more invasive treatment won't become necessary, particularly if she continues to defy me," Giles said.

Foxhall cleared his voice. "She doesn't want to marry you, Giles. Forget about that plan."

"She will marry me. She has to. That's part of our devil's bargain, Senator. I brought her back from near death. I saved her life. I saved her mind. She belongs to me."

I heard a noise and turned around. I had no time to concentrate on the devil's bargain of which I was the jackpot. Brendan walked in on me in the sunroom. I had no idea where he'd come from. Why was he here so late? I put my black phone in my pocket.

"Hey, Tennyson. Don't mind me, I'm just making off with some leftovers from lunch." Brendan carried a big sack full of plastic containers. "Graciela outdid herself today for the stable tour, doesn't want it to go to waste. Don't worry, I'll share the wealth with my crew."

"That's nice."

"Where's Dr. Frankenstein and the folks?" He bent down and stared at me. "Hey, you don't look so good."

"I'm going to be sick." I ran out of the room, into the powder room off the hall, and threw up. I washed out my mouth and cleaned my face. When I emerged, he was waiting.

"You're pale, Tenn. Something you ate?"

"Something I couldn't swallow."

He put his arm around my shoulder and let me lean on him. He smelled nice. His shirt was fresh and clean.

"Let's get some air."

We wound up at the stable, brushing Blacksburg Downs. The horse seemed happy I was there, despite my impaired brain. Horses aren't snobs about brains. I leaned against his soft head. Princess the beagle found us, and after jumping up and licking me repeatedly, she settled down to chaperone.

"You want to talk about it?" Brendan asked.

"It would sound insane."

"Heck, Tenn. Nothing new coming from you." Brendan took the brush from my hand. "Blacksburg's had enough."

I needed a friend, but I found it impossible to tell Brendan that Giles planned to blast my memory to cosmic dust, no matter what my grandparents said.

Get away was the refrain playing in my head. *Get away before Giles blots out every true memory.*

಄

I don't remember much about the nightmare that came to me later, but I was standing by a grave and a voice that wasn't mine kept saying, "Wake up, Marissa. Please wake up."

My head throbbed. I couldn't get back to sleep. Princess was by my side, whimpering in sympathy while I picked up *The Odyssey*.

> **Thus solemn rites and holy vows we paid**
> **To all the phantom-nations of the dead;**
> **Then died the sheep: a purple torrent flow'd**
> **And all the caverns smoked with streaming blood.**
> **When lo! appear'd along the dusky coasts,**
> **Thin, airy shoals of visionary ghosts.**

Ghosts. I'd been dreaming of ghosts.

Chapter 35

S T. STEPHEN THE Martyr Catholic Church was calling me. With its stark steeple and handsome brick steps, it looked to me deceptively like a Protestant church, which suited the understated elegance of Middleburg. It was right off the main road into town, the John Mosby Highway. Graciela had told me where to find it.

"Where are you going all dressed up?" Octavia inquired before I fled that Sunday morning.

I smoothed the skirt of yet another expensive dress. This one was a white silk blend with a rainbow of colorful bands around the skirt.

"St. Stephen's for Mass. I can't remember the last time I went. Needless to say."

"Fine, if that's what you want. But you know, Magpie, our family is not Catholic."

I had suspected. "I know. Must have picked up a little of it while I was at Georgetown."

She looked skeptical. I could see her thinking I hadn't picked up much in the way of an education while I was there, why pick up being Catholic? And swimming? But she was too nice to say it.

"Well, sugar, times have changed. I'm sure you'll be in good company. Jackie Kennedy attended St. Stephen's when she lived in Middleburg. And it is a sweet-looking little church."

I reached for my keys and jingled them. The sound of freedom. I paused.

"Do we actually have a religion?"

"Of course we do. Do you think people would elect an atheist hereabouts? We're Episcopalian twice a year, dear, not including various church fund-raisers." She said it without irony. "You're the one who always refused to go to church."

"Sounds like me." I picked up my red purse. "Tavia, please don't tell Giles where I'm going. He's very anti-God."

"No man needs to know everything, Magpie. I don't think he'll be coming around today."

"Even Giles needs a day off from me?"

"He said he has lots of things to do."

Probably doing Jordana. I kissed my grandmother's cheek. She really was my grandmother. I had proof. Our DNA said so.

"I have no idea when I'll be back."

"You'll wear out your knees in that church, sugar. Catholics! Up, down, up, down, up, down."

I thought about what Octavia said as I knelt and recited the prayers by heart. High Church Episcopalians and Catholics were fairly close, I knew. Maybe that accounted for my being here? But I didn't remember being Episcopalian. I couldn't even remember most of my sins. How could I pray for them?

I chose the last pew nearest the door. I thought of it as the "sinners' pew," handy for a quick exit if I wanted to duck out early. A few people seemed to recognize me, but I bowed my head and prayed. I tried not to worry about what they might think. *Take the thorn from my heart and let me find my life again.* There was a small measure of comfort in the ritual, in the hymns, in the familiarity of the Mass. I didn't leave until the last note sounded.

೮౩

"Tennyson Claxton at church? I suppose it's true: Miracles will never cease. You weren't afraid lightning would strike you at the threshold?"

Brendan Troy stopped me on my way out. He looked spiffy out of his jeans and work shirt. He wore slacks and a light polo shirt. He was handsome in a real-world way.

"I assumed no one would look for me here," I responded. "It worked, until you showed up."

"Trying to evade the good—or is it the *bad* doctor? Don't worry, he wouldn't dare show up at St. Stephens. The smell of sulfur would announce his presence. Cut right through the incense." He smirked at the thought.

I laughed. "No doubt. Why are you here, Brendan?"

"Habit. And good coffee and doughnuts after Mass."

"Yeah? I should have figured you for a coffee-and-doughnuts man."

I was about to flee to my car when he took my elbow. He steered me away from the priest who was greeting parishioners and directed me down the steps. I wondered if we were heading toward the coffee and doughnuts. He stopped and examined me closely.

"Who are you, Tenn? What's happened to you?"

I stared at the departing churchgoers.

"I'm infamous. Ask anyone."

He stepped in front of me. "And you sure look like her. But there are differences. She was hard, in her heart. You're not. Maybe I can't believe Tennyson Claxton, spawn of Satan, would step inside any church, let alone this one."

"I couldn't have been that bad."

Spawn of Satan?

"I didn't pay much attention to the good Father after you walked in."

"I sat in the back, how did you even notice me?"

"Eyes in the back of my head. You know all the words? How did that happen? Someone plant a microchip in you?"

"I went to college. I learned a few words. How could I be anybody but myself?" Or could he see something different in me, because he wasn't part of some conspiracy?

"Don't know. At the very least, you had a personality transplant over the past few months. And you know something, Tenn?" He rubbed the back of his neck. "I don't think Embry even likes you, not the way he did before."

"What do you know about that?" Suddenly I was interested in this conversation.

"I stay well away from that phony. Embry and I despise each other. Politely, of course. But I saw the two of you together occasionally, social things, horse country things. I don't know if it was all hearts and flowers and rainbows, or just a twisted mutual obsession, but there was something between you. What's going on now isn't the same. What happened in that accident?"

"I don't know." I had a sudden urge to run away, but I controlled it. "I have memory issues, didn't you hear? And are you Giles's spy? Or my grandparents'? Or maybe Porter's?"

"That's what I like, a little faith. Don't insult me, Tenn. I wouldn't trust your family as far as a fly can spit. I imagine it's the same for them, our riding lessons notwithstanding."

"Why'd you agree to teach me to ride?"

"I thought you were lying about not being able to."

"So you agreed to teach me just to catch me out? That's what I like, a little faith! Well, if I knew how to ride once, I've forgotten."

"What's going on? You're so scared of something, you ran to church. And not even your own people's church."

Words failed me. He was right, I was scared.

"Long story," I managed to say.

"Good thing it's Sunday. I got the whole rest of the day. You hungry? You're skinny as a scarecrow."

"This flattery thing work for you much, Brendan?"

"Don't want you fainting dead away before I satisfy my curiosity. You need some food and I'm talking more than doughnuts."

He suggested that we escape to Purcellville for a lunch away from everyone else. I'd never been to Purcellville, as far as I knew. It sounded like more fun than heading back to Foxgrove alone and searching my family's lying faces for a clue to the truth. I started for my car.

"You're driving a Volvo? Since when?"

"Why not? I wanted something safe. And there weren't any armored cars on the lot."

He shook his head. "I'll drive. Besides, I know where we're going." He opened the door to his truck. I hoped I didn't expose too much leg climbing up into it.

Purcellville wasn't far away, a tiny Hunt Country hamlet with a decent restaurant or two. He chose one. Flickering candles in amber glass cast a cozy glow over the room as we walked in. The restaurant was set in an old mill where heavy timbers and iron tools hung from the ceiling, ghosts of a bygone farming era. The wooden walls and floors reminded me of our stable at the Farm. Tall windows on the second and third floors shed soft light down on the center of the room, which held the bar.

There was the faintest aroma of clean sawn wood and fresh home cooking. Suddenly, I was hungry. Very hungry. I reached for the basket of warm bread. I caught Brendan staring at me.

"I haven't had much of an appetite in quite a while," I admitted. Perhaps I'd tried to become a shadow so Giles couldn't see me. I pulled the bread apart and enjoyed the aroma.

"You may not think so, but you can trust me, you know."

"Call me skeptical, Brendan."

"I get that, but I've always been honest with you, even when you didn't like it."

I wanted to trust somebody. I trusted Mercy and Hailey, but my universe of trustworthy friends was very small.

"I gather you never believed me."

"You were always so full of—bull. Always so impressed with yourself."

"Ouch."

"Arrogant. Conceited. And yet you fell for every flimflam artist out there."

"Are you talking about therapists?" I slathered a piece of bread with butter and popped it in my mouth. At least I didn't think Brendan would try to drug me.

"Those too. And the biggest con artist of all, Giles Embry."

"That's him. Why do you know so much?"

"Grew up right next door. Next door, in country terms. If I tried to ignore you, there were always those sleazy magazines with your latest escapades. And people like to gossip."

"So I can trust you because you're the boy next door?"

"Yes." It was his turn to reach for the bread.

"How can I be sure you're not just gathering info for my family?"

He snorted. "I could sign an affidavit."

"Even if what I have to say sounds crazy? Beyond crazy?"

"Even if you tell me you were abducted by space aliens and given a new personality. Hell, that would be easy to believe."

"It would explain things. However, from what I've read, space aliens prefer Maryland to Virginia. Highway Forty."

"The old Tennyson Claxton's frame of reference extended no farther than a ten-foot radius in front of her. She wouldn't joke about aliens."

I dropped my eyes and looked at the menu. "Or horses."

The waiter sailed up and took our orders. I splurged on eggs benedict and Brendan ordered something served in a skillet with scrambled eggs, potatoes, extra bacon, and a side of grits—a heart attack in a pan. After the waiter rushed off, he waited for me to speak.

"If you break my confidence, I'll deny everything. And I'll trample you with Blacksburg Downs."

"I would expect no less. Don't worry, no one on the Claxton side of the fence would listen to me anyway."

Before I could begin, I swallowed some coffee. It was black and bracing, though not as strong as my grandfather's brew. I cleared my throat.

"For the longest time, since I woke up at the Campus, I've had this out-of-place feeling. Basically, I woke up in a nightmare with two sets of memories. Two different women: Tennyson and Marissa. In the beginning, I thought I was the latter. Giles insisted she was a false memory."

"Some kind of split-personality thing?" Brendan didn't laugh. No mockery. Just curiosity.

"Giles said no. First he said Marissa was just a fantasy. Then he said she was a false memory implanted by one therapist I'd had, with my help. He slipped and told me the name. Jensen. David Jensen. I managed to find his number and arranged to meet with him. He had a piece of my history. Something not laundered by Dr. Embry. He was going to come to the Campus to talk with me." I ran my hands through my hair. "Giles found out. And Jensen died the night before he was supposed to see me."

"How did he die?"

"The newspaper said suicide. Gunshot. My memories seem to live side by side. There are thousands of things I don't remember. Places gone. Years vanished. And what I do remember flips back and forth between Marissa Brookshire and Tennyson Claxton."

"That could give you whiplash. Tell me about Marissa. Who is she?"

"A dead woman. She worked hard, never had enough money. She was a teacher, going to grad school." He stared at me in surprise. "Yeah, I know my spotty history with college. Doesn't sound like me, does it? I remember Marissa's grandparents, not mine. I remember the ocean, not horse country. I can swim like a porpoise, for God's sake, and I cannot ride a horse."

"And yet there are times when I see a glimpse of the old you. You love that horse. Can't hide that."

"Blacksburg Downs doesn't judge me." I laughed. "Much. As long as the apples keep coming. Want to know a secret? Since I escaped the Campus, I secretly had a DNA test done. Comparing my hair with Octavia's and Foxhall's."

The waiter came by and slid our plates onto the table. He poured more coffee and vanished.

"Quick work," Brendan said. "You haven't been out that long."

"Money talks."

"Still awfully quick. So you wanted proof you were, or were not, Tennyson Claxton?"

"Looks like I'm a Claxton."

"Okay, you're a Claxton. My old friend Tenn, according to DNA. So is this Marissa a figment of your imagination?"

"No. Now Giles admits she existed. She's buried in Leesburg in the Union Cemetery. He took me to her grave. He said I killed her in the car accident that night. My memories of being her are from the guilt of killing her. Or something like that. His story changes all the time."

"He says you killed her? God, why would he tell you that?" He stabbed his eggs. Then he lifted his gaze to mine. "You were alone in that wreck, Tenn. I know. I drove the same road that night. It was cold and icy. I had to pull off the road to let the ambulance and cop cars reach you. It made an impression."

I could hear the sound of the crash in my mind.

"You saw it?"

"Just the aftermath. I saw your Porsche, what was left of it. No other cars in that crash. If Embry would tell you you'd killed someone, he'd tell you anything. I just don't know why."

"Lie after lie after lie." I took a bite of my breakfast.

"You were always fooled by him," Brendan said. "I, on the other hand, never believed anything he said. I'd like to knock some sense into him."

"Don't. He's dangerous. No one is going to take the word of a crazy drug-addled flake like me over the distinguished doctor. He's got a golden pass."

I dug into my Hermès bag and pulled out the picture of Marissa. Brendan stared at it, then at me, then back again.

"Damn. Except for the eyes—"

"Hers were green. I've heard that eye color can change. Glaucoma medication?"

"I know." He dug into his scrambled mess of eggs and bacon. "My grandmother used eye drops for that. One of the side effects they told us about. Didn't affect hers though, they were already brown."

The waiter returned with a coffee refill. We ate in silence. Finally, Brendan leaned back.

"You got one side of the DNA equation. Now it seems to me you need to try and find a DNA match for this woman Marissa. Get her exhumed. See who she is. You mentioned her grandparents?"

"They're dead."

"Parents? Siblings?"

I shook my head. "Marissa never had a father. Her mother died when she was young."

"How do you know that?"

"I just do." I knocked a couple of fingers against my head. "And I know something else." I fluttered my ringless fingers. "Giles Embry is not my fiancé. It's been difficult to get it through his head, what with him saving my life after the accident."

"You sure he did all that? Saved you? Or tortured you? And the Claxton clan hails him as the Conquering Hero?"

"They seem to." I leaned in close and lowered my voice. "I don't love him. I don't even like him. I can't stand him." I didn't go into my jaunt to Georgetown and Giles's affair with Jordana.

"You know, Tennyson, not a lot of people would try to talk themselves out of a fortune."

"That fortune is attached to a pretty awful person."

"Not anymore."

I didn't know what to say to that. As small as it was, it was one of the nicest things anyone had said to me lately.

"If we're talking wildly outlandish theories here," I began. "If the real Tennyson died in that accident— Could Giles have made a substitution? With a look-alike?"

He frowned. "With the same DNA? That's a stretch."

"Exactly. How could he do that? How many people would have to be bribed or silenced?" I rubbed my nose and thought about how, long before the accident, Giles had encouraged me to change my nose with the rhinoplasty that made Marissa and Tennyson practically identical.

"So how did he coerce this Marissa into his preposterous scheme? Anyway, you said the DNA proves you're a Claxton."

"I know. I have no idea what it all means. None of it fits together. But I know Giles has this experimental drug that can erase memories. I overheard him telling my grandparents that if necessary, he'll use it to erase all the memories I have left." I didn't tell Brendan exactly how I overheard it.

"He can do that?"

"He could try. I don't know if he's tried it before."

"On you?"

"Oh my God. I don't know. I hope not. It didn't sound like it when he talked with the Senator and Octavia."

I'd gone that far. In a rush I told Brendan other things. Roy's overdose. Miss Jasmine's demise. Death seemed to follow Giles around. Or did it follow me?

"By my count," he said, "there are four dead people. Did he kill them all?"

"Miss Jasmine was very old. And every death can be explained away. Accident, suicide, overdose, old age."

"You cannot ever be alone with him, Magpie. You know, you used to hate it when I called you that."

"I'd rather be a magpie than a million-dollar guinea pig."

"Don't sell yourself short. Could be billions."

"Is that what everyone sees in me? Just a big pile of cash?"

"Not everyone." He reached for my hand and squeezed it. "Not me, for instance. But then, I don't see the Tennyson I grew up with anywhere around here."

Chapter 36

M Y BIGGEST OBSTACLE to escaping Giles is *me*.
My personal history and my recent hospitalization make everything I say unreliable, if not preposterous. Giles is my doctor, the famous memory expert, the concerned professional. He's set the scene by telling everyone that, in addition to my memory lapses, I'm unstable and paranoid, delusional and incompetent. I can't remember who I am from minute to minute. Who would believe me? I should be under a doctor's care. Dr. Giles Embry's loving, and lethal, care.

Brendan seemed to understand. I could still feel the warmth of his hand on mine, and the temporary thawing of my heart. But would he be there if I needed him?

When I got back to the Farm, the place was empty, except for Graciela and Hector. No one to eavesdrop on. The least I could do was to read the stupid diary I'd been avoiding, the one I'd hidden between the lines in *The Decline and Fall of the Roman Empire*. I had to be brave enough to face the inner Tennyson.

Giles thinks he is so smart and he can have secrets from me, it began. *But he can't.*

The first entry was dated a year ago, last spring. The entries were sparse. Most were sparked by something that angered me.

Let Dr. Giles try and find this journal. He has no use for books or anything that's not about science. Except me. Unfortunately he believes he can play around and not get caught. Does he think I don't know he slept with that SLUT Lavinia? I got there first Lavinia. So back off BITCH.

Lavinia. The woman we met in Middleburg the day I left the Campus. No wonder I didn't like her. And Giles? I wasn't surprised at that. Not after his performance with Jordana.

I can have secrets too.
To get even with Giles I slept with Hudson. Everyone knows that

pig Lavinia has her eye on him. And Hudson, well he's nice enough. Nothing to complain about. But he's not the one I love. Giles's transgression required an in-kind payback. Double payback. So then I slept with a cute bag boy at the grocery store. Jason or Jeremy or something. He was BIG! And enthusiastic, if not very accomplished. And very willing to do it again anytime I want. Take that, Giles.

Oh, God, could I have possibly done that? I was embarrassed just to read this stuff.

I'm going shopping tomorrow with Lavinia. I'll talk her into buying something really ugly that will make her look super fat. That bitch has to understand that Giles Embry is MINE! Hudson is mine if I want him and anyone Lavinia looks at is mine! I love that Giles is so handsome and he belongs to me. I hate that he is weak. I hate that everyone is after him. Even some boring lab assistant in GLASSES. He's not their trophy. He's MY trophy.

Oh dear. I flipped through a few pages before a new entry appeared in pink ink. Something had happened, a quarrel, but I didn't explain it. I should have known all about it. But now I didn't.

We had a terrible fight over that other BITCH. Of course he came crawling back to tell me how sorry he was. We had make-up sex all night. I want to believe him. I really do.

It went on in that vein. Gossip and fights and make-up sex. A few entries about the family and how much I hated them all. Not merely Octavia and Foxhall. I hated my mother and father and wished them all dead. Anyone who offended me. Dead, dead, dead.

It sounded like it was written by a bitchy, boy-crazy thirteen-year-old in the grip of hormonal angst. I wished harm on everyone except Giles, about whom I had an obsession. I fawned on him inexplicably even when he made me cry. I sounded mentally ill.

I skipped ahead until I found entries from late last summer.

We're shopping for a ring tomorrow!!! Giles's first proposal was not romantic. I had to patiently explain to him that I am not an oh-by-the-way-do-you-want-to-get-married kind of woman! I told him so and I refused him the first time. I told him to stay in his apartment. That shocked him. Just when he thinks I'm eating out of his hand I surprise the good doctor. Giles is awfully fond of my townhouse, my money, my name. I know that's part of it, it comes with the Claxton territory. Male gold diggers, Tavia calls them. But underneath it all, Giles loves me. I know he does! He has to! He's so smart and so perfect for me!

He crawled back later carrying an armload of yellow roses. My favorite. Pretty soon, we wound up doing the deed on the living room floor in front of Great Granny's pink marble fireplace. He apologized for his first pathetic proposal. He asked me again. On his knees! I said YES! I want a great big ring!

The ring expedition was successful, as noted in the next entry.

Giles says my engagement ring is not tasteful. As if I care! I love it. I'm a Claxton. Whatever I wear is what everyone else wants. That's how it is when you're ME!

I wished I could tell the woman who wrote that how wrong she was. Shame made me cringe, but I read on.

My engagement ring has a huge pink diamond in the center surrounded by white diamonds. I could have had something designed specially, but they swore it was one of a kind, and I couldn't wait! As it was, I had to wait all day to have it sized. I had to pay more to have the jeweler stop everything he was doing to do it. But he did and I am looking at it now! Yes, I want everyone to know Giles Embry is mine and he gave me this ring!

Of course not exactly. I had to pay for it myself. He couldn't afford a diamond this big. This is the one I wanted. Who does he think I am? I am an expensive person. So I'm high maintenance and PROUD. He doesn't want to KNOW what low maintenance looks like. Giles doesn't really even have a say in the matter, does he? It's my finger after all. He actually pointed out a one-carat diamond he could afford, not that he would have paid. He never does. Somehow it always seems to be me. It makes me sad sometimes. But he's a genius and he's helping the world and all that with his brilliant research. So maybe it evens things out.

Poor confused little rich girl. This entry made me wonder why

Giles was so keen on me wearing the damn ring. Except that it fully reflected Tennyson's taste. He was right. It wasn't tasteful. That ring was even more appalling to me now.

This volume really should have been subtitled *The Decline and Fall of Tennyson Claxton*. I'd been worried about being brain-damaged after my accident? Apparently I was brain-damaged long before that. I closed the book, disheartened.

It was time to put in an appearance before dinner. I dreaded every second of it.

Chapter 37

"TENNYSON, YOUR MOTHER has arrived. She'll be staying in the annex."

Octavia's tone was ice-cold, but she was still bound by the code of behavior of the Southern hostess, pressed up against the etiquette wall built by those who had gone before her. The beagles crowded round her, furry court jesters attempting to cheer their queen.

If I had inspired such a frosty reception, I'd have headed for the nearest roadside motel, but there was none. Perhaps the Red Fox Inn was full. And just what was the annex?

"My mother? Where is she?" My heart jumped at the very word, mother.

"Yes. Your mother." Octavia's pained expression bore this new martyrdom with a certain grace, but she made it clear she was suffering.

How I'd longed for a mother! I had the sense that my mother was long dead. Perhaps it was simply being part of the Claxton clan that gave me that lost feeling. Perhaps, reading that awful diary upstairs, I'd simply wished her dead so many times I believed she was. And it seemed Priscilla Claxton was practically dead to my grandparents. I hoped I would know her when I saw her.

"She's unpacking. She'll meet us in ten minutes in the solarium."

"I don't know what to say."

"Don't let her upset you, Magpie. I know you've had trouble in the past. Your father is briefing her on your recovery."

My grandmother followed me into the appointed room.

"Without a fight?" I was joking.

"Hopefully the fireworks will be kept to a minimum. And if those two can get through a conversation today without bloodshed, heaven knows you can as well. So be good, sugar." She gave me her special I-brook-no-nonsense look. It made me laugh.

"This should be interesting."

"Less interesting than usual. She left the Argentinian polo player at home." My grandmother smiled. This apparently was a blessing. Whether Tavia didn't like my mother's new companion or simply didn't want him to ride our polo ponies, I didn't know. "We're going to be civilized about all this," she continued, straightening her shoulders.

My throat went dry. "I need some lemonade." I fled to the kitchen, followed by Princess, who was determined to claim me as her own. I helped myself to lemonade and ignored my special beagle's plea for some of whatever I was having. We scooted out of there to avoid annoying Graciela, who was in the midst of preparing dinner.

Surely my mother would know me for who I was. If I were a fraud, she'd be able to tell. She wouldn't care what the Claxtons thought. She hated the Claxtons, they hated her, so why should any of us lie? I carried the glass with me. I paused in the hall to gaze into the mirror and decided that perhaps I needed a different outfit. Something fresher. Prettier. I wanted to please this woman I only vaguely remembered. Princess sat at my feet.

The family had briefed me about Priscilla Alden Claxton, who was living comfortably in South America with her handsome man-toy on Porter's generous alimony. The Claxtons accused her of willfully remaining un-remarried just so she could stay connected, not only to the family money, but also to the illustrious family name. Matrimonially, Porter had moved on, and on, and on, so why shouldn't she?

The Claxtons united were a tank without brakes, hurtling down a hill, mowing down everything in their path. I was prepared to feel sorry for Priscilla. She was an outsider, and so was I.

After my parents divorced, I knew, I was warehoused in a succession of boarding schools, bouncing between them like a pinball. On school breaks and between custody fights, I sought refuge with Octavia and the Senator at Foxgrove, where I would inevitably melt down, scream and shout, wish they were all dead, dive into the gin and vodka (after age sixteen or so), then move on to the next boarding school.

Tell me again: Why does everyone think I'd be thrilled to be a Claxton?

I ran upstairs and changed into a yellow silk sundress and high-heeled gold sandals. I was swimming and riding and eating on a regular basis, I was drug-free and alcohol-free, and I looked much healthier now than the Tennyson I had seen in so many videos, not so pale and gaunt, hollow-eyed. I touched up my makeup and fluffed my hair. Because Giles disliked my blond highlights, I loved them out of all proportion. I looked more or less acceptable, at least to me, in spite of my doubtful brown eyes.

I trotted back down to the solarium, followed by Princess. Octavia made herself scarce, perhaps not trusting herself to deal with Priscilla alone, with the gloves off and the claws out. Fights between these two were the stuff of family legend.

I paced up and down. Was this one more test to see what familial remembrances I could cough up? To reveal how much I didn't know? Behind me I heard heels tapping staccato on the stone floor. I turned and gazed at the woman who stood there. As is often the case with those whose reputation precedes them, she was smaller than I had imagined. We were the same height. Unexpectedly, I felt a sense of familiarity. At last.

"Mother?" I stood still, waiting.

"Tennyson Olivia?" Her voice had a musical Southern lilt to it. She peered into my face. "You're looking well."

Did she really recognize me? In spite of my efforts to stay calm and sophisticated, I felt a tear slip down my cheek. I'm not usually a crybaby, it had just been a couple of very intense days. She moved closer.

"Tennyson, are you all right?"

"I'm sorry, it's been so long—" I wiped my face.

Priscilla pulled me into a big long hug and I heard her sigh. I smelled her perfume. I thought I recognized it, though I couldn't name it.

"Yes, it's been much too long."

She seemed so very much like what I remembered about my mother. The shoulder-length blond hair, the slender build. Her eyes were brown, but large and expressive. I didn't remember that. She was beautiful. She had aged very well and could pass for my older sister. Priscilla was lightly tanned, which she showed off in turquoise slacks and a white silk blouse. Large turquoise and silver drop earrings dangled from her small ears. She certainly didn't look like the fabled man-eating shrew Octavia made her out to be.

"How long are you staying?" I asked.

"A week," she said. "Perhaps we can manage it peacefully." We looked at each other and laughed at the same time. Her laughter had a clear crystal tone. "I thought this would be harder."

"I've missed you." I meant it. I missed my mother.

"Really, Tennyson? You have? Porter says you've changed a great deal. More than your nose." She reached out one finger and almost touched it. "Now you look more like me, and not so much like your grandfather." She smiled.

Well. At least she liked my nose. I smoothed my hair, not knowing what to say.

Octavia chose that moment to make her entrance. We both made way for the imperial dame. She wore a cream-colored silk and linen shift dress and a matching sweater with three strands of pearls.

"Ah. I see you two have met." She gave me a warning look and turned to Priscilla. "And how is Marco?"

"Polo." I couldn't stop myself.

Priscilla groaned, but she was still smiling. "Such an old joke, Tennyson. He's fine, Octavia."

"He sent you into the lion's den alone," Octavia commented.

"I'm a better lion tamer that he is."

Her former mother-in-law didn't rattle this woman. I wanted to know all about her, but I was tongue-tied. It seemed like a trick of time to have my mother here with me. Time travel, or magic, or a dream.

"Cat got your tongue, Magpie?" Octavia asked.

"I don't know where to begin," I said. "How long has it been?"

"Quite a few years," Priscilla said. "Maybe five? Of course I was here to see you after the accident, but you were in that coma, and then—"

"And then she hurried right back to South America." Octavia's smile was wicked. "And Marco Polo."

Porter strolled into the solarium. He was even tanner than the last time I saw him. Did these people know nothing about the dangers of skin cancer? He sported a cocktail in each hand and presented one elegantly to his ex-wife, like a movie star out of the 1940s. He kissed me on the forehead.

"I'm sure Giles kept you away from me, like he did everyone else," I said. I wanted to make her feel comfortable. I liked her. At least, I wanted to like her, knowing that the family liked to gang up on her. We outcasts need to stick together.

"You were in no condition to see anyone." We all turned toward the speaker.

Like the serpent in the garden, Giles slithered out from behind a magnolia, though I'm not sure there were magnolias in the Garden of

Eden. It was just like him to ruin the moment for me. Priscilla took a step back. He had that effect on a lot of people.

"I'm sorry he did that," I said to her.

Giles was about to speak again when Foxhall entered from the hallway and put his arm around my shoulder. "This is a scene I never thought I'd see again, our little family all together."

"Even me?" Priscilla inquired.

"Yes, even you, my dear." He smiled widely, his senatorial smile that always offered much and hid a little something.

"We should take a photograph. It is a momentous occasion, after all." Giles pulled his phone from his inside jacket pocket. He would now have another picture for *The Big Show,* another learning tool for me. But I would never forget this moment.

"Excellent idea," Foxhall said. He herded us all into the frame.

And that is how I wound up in the middle of the picture, surrounded by my family. Foxhall and Tavia to my right, Priscilla and Porter on my left. I tried to ignore Giles, but of course he insisted on more photos, with him standing right next to me. He smiled. I scowled. He finally put the phone away.

At that moment, I wanted to apologize to all of them, except Giles. It was difficult to know where to start, there were so many past sins.

"I must have caused you all such sorrow," I began.

"Hush now, Magpie," Octavia said.

"My goodness," Priscilla laughed. "This doesn't sound like the girl voted most likely to fight with her mother."

"The past is past," Porter said.

"Tennyson still has gaps in her memory," Giles said. "She's continuing intensive therapy to reclaim them. In fact, she's about to go into the phase I call Pegasus."

"Giles loves to pretend I'm not in the room when he talks," I said.

"That's not true, Tennyson, I was merely explaining." He put his hand around my waist and pulled me to him. "You're doing so wonderfully, Tennyson. Don't you think it's time you came back to Georgetown, to the townhouse, and live with me?"

I didn't bother to correct him. It was *my* townhouse and he would have been living with *me*, not the other way around.

It was Octavia who spoke first. "Do you really think so, Giles?" She hadn't overheard his moment with Jordana, like I had. "But you wouldn't like to be alone in that empty townhouse all day, would you, Tennyson?"

"I'll be taking some time off from the Campus," Giles hastened to add. "Tennyson's recovery will be my sole focus. We'll be together full-time, and we'll be able to make so much more progress that way. Together."

I'd be caged like a tiger.

"Why, Giles, I'm surprised," I managed to say calmly. "You were against me coming here and now you want me to live on my own? I'm very happy here for now. I'm not ready to live with you. The answer is no."

I wanted witnesses to my declaration. My mind was racing. Surely he couldn't physically force me. And where and how did he plan to administer the Hypnopolethe that would make me a blank slate? How much would he use? Could it kill me? Would there still be some memories of me hiding in the dark recesses of my brain?

"You've made amazing strides here. You'll make even more there. The sooner the better." He turned on his charming smile. It chilled me to the bone.

"Absolutely not while my mother is here. It's been years since we saw each other. I'm still getting used to being with my family again. And don't forget Blacksburg Downs. I can't abandon him."

"You shouldn't be on that horse," he grumbled.

"If she's not ready to leave, she's not ready," Foxhall said firmly. "If she wants to ride her horse, she'll ride."

I broke Giles's hold and slipped away from him. I joined the Claxtons in a line against him. I hoped it was clear to everybody that Giles was afraid of losing control of me.

"I remember the days when you couldn't wait to get away from all of us." Priscilla stared at me. "I've never seen such a change."

"It's been a long time since you've seen her, Priscilla," Foxhall said.

"True. I didn't even know about the plastic surgery until Porter told me." She gave me a small hug. "We parted on very bad terms, Tennyson. I am sorry about that."

Octavia moved in close on my other side. "She has grown up since you left. As for you, Giles, Tennyson can stay here as long as she likes. Foxgrove is her home too."

If Giles felt outnumbered, he didn't show it. "As her doctor, as well as her fiancé, the time is ripe to move back to her own townhouse. Living here, she's become too dependent on you."

"Don't worry, Giles, you'll be the first to know when I'm ready." To Priscilla, I said, "I have a riding lesson first thing in the morning, but maybe we could have lunch and go shopping in the village, if you don't mind."

"Mind? It would be a first, and I'd be delighted."

Giles reached for my hand. He gazed into my eyes, an approximation of affection.

"Not too much excitement. You might be disappointed if you don't remember everything you think you should."

"I'll be disappointed if I don't get to be with my mother. You don't want me to be *disappointed*." I wished I knew how to veil a threat as well as my grandfather.

"You've forgotten your engagement ring." He squeezed my finger, hard. I pulled away.

"It's not really tasteful, is it, Giles? Too big. Too pink. Too gaudy. Too much the old me."

Foxhall inserted himself between us. "Time for dinner. Magpie, my dear, would you accompany me?"

 CB

Following a dinner he made more tense with every word, Giles asked me to walk him to his car to say good-night. I went as far as the front door, and I kept Octavia and Priscilla on either side of me. He scolded me again for not wearing the ring. He pushed for a date for me to move back to the townhouse. I promised myself I would change the locks on the townhouse as soon as possible.

Giles left without kissing me good-night. He slammed his car door shut and drove off. Much to everyone's relief.

CB

Back in my room after a little old-fashioned ballroom dancing in the library, I opened *The Decline and Fall,* determined to finish reading what I must have written before the accident, no matter how distasteful. There were tear stains on the next page I read.

This devil's bargain between Giles and me is at an end but he doesn't know it yet. He has lied to me once too often. He has kept one more secret from me. The worst of all. He didn't think I'd find out. Oh and yes that bastard father of mine didn't bother to mention it either. And I bet he never told my mother. It would shock her.

I have a sister!

Her name is Marissa. She is two years older than I am so she was born before my parents married. I always wanted a sister! Everyone has been lying to me all these years!

Maybe it was wrong to go through his desk but I don't care. When will Giles learn that I can find out all his dirty little secrets? Now I'm wondering if my mother knew when she married my father there was another deep dark family secret. Did anyone ever think of ME? Giles has a freaking file on her! There are pictures. I took one.

I had to close the book for a moment. A file? He'd been keeping information on Marissa. For how long? My hands shook. Here it was. What Mercy and I suspected. This was how I found out about Marissa. I was as rocked by this information as I must have been the first time. I'd had a sister all along. Now she was lost to me.

The weird thing is that we look so much alike. I don't know if it's creepy or just strange or if that's the way families are. Her eyes are a different color and she obviously dyes her hair. I mean, she's blond and her dark roots were showing. But she's not a dark brunette like me. More medium brown. She's the same height too.

It's so unfair! All my life I wanted a brother or a sister. Are there more of them hiding out there? Any more secret kids, Porter? You lying lying lying BASTARD.

Marissa and I could have been sisters and friends and she could have shared this stupid weird rich girl life. Maybe I wouldn't be so ANGRY all the time. Maybe I wouldn't HATE everybody. Instead I'm ALONE and I HATE it! She grew up poor, really poor, so I guess that prick Porter never even did the right thing and helped her mom. I am DISGUSTED by him. He never even sent her money. I wondered if maybe he didn't even know about her. But if he didn't know how could Giles find out?

Giles hoards his secrets like a miser. I don't know how he's using this one. Marissa was born out of wedlock because as far as I know Porter didn't get married until he met Priscilla. I wonder if my mother or my grandparents knew about this little surprise. I don't care how bizarre or strange it will be. I want to meet Marissa Brookshire. MY SISTER!!! You can tell just by looking at us!

I copied the whole file on Marissa and read it so many times I feel like I know her. She was raised by her grandparents sort of like me. Only she seemed to like hers even though they were poor. I wonder if she's going to be as MAD as I am that we were kept away from each other?

"I feel like I know her." Giles's file must be where I found out the details I knew about Marissa. The hitchhiker my mind had picked up along the way. I had to put down the book again. To cry. I picked it up again. The last entry was dated the day of the accident in January. The day I nearly died. The day before Marissa died.

I'm breaking it off with Giles tonight. I thought about it for the last week. I want him but I hate him so much. I cannot live with such a LYING cheating WEASEL. Oh yes there is going to be a SCENE! A huge scene. The biggest scene ever. In a public place so I can't take it back and forgive him. So everyone will know. I'm not going to let sex get in the way this time. I'm going to tell Giles and throw the file in his face.

I'd throw my ring in his face except I bought it. And I like it. Everyone is going to know I'm free again.

Tomorrow I'm going to call Marissa Brookshire. Won't the family be surprised?

It was a risky plan and it didn't work. After what I must have said to Giles that icy night, both Marissa and I were in awful car accidents. The same night, though hers happened hours after mine. One of us died. I had no doubt now that Giles engineered both accidents. But why exactly?

As for Ulysses, he was chatting with the dead. Greek gods and goddesses and heroes in Homer's era did that all the time. Why can't I? I wish I could talk to Marissa.

The tribute of a tear is all I crave,
And the possession of a peaceful grave.
But if, unheard, in vain compassion plead,
Revere the gods, the gods avenge the dead!

The gods avenge the dead. And so will I.

Chapter 38

"YOU DON'T SEEM very fond of your fiancé," Priscilla noted.

"I'm not. I'm trying to find a way to free myself of him once and for all. It's not easy."

We were having lunch in another horse-themed Middleburg restaurant, slightly old-fashioned but comforting. Priscilla ordered the featured wine from a local Virginia vineyard. I stuck with iced tea.

"Are you afraid to leave him because Dr. Embry works for your grandfather?"

"I'm afraid of him because he's a monster. But everyone thinks he saved me, that he's a hero."

"Whoever saved you, I'm glad they did. So many changes. No more drinking, no more drugs?"

"Not even the ones Giles keeps trying to shove down my throat."

"He doesn't seem to have a sense of humor, but he is rather handsome."

"Pythons are probably pretty handsome too, right up until they squeeze the life out of you."

"That's the rub, isn't it, Tennyson, honey? It's hard to find a man who can see beyond the bank account. You're a Claxton, after all. It's sort of a devil's bargain."

That phrase again. "That's something I've been wondering about." I wrote my initials on my frosted glass: TOC. I lifted my brown eyes to her. "Do you know me, Priscilla? Do I really seem like your daughter? Could I be a stranger?"

She stared back, then she started to smile. She looked at me with love and my heart clenched. "Of course I know my own daughter, even when she's changed so dramatically. Your hair is different, but now it's much more like mine." She reached out and touched it. "You're more thoughtful, but I hope you don't brood over things, like I can. Your father tells me you want to go back to school. I hope you do. I always loved school."

"What was I like before?"

"My little rebel without a cause. You had more of your father in you, Porter when he was your age. An attractive hellion. You know what I think, Tennyson? You were changing before the accident. You conquered your fear of the water. You even learned to cook. I like to cook too, now and then. Even Graciela's impressed with you. You know how hard that is to do?"

My cell phone, the one from Giles, interrupted us with a muffled ring, because I had wrapped it up in a scarf and stuffed it in the bottom of the bag, without Mercy's special pouch. She suggested I keep it with me when I went to ordinary places around the neighborhood, so Giles wouldn't suspect I was on to him. The scarf and the bit of tape on the microphone would keep my conversations private. But it was still disturbing to realize I was on Giles's electronic leash.

"Are you going to answer that?" Priscilla gestured to my purse.

"Might as well. He'll just keep calling." I reached in and grabbed the phone. She smiled at the elaborate unwrapping I had to do to answer it. "Yes, Giles, what do you want?"

"You bought a car without my knowledge! Or my approval!" His tone was blistering.

"Approval? How dare you! I don't need your approval." As if I wanted him to put a tracking device on my Volvo. "Your permission wasn't needed or wanted and I needed wheels."

"Did you forget you were in a terrible car crash this year? And it was your fault?"

"*Mea culpa, mea culpa. Mea maxima culpa.* How sweet of you to never let me forget that."

Priscilla raised her eyebrows, but said nothing.

"Then how could you go behind my back—"

I cut him off. "Is there some problem, Giles? Are you telling me I shouldn't have a car?"

"You should have asked me. In a few months, I could have arranged everything for you."

"In a few months?" In a few months I'd be as blank as a sheet of paper, if Giles had his way. "Go to hell. I can arrange things for myself."

"You're under stress."

"You are the cause of my stress! I'm lunching with my mother. Go away. Lecture me later."

"I'm not lecturing, I am merely—"

"Bye. I'm busy." I cut him off and wrapped the phone up tight and shoved it down to the bottom of my bag.

"He's a controlling bastard. I know the type, honey," Priscilla said. "Dump him."

I liked her more and more.

"I'm trying. I might have to flee to South America to escape him." I was only half kidding.

She gripped my hand. "Tennyson, that would be wonderful. It could be arranged. Believe me."

"Who knows? Maybe I'd love Argentina."

Chapter 39

HOW MANY OF life's answers are found in a magazine from the supermarket checkout line?

I don't know. I only know that's where I found mine that day. I found a picture. A memory. A storm of emotions.

Priscilla wanted to pick up some special coffee and cheeses on the way home. We'd already stopped at the pricey little farm market on Washington Street and scooped up some delicacies. But after spending time in South America, she wanted to visit a regular American grocery store too.

"You miss the funniest things when you're out of the country," she said, picking up a package. "Krispy Kreme Doughnuts. Yum."

I offered to take her to a super-sized grocery store in Leesburg. But she said no, the little one in Middleburg would be fine.

"I used to come here with you when you were a baby."

She wandered through the aisles while I paused at the magazine rack. I don't know why, but I reached for the one with the Maine seacoast on the cover and tossed it in the basket.

As we checked out, the bag boy winked at me. "Hi, Tennyson. Call me." He waggled an imaginary phone at his ear. His nametag identified him as Justin.

Oh God, was Justin the guy I mentioned in that awful diary? The bag boy that I'd cheated with? At least he looked like he was of legal age, in his early twenties. He was cute, too. Hot shame covered my face and I fled to the car.

"Who was that?" Priscilla asked, bringing up the rear with a couple of bags.

"I'm not really sure. It happens a lot."

"You're handling it well."

I drove us back to Foxgrove Manor.

Giles called me several times on the way home. I refused to answer the phone in the car. When I did answer, after we parked behind the main house at the Farm, he demanded, "Have you been thinking about the move to Georgetown?"

"I've thought of almost nothing else."

"Good." He took that as a positive sign and hung up. He called right back to explain he couldn't come for dinner. My spirits rose. Why did he think he had an open invitation to every meal at Foxgrove? I certainly hadn't tendered one.

"Don't worry, Giles. You won't be missed. And do give my regards to—" I nearly said to Jordana, but I didn't want him to know that I knew about her. "To someone who cares where you're having dinner. I don't." I hung up, resolving that if I ever lived in that town-house again, I would have to buy a new bed. Not to mention sheets and linens. I'd have the place cleansed with bleach. Fumigated. And exorcised by a priest.

Priscilla and I made our way through the pack of barking dogs and wagging tails to the kitchen to unpack our loot and startle Graciela. Princess stayed by my side. I was growing awfully fond of her. My favorite beagle didn't care who I was. Like my horse.

My mother made coffee and picked out a doughnut. She offered me one with an impish smile. I couldn't picture her actually indulging in sweets, she was so thin, but she surprised me.

"Our little secret." She winked at me.

We took our treats outside and sat in companionable silence, watching the shadows deepen and the doughnuts disappear.

Later, Graciela outdid herself for dinner. Beef Wellington, crab cake appetizers, salad, and fresh roasted vegetables. Dessert was homemade sorbet and fresh berries from the garden.

There was no occasion, simply a family supper on a lovely Virginia summer evening. The dress code was casually elegant and I was getting used to it. Perhaps too used to it, too used to having things done for me. We sat at the vintage glass-and-wrought-iron table on the stone patio, beneath the green-and-white striped canvas awning. It looked west over the fields and trees and the pond. As the light faded, candles and tiny white lights illuminated the space and fireflies dropped by to wink hello. It was magical.

I was as happy as I'd felt since leaving the Campus. Even Priscilla and Octavia were getting along. Porter and Foxhall had a good evening, discussing various arcane aspects of the Claxton Empire.

I didn't realize how pleasantly tired I was until I yawned. I excused myself after dinner and retired to my serene blue retreat, followed by a sleepy beagle.

ॐ

I would never forget that June evening, because it was the night my memories—many of them—came flooding back. Flooding, cascading, breaking over me like waves in a storm.

I settled on the cushions of the window seat in my room and started flipping through the pages of *Down East,* the glossy magazine I'd found at the supermarket. It was all about Maine. Gradually, I realized I knew some of the places mentioned. I recognized the rocky shores in the photographs. Not from a geography class or Tennyson's *Big Show,* but from life. I had dug my toes into the sand on those shores. I could almost smell the sea.

It wasn't the articles that opened the door into my brain. It was a small photograph in the back, in the real estate section. A property listed for sale in Camden, Maine.

It was a two-story, center-hall, white clapboard cottage with a peaked roof and green shutters. It was the dollhouse of my dreams and my nightmares, come to life.

"Oh my God," I whispered to myself. "I know that house. I grew up in that house."

Princess opened her eyes and settled her head on my lap, where I could stroke her fur.

I started to remember. To really remember. No false memories this time. I could tell the difference. All it took was seeing that one picture of that one house.

I'm trying to write down everything I remembered, but it came so fast.

I was born in Camden, Maine. After my mother died—my real mother—I went back to live with my grandparents in Camden. Grandpa Tom was a carpenter who crafted custom woodwork for ships' interiors. I loved the smell of new sawn wood, the sea, and the Maine forest. He built the dollhouse for my mother to look like their home in Camden, a miniature version. With a few fanciful additions. My Grandma Anne painted it and stocked the dollhouse with doll figures representing all of us, including one for my late mother, so I wouldn't forget her. So I would feel at home.

Camden is a jewel of a town on the Maine seacoast where the mountains meet the sea, with a snug little harbor on Penobscot Bay, protected by a ring of islands. Camden Harbor is full of sailing ships and fishermen, ready to sail off to adventure or to fish for herring and lobster. That's the way I remembered it. Whether I climbed to the top of Mount Battie or sat on the grassy parkland near the bay, I could always look to the rugged shoreline and know that I was home.

From the time I was eight until I was fourteen, my grandparents and I lived together in that pretty postcard town. I saw the leaves of Camden color to flame in the fall, shivered in the chill of winter, felt the welcoming warmth in the spring, and the heat of the summer. That was my town.

And now, that little white house with the green shutters was for sale.

I stared at it for the longest time. In my mind, I moved through each room, running up the wooden steps to the porch, opening the front door, dashing into the living room, then across the hall to the dining room and back to the kitchen, where there were always delicious aromas. My grandmother loved to bake. And my grandfather and I loved to eat.

I mentally climbed the stairs, heading for my grandparents' bedroom in front. The place where I hid my very first secret diary, just before we moved. I've always been a diary writer, ever since I was twelve and Grandpa Tom gave me that pink-covered book with the little lock on it.

"This is for your thoughts, Marissa, anything at all you feel like writing. And you see this? It's a key, the only one, so nobody else can snoop on you."

"Nobody?"

"Not even Grandma or me. Because everyone is entitled to their own thoughts."

The magazine photo was my immediate memory prompt, my trigger. But it might have been self-defense, as well. My soul knew I had to remember these things *now*, because time was running out. Giles was planning to strangle my soul and leave an empty shell behind. A shell that he could fill with selected bits and pieces of my sister Tennyson.

I am Marissa Brookshire.

I know who I am. Tennyson's sister. But how exactly did I wind up here at Foxgrove? How precisely did Giles Embry discover who I was and manipulate my fate? None of those answers were to be found in the latest issue of *Down East.*

So many thoughts careened through my head, crashing against my skull. Months spent at the Campus in the Fog. Waking from a nightmare that was warning me, telling me to run to the dollhouse. Escaping to the Farm. Finding Mercy Underhill, the DNA test, swimming, riding, overhearing voices in the library, finding a photo-graph in a magazine.

Where did I fit into this picture? Octavia was my grandmother, so Porter, her only child who lived to adulthood, was my father. Priscilla, whom I liked very much, was not my mother. I began to remember my real mother. Her name was Marisol Brookshire.

My mother died when I was a child. From what I recalled, she looked a great deal like Priscilla. They could have been sisters. Porter Quantrell Claxton clearly went for a type. Marisol had silken blond hair and large green eyes. She was small and delicate. She was the world to me.

"Where is my daddy?" I often asked her.

"You don't have a daddy, sweetie."

"Other kids have them."

"You're not other kids. You're mine, all mine, and I love you more than any daddy ever could."

We never had any money and I never knew my father. We were always on the run, before she died, before I went to live with my grandparents in Maine, where I gained the only stability I had known.

My beautiful, breakable mother, Marisol, died when I was eight. I loved her, but even as a child, I understood she was sad and delicate. She cried too many tears. She relied on me to keep her spirits up. We lived on canned soup and peanut butter sandwiches in cheap apartments where the lights and phone were sometimes cut off because Marisol couldn't pay the bills. We were often cold and often hungry. She always worked, but she'd had me very young, never finished college, never married, never found a job or a place that would change our lives. We moved around as if we were trying to outrun the devil. I was little, I was loved, I didn't know any better.

She admitted one night that I had a father, and I hadn't hatched from a random carton of eggs. But she told me we couldn't see him, because he would try to take me away from her. We had to hide.

We were both sick with flu the winter I was eight. We didn't worry about the lack of heat in that freezing Chicago apartment, because we were feverish. Or the lack of food, because we were too sick to eat. Marisol finally called my grandparents, who flew to Chi-cago just in time to take us to the hospital. Children bounce back, but my mother was much sicker than I was. I recovered. Marisol died of pneumonia.

My Brookshire grandparents, Grandma Anne and Grandpa Tom, never told me I was "illegitimate." The word wouldn't have meant anything to me. I didn't know my mother's story or how she became involved with my father. With the man I now knew had to be Porter Claxton.

My mother had been my world, but my grandparents became my rock. I was alone and scared. Thomas and Anne Brookshire stood between me and desperation.

"You're going to come and live with us." Grandma Anne wiped my face and hugged me hard. "You'll like it. It's a wonderful place, perfect for a little girl. You'll have your mother's old room."

Tom leaned down and put out his big hand. I put mine in his. "Can you be a brave girl?"

"I am a brave girl. My daddy won't try and take me away, will he?"

"No, Marissa, we won't let him," Grandpa Tom assured me and he took me to the big white house where Grandma Anne had painted colorful murals on the walls of the rooms. Marisol had grown up there. I was put in her childhood room. I was never hungry again.

Now somehow I was masquerading as Tennyson, a woman I'd never met. Except through *The Big Show of Tennyson O*, and now her brief, heartrending, angry diary.

Marissa Alexandra Brookshire: To the world I was buried and forgotten, my name on a granite slab in Virginia. Tennyson must be in that grave, put there by Giles. I wanted to shout. But the warning voice from my dreams stopped me.

What on earth am I supposed to do now?

Giles murdered her. By his own hand, or he arranged her death, as he did the others. Everywhere I turned, Giles was there before me, behind me, blocking my way, his hands full of death.

A wave of pure grief hit me.

I had a sister and she was dead. Like Tennyson in her secret diary, I had longed for a sibling. We were sisters after all, two women worlds apart, not soulmates, but both of us writing secret diaries between the lines of old books, both of us afraid of the same man.

I stared at the picture of my house in Maine for hours. The more I looked, the more I saw, and the more I remembered. It might still hold my first diary. If my diary was still in that house where I'd hidden it, I would have all the proof I needed. It contained more than ink. My DNA would be on the pages where I recorded the private thoughts of my teenage life. A tear stain, a smudged fingerprint, a strand of my hair. Being Marissa would no longer be my word against Giles.

Down East said my house was for sale. Tennyson Claxton had the money to buy it.

It might be wrong, it might be criminal, it might be fraud or embezzlement or grand larceny to knowingly use another woman's money for my own purposes, but I could buy it. Secretly, I hoped. Perhaps Mercy would have an idea how to go about buying a house on the quiet. Maybe I would only have it for a little while before they sent me to jail for it. I wasn't going to worry about that now. There were pieces of my past in that house and I had to find them.

Tennyson would have to help me. We shared the same devil, and now we were in the same fight. And after all, what are sisters for?

'Tis not the queen of hell who thee deceives;
All, all are such, when life the body leaves:
No more the substance of the man remains,
Nor bounds the blood along the purple veins.

With Princess resting her head in my lap and approving my decision, I reached for my safe phone and called Mercy. It was after midnight, but she picked up on the first ring.

Chapter 40

"THERE'S A HOUSE for sale in Camden, Maine."

"Probably more than one. What's so important about this one?"

"I have to buy it, Mercy. It's terribly important. But it has to be a secret. Is that possible?"

Mercy laughed into the phone. "You're coming along fast, Tennyson. To answer your question, if the house is for sale, you can buy it. Your accounts are in order and shall we say, well stocked. How much is it?"

"Around three hundred thousand. Good location, but it's a fixer-upper."

"I don't see a problem. Is there anything you'd like to tell me, Tennyson?"

"Maybe later. Right now, I want to buy that house before anyone else takes it."

I couldn't risk Mercy getting in trouble for my crime. If I never actually admitted I wasn't Tennyson Claxton, she would be in the clear. My theory, anyway. She understood our unspoken agreement.

"All right then. This house, this fixer-upper, may still be for sale, but what if there's a bid or a contract on it already?"

"Offer whatever it takes." Brave words as I started to tally up the years I might spend in jail for this stunt. Yet they would be years spent knowing who I was. The way Octavia always knew who she was. And they would be years spent locked safely away from Giles Embry.

I gave Mercy the pertinent details: the address, the realtor, the Web site where she could find more information. After some discussion, we agreed Mercy would arrange to buy the house with funds I would transfer to her, and instead of using Tennyson Claxton's name, we would establish an offshore corporation to make the purchase. Mercy had done that before. Tennyson would own the corporation. If there were other bidders, she would outbid them. It would be a cash deal, price no object.

I didn't have time that night to worry about Giles Embry and what he was doing or planning. There were so many details to think about in making my escape. I'd never bought a house. Up until a few days ago, I'd never bought a brand-new car.

ᚠ

Mercy Underhill showed up in the stable before my riding lesson the next morning. I'd told the guys at the gate to let her in and not alert anyone else. Princess greeted Mercy with a happy dance, settling down after she got a brief petting. Blacksburg Downs was anxious to get running, but I soothed him.

"This is my friend Mercy. You remember her. She has things to tell me, big boy, so be patient." I brushed his coat, and he dipped his head and neighed.

"He understands you?" she asked.

"More than you think. He knows who I am."

"And you are?"

"Interested in what you've found out," I said. I didn't want to spell out what I recovered last night. The less she knew, the less trouble she would be in when it all came crashing down.

"I'm interested too." Brendan strolled into the stable with a carrot for my horse. He was early. He leaned against the wall and crossed his arms. I didn't know what to do about Brendan, but I didn't fear him. However, our riding lesson would have to wait.

I introduced them. Mercy didn't seem too surprised to see Brendan, or too concerned. There was an ease to their stances and they weren't on their guards.

"Oh. You two know each other?"

Brendan was the first to cave in. "You might say Ms. Underhill and I have met in passing."

"You could say that," she agreed with a smile. "We've solved the occasional problem together. As colleagues."

"Okay then. Presumably you're both on my side? Or do I need a lawyer?"

"Not to worry, Tenn," he said. "And I already disabled the cameras here in the stable, by the way."

"Um, thanks."

"Some strange things have been going on here. We all need to talk."

"Indeed we do. Let's start with Embry." Mercy opened one file on a pile of hay bales.

"You're having Giles Embry investigated?" he asked me.

Mercy's report on Giles Embry was partly a list of glowing accomplishments, including his Harvard education, his publications in scientific and medical journals, and his presentations at major conferences. But certain terms kept cropping up in his press clippings: "maverick" and "controlling" and "unconventional" among them. Dr. Embry was not a team player.

More enlightening were comments from his colleagues who had agreed to speak to Mercy on assurance of confidentiality. They didn't go so far as to say he was unethical, but they questioned his need for absolute control, and his reputation for never letting anything or anyone stand in his way.

One former colleague of his divided scientists roughly into two groups. First, the "super nerds" who lived in their labs, wore mismatched socks, and survived on pizza delivery. They would rather work all night, getting lost in their research, than receive an award at a fancy dinner. Their dedication to breakthroughs, to the truth, and to the scientific method made them, she said, the unsung heroes of science.

Then there were the "peacocks," scientists in sharp suits who were equally interested in their image, their funding, and the sound bite that would make them media celebrities and garner more financial support for their projects. They chased awards, grants, and recognition. This colleague called Giles "the über peacock."

A coworker who asked not to be identified termed him a "ruthless fame whore" who skirted ethical rules for his own purposes. She accused Giles of exaggerating the results of his early memory research and taking credit for others' work. Although he had been suspected, Giles was never caught in an outright ethical breach.

Several others pointed out that because of his mother's dementia, Embry was driven by fear the disease would seize him as well. "Trying to outrun the Brain Reaper," as one colleague put it.

"That's got to be part of it," I said. "He's afraid he's doomed to get Alzheimer's." Was he already planning ahead? To re-implant memories he feared he would lose? Did it even matter to him if they were false memories?

"Not soon enough for me," Brendan said. "Or for you."

"You asked for something else as well," Mercy said. "I don't have much on David Jensen yet. You and I have a rough idea what really happened to him, but I want the gory details. It's officially suicide. The police don't like to mess with it once that determination has been made, but I will." She opened another folder on the hay bales. "But this morning I have—"

"Marissa," I said.

Marissa Brookshire had taught at the Quartermaine Academy, a private Falls Church, Virginia, elementary school, until Christmas vacation. According to friends and other teachers there, she was always worried about money, always thinking of new ways to pay for her master's degree. Her free nights and weekends were spent in the library studying. Although she had dated a guy in North Carolina who joined the service before she started grad school, she apparently had no more time for men in her life, at least recently. She loved the classroom and the kids, and the children loved her.

Mercy was still waiting for her birth and death certificates, but she'd obtained a few more photographs of her from the school. I tried not to give anything away when I gazed at them. I remembered one, taken at a birthday party for another teacher. I baked the cake. Everyone was smiling.

"Her life sounds a little dull when you put it like that," I said. My little life was nothing so outlandish or outsized as Tennyson Claxton's. "Did you find out whether she knew Giles? Or how they might have met?" The months leading up to the accident were still a blank. That particular Fog hadn't lifted.

"I don't think she did know him. She was too busy, too focused on her career, not part of his world. She wasn't his type. Nor do I think he was hers. Sounds like her life was a bit of a grind, to be honest. But a great teacher, everyone says so, and you never know what's going on inside someone, looking from the outside in." Mercy offered the whole file to me. "Maybe she had a secret wild life." She lifted one eyebrow at me.

"The kind of woman who doesn't realize how attractive she is." Brendan lifted a picture. "Worked hard, kept her eyes on the prize, while the guys had their eyes on her."

I read quickly through the report as they watched, wondering how I'd lived my whole life making such a small impact on the world. I'm not that old! Give me time! Just let me live and be who I really am. I handed the file back.

"Thanks, Mercy. Thank you so much. Will you keep this and lock it up for me? Make a copy?"

"Already done." She took it back and gathered her things to leave. "By the way, Barnaker's remains were cremated. No memorial service. And that other matter? I made a call this morning and it's looking very promising. I'm working on it today."

Thank God. I handed her a check. This one had a lot more zeroes than the first one. Enough to buy a house, plus expenses. It didn't feel real.

Mercy glanced at the check, considered me with a knowing look, and smiled. "I'm heading to the bank right now." She walked through the stable to the parking lot.

Could Mercy and I pull this off? How do you resurrect someone who's been declared dead?

Blacksburg Downs was prancing in anticipation of a run, and so was I. I turned around and there was Brendan.

"For the record, Magpie, I don't care who you are or what you're up to." He took me into his arms. "But just in case you are Tennyson Claxton and you ever remember how much you hate me, I say let's put the past in the past. Start over."

This was different! Unlike the way I always felt with Giles, I felt no desire to pull away from Brendan and run for my life. I felt safer now with him than any time since waking up at the Campus. I rested my hand on his cheek. It was a nice face, a strong face, a very real face. I inhaled his spicy, musky scent. His aftershave, I wondered, or did he just always smell so intoxicating? I took a chance and kissed him. He kissed me back. That kiss could have lasted for hours, but Blacksburg Downs interrupted us with a loud neigh.

I laughed and turned and caught sight of Giles at the stable door. I jumped back from Brendan's embrace. I don't think Giles could see our kiss—we were inside the horse stall. Still, his early morning appearance startled me.

I swung up onto Blacksburg's back and Brendan led us on foot out into the paddock where Boomer was waiting. I stared down at Giles, who glared back.

"Good morning, Giles. It's very early for a visit. Good-bye."

"I want to see you."

"Here I am. See ya."

"Get down from there."

"No. Riding lesson. Is it important?"

"I'm here to see Foxhall. I thought you'd like to have coffee with me."

Coffee with the devil. He was capable of slipping something, anything, in my coffee.

"No way. What are you seeing Foxhall about?"

Giles's smile was closemouthed and turned up like a troll at the ends. I'd seen it before.

"Someone to replace Roy Barnaker."

"I don't think so. Roy was so special. Who could replace him?"

"You shouldn't be on that horse, Tennyson. You're on meds. It's not safe. How many times have I told you?"

He tried to grab the bit in Blacksburg's mouth, which made the horse rear up and back away from him. The sudden movement startled us both. I held on to the reins, leaned into Blacksburg's neck, and hung on. Brendan held on tight to the horse's harness with one hand, and with the other he shoved Giles away, hard. Giles sprawled on his butt in the mud. Brendan raised a closed fist at him.

"Embry, what the hell is wrong with you? You want to get trampled by that horse? You want this woman to take a fall? Not on my watch, you dumb ass."

Blacksburg settled down, but he jittered and danced. I stroked his neck as Brendan rubbed his nose.

"Whoa, boy," Brendan murmured to the horse. "You handled that real well, Tenn."

"Good boy, Blacksburg." I leaned down and kissed my horse.

Giles picked himself up and brushed mud and straw from his clothes. His face was bright red. He readjusted his jacket, burned me with another hard stare, and cleared his throat.

"I'll attend to you later." He spun on his tassel-loafered heel and stomped off.

"Next time I'll just let the horse trample him," Brendan said. We watched him go. Brendan mounted Boomerang, and we left the stable behind, cantering into the meadow before slowing to a walk.

"Brendan, he wants to put another spy on me." He inclined his hat to indicate he was listening. "I was wondering, and I know it would be a terrible inconvenience— But do you think— Would you be willing—"

"Do you want to tell the Senator, or should I?"

"I'd better do it alone. You wouldn't mind being my body-guard?"

"No one else's body I'd rather guard, Tennyson."

This guy could flirt with me and make it sound like he was pledging allegiance at the same time. I liked that.

"It wouldn't be for very long. I hope."

"No getting out of it now, Magpie. Long as it takes, I'm your man. You know, I'd like nothing better than to knock Dr. Frankenstein out of the ring. Maybe it's those tassel loafers he wears. I want to get them good and muddy."

"Exactly." I leaned forward on Blacksburg Downs. "You and Boomerang? Me and Blacksburg. Right now. Let's run."

Chapter 41

"SENATOR, COULD YOU tell me something about—"

I hesitated at the door of the library after lunch. What I needed to discuss with him was awkward.

"What is it, Magpie?" Foxhall settled into his wing chair and gestured me into the room.

I took the seat opposite him. I sat on the edge. "I'd like to know about my money. The alleged, ah, fortune."

He folded his newspaper. "We don't usually discuss money much in this family, Magpie. We have accountants and wealth managers for that sort of thing. You could ask one of them."

He watched me.

"I'm sure we have those people, but right now, I don't remember who they might be. So could we talk, um, ballpark?"

"What do you want to know?"

"How much am I worth? Round numbers would do."

He put the newspaper back down and fixed me with a penetrating glare. I could see how he could make opponents quiver in their boots.

"Why do you need to know this, all of a sudden? Do you want to buy a small nation or something?" He grinned.

I grinned right back. "I don't personally care if I have a lot of money, although I'd like to think I've got enough to live on for a while without worrying about it. Until I get back on my feet and get a job."

"A job?" It was the first time I'd seen the Senator look that surprised. Well, that morning, anyway.

"Eventually, yes. I want to go back to school. Then, of course, I'll think about a career. 'To whom much is given, much is required,' as they say. I can't just sit around and do nothing."

"No, of course you can't." He patted my hand. "I'd nearly given up hope for this change of heart. Maybe someday, you'll even take an interest in the family business."

"That's a lot to think about. Perhaps I'd better start small. With a subsidiary. Or a really tiny nation." We both laughed. "Senator, I must know why Giles Embry wants to marry me. I know it has to do with the money, and not me. I'm not just his lab rat. I'm his cash cow. Isn't that right?"

"Now Tennyson. Don't discount your charms."

"Please. He may have cared for me once. But not anymore. Is there a prenuptial agreement?"

"Of course, there is a prenup. You don't think the family would let you run off with some opportunist." He put up his hand. "Now, Giles likes money, don't get me wrong. Don't we all? But he's different. He's far more interested in his research than any kind of personal wealth, and he needs money for the Campus. I know the man very well. So did you, once. He has been vetted by the Claxton clan."

"Vetted? He's not exactly running for husband, is he?"

"You've had another spat?"

I willed Abercrombie Foxhall Claxton to see me as I was. But he wouldn't. Perhaps he couldn't.

"Not just a spat. You are well aware that I don't have any feelings for him."

That was another lie. After the episode in Georgetown, I despised Giles, and not for my sake alone. For Tennyson's too.

"Are you sure? Every couple goes through these little episodes."

"Isn't it perfectly obvious I can't stand him?" I jumped up, agitated. "Why is he so interested in me if it's not just the money? Is it because of my memory issues? He wants to prove he can make me do whatever he wants me to do? Remember whatever he tells me to remember? I'm merely an experiment to him. A lab animal with a trust fund."

"No, my dear. I don't believe that." Foxhall's expression was troubled. I was making progress.

"Don't I have some stupid rich girlfriends I can introduce him to? An idiot cousin or two? Let him chase someone who might actually be able to stomach him?"

He reached for his coffee.

"Round numbers, you said? All right. By the terms of your trusts, you have about thirty million available to you right now. Since you turned twenty-one. You won't come into control of the full trust principal until six months from now, when you turn twenty-five. You'll have personal funds of about a hundred and fifty million. That sum is still growing, and it's being well managed. The family as a whole, of course, is worth considerably more. By, well, let's say an order of magnitude or two. And then there are the various partnerships, corporations, foundations, overseas investments. Someday you'll inherit everything."

"Good God!" I gaped at him. "This is even worse than I thought!" I stumbled back into the chair and sat down. Money only meant trouble and Tennyson had died for it. Now it was my turn as the target. "If I married Giles and I died, what would he get?"

The Senator was taken aback. "This is a rather morose turn of the conversation."

"How much? According to the prenup?"

"Well. Quite a lot. Some would go back into the family pot. Depending on how long you might be married, and your age, his allotment would rise. He would receive more if you have children and he was left the custodial parent. If you had children, half of your estate would go into trust for them."

"Which Giles would control?" Never mind the insanity of having Giles's little psychopaths.

"Yes. Which he would control."

"No wonder he wants to marry me. He'd marry a trained monkey for that kind of money."

"That's very cynical of you, my dear."

"No. Realistic."

With more than a hundred million more coming to me at the age of twenty-five, I figured my life was safe for the time being. At least until Tennyson's birthday.

"I can't say you've made my morning brighter, dear. But you have a right to know, I agree. Something else on your mind, Magpie?"

"Giles wants to hire a new spy to watch me."

"I wouldn't call it a spy, exactly."

"Hire Brendan Troy. Please."

Again his eagle eyes were on me, measuring me. Was he amused?

"That would be most interesting. Giles would disapprove."

"Are we supposed to do just what Giles wants, when he wants it?" I felt like a human sacrifice. My boring little life never looked so good. No money? Long hours? Night school? A classroom full of hyperactive kids? *Bring it on.*

"Young lady, Dr. Giles Embry is vital to the success of our memory research institute. Yet, as you well know, I do not bow to his every wish. I follow my own counsel in business decisions and in family decisions. Do you think you could live with Brendan Troy in such a position?"

"Could you? I won't agree to anyone else. He's already said yes."

"You want fireworks with Giles?" He sighed. "I have never cared for Brendan's politics, but I've known him all his life, and his family. Brendan Troy has always behaved with integrity. He has come to enjoy your company. I could live with him guarding you. Now answer me."

"I am afraid of Giles. I was afraid of Roy Barnaker. I'm not afraid of Brendan. He would protect me."

"And give you the freedom you crave? Can he do both?"

I stared at him. "Maybe."

"Very well."

Cઠ

Giles went purple with rage when he found out later that Brendan would be my new bodyguard.

"Absolutely not!" The veins in his forehead stood out like ropes.

"Brendan is in the security business, when he's not tending his own horses," Foxhall said.

"He's a fortune hunter!"

I gasped at Giles's sheer temerity. "Pot, meet kettle," as my grandfather—my other grandfather—would have said. Brendan owned his own farm, his horses, and his business. He was financially secure. He might be as rich as the Claxtons, for all I knew. He seemed less like a fortune hunter than anyone I'd met in the Claxton Empire.

"Tennyson and Mr. Troy and I are in agreement," Foxhall said quietly. "It's him or no one."

Giles stormed out of the house without saying good-bye. Or issuing some imperial command. He was heading back to the drawing board. I hoped I'd be gone by the time he came up with his new blueprint for my destruction.

CЗ

The moral and ethical questions of continuing the impersonation that was forced on me were something I'd tangle with later. Even though my grandparents had to know, or suspect, who I really was, they seemed invested in me being Tennyson. They certainly seemed to like me better than the original. But I couldn't risk having them agree with Giles that I needed to return to the Campus. Not for any reason, under any circumstances. Proving my identity required extraordinary measures.

Time to run.

I had no luck listening in on other momentous conversations. Giles kept up his fantasy of our engagement and impending marriage. He seemed to think if he kept saying it, it would come true.

Magical thinking is bad form in a scientist.

In the meantime, Brendan moved temporarily into the very masculine suite down the hall from my blue rooms. My personal security force.

I canceled all my future therapy sessions with Dr. Chu, and Foxhall backed me up. Giles said nothing.

Giles popped in each day to check in with Foxhall, but he spent less time with me. He could barely stand the sight of me. He said he was preparing the Georgetown place for "my return," but I kept telling him he was out of his mind. I didn't plan to go back there any time soon, certainly never with him. Before I ever walked through the door again, I would surely have it cleansed with fire.

Now that the Stable Tour, one of the highlights of the Hunt Country social calendar, was over, the Claxtons would soon scatter in every direction. Foxhall and Octavia were slated to travel to Palm Beach the day after Priscilla returned to South America. They had to look after "family interests" there. I was unclear as to the scope of those interests, except for the polo ponies, which at the moment were still frolicking in the early morning dew. Porter was due in Los Angeles to speak to one of C&B's subsidiaries and buy some tech startup or another. He would be gone at least a week, with a side trip to Cabo San Lucas to fish for marlin.

Best of all, Giles was scheduled to present a paper on his latest research at a scientific conference in New York City, where his ego would be polished to a high gloss. At one point, he suggested that I travel with him, but I refused. Vigorously. Mercy dispatched an associate to New York to keep an eye on him. Two could play his game. If they had a little help.

I lobbied to be left at Foxgrove on my own for a few days,

watched over by Brendan, until I could join my grandparents in
Florida.

In the remaining time, I wanted my mother. At least the illusion
of a mother. I ached over the coming moment when Priscilla would
discover that Tennyson was dead. She would hate me, but in the
meantime, I wanted to pretend we were family. She was here for just
a few more days. I'd never had so much fun.

She and I lunched together and shopped together and surprised
the rest of the family (and ourselves) with our new relationship. My
grandparents were delighted. I even managed to be civil to Porter. I
didn't know what I thought about him, but he was a good dancer,
nearly as good as Foxhall. He clearly wondered about me too. We
danced around each other carefully. He didn't really know either of
his daughters, so at least his confusion was genuine. Despite that,
whenever Giles was absent, harmony reigned at Foxgrove Manor.

Mercy Underhill called me every day with an update. Things
were falling nicely into place, she reported, and the white house with
green shutters would soon be mine. I couldn't wait to claim the keys.

To whom with sighs: 'I pass these dreadful gates
To seek the Theban, and consult the Fates:
For still, distress'd, I rove from coast to coast,
Lost to my friends, and to my country lost.

Chapter 42

"THIS WEEK WAS wonderful."

I walked Priscilla through the Dulles airport terminal to the security line hand in hand. I wanted to remember the last moments I would have a mother.

"For me too. You talk as if it won't happen again. It will," she replied. "I'll be back sooner than you know. Christmas at the latest. And you have an open invitation to stay with me in Argentina."

"After I settle things, I'll let you know."

"Still planning the Great Escape from Giles?"

"His tentacles have suction cups." I had shared my doubts about him with her. Not the entire sordid story, of course. Priscilla agreed that my grandparents and father seemed blind to his true nature.

"Don't wait too long. Trust your instincts, Tenn."

If only she knew. "I'm sorry you have to go."

"Me too. Maybe we just didn't have enough time to get on each other's nerves. We will someday."

"Promise?" We laughed at being so sentimental. She reminded me so much of Marisol, but she was sturdier, more resilient. It was so easy to pretend she was a stronger version of my mother: a Marisol who survived.

By Christmas everything would be different. My identity would be known. I'd be dead, or reprogrammed, or in jail or— Who knows? Priscilla would hate me because I was not her daughter, but I'd pretended to be. Her daughter was dead and I was the bastard child of the man she despised. This parting was bittersweet for me.

After kissing her good-bye, I drove past the little private school in Falls Church where I had taught, the Quartermaine Academy. For three and a half years, before I was reported dead, I was a teacher there. I missed the classroom and I wondered how I could possibly resurrect the life that had been stolen these past months. Could I go back? Would I still even want to teach? Would I be able to give up the things I'd become accustomed to, the seductively comfortable life of a Claxton heiress? Those questions were academic. I would be ruined. But it wouldn't matter. Because Giles would be stopped and I would have my soul back.

I parked the Volvo several blocks away from the Academy and stopped at the coffee shop where I used to go before starting my day, when my days had a comforting regularity. I was wearing designer sunglasses I'd found in Tennyson's dresser and a camel-colored silk dress. Things I'd never be able to afford before everything happened. I didn't look much like the old Marissa.

School had just let out. Several teachers stopped in for their afternoon hit of caffeine and something sweet, to replenish their energy after a day spent with active, curious, intelligent children. I could almost smell the chalk in the classroom. The Quartermaine Academy was old school. They still had chalkboards.

One of the older teachers stared at me and nudged her friend. They caught me looking back. They looked familiar too.

"I'm sorry," the first one said. "It's just that you look like someone who used to teach at our school."

"Really?"

"Yes," the other one said, "but sadly, she died. An awful car crash. An icy night."

At least they didn't take me for the infamous Tennyson Claxton. I pushed my sunglasses to the top of my head. "That's a shame."

"You look so much like her. Except—" She stared at me and shook her head. "Miss Brookshire's eyes were the most unusual shade of green. Sorry to have bothered you." The woman turned away and gave her order to the barista at the counter.

I would have to learn to deal with moments like this in the future. *You look like Marissa, but what happened to your eyes? How could they turn brown? I don't understand.*

How would I explain that Marissa Brookshire wasn't in a grave in Leesburg? It wasn't even the first time Marissa was supposed to be buried.

ᘔ

How would my life have turned out if my mother had lived?

My grandparents took my mother Marisol home to Maine and buried her in the local cemetery, when the ground thawed. The tombstone read: MARISOL AND CHILD. But I wasn't in that grave either. When I asked about that, years later, Grandma Anne said the stone carver had made a mistake. It was supposed to say: MARISOL, OUR CHILD. It was a sweet lie, and I believed it. Now I realized the headstone said exactly what they wanted it to say.

One day, a few months after my mother died, the phone rang. Grandpa Tom answered it and I knew from the look on his face something terrible was about to happen. When he hung up, there was a bustle of activity. My grandmother grabbed my clothes and threw them in a trunk. In went my pink bedspread and all of my little girl things, dresses, shoes, books, toys. The trunk went under their bed. I never saw my grandparents move as fast as they did that day. I was eight.

Grandma Anne took me to their bedroom, to the sloping back wall of their deep closet, behind their old suitcases, and unlatched the door to the crawlspace. I'd never seen that little door open before. The crawlspace was low and dark. The air was musty and so still. Grandpa followed with my dollhouse with all its furnishings, my happy doll family.

"Are you my brave girl, Marissa?" Grandma asked.

I nodded my head. "You know I am." I held tight to my favorite old cloth doll, faded from many trips through the washing machine. We were both on our knees. I tried to be brave, but I was afraid of a monster in the crawlspace.

"We're going to play a game today." She pointed to the crawlspace.

"Hide-and-seek?" I loved playing hide-and-seek, but I was afraid of that narrow crawlspace leading into the darkness beneath the eaves.

"That's right." She smiled at me, reassuringly. "Only this time, you have to hide until we come and get you."

"It's dark." I peered inside and held my doll tighter.

"I'll get you the little lamp, honey bunny. A bad man is coming here and he wants to take you away from us." I clung to my grandmother. I begged her not to let that happen. She held me tight, whispering. "We won't let him do that."

"A bad man? The *very* bad man?" My mother had told me about him.

"The very bad man. Don't cry, sweetie, everything is going to be all right, Marissa. You just have to play quietly in the crawlspace, for just a little while. You have your dollhouse right here. But you have to be very, very quiet. That's part of the game. Like hide-and-seek."

Someone rang the doorbell. My grandparents and I looked at each other. The ringing turned into knocking. Then pounding.

Grandma Anne laid a duck-print sleeping bag on the floor for me and gave me their battery-powered camping lamp. Grandpa carefully set the dollhouse inside the door of the crawlspace and slid it deeper into the dark. He pulled the tiny family of dolls from his pockets and handed them to me. Grandma rushed downstairs and came back with milk and cookies for me.

All this time the pounding continued. The monster wasn't in the crawlspace. He was at the front door.

"You'll be safe," Grandma said. "We won't let him take you, sweetie. It's just a game."

"I know. I'm not scared of the dark. I have my dolly." After living with my mother, I was used to the dark. I was much more afraid of the unknown. Of the Bad Man.

"Now, Marissa," Grandpa Tom said, "you know it's wrong to tell a lie, but today I'm going to have to tell a whopper about you to that man at the door, so he'll go away and never bother us again. There are extenuating circumstances for this lie. You know what 'extenuating circumstances' means?"

"Yes," I said, although I didn't. I was frightened, but I knew the hiding game. My mother and I used to hide when landlords and bill collectors came to the door. And I already knew grownups lied. "But why does he want to take me?"

"Because he doesn't understand what 'no' means. We're going to tell him no and make him believe it."

He hugged me. Then it was Grandma's turn. She kissed me on the forehead.

"Now Marissa, you be quiet as a mouse! Keep that door closed tight, don't make a sound, and don't answer to anyone but Grandpa or me, do you understand?"

Even if monsters come knocking on the door.

I put my finger to my lips, nodded my head, and crawled into the dark space. Grandma reached in and turned on the camping lamp and latched the door tight. I wasn't afraid at first. I put the little lamp inside my dollhouse, and the light streamed through the windows. The crawlspace was shadowy and the sloping rafters were covered with cobwebs, but it was cozy and warm. I heard their footsteps retreating down the stairs. The house was old and drafty, and sounds passed easily through the floors and walls and furnace vents. I couldn't hear everything that happened, but I heard a lot.

The knocking went on furiously. A man's voice, shouting.

"Damn it, Brookshire, I want my child! Where is she?"

"Keep your shirt on." Grandpa Tom opened the door. "Why are you disturbing us in our grief?"

I heard more shouting. Grandpa protested that Marissa wasn't here. The angry man went on and on, about my mother and me living in squalor and he was doing the right thing and why were they standing in his way?

"You can't keep her from me, I'm her father, I'll get a court order, I can take care of the child better than you can. She is mine!"

The shouting man must have been talking about the child on the tombstone. I heard the front door slam. The shouting was in the living room now.

"Get out of my house," Grandpa Tom was saying. "Right now, or I'll call the police."

"I'm calling them now," Grandma Anne said. "You get out of here!"

I heard loud footsteps pounding through the house into every room and up the stairs. I could hear them in the hall outside the bedroom. It was the Bad Man my mother always talked about, there in our house, looking for me.

"Marissa is not here, you fool! You know why? Because she's dead!" Grandpa lied. "She died with her mother. Last winter. In Chicago. Now get out!"

That was an awful lie to tell. But I knew there were extenuating circumstances. I put my finger over my doll's mouth to keep her from screaming.

"I don't believe you," the man said.

The bedroom door slammed open against the wall. He stomped into the bedroom, just a few feet away from the crawlspace, and me.

"My granddaughter is dead! Go to the cemetery if you don't believe me."

"I went there. 'Marisol and child,' it says. Why does it say that?"

"Because they're buried there! Side by side! And you weren't man enough to give the child your name. Why do you care now, Claxton? You lied to our daughter. You abandoned her and the child. You let them suffer. You let them die. Marisol wasn't good enough for you to marry. And you know something? You weren't good enough for her or her child. A dog in the street would be a better father than you."

At this point I'm not quite sure I really remembered him saying the name "Claxton," but I inserted it into the memory because it fits, now that I know Porter is my father. No wonder I'm uncomfortable around him. I know what he can do. And what he can't.

"You don't understand, old man. It's Marisol's fault. She would never let me see Marissa."

"Good! All to the good. You didn't deserve her. You're a pathetic excuse for a man. A child is not a pawn in your sick game. Did you think your new wife would let you bring another woman's child home? Besides, Marissa belonged to my daughter, my Marisol. That child was the only thing she ever had. And they're both dead. Dead because you threw them away! Like trash!"

Everyone was shouting now. I stopped listening, to try to stop being afraid. My cloth dolly and I played quietly in the dark with my dollhouse, where the dolls were happy and the mommy doll was still alive. The next thing I remember is my grandmother waking me up and carrying me to bed.

"Is the bad man gone now?"

"Yes, sweetie. The hiding game is over, and you were so good and so quiet. He's gone and he's not coming back," she said. "There are no more monsters here."

"Do you promise?"

"Of course I promise."

"Cross your heart?"

"I cross it a hundred times for you, Marissa."

She was right. There were no more monsters in my world.

Until I met Giles Embry.

Chapter 43

ONCE I STARTED to remember, really remember, it was hard to stop.

I didn't bother to try. These memories told me I'd once had a family and a home where I was loved. They made me feel alive.

We left Maine when I was fourteen, my grandparents and I. We moved to North Carolina for my grandfather's health. We loved Camden, but the winters were getting harder on him.

When we left, I decided my dollhouse would stay behind in the Camden house. Perhaps it would comfort some other child as it had me. Maybe it would be a delightful discovery, a treasure for someone to find.

Grandma Anne and Grandpa Tom never questioned me about it. Besides, it was a copy of the big house. My grandmother had even painted miniature murals on the walls to match the full-size murals she'd painted. I loved that dollhouse, but I knew it belonged there. And at the sophisticated age of fourteen, I was sure that playing with dolls and dollhouses was something for little girls, not for me.

At my school, we had a class assignment to write a true story about ourselves. I wrote about my hiding game in the crawlspace with my dollhouse. *My name is Marissa and this is my story,* it began. My teachers must have thought my imagination was in overdrive.

The day we left for the South, I unlatched the small door inside the closet that opened into the crawlspace. I carefully set the doll-house inside. In the dollhouse I placed my little doll family, my first diary (the pink one with the lock), and my class assignment. My "true story."

I had learned about time capsules at school. This was my time capsule, the childhood I was leaving behind. I slid the dollhouse deep into the protected space under the eaves, where it couldn't be seen by merely peering through the door. I threw an old blanket on top of it so it wouldn't get too dirty. That blanket would be coated in dust and cobwebs, if it was still there.

Most likely, I knew, it had been discovered long ago, played with, given away, or sold at a yard sale. I still wanted to look for it.

Whether it was there or not, just knowing it had existed was more proof to me of who I really was.

I would know soon.

C<

Even as I clutched my plane ticket to Portland, Maine, in my hand, I wondered whether I could truly break away from the web Giles had spun around me. I'd barely seen him all week, by design. He came around every day to see Foxhall, but when he entered a room I left it. When he spoke to me, I ignored him. When he stayed for dinner, I cut him dead.

Giles started sending me flowers every day. Yellow roses, Tennyson's favorite. They were creepy. It was so out of character. Was his next plan to stage a romantic farce? A moonlight serenade? He even asked me out on a date, to the restaurant where Tennyson had her last meal. He said it was to make everything right again. I said it was pure sadism to take me back to the scene of my accident. I refused.

Brendan was generally nearby, except in my blue bedroom, and he and I had a running bet on which of us would first put a fist in Giles's face. Giles gave Brendan a wide berth. I couldn't tell, and neither could Mercy, whether he was truly plotting something, or he'd given up on me, or he was preoccupied with his big presentation in New York. Mercy said all he seemed to do, besides annoy me, was to go to work at the Campus and sleep with Jordana in Georgetown.

Hailey reported that she was "doing her Southern girl blather" so well that Giles had taken to turning the other way whenever he saw her. "Bless his icy little heart," she added.

If I made it to Maine, I would rent a car at the Portland airport and drive straight to Camden. I was counting the hours. Foxhall and Octavia would leave the Farm first, followed by Porter, later the same day. The following day Giles would be off to his conference. And then I would fly north.

Blacksburg Downs had always known I wasn't Tennyson, I think, but he didn't talk much. He'd become a faithful friend. I'd miss him when I left. And Princess, who had crowned herself as my royal companion. She sensed a change in me that week, and she seemed worried, putting her paws on my hands and peering up at me, whining. Her tail tapped mournfully on the floor.

My trusty bodyguard Brendan remained by my side after everyone went their respective ways. Once they'd flown, I let him in on my imminent travel plans to Maine, though I didn't tell him why, or that I was not Tennyson. I didn't want anyone else to suffer the consequences of my actions. No one could call this a conspiracy, despite all the help he and Mercy and Hailey had given me. But I was sure Brendan knew I wasn't Tennyson.

"The Claxtons are going to be mad when they find out I've gone. I don't want to get you in trouble," I told him in the library after dinner. He and I, and Graciela and Hector, were alone in the big house.

He laughed and held me close. He kissed my hair. We hadn't gone any further than kissing and holding each other tight, because I didn't want to make things any more complicated. He didn't push things. We were like seventh-graders, making out after school in my grandparents' library. It felt a little silly, but it felt great.

"I'm a big boy, Magpie. Trust me, I can take care of myself. I'm not afraid of Dr. Frankenstein or your family. Besides, I'd like to come with you."

"You would?"

"I've never been to Maine. I hear it's pretty. Moose. Lobster. Atlantic Ocean."

"Where there's a will?"

"I've got a way," he said. "Say the word, and I'll buy my ticket."

"Word. But let me go first. On my own." I couldn't rely on other people forever.

ဆ

The day finally dawned.

With visions of prison dancing in my head, I packed the expensive green jacket I bought in Middleburg. I took my copy of *The Odyssey*. I left the journal Tennyson hid inside *The Decline and Fall of the Roman Empire* with Mercy Underhill. I explained it was my old diary and detailed the days leading up to the accident. I included a sealed handwritten letter she was to open if anything happened to me. It revealed my identity and everything I knew about Dr. Giles Embry, Tennyson Claxton, and Marissa Brookshire.

Unlike the reality game show it sounded like, there was no grand prize.

I met her at the coffee shop in Middleburg for a farewell and conclusion of current business.

"Good-bye, Mercy." I handed her an additional retainer check, a big one. As far as she knew officially, I had merely discovered Marissa's childhood home and she was helping me preserve it, to honor her memory. That much was true. "Deposit immediately. And be careful."

"You'll be fine, Tennyson. Nothing's going to happen to you. I'm tracking the bad doctor and I'll keep you posted. And call me every day."

"Watch out for Hailey too." I would be on edge until she was clear of the Campus and Giles. Until we all were.

రాజ

Back at the Farm, I took one last tour of the house, followed by a grumpy slow-moving beagle. Graciela seemed to be expecting something from me when I stepped into the kitchen.

"What's up with you, huh? I know that look, Tenn. And what's with that dog?"

"She's a little sad. I don't want to get you involved in my troubles."

She blocked my way to the coffeepot. "What troubles?" She poured us a cup of coffee. "Talk to me, Tennyson. You think I'm going to rat you out? I don't do that. But I will, if you don't tell me what's going on. And don't tell me nothing is going on. Something is going on. Sit."

We settled at the breakfast table. Princess snorted into her water bowl and slumped under the table. She was soon joined by King and Duke, who came in all excited from tearing up the garden.

"I'm leaving Foxgrove. Just for a few days, Graciela." I left out the part about how I would probably end up in jail and she would never see me again.

"Leaving? Why?"

"I have to find out certain things. About me. I'd appreciate it if you didn't alert the family." At any rate, even if she did, I would be gone, hours ahead of anyone who would try to follow.

"Do I look like a fire alarm?"

"No." I took a sip of her tasty coffee. "You've been wonderful to me." I choked up and drank more coffee to cover it.

"Tennyson, what do you want to tell me?"

"I have to find out the truth about Tennyson Claxton."

"And you don't want me to tell nobody?"

"That's right. I know it sounds crazy, but this is life and death to me. I hope to answer some questions about—my memory. My life. Who I really am."

"I think you might already be remembering who you are."

"Who am I?"

"Everybody needs to know who they are." Graciela patted my hand. "You gotta do what you gotta do. Besides, I knew you were going away."

"How?"

"That dog told me. She's been moping around like a lost soul for days."

"Do you think I'm Tennyson?"

She looked at me for a long time before speaking.

"You were here once before. One time when you were a baby, maybe two or three years old. A pretty little blond girl. With your pretty mother. So sad, that one. Porter! So mean as a young man. What a scene that was! He wouldn't give her a dime unless she gave you up to him. She never would. You just sat quietly and watched everyone scream at each other."

"You knew who I am? When did you know? Why didn't you tell me?"

"I don't know nothing." She threw her hands up and winked.

"What was I doing here? And what do my grandparents know about this?"

"I'm not their snitch. You're not the only one with memory problems. Sometimes I have a real bad memory. I don't even know my own name. Call me Princess Grace. Now, what do you want for lunch, Tennyson?"

"Why don't I make it today, Your Highness? Would you like an omelet?"

"That would be nice." She waved me on to the kitchen. "It's like you worked in a restaurant someplace, you know?"

"Who knows?" I hadn't, that I remembered, but I had learned a lot from my Grandma Anne. It was a great breakfast, if I do say so myself. I have a knack for omelets and Graciela made only a few suggestions. Like the Stilton cheese.

It was harder than I expected to say good-bye to Blacksburg Downs. I rested my cheek against his big soft head. He could read

my mood, his dark eyes knowing. He neighed softly. But as I turned
to go, he reared up and bellowed, as if to say "Don't go!" He shook
his head from side to side: "No, no, no!" He'd already lost Tennyson
once.

I choked up and ran out of his stall, followed by a pack of
beagles howling for my attention.

Damn, I'd come to love this place. Monsters and all.

ଔ

Brendan drove me to the airport and walked me inside to the
security line.

"I'll be there with you tomorrow night," he said. "I just have to
get my crew rounded up, take care of the horses."

"I know." I put my hand on his chest and leaned in. "I can't tell
you how much it means to me."

"We'll go on a real date, I promise. When I get there." Brendan
kissed me. My heart twisted.

"You'll love the lobster. I miss you already."

"You're not wearing his ring," he said.

"I left it in my jewelry box. I suppose I should have locked it up
somewhere."

"You look more like yourself without it."

I had come to rely on Brendan. He was a rock, a warm, kissable
rock. I could feel myself light up when he was around. I loved
looking at him, at his eyes, which crinkled around the edges when he
smiled. I loved the set of his shoulders and his powerful arms. I
loved his voice when he was gentle with the horses. And when he
spoke to me in that deep whisper of his.

I was in danger of falling in love with Brendan Troy. I had to
leave quickly or I'd miss my plane.

He kissed me again. "So you don't forget."

I wouldn't. I walked to the security line and didn't look back.

Whatever toils the great Ulysses pass'd,
Beneath this happy roof, they end at last;
No longer now from shore to shore to roam,
Smooth seas and gentle winds invite him home.

Chapter 44

THE LATE JUNE day was hot and humid when I left Virginia. It was cool and fresh and salty when I disembarked in Maine.

Even the air smelled different. To my surprise, I'd slept deeply on the plane. I awoke when the pilot announced we were descending into Portland International Jetport. It was delicious to know that Giles couldn't touch me there. I hadn't bothered to take his spy phone. I left it with Brendan, who could deal with Giles if he wanted. He could punch him in the face and throw him in the mud if he wanted.

I told myself not to get too giddy with this temporary freedom, but it was hard. I felt like dancing.

The drive up the coast to Camden delighted me, pulling up memories of shopping trips to Portland and Freeport, buying camping equipment and plaid flannel shirts with my grandfather at L.L. Bean, picnics in parks that hugged the rocky shore, the day I went to live with my grandparents, and the day we left for North Carolina. The day I hid in the crawlspace.

Graciela had dropped a bomb on me: Whenever I mentioned Marissa Brookshire, the Claxtons knew exactly who I was talking about! But they played dumb. Except perhaps for Priscilla—they had good reason not to tell her about me. As for the other three? Giles had played them, and they played along. I was glad to leave behind their conspiracy of silence and denial.

There was no heiress to the Empire without me. My only consolation was that they thought Marissa was long dead, for eighteen years now. Either that or they'd given up trying to find me, for their own reasons. But I would soon be resurrected.

What would I do after I proved who I was? Expose Giles for the scheming murderer he was? Confront Foxhall and Octavia with their lies? Condemn Porter to Hades once and for all? Crown Graciela as Princess Grace? It was all academic. First, I had to get to my house, find my dollhouse, my diary, and my handwritten biography. Proof of my existence.

Cruising my rental Toyota up Route One, through Freeport and Brunswick, up to Bath and pretty Wiscasset, I opened all the

windows and smelled the scent of pine, the scent of the sea. Finally, I
was on Camden's main street: Main Street. There were changes in
the storefronts, changes in the names, but everything felt familiar.

I forced myself to check in at my hotel, the Lord Camden Inn,
before stopping by the real estate office to pick up the house keys
and papers from a young woman named Shannon. She seemed very
bubbly for Maine. Perhaps she was a transplant.

"You're here! Welcome to Camden, Ms. — Um." Awkward
pause.

"Olivia Claxton."

"Welcome, Olivia! Not many people buy a house hereabouts
sight unseen." She looked at me as if she were trying to guess my
native planet. "Unless they just want to tear it down and build condos
or something. I wondered when I saw a corporation doing the buy, I
thought you must be a developer." She raised an eyebrow.

"Not me," I said. "Just a tax thing."

"Well, then, these are for you. It's a pretty house. Not far, I
drew you a little map, it's in with your paperwork." She smiled
brightly and dropped the keys in my hands.

I hefted them. There were a lot of keys, some of them old-
fashioned skeleton keys—the keys to the bedrooms upstairs. I almost
mentioned I grew up in that house. Then I remembered I was still
supposed to be a Claxton. Not just a bastard Claxton. If they had a
coat of arms, I would add the bar sinister. To be truthful, I had begun
to think of myself as part of the family, in an odd way. And I was. In
a very odd way.

"It looked like the perfect house for me," I said. "Like one I've
had in my mind for a long time."

"Oh, I could show you half a dozen just like it with better
upgrades. You know. Granite. Stainless steel. Don't get me wrong,
it's a nice little house, but it hasn't been lived in for a few years. The
owners took care of it though. No leaks. Water's running, lights will
be on tomorrow, and you've got oil heat, plenty of oil. There's a
wood fireplace, but you'd have to get some wood delivered. Nights
can turn chilly up here."

"Anything else I should know about?"

"Inspection was clean enough. The stairs to the second floor are
solid, but there may be a tiny problem with a banister. Loose. Some
of the doors are a little warped. You're going to want a handyman in
there." Shannon handed me a short list of people she recommended.

"Kitchen's old. Needs a total rehab. Oh, they tried to make it look better. Painted the cupboards," she confided, shaking her head sadly.

"The horror," I agreed, trying not to laugh. I wondered if they left any of my grandmother's murals. I indulged in a fantasy of fixing up the place and moving in, living there. But the charade would be over soon. I didn't know how my grandparents would feel about their illegitimate kin buying a house with their dead heiress's money. My long-lost sister. I felt a pang. I held out a small hope I could prevail upon Octavia to let me keep the house and the Volvo and work out a payment plan. If they didn't have me arrested and thrown in a dungeon for disgraced heiresses and scandalous scions.

"Want to see your house while there's still light?" Shannon inquired. "I'll be happy to give you the tour."

I jingled the keys in response.

It was practically around the corner, past the town library, and although I knew a shortcut, I followed her in my rental car, parking behind Shannon's SUV. I took a photo with my phone, but it would never capture my excitement.

There it was. The front door was painted a cheerful red, but the rest looked the same, white clapboard and green shutters. The porch needed some paint. The lawn needed new sod. One shutter was sagging.

Shannon insisted on giving me a walkthrough, even though I couldn't wait to explore it on my own. Most of the interior had been repainted a boring white, although part of the Camden Harbor mural still greeted me in the front hall. I was disappointed that my grandmother's Mount Battie mural no longer decorated the dining room walls, but it was more than a decade since I'd lived there. The stone fireplace's mantel in the living room no longer boasted my grandfather's handsome handmade clipper ship. That model was one thing of his I saved when he died. Grandma Anne died soon after. I'm sure I would have taken it with me to Virginia. Who knows where it went after my reported death?

The rooms were smaller than I remembered. The kitchen was rudimentary, yet many fine dinners had come from it. The large pantry was intact. I was relieved it hadn't become a shrine to subzero refrigerators and polished granite. The countertops were the same old butcher block. I let my hand linger on the painted wooden shelves and wondered if Graciela would approve.

"More rooms upstairs," Shannon interrupted my thoughts. "Is

everything all right? Like I said, I have other houses with better upgrades, but the contractors I know can work wonders with this space. Knock out the walls between the pantry and dining room for a great room? Open concept, you know."

"I wouldn't change a thing," I said. "It's exactly what I was looking for. Lead on, please."

She charged upstairs, in a hurry to be done with this. I was willing to bet she had a date. Bubbly girls always do.

The front hall stairs circled round the second floor landing, overlooking the downstairs entryway. The banister swayed as I grabbed hold of it. "Whoa."

"See what I mean?" she said. "A few little fixes, that's all it needs. But it's so cute! The original decorative molding here is impossible to get nowadays."

"I'll call someone tomorrow." I followed her past the hall bathroom and the tiny guest bedroom. A small bathroom had been added to the master bedroom, by breaking into the hall linen closet.

Memories raced through my mind at top speed, along with the voices of my grandparents. *Marissa, wake up, sweetie, time for school. How was school, my girl? More apple pie? Marissa, time for bed. Marissa, lights out. Good-night, sweetie, sleep tight...*

Shannon opened the last door to the smallest bedroom, where the last western light illuminated the space. "No one had the heart to cover this one over."

I stepped in and gasped. "Oh yes. It's lovely." I could feel myself smile.

"I was kind of hoping you'd think so." Shannon raised the shade over the window seat to let in more light. "It was the nursery."

It wasn't a nursery. It was my room, and my mother's before me, exotically painted by my grandmother. The walls were a light blue-green, filled with exotic birds and trees and flowers in pastel colors. It resembled hand-painted Chinese silk. There were generous glints of gold, adding energy to the scene. I gazed up to the ceiling, with its heavenly blue sky and fluffy white clouds. Only the wood-work and moldings had been brightened up with fresh paint.

"Oh my God. I'm so glad this is still here."

I had forgotten how extraordinary it was and how talented my grandmother had been. I could hardly speak.

"Alrighty then," Shannon said. "I guess it'll be safe with you. We have the rental agreement in place until the closing, day after tomorrow. We got your deposit, of course, and the paperwork is ready for you. I have an appointment. I could leave you here with the keys, if you want."

"Thank you. This is definitely my house."

It was amazing what a little money could do. It could unlock the doors to my childhood home and my memories. As much as I wanted this house, I couldn't let myself forget it wasn't my money. Or my house.

Shannon let herself out. I heard her car door shut and watched out the front bedroom windows until her SUV drove down the street. I selfishly wanted the moment to myself.

I went back to my old bedroom and sat down on the floor, admiring the way the fading evening light sifted through the leafy trees. In the fall, the maples would blaze like fire in the setting sun. The room felt magical to me.

An intense lethargy overtook me. What a day! I lay down and placed my red purse under my head for a pillow, gazing up into the painted forest of birds and trees that surrounded me. Within minutes, I was asleep. No dreams came to haunt me. No nightmares in the crawlspace.

I was home.

O Queen, farewell! be still possess'd
Of dear remembrance, blessing still and bless'd!
Till age and death shall gently call thee hence,
(Sure fate of every mortal excellence!)

Chapter 45

MY CELL PHONE woke me up. The room was dark. I checked the ringing phone for the time. I'd slept on the floor for a couple of hours, better than I had in months.

"Hey, Mercy. What's up?" I yawned.

"Maybe nothing, but you need to know." There was an edge in her voice.

"Go on."

"Your boyfriend is checking up on you."

"Brendan? I wouldn't worry. I've told him— Almost everything."

"Oh, Brendan's your boyfriend now?"

"Um, forget that. What are you talking about?"

"Your fiancé."

"Giles?" I sat up straight.

"Dr. Giles Embry hired a private investigator to look into what you do when you're not with him. Apparently he didn't care for your choice of Brendan Troy."

"He's following me now?"

"No, but he has someone looking for you. A pro."

"How do you know?" I peered out the windows, where a streetlight confirmed that all was quiet. There were a few empty cars parked on the street, but no movement.

"Another investigator I know, call him Groundhog—he looks like one—came to me today. Asked if I wanted some of his action on a case, because it might involve traveling to Maine and he's tied up on some surveillance in the District. Of course, I said sure, I'd love to go to Maine. So I'm the pro who's looking for you. Hey, I found you."

"Oh my God, Mercy. Are you sure Giles doesn't know it's you looking for me? He could be setting you up."

"Embry's smart, but Groundhog thinks it's a simple surveillance, he's just subcontracting it out, and Embry won't know the difference. So now I'm a double agent. Embry is telling Groundhog you're his patient, you're ill, PTSD, a danger to yourself and others, and you need immediate treatment. Or you'll explode or something.

But he cautioned Groundhog to go about it carefully, because despite all your deficits you're still intelligent and wily. He said 'wily.' "

My spine was beyond chilled, it was frozen. I sat down on the window seat and put my head between my knees. "Go about what, exactly?"

"Rounding you up. Embry set the scene and this guy bought it, hook, line, and *stinker*. To quote Groundhog, 'It's, like, she could forget who she is! She could go wandering and hurt herself! She needs her meds, man!' He's worried about you. Groundhog's not a bad guy, just a stooge."

"Oh, God. Giles doesn't know where I am, does he?"

"I don't think so. Groundhog is tied up, so I'm on the case. I'll just report you're nowhere in sight. He'll pass it on as if it were his own work, my name won't be on it. But get this: He said Embry expected you to take a powder while the cat's away."

"You mean flee while he's out of town?"

"Yes. I sometimes have a fondness for noir slang. It's the root beer talking."

"Where is Giles now?"

"Still in Richmond today. Tomorrow I can't be sure. He's supposed to be in New York for that conference, but I have a feeling he may go off course. Be careful."

"Thanks, Mercy."

"Call me anytime, Tennyson. Day or night. Say hi to Brendan for me."

I clicked off. I tried to get ahold of Brendan. My calls went to voice mail. He often turned his ringer off when he was with the horses.

I told myself to calm down. Giles was not in Maine. Did he know where I grew up? My most recent tracks would have led him first to North Carolina. Still, I was sufficiently spooked to lock up the house and go back to my hotel. Before I left, I checked the closet of the master bedroom. The crawlspace door was still there, still latched the way I remembered it.

It was fully dark outside now. The house's electricity wouldn't be on until tomorrow. I didn't feel like searching for my dollhouse in the dark crawlspace. That was a job for the light of day.

At my hotel I chatted up the concierge and made a production of asking about local restaurants. If Giles followed my trail, I wanted it to dead end there. I went to my room, picked up my suitcase, and slipped out to my car through the back door. I didn't think anyone saw me. I looked for another place to stay.

A roadside motel a mile down Elm Street had an open room. I checked in with cash and used another name, Anne Thomas. I asked the young guy at the desk not to give out any information about me. He shrugged. "Whatever." I parked behind the motel, out of sight.

The room looked like any other motel room in America. A desk, two beds, and a bathroom at the back. The palette was a nice nautical blue and it had a security lock. My cell phone rang. It was Brendan returning my call.

"What's wrong, Tenn? Your voice sounds funny."

"Giles hired a private eye to track me down while he's in Richmond. Mercy got herself in the middle of it and she's running interference, but I'm afraid Giles will eventually figure out where I am."

"I'll talk to Mercy and move my flight ahead. I'll be on a plane first thing tomorrow and grab a rental in Portland. Ethan can take care of the horses."

That sounded good, but I was feeling frantic.

"Giles is telling the world I've got PTSD and I'm dangerous. It's his cover so he can destroy my mind. It sounds like science fiction, I know."

"Not to me. Where is Giles now?"

"Still in Richmond, Mercy says. Brendan, if something happens to me—"

"Nothing will happen. I'll be there. Hey, Magpie, promise me something."

"What?"

"Try to relax. Go eat something. You're probably running on fumes. You'll feel better after you get something in your stomach."

"You're a know-it-all." He was right, I was starving.

Just hearing his voice made me calmer. I was safe for the moment, at least, and Brendan would be here tomorrow.

ᘓ

The restaurant featured a view of the water and a "famous" lobster supper. It was buttery and delicious, but I couldn't finish it. The red checkered tablecloth suggested the chess game Giles and I were playing. I was so tired of it. *Spy vs. Spy*, like the comic strip in *Mad*. Only we weren't playing it for laughs.

How did he plan to drag me back? With a court order making him my custodian? By brute force? With drugs? With the legendary Hypnopolethe? Would I wake up in a fog of confusion, the way I did at the Campus? Would Marissa Brookshire wake up at all? I might be nothing but a robot called Tennyson. I felt the heartache of not knowing my sister, but ironically, because of Giles, I had some portion of her memories. I knew a great deal about Tennyson. I had moments of pity for her, moments of empathy, but I didn't want to be her. She'd made a name for herself with drugs, partying, scandals, notorious sex tapes, wrecked Porsches, and a wasted life. That might be me if the Hypnopolethe worked.

After all, DNA doesn't lie. Only Priscilla could prove I wasn't her daughter, though she might be the only one in the family who really thought I was. She hadn't been around me enough to have doubts. None of them would save me. Why would they? They wanted a docile, well-behaved heiress. Giles wanted to erase my soul. To do that, he'd left a trail of dead bodies in his wake: Tennyson, David Jensen, Roy Barnaker, and perhaps even Miss Jasmine. How many others before me? How many after me?

I have only one weapon: the truth. To launch that weapon, I need proof that I am who I say I am. I want my name back. I want Giles stopped. After that, the world can lock me away and tow the whole Claxton clan and their millions out to sea in a leaky boat for all I care.

Tomorrow I'll have my evidence. If Giles shows up, I'll meet him with Brendan at my side.

Behold the long-predestined day! (he cries;)
O certain faith of ancient prophecies!
These ears have heard my royal sire disclose
A dreadful story, big with future woes.

Chapter 46

THE NEXT MORNING, I threw on jeans and a blue work shirt and sneakers.

I packed a tote bag with a change of clothes. I bought a hammer, a screwdriver, a box cutter, and a large flashlight at a hardware store near the motel, and I picked up provisions from a bakery on Main Street. I was ready to explore my house.

I let myself in and locked the door against my fears. As promised, the electricity was on. I turned faucets on and off, tested the sticky doors, and found my favorite views from every window. I pretended that I really owned this house. I moved slowly, luxuriously, from room to empty room, with a large cup of coffee and a fresh blueberry muffin.

I sat on the dining room window seat to eat my breakfast and watch two squirrels play outside in the yard. They dove from rocks to trees to grass and chased each other around the trunk, and never seemed to tire of their game.

My inspection continued upstairs. The wobbly banister reminded me I needed to call that handyman. One good push and it might tumble over. Sunlight streamed through the east windows of my grandparents' bedroom. I could have lingered, but I had a mission.

I stepped into the empty closet and flicked on the overhead light. Like the rest of the house, the closet was smaller than I remembered. But then, I was bigger than the little girl who grew up here.

I got down on my knees. The crawlspace door was painted shut. It had been a while since anyone had been inside it, which gave me hope against hope that the dollhouse was still there. I dug the paint out of the cracks around the door with my box knife.

It was hot work in the little closet, and soon rivulets of sweat ran down my back. I had to wipe my eyes repeatedly. Whoever had painted over my door had done a fine job of it, thank you very much. I hammered the screwdriver into the seam, and finally the little door gave way. I opened it and peered into the black hole. Chills chased each other up and down my spine. I caught my breath. I couldn't imagine why it was so difficult to take the first step inside. After all, I needed the truth. I needed proof. If it was anywhere, it was in the crawlspace.

The memory surfaced again: Porter Claxton, my father, screaming at my grandparents, pounding up the stairs, ripping open the doors to every room. Looking for me.

I took a break, washed my hands and face, and swallowed some more coffee. I uttered a few prayers for my grandparents, for Tennyson, for myself.

I returned to the closet, crouched down, switched on the flashlight, and plunged into the dark. I inched along on hands and knees, beaming the light around the walls. I bumped my head on the sloping rafters.

The past owners had left a couple of old wooden chairs in the space, which I dragged out into the room so I'd have something to sit on. I crawled back inside. I began to fear there was nothing left in there when I saw a filthy blanket covering something lumpy deep in the shadows at the very back, and I thanked God. No one had gone this far into the crawlspace.

I tore the blanket off and pushed it behind me. A cloud of dust made me sneeze. I couldn't turn around, it was too narrow, so I crawled backwards, dragging the dollhouse behind me, out onto the closet floor. I sat there for a long time with my arms wrapped around it, around what was left of my childhood.

I marveled at the little replica of the bigger home. The dollhouse was beautifully crafted by my grandfather, a master woodcarver and carpenter, and it was shaped by his love for my mother and me. I was humbled and my throat tightened.

"How do you like it, Marissa?" my grandmother asked me when Grandpa Tom unveiled it. He had spent weeks in his workshop, repairing it, repainting it, making it perfect again.

"For me?" I was so excited I was bouncing on my heels, reaching out to touch it, but afraid something so wonderful might not really be mine.

"Who else do you think it would be for?" Grandpa Tom teased me. "It was your mother's dollhouse first, but I know she wants you to have it now."

I turned my attention to the small dolls. There were four of them, a bit faded, but still a family: the grandmother and grandfather dolls, one for my mother, and one for me. Their clothes were made from scraps of my old dresses. There was no daddy doll, but now I knew who he was and why he was never part of the picture. His absence was part of the picture. This was my family in miniature.

Each new piece of furniture, each small rediscovery, delighted me. The miniature painted murals in the dollhouse mimicked the ones my grandmother had painted in the house. It still amazed me that she had copied her originals for me. They were a life story writ small. I wondered if the large murals downstairs could be restored someday, if I could figure out a way to keep the house.

My little pink diary was tucked inside, right where I'd hidden it. Still locked. The key was long gone, and I'd have to pry it open later. I pulled out the envelope slipped inside it. My childish scrawl was on the outside: "Marissa Brookshire. My Story." Inside was my school assignment, my missive, my brief. On the cover I had added a note for my time capsule: *My name is Marissa and this is my dollhouse.* My school picture was stapled to the back page. I laughed at my unfortunate teen hairstyle, cool at the time. I'd forgotten that I'd included locks of our hair braided together, my grandmother's and my mother's and mine. My grandmother saved everything.

Something else fell out of the envelope. A heart-shaped gold locket I had never seen before, with my mother's initials set in diamonds, or more likely, rhinestones. I popped it open. There was a picture of her, Marisol, on the left. The right side of the locket had a picture of Porter Claxton as a young man, a preppy college boy. If I weren't sitting on the floor, I might have fallen.

"Grandma?" I said aloud to nobody.

She must have placed it in the envelope for me. I examined the locket in the light. I slipped it over my head and moved to the bathroom to admire it in the mirror.

I pulled out my phone and called Brendan. He was at Dulles, waiting to board the plane to Portland.

"I'm inside Marissa's house, Brendan. I think you'll like it."

"I'll like it if you're inside it. I can't wait to see it. I'll be there tonight, Magpie. I'll take you out on the town."

"It's a pretty small town. Listen, when you get to Camden, come straight to the house. I'll text you the address. I'll have a little something ready for us. I miss you. I have a lot of things to tell you."

"Magpies always have a lot to say. See you soon."

I headed out for lunch and a look around town. I peeked into a cute little bookstore, The Owl & Turtle, and promised myself I'd return to browse. On the corner of Elm and Main I found French & Brawn's Market Place, right where I left it years ago. It had been there forever. I bought a fresh coffee, wine and two goblets, gourmet cheeses and sausage, grapes and other fruit, and a large tray to hold it all. I also bought sponges and cleaning supplies to wipe down the chairs I'd found in the crawlspace.

At another shop on Main, I picked up several large bright pillows for the floor in front of the fireplace, where I could tell Brendan my story. I picked up flowers for the mantle and some fat candles.

After a deli sandwich, I spent the afternoon back at the house in a happy daze of preparation, washing the chairs and the dollhouse, polishing the small tables and chairs. I spread the pillows on the floor and set out the candles when the sun was setting. I dragged the wooden chairs downstairs, in case the pillows weren't comfortable enough. I arranged the cheese and meats and fruit on the tray and took it to the living room. I showered and changed into a fresh pair of white slacks and a bright green blouse.

I expected Brendan soon, but he texted me that the flight had been delayed by storms and he wasn't sure when he'd arrive.

The doorbell rang. I checked my watch. It was too early for Brendan. I thought it might be Shannon, the real estate lady. Or perhaps she'd sent me a handyman to fix the banister, the sticky doors, the sagging shutter.

I opened the door wide without another thought.

Chapter 47

GILES LEANED INTO the doorway with a triumphant smile on his face.

That smug little smile I despised. I jumped back and tried not to let him see I was afraid. I held onto the door.

"What are you doing here?"

"Not happy to see your fiancé? I'm happy to see you."

"Go away. You're not my fiancé. We have nothing to discuss."

"I don't think so. You forgot your engagement ring, Tennyson. Yes, *Tennyson*. That simply won't do, not if we're going to be married. And we are." He unfolded his hand, revealing the ring I'd left behind. He took a step forward.

"I didn't forget."

"I suspected you were remembering things you ought not to. If you ran, I suspected you would run here."

"Did you find that out from your private investigator?"

Giles looked slightly surprised. "He wasn't much help. Good thing I already had a destination in mind."

I instantly regretted not carrying the hammer with me to the door. I tried to slam the door in his face, but he blocked it and forced his way in. I retreated. Giles looked like a volcano about to blow.

"Is that any way to treat your fiancé, Tennyson?"

"We're not getting married. I am not Tennyson Claxton and you are well aware of that fact. I'm Marissa Brookshire."

"Are you quite certain? Sure you're not Queen Elizabeth? Teddy Roosevelt? Napoleon Bonaparte?"

"I can prove who I am."

"You've been most enterprising. Resourceful. Very impressive. It must be a personality trait. Not one of your sister's. She had her own particular set of traits."

"My half-sister, Tennyson."

"That's the one."

"You admit it?" I was surprised. I expected another blizzard of lies.

"Why not?" He waved his hand around the room dismissively. "So this is where Porter's illegitimate spawn grew up. Way up here in Maine. I'm just relieved you didn't grow up at the North Pole. One question: How could you possibly prefer this dump to the Claxton mansion?"

"Because it comes without Claxtons. Or you."

I was still backing away from him. But Giles was quick. He grabbed me and pushed me toward the fireplace and down into a chair. He held me down and jammed the ring on my finger. Then he took the other chair and placed it opposite me, very close. I waited for a chance to run. I watched his face the way the trapped rat watches the snake.

"So nice of you to think of chairs for the two of us. In fact, this place, this cottage, it's not bad. Quaint. Nice little town. We'll keep it, after our marriage, shall we? Make it cute and cozy with endless buckets of Claxton money. It'll be nice to take an occasional break from the Claxton Empire, somewhere my work and I aren't under the C&B microscope. I'll say I gave the place to you as a wedding present. Using your money, of course. Our little honeymoon cottage."

"Never," I said. I couldn't say another word.

Giles glanced around at the wine chilling, the new goblets, the tray of appetizers.

"Never? But you've thought of everything, my dear. Such a shame that your sister didn't have your brains and resilience. She, on the other hand, was crazy about me."

"Maybe you drove her crazy."

"We had our disagreements at the end. But in the beginning she adored me. You? You never even liked me. Why is that? And yet you arranged this little romantic feast for us."

"I despise you."

"That's unusual, you know. Women, well, they usually like me."

I said nothing. I mentally measured the distance to the door. Giles took the corkscrew and opened the wine. He sniffed the cork.

"Nice vintage, not too expensive. Tennyson would insist on the most expensive bottle wherever we went, no matter if it tasted like swill." He poured the wine into the goblets and handed me one with a flourish. "It's a special occasion, so you may have a glass this once. Unlike your sibling, you haven't had a drinking problem, or a drug problem for that matter."

"Tennyson died in that accident in January," I said.

He was unperturbed. "As a result of her injuries. Yes."

"You had a terrible fight with her. But how did I—"

"Happen to fall in love with me? All in good time. You'll appreciate this tale, Marissa. You have the brains to appreciate it, anyway. You surprised me with that. You look so much like her, but you're so different inside. It's been a challenge, I can tell you that."

"And then what? After you satisfy my curiosity?"

"And then, you'll go back to being Tennyson." This entire conversation was perfectly insane. Giles, me, the whole world, we were all insane. Go back to being Tennyson? Back to the Fog? I would mount a flying pig and sail away into the skies before that happened. Or I would die.

"Never."

"There's that word again." He laughed, which always unsettled me. It was so out of character. His face wasn't made for laughter. "Don't worry, Marissa." He patted my knee. "You like that name better? It might be helpful that you've remembered a few things. It will tell me how to adjust your therapy."

"The Pegasus protocol?"

"Beyond Pegasus. Narcissus. This time I'll start with a blank slate. Wipe away all that leftover Marissa crap. This time I'll know how to make sure you become Tennyson, the whole Tennyson, and nothing but Tennyson. Forever."

I jumped up from the chair, kicked it over, and ran for the front door. My hand was on the lock when he caught me. He dragged me back, righted the chair, and pushed me back into it again.

"You think you're going to brainwash me again? Never!"

"Brainwashing is such a negative term. What I'll do to you is so much more permanent than mere brainwashing, Tennyson."

"I am Marissa. And I am not your lab rat."

He patted my head and I swatted his hand away. "Oh yes, you are, my dear. You are my perfect little lab rat. My pet. You see, I need Tennyson and you are the closest genetic match. Her illegitimate half-sister, who looks remarkably like her. Prettier. Smarter. Stronger. I'll use you to build a better Tennyson. Tennyson Two Point Oh." He grabbed my wrist and squeezed it painfully. I yelped.

"You bastard."

"Don't be like that. Your memories and what I can do with them will give hope to millions. Your little life will have meaning in my hands."

"You implanted those memories. Not David Jensen. You murdered him."

"Jensen was in the way. I put him down like the dog he was. And murder is an ugly word. I must do something about your vocabulary. Tennyson Two doesn't need to know big words like *murder*."

He sniffed his wine, swirled the glass, and sipped.

"You chose me to do this to me? You knew all about me?" I was on autopilot. Waiting for that winged pig to fly through the window.

"No need to give me all the credit," Giles said modestly. "I learned about your existence from Porter. Your loving father." He laughed.

The scene in the crawlspace replayed in my mind. I could hear Porter—it *was* Porter—yelling at my grandparents.

"He thought I was dead, didn't he?"

"Porter gets sloppy and sentimental after a few drinks. Sentiment, it's a Claxton trait. You, for instance, are sentimental about this crummy old house." I looked around at my house. My poor, doomed little house. "You're shocked it was Porter? You shouldn't be. He and I worked together on the Campus project from the beginning. He was grateful to me when I started seeing Tennyson. She was 'delicate,' shall we say. So sensitive, always having her feelings hurt. Temper tantrums. The little bipolar prima donna. He and your grandparents were very happy to have her in my capable hands. I could handle her scenes."

"By drugging her?" Oh Tennyson, I thought. I wish I could have saved you, but I didn't even know you.

"She loved drugs. All kinds." Giles settled back in his chair and took a sip of wine. He always enjoyed having a captive audience. I wasn't bound, but he was too close for me to run again.

"How did you meet Tennyson?" Talk, Marissa, I told myself, just talk, and keep him talking too. As long as I'm talking, I'm still myself, I'm still Marissa.

"At a fund-raiser for the Institute. Tennyson was there for her father, a command performance. Sulking, as usual. Wearing practically nothing. Drinking too much. Acting out. Whenever Porter asked her to do anything, she got loud and drunk. She did that night. I managed to get her out of the room before she passed out and further embarrassed the family. Soon enough she was crying on my shoulder."

How easily Giles said *the family*, as if the Claxtons were his family.

"Did you care for her at all?"

"Oh yes, I did. She amused me. She was beautiful and full of life. It's funny how a woman's attractiveness increases when she's worth a hundred and fifty million dollars," he mused. "That's not the kind of girl you bed and forget. Exhausting, though."

"How did I come up in the conversation?"

"Porter was disappointed in Tennyson. More than that, disgusted, in despair. His words. He knew she would never get any better. And he mentioned there wouldn't be any more children for him. Some medical issue. 'If only the other one had lived,' he said. 'If only we'd found her in time.' Turned out he was talking about *you*." Giles patted my hand and put the other wine glass in it. "Do have a sip of the wine. You picked it out and I haven't slipped anything into it, if that's what you're afraid of."

I put the glass to my lips and wet them with wine. "There."

"Good girl. Porter spilled out a sad story about this love-child, a daughter of his who died young. He was fond of the girl's mother, some townie he bedded when he was at that preppy little rich-kid college in Maine, but he couldn't marry her. Not the right class, you know. And Catholic." Giles watched for my reaction. Everything was a test with him. "I find it fascinating that the grandparents who raised you would rather report you dead than hand you over to the Claxtons. You would have had everything as a Claxton. He was sorry he didn't find you in time. Before you *died*," he smirked.

"Hard to believe he was sorry."

"Hard to believe you're related to Tennyson. You have a mind of your own, intelligence, curiosity, and I really hate to say it, spunk. It's endeared you to Foxhall and Octavia. Why did you have to be so troublesome?"

"Why did you have to ruin my life?"

He shrugged. "For the greater good, of course."

"And they went along with your switch? They don't seem like the 'greater good' type of people."

He cocked his head, considering. "They're not. And I never told them. They believe what they want to believe. They wanted to believe you're really Tennyson, a new, improved Tennyson. They were amazed at your transformation, but it was all believable. Although the swimming and cooking? That was almost too much."

"But if Porter thought I was dead—"

"Something happened that I'd never believed in. Serendipity. Chance. Luck. Roy Barnaker spotted you donating blood for a medical research project at NIH."

"I donated blood?" Oh yes, I did. I remembered it as he said it. There were all sorts of research projects at the National Institutes for Health, and every day on the Metro I read the ads in the paper: 'Healthy females needed between the ages of...' or 'Men and women wanted for an investigational study of...' I always needed an extra couple of hundred dollars in grad school. I thought those studies might help somebody. I didn't think giving blood would be the end of my life as I knew it.

"I used to send Roy over there to pick up lab reports. He was more presentable back then. One day a year or so ago, he came back with news: Tennyson Claxton, my girlfriend, had this amazing look-alike. He swore you could be sisters. That pricked my curiosity. Tennyson's half-sister was supposed to be dead, but who knew where Porter had sewn his oats? There might be another one. I sent Roy back to find you."

"How did he find me? Those tests were supposed to be private. Why?"

Giles stretched out in his chair and sipped his wine. "Roy followed you from NIH to your school. And why? Knowledge is power. Roy also found the coffee shop you frequented after school. I even stopped by there one time to see for myself. I was astonished when I saw you."

That was where I'd seen Roy before the Campus. At a table in the back with his coffee, Roy was staring at me. Always staring.

"You spied on me even then? Before the Campus?"

"Research is always the first step." Giles stood and loomed over me. He held my face gently in his hands. "The resemblance was incredible. I didn't know how you might be of use to me, but I was sure you would. Possibility soon turned into a plan. But I had to confirm that you were a Claxton. Your DNA wasn't hard to get. Roy collected your coffee cup as you discarded it. Porter was always drinking. I took his bourbon glass."

I couldn't control a shiver. "Roy Barnaker gave me the creeps."

"He had that effect on women. To my chagrin, and his embarrassment. It limited his usefulness to me. I think women sensed some things in him he'd—forgotten."

"Did you make him forget? Was he your lab rat too? Did you give him Hypnopolethe?"

"Impressive how you put things together."

"He was one of the soldiers who screamed in the night at the Campus."

"Worst case I ever saw. I helped him."

"You told me Hypnopolethe had never been used on humans."

"I did, didn't I? You don't think I'm the first person to lie to Congress, do you?" Giles sipped his wine. "Back to you. I sensed there was a higher purpose to your existence. For me."

"You, as well as God?"

"Really, Marissa, that religious bent of yours is annoying. Boring and low-class. Not like Tennyson. But it was tantalizing to see how close you two were physically, the closest person on earth to Tennyson Claxton. There were minor differences. Her nose always bothered her. It was easy to encourage her to fix it. I recommended the final shape: yours."

"I knew I never did that." I touched my nose. I was absurdly relieved it was my own.

He patted my shoulder. "You would find it interesting how easily led Tennyson was. She didn't have that mulish streak you have. Maybe you got that from your late mother."

Unlike Giles, I had read Tennyson's diary. I wanted to tell him that she tumbled to the truth and she knew all about him. About him and his dalliance with Jordana and others. She found out about me. She wanted to meet me. A pure jolt of unadulterated rage hit me.

"I always wanted a sister."

"So did she."

"You son of a bitch! You killed her. I had green eyes! Green eyes! You changed them."

"Poor Marissa. Quite an unusual shade of green, almost emerald." Giles had the nerve to sigh, as if it pained him slightly. "But Tennyson's eyes were brown, and you weren't any good to me without brown eyes. As it is, they aren't an exact match. Hers were darker. But close enough."

"I hate you for that and for so many things I can't even count."

"All in the service of science." He filled his wine glass again. "You haven't made any progress on yours. Please drink. More than a sip. We're having a moment here."

I put it to my lips again. "Why are you telling me this now?"

"Why?" He smiled broadly. "Because, my dear Tennyson-Marissa, you're never going to remember this conversation."

Hypnopolethe.

"You're wrong, Giles, I'll never forget this conversation."

"Yes, you will. It's a shame I can't share all my breakthroughs with the world. There are those who consider my methods unorthodox, even unethical. But you, with your intellect, you can understand. You can appreciate what it will mean for the world. That's one reason I'm telling you all this."

"How did I get to the Campus? Was it you? Did I ever know you before the Campus?"

"I only saw you that once, before. I didn't want to contaminate the experiment. And I was busy with her that night."

"The night of the accident?"

"Yes. Aren't you paying attention? I sent Roy for you."

Now I remembered. The doorbell rang at my apartment and I opened the door. Roy Barnaker was there. After that, nothing.

"How?"

"Something like chloroform, but better. When he brought you to me unconscious, I supervised the blows."

"You hit me? You broke my arm!" It throbbed, right on cue. I rubbed it.

"Technically, Roy broke it. And he administered superficial blows about the face. You had to look like her and like you'd been in a terrible accident. And she had to look like you. It was a masterpiece of timing. At any rate, your arm is healed now. Tennyson was completely destroyed in her wreck. You escaped relatively unscathed."

"Unscathed? You stole my life. Have you no shame, Giles? None?"

"Science has no shame."

"How did you blackmail Roy into it?"

"Not blackmail. Loyalty. Roy owed me his new life, after the Army. I saved him from those things he couldn't forget. Even so, he didn't want to hurt you. He said he thought you had a nice little life already. But I told him no, Roy, little lives don't matter. Now you would have a wonderful life."

Chapter 48

L ITTLE LIVES DON'T matter.
His words echoed in my head. *Little lives don't matter.*

"Light the candles, Tennyson. It's getting dark."

"All right."

I needed to stretch my legs. I needed a plan. The candles were lined up on the mantle in a row of colored glass containers. I struck a match and lit them one by one and thought how nice it would be if Giles weren't standing behind me.

If this were all just a nightmare.

"Don't do anything stupid," he warned. "I'm right here. Turn around."

I faced him. "Now what?"

He trailed his finger down my face. "I compared you with Tennyson that night. Side by side. By then she was dead. There are photographs."

"You took me to the morgue, didn't you?" My head was spinning. I held onto the mantle for balance. "The cold pale woman on the table? The woman in my nightmares."

"See what a funny thing memory is? I thought you had forgotten. Yet you do recall that moment. I must write that down. I had no idea you'd wake up. It was very traumatic for you to see your dead double lying on that table."

"You thought I would forget something that horrible?"

"I hoped you would. Trauma like that can, and often does, trigger severe amnesia. That was why I did it. You did forget for a long time. The drugs and therapies at the Campus helped too."

Giles was made of ice, not blood and bone. I had seen my dead sister on that metal table. My nightmares never forgot. They warned me. My sister came in my dreams and warned me.

"You have no soul, Giles. Why bring me there?"

"To confirm the resemblance, of course. To see if you were really identical. With her adjusted nose, it was remarkable. Your eyes, though. It took some time for them to turn brown. That's one reason why I had to keep you away from everyone in those first few weeks, in a medical coma. Luckily the underlying pigment was there.

And thanks to you, now I know the trauma-induced amnesia was temporary."

"You think you can brainwash me twice?"

"Probably. We'll see. Don't you think it is fascinating how the brain can recreate a memory, reconfigure it, change the details, smudge it and smear it and turn it into something else over time? Like a charcoal drawing. A touch here, a touch there, and one face becomes another."

"And you're the artist."

Giles always enjoyed it when I fed him a cue.

"Exactly. You see, I had to start with a clean slate, as clean as I could without damaging your ability to create new memories. That's why I was interested in how much suppressed imagery you incorporated into your nightmares. Sleep is vital to learning and you were doing so well. But then you started having nightmares that told you other stories." He paused for more wine. "It was a mistake to let you wean yourself off the drugs with that little sleight-of-hand trick of yours. I shall be more careful in the future."

"You should go, Giles. Leave now. This can all end differently if you leave now."

"I will never leave you. We have a future together, Tennyson. As long as you live."

"My name is Marissa."

He grinned.

"I can see where I went wrong. No, 'wrong' is not the right word. An experiment is never wrong when you learn something. I can see now where I need to go. It's been hard for you. Don't worry, this time it will be easier to become Tennyson."

I looked into his cold, clear eyes. I thought if I locked my eyes on his, I could make him look away first. When he did, I might have one single moment before he could react. I silently counted seconds. *Six, seven, eight, nine—*

He dropped his eyes to his wineglass and I broke away. I dodged around him and ran to the hall. His legs were longer. He body-slammed the front door as I opened it. He grabbed me and held my wrists.

"I'm not Tennyson!"

"You will be! It'll be easier this time. You already know Foxhall and Octavia are your grandparents. You understand Porter is your father. You even bonded with Priscilla. Not even Tennyson did that. The foundation has been laid in your brain, like muscle memory. This will work. I'll make it work."

"I won't let it work! I'll never be Tennyson! Let me go!"

He held me tight, his breath in my face.

"No, Marissa, my clever little impostor, you can't leave. I'm almost sorry your brain will never again be as curious or as sharp. You saw what happened to Roy. You must understand that my work—the mystery of memory—is more important than you."

"Then it's more important than you too. You said little lives don't matter."

"Ultimately, yes. Right now, however, I can make a difference and so can you. In your own little way."

I kept struggling, but he was much stronger, and he was made of stone. He yanked me up with one arm, picked up a chair with the other, and half-dragged me upstairs with him. All the way up, step by step, I fought, clawed, kicked, screamed.

He stopped on the landing overlooking the entry hall and the front door. We turned toward the middle bedroom, not mine, and not my grandparents' where my dollhouse was. He threw me to the floor. I landed on the arm Roy had broken for him. Pain shot all the way up my arm to my shoulder. Giles positioned the chair, picked me up, and pitched me into it, and standing behind me, pinned me there with his arms.

"I like the view from up here. We can welcome your boyfriend when he walks through that door," he sneered.

How did he know about Brendan? Oh my God, Brendan would get here too late. After I was—

"Tennyson couldn't stand Brendan Troy, you know," he confided. "Her pet name for him was Captain America. I can't imagine what you see in him."

"He calls you Dr. Frankenstein."

"But you're a smart-mouthed bitch, just like she was." Giles put his hands around my neck. "How I'd like to shut you up forever. You've cost me so much time and energy, Tennyson."

I clawed at his hands and he squeezed. I was seeing darkness when he stopped squeezing, but he kept his hands where they were. I could barely talk.

"You said it's been informative." My voice was a croak. I coughed.

"Right you are. We are on the brink of a discovery."

"You think you'll get away with this?" I coughed again and tried to open my throat.

"I already have." He pulled my hands behind me and snaked a length of rope from his pocket. I couldn't believe this was really happening. I jerked my arms away, but he caught them. "Duct tape is messy, don't you think?"

He wrenched my arms behind me again and bound them at the wrists.

"You're hurting me, Giles. You'll leave bruises. Everyone will know what you've done."

He snorted. "We can't leave bruises on the famous Tennyson Claxton, can we? No, we can't have *that*."

He squeezed hard, not caring if he bruised $150 million. I spread my wrists as he tied them, trying to stretch the rope, and he tied it with a simple granny knot like he was tying a package. Giles had never been a Boy Scout. I, on the other hand, had learned a few corny tricks from Grandpa Tom, in addition to making pills disappear. Like sailor's knots and rope tricks.

I strained my fingers to reach the middle of the knot, working slowly while he jabbered on. It gave me something to do and think about. It was either work on the knot, or give in to despair. I worked on the knot.

"Why do you need me, Giles? Aren't there enough brain-damaged people out there to play mad scientist with?"

"I do need you. You're my Tennyson Two Point Oh. And I'm happy to share this with you. After all, I won't be able to write a paper on this experiment. Yet I will always enjoy talking to my soon-to-be-mindless bride."

"Mindless?" My thumb and index finger reached the knot and started probing into the center of it. The rope cut into my wrists. I prayed I wouldn't dislocate anything. Giles reached inside his suit pocket and pulled out what looked like a pen case. He snapped it open for me to see.

His weapon was a syringe.

"Hypnopolethe. You already guessed that, didn't you? You're going to forget everything we've said here tonight, Marissa Alexandra Brookshire. All your troubles, all the trauma of your experiences here, it will all be gone, not even a whisper of a memory. If it works the way it's supposed to," he added cheerfully. "It's an experiment."

Hypnopolethe. The experimental drug that promised to erase unbearable memories. But those victims wanted to forget. I wanted only to remember, remember everything.

"Roy Barnaker."

"Poor Roy, always in a fog. That's one side effect. But the trauma, the horrors he'd lived through, all that was gone. I took it away."

"You took his soul."

"No great loss. His soul wasn't a shining example."

"That's crazy. Unethical. Immoral. Even you should know that."

He placed the syringe in its case on the floor next to me. He leaned on the guardrail and stared at me.

"Ethics? What about the ethics of saving the memories of millions of others? Yes, that's what I will be able to do. Save millions. Save their lives."

"By destroying me?"

"Not you. Only your memories. Only Marissa's. I promise. That's why I'm telling you all of this. To bring the memories forward. One by one. It's essential. The experimental protocol calls for repeated injections during intensive talk therapy, to bring the targeted memories to the forefront of the patient's consciousness so they can be erased. I'd say we're doing that right now, wouldn't you? We're also supposed to measure our progress with a continuous brain scan, to achieve precise dosage control. We don't have the luxury of a clinical setting here, so this conversation and one full syringe will have to do. I can give you a booster shot later."

"It could kill me."

"Always a risk."

"What would you tell my grandparents?"

"Suicide."

"They know who I am, Giles. They know I'm Marissa."

He was still for a moment. Then he continued his preparations. I knew he was thinking about what I said.

"I know Tennyson broke up with you the night she died." I kept my legs still, hoping he wouldn't think to bind them.

"How do you know that? Message from beyond the grave? Or one of her own secret memories? One I didn't implant in you? Now, that would be interesting. That would be a breakthrough." He got back to his feet and placed his hands on my shoulders. "No one breaks up with Giles Embry. Not Tennyson One, and not the new improved version, Tennyson Two. You."

Lights from a car in the street outside refracted through the sidelights by the door. I watched them slide past the house. Giles did too. Could it be Brendan? But no, the car didn't stop.

The dead woman on the table, the dead woman in my dreams flashed into my head. I didn't want to be that woman. What if I came back alive but an empty shell? Would the Claxtons care? Would Mercy pursue the case? Would Brendan remember me the way I was?

I was trying, trying, trying to spread the knot open and pull the rope away. Unfortunately it wasn't a magic rope, but I didn't need much slack, just enough to slip one hand free. I closed my eyes and kept working on the rope.

I felt Giles's hand on my shoulder, patting it.

"It is remarkable, isn't it? Science."

"You killed her."

Giles opened his blue eyes wide, innocent. "Tennyson killed herself. She drank too much, she drove like a madwoman, and she had a lot of cocaine in her system. Disabling her Porsche's steering gear, knowing that an angry drunk would drive too fast on an icy road? That was just giving fate a helping hand. Tennyson didn't die right away. There was time enough to make sure she knew that I had won the game."

"You disgust me."

"It was a busy night," he continued. "At the same time, Roy was busy collecting you."

"You killed David Jensen too."

"What a team we could have made, if only you liked me a little, Marissa. I made a point to have a drink with Jensen that fateful night. He didn't trust me either, so I slipped something in his Scotch. When he got a little too drunk, I drove him to a quiet place, put him in the driver's seat, put my hand around his and pulled the trigger. Did you get all that? You know why I'm telling you all this now, don't you? So it will be fresh in your conscious mind, where the Hypnopolethe can find it. And kill it."

I felt the knot in the rope give just a little, as the knot in my stomach squeezed tighter and tighter. "And Roy?"

"Roy had served his purpose, and he was falling apart. He was beginning to feel sorry for you. He started to keep things from me.

He wanted to tell you things. I couldn't have that. Roy had been my right-hand man. I realized his death could serve another purpose."

"To traumatize me so you would have an excuse to keep me at the Campus."

"You get another A plus."

"It didn't work. And you wrapped your tie around his arm."

"I was in a hurry. I explained to the police that I kept extra ties in my office and Roy must have taken one. Roy drank a soda with Rohypnol in it. Like your guru Jensen. Fast-acting and gone from the bloodstream in a matter of hours. When he woke up, I explained a few things to him. Why he was going to kill himself with heroin. It would at least be pleasant for him. He always loved heroin."

"You are evil."

"Evil is just a word. I can't let emotion get in the way of my work."

"Except when it comes to your mother."

"My mother?"

"You're afraid, aren't you? Afraid you'll wind up like her? With Alzheimer's?"

"You don't know anything about my mother."

"I know the Brain Reaper is going to get you, Giles. That's what you memory wizards call Alzheimer's, isn't it? The Brain Reaper. You won't even remember saving the world."

He slapped my face hard. "Don't make me angry, Tennyson."

"What's your next step, Giles? A brain transplant? You'll need one." I felt the knot give a little more. I flexed my wrists and the rope gave an inch. The next pull would free me, but I had to choose my moment.

He leaned against the wall and looked down at me. "Never mind that. We're going to be married. Very soon. You'll be a bit groggy, confused, but pliable. Suggestible, you might say. An elopement is so romantic, don't you think? We can have a formal wedding later. Octavia will insist."

"My grandparents will figure this out."

"They won't want to. I am a genius. A star. Their star. My research will change so many lives. A shining example of your family's money and C&B power going to a good cause, making the world a better place. Think about the greater good, Marissa. And you can buy all the shoes and dresses you desire, if you still desire anything. I wouldn't stop you."

"You think I care about shoes and dresses?"

"Not you, but Tennyson does. I never understood why you wouldn't want to be rich and have a wonderful life."

"I had a wonderful life. My own."

He stepped in close and ruffled my hair. I stilled my hands.

"This blond hair will have to go. Tennyson has short, dark hair. Her signature look." God, how I hated him. I wrenched my head away. "And we will sleep together. Every day. Every night. Tennyson was a girl with appetites. She loved to please me."

"When you're not cheating on me," I said. "With Jordana and Lavinia."

"How can it be cheating when there's no one inside there to cheat on?" He tapped my forehead. "But you and I will marry. We will have children. The perfect couple." He leaned in close to me and kissed my lips. I tried to turn my head, but he held it there.

"You are out of your mind!"

"And then, Marissa." He leaned in close and whispered. "I mean, Tennyson. One day in the near future, just a few years, when you've fulfilled your purpose, when you've given me a child or two, and when my role in the Claxton Empire and my fortune are secure, you are going to die. I'm going to kill you."

My eyes were wide, my pulse hammering. "What?"

"For all the trouble you've caused me, I'm going to kill you. It will be a terrible shame, a tragic suicide, but after all you've been through, everyone will understand."

"You're not even human, Giles." My hands were itching to act. I pulled my right hand free and caught the rope before it fell. I forced myself to wait for the right moment. "How are you going to do it?"

"One day, Tennyson will lapse into her old bad habits again and overdose on some drug or another. Whatever's handy. Don't worry, a drug overdose is quite humane, as deaths go. It won't hurt. You may even enjoy it. Roy enjoyed his."

"I won't let you."

"How can you stop me? You'll never even remember this conversation."

Giles bent down and reached for the syringe.

Chapter 49

I KICKED HIM hard in the face.

I pulled my hands free and jumped to my feet. Giles staggered backwards against the banister. It creaked and the post at the top of the stairs wobbled, but it held.

I leaped back and scrambled away from him as he grabbed my leg. I kicked at him again with the other foot, and my heel scraped his face and ear, making a long red gash. I'd drawn blood. He rubbed the side of his head and looked at his bloody hand. He stalked toward me, flexing his fists in rage. I backed away toward the bedrooms.

He grabbed for me. I ducked, off-balance, and tumbled to the floor. He lunged toward me, half on top of me. I just managed to pull my leg up and knee him hard in the groin. He bellowed and rolled off of me, gasping, clutching his crotch in agony. I rolled away from him and staggered to my feet, trying to catch my breath.

He roared up off the floor like a bull and lunged at me again. His back was to the open staircase and the railing overlooking the front door. Giles stood full height, blocking my path. He was panting. So was I. There was no escape, no other direction for me to go: Straight through him? Or let myself to be cornered in one of the bedrooms? I put both hands out in front of me and charged. I caught him off guard, one hand wiping blood from his face, the other still holding his groin.

He fell back and the banister wobbled, swayed, sagged. Giles tried to catch himself, but there was nothing to grab but the rail. He put all his weight on the wood. It creaked. I heard wood cracking. It held again.

We would have to go over together. It was the only way.

I charged once more, and I put my right shoulder straight into his gut as hard as I could.

His back hit the railing with all his weight, and all of mine too. The post snapped, the screws pulled out of the wall, he grabbed for the railing as it tore loose. Falling backwards, he twisted in midair. I just tried to hold on to him. We plummeted together, twelve feet down to the bare wooden floor.

I landed flat on top of Giles, holding on to his jacket with both hands. Neither of us moved for a few seconds. The air was knocked out of my lungs and my whole body was shaking.

I moved first, pushing myself up on my elbows. They hurt. My knees hurt. Everything ached, every bone in my body, but I was alive. Nothing felt broken. I crawled off Giles and sat on the floor, holding my head in my hands.

I stared at Giles. His back was twisted beneath him at an angle, his legs splayed out. His left arm was flailing, trying to lever himself up to a sitting position. His right arm was pinned under his back. Splintered wood was scattered around us like straw. The entire banister, the handrail and all the staircase posts, from top to bottom, had been torn off as we fell.

"Help me," Giles was gasping. "Tennyson, help me! I can't move."

"I'm not Tennyson," I said.

I would have to call the police. Soon.

My wrists stung, bleeding where I had rubbed them raw untangling the knot. Giles was speaking again, but his words were muffled. I blocked them out for the moment.

I was moving in slow motion.

The syringe was still lying on the floor upstairs. I couldn't leave it there and I couldn't get it out of my mind. Standing up hurt. Walking hurt more. So I crawled back up the stairs, staying close to the wall so I wouldn't get dizzy and tumble off the unguarded edge of the steps.

Not sure what I was going to do, I gazed at the needle before picking it up.

I staggered back downstairs to Giles's side. I crouched down and looked him right in the face. He seemed to be in shock. There wasn't much blood, except where I'd gashed his cheek and ear. His eyes were unfocused, his pupils dilated, his breathing fast and shallow.

"Are you all right?" I asked. It was the automatic thing to say and I was still on autopilot.

"Tennyson, Tennyson, I can't move my legs, I can't feel them! My back— And my arm— My arm is broken." He clutched at me with his left hand, trying to pull himself up. He couldn't. "Tennyson, help me!"

"I'm not Tennyson, Giles. I'm Marissa. Remember?" I slapped his face. His eyes focused on me and went very wide. I knew he remembered me now. "Take it easy, Giles. Everything is going to be all right now."

I pressed down on his forehead with one hand, forcing his head back to the floor.

"What are you doing?" For the first time, he was afraid of me. I moved very calmly now. I tried to slow my breathing, my pounding pulse. The balance of power had shifted.

I leaned my full weight on his chest, pinning his flailing arm down with my legs. I didn't care if he was broken, I didn't care if he couldn't move, I didn't care if I hurt him even more. I held the syringe up as if it were the sword of justice. He squirmed and tried to throw me off, but he was too weak, the pain drained his strength. He coughed. Even shallow breathing made him groan. I wondered if he had shattered his ribs too. His entire torso was twisted like a broken doll. His back, one arm, his ribs, maybe a collarbone or a hip? That would do for now.

"I'm helping you. You're going to forget everything that happened here, Giles. Everything we did and said. All this ugliness. You left me the magic needle." I took off the protective cap and let him look at the needle. It was big and sharp. It gleamed in the light.

"Don't do that! You're not a doctor! You don't know what you're doing!"

I smiled at him. "Then I can't be held responsible, can I? You'll be one of the chosen ones, a sacrifice for science. Think of the honor. Do you want me to take notes? Publish a paper?"

"No! Put that down! I forbid you to do that!" He tried to sit up, but the effort made him scream. His eyes rolled back and the tendons in his neck bulged. I slapped him again to keep his full attention. He focused on me. His blue eyes were filling up with raw fear.

"You forbid me? You can't stop me now, Doctor Embry. You're going to forget Marissa Brookshire and everything you tried to do to her. You'll forget she ever existed. You're going to forget you were engaged to Tennyson Claxton. You might forget everything you ever knew. Believe it or not, I even want you to forget the horrible monster you are. You might be lucky enough to have a fresh start. You'll be a bit foggy and stupid afterward, but that's a small price to pay for science, don't you think? At least you can't lose your soul. You don't have one. And remember what you told me? Little lives don't matter? Your little life is about to get much, much smaller."

"NO, NO, NO, NO, NO! Tennyson, please don't do this!"

"I keep telling you, Giles. I'm not Tennyson."

I looked at the gash I'd made across his cheek. It was seeping blood, and I thought the wound would hide the needle stick. I held his head down and jammed the magic needle deep into his open wound. I didn't know what the Hypnopolethe would do if it went straight into his brain. Would it wipe his mind clean? Would it kill him? I pressed the plunger down as hard as I could. He screamed until he ran out of air. When the syringe was empty, I pulled it out of his face with shaking hands. Giles Embry's eyes rolled back in his head, and in a moment he was unconscious.

I slipped the syringe back into its case and took it upstairs. I stumbled to my grandparents' bedroom and tucked it away in a deep, dark corner of the crawlspace. Later, I would think of something else to do with it.

I called the police.

Chapter 50

"THANK YOU FOR coming so quickly. There was a terrible accident."

My face was smeared with dirt and tears. I could feel it. The lone Camden police officer asked for my name and ID and surveyed the wreckage. Giles lay on the floor, unconscious, surrounded by chunks of wood and debris that came down when we fell through the banister. The officer leaned down to check for a pulse. Giles was alive.

"I'm Officer Morris, ma'am. I was just a couple of blocks away when you called. The ambulance will be here in a minute." As he said it, I could hear the siren approaching. I nodded. I didn't know what to say. My limbs felt impossibly heavy and I started to sway. He caught me and led me to the staircase, where I sat down on the bottom step and leaned my head against the wall. "Are you all right, ma'am?"

"I'm alive," I answered. I knew who I was and what I had done. I was horrified.

Another officer came through the door, and after making eye contact with Morris he headed up the stairs. He dodged around me and stayed against the wall, away from the missing banister.

"Looks like an altercation took place," Morris prompted me.

"He tried to kill me." It was the truth. Giles had planned to kill what was left of Marissa. Later he would have killed whatever was left of Tennyson Two.

"Excuse me, ma'am. Would you mind lifting your hair for me?"

He inspected my neck with his flashlight. I gathered from his low whistle that there were impressive bruises around my throat. Morris asked me to turn my wrists over so he could look at them too. Bruises had already formed and my cuts were beginning to scab over the rope fibers. The police officer upstairs reported that the rope Giles had used was still on the floor near the overturned chair.

Officer Morris gave me a puzzled look. "You know, ma'am, this has nothing to do with anything, but you look just like someone I used to know in middle school. She had the most amazing green eyes, though. No offense to your eyes, ma'am."

"None taken," I managed to say.

He scratched his head. "Funny thing, she might have lived in this same house. Long ago."

"Funny thing," I agreed.

I realized I had known him too. His badge read Ted Morris. He sat behind me in the seventh grade. I'd had a crush on him once. I smiled at the memory. He was the first boy who ever kissed me, at a party when I was thirteen.

He paused for a moment, perhaps remembering that kiss. The gawky boy I had known was gone. Now he was all authority and swagger. A police officer.

"Tell me more about this—what happened." He clearly wasn't sure what to call it yet.

"I'm buying the house. My real estate lady told me the banister was loose. The guardrail, across the landing." I gave him her phone number. "It was on my list of things to fix."

He jotted down a note. "Can you try to explain what happened?"

The simplest version of the truth was the best. "I was running away from him. He found me."

"You're Tennyson Claxton? Now I know why the name is familiar. Aren't you supposed to be engaged to some doctor? Is this the guy?" he said. "Listen, I'm sorry, my girlfriend reads the tabloids and all that stuff on the Web, and well, you do look so much like the girl I knew in middle school that it kind of stuck in my mind."

He focused on the ring. The big pink ring. I brought my hand up to show it to him. My finger was bruised. The ring would not slip over my knuckle. I was aware it was throbbing.

"The engagement was over. Giles wouldn't take no for an answer. Dr. Giles Embry. He brought this with him and jammed it on my finger. I think it's sprained."

"When the swelling goes down, it'll probably come off again. Or they can cut the ring off." He lifted his eyes and peered into the living room. "Seems like a pretty cozy scene. Wine, cheese, candles."

"I was expecting someone else. I still am. He was delayed."

"I see. Then this Embry guy found you waiting for someone? He was angry? He tied you up?"

"Yes." I turned my wrists over. I needed to clean the wounds. "He's much bigger and stronger than I am. Marine Corps Marathon runner. He tried to choke me— My neck. I— He tied me to that chair up there." My throat was dry. I swallowed. I touched my throat. It hurt.

Flashing lights from the ambulance lit up the front of the house. EMTs stormed through the door and the second officer directed them to Giles.

"You managed to get loose?" Officer Ted Morris asked.

"I had to. He was going to kill me. I worked the knot free— He came at me again and again. I got loose and pushed him back. I kicked him. He grabbed me and we went through the railing. Together."

Might as well keep it simple. I shut my eyes, but the scene replayed in my head. The sickening sound of the splintering wood and the thud of his body hitting the floor below, with me clinging to him. I jerked my head at the memory.

"Lucky break for you, landing on top. He broke the fall for you."

"Lucky." I nodded. Officer Morris asked one of the paramedics to attend to me. I waved them off. "I'll be fine," I said. "I just need some air." I stood up.

That's when I fainted.

When I came to, I was on a stretcher and paramedics were loading me into a second ambulance. Brendan was by my side as they shut the back door and we took off, siren screaming. His fingers traced the bruises on my neck. He kissed my bandaged wrists.

"I'm so sorry I'm late, Tenn."

And now appear, thy treasures to protect,
Conceal thy person, thy designs direct,
And tell what more thou must from Fate expect;
Domestic woes far heavier to be borne!

Chapter 51

I'M STILL SURPRISED I wasn't arrested.

I'm still surprised I'm not currently residing in some forgotten prison. After the Claxton family damage-control conference I lived through later, prison might be a relief.

The little hospital down the coast treated my injuries and kept me until almost one in the morning. I was X-rayed, bandaged, poked, and prodded, but not drugged, except for some extra-strength Tylenol. Bruises and abrasions, no concussion, no broken bones.

Eventually, I was cleared to leave with Brendan, with an ice-pack on my swollen finger. They cut off the pink gumball ring and put it in a plastic bag for me. My house in Camden was a mess, so we returned to the roadside motel for the night, and Brendan slept in the second bed. When I woke up at dawn, he was wrapped around me protectively, sound asleep.

I called Octavia and Foxhall in Florida the first thing in the morning, and I informed them as tersely as I could about Giles's "accident" and what he tried to do to me. They expressed the predictable shock and disbelief. I told them to come up and see for themselves, if they cared.

Later that morning, the Camden police declined to arrest me, at least for the moment. They wanted to hear Giles's version of the accident first. He was in the ICU at the Pen Bay Medical Center in Rockport, Maine, five miles away. When he regained consciousness that afternoon, he didn't remember anything about what happened, or being in Camden, Maine, with Tennyson Claxton. They let me see him, just for a minute, through the glass. That was all I needed. I had to make sure he couldn't come after me again.

He would be flown back to Virginia, I was told, when his condition was stable, with his head screwed into a steel halo. His back was broken, his right arm and shoulder were smashed, and he was paralyzed from the waist down, at least temporarily. Full recovery of his mobility or memory seemed out of the question. But as soon as he could talk again, he told everyone in the ICU that he was a brilliant doctor, so his ego wasn't paralyzed.

The DA interviewed me. She told me Giles might eventually be charged with assault and attempted murder, but that was up in the air.

In the meantime, the police report supported my version of events, and so did the DA. She asked me not to leave the area until the police closed the investigation.

My grandparents and father arrived in Maine the following day by private jet. After viewing Giles at the hospital they went unerringly for the Lord Camden Inn, the most expensive hotel in town. They wouldn't hear of me staying another night at a roadside Bates Motel, so I checked back into my own suite at the Inn. Next door to Brendan's.

For this tender family reunion, Brendan made himself scarce at my request. He said he would go look at the harbor.

"This is one hell of a mess," the Senator said, as we took our seats around a conference table at the Inn. The hotel supplied coffee, which had to be refilled, and pastries, which went untouched. Later a bottle of wine was delivered. When it was, I filled my glass, because after all, I wasn't Tennyson.

"The kind of mess Tennyson Claxton might find herself in," I agreed. I was wearing my new heather green jacket. I hoped it would be my suit of armor.

"At least it's a small town," Porter said. "We can contain some of the fallout. An old house in need of repair, a tragic accident, Tennyson's quick thinking saved his life. That's what we're telling the press."

In fact, a C&B public relations team was already there, preparing a statement. Porter read part of it to us.

"Ms. Tennyson Claxton and her fiancé, renowned research scientist Dr. Giles Embry, were viewing vacation homes for sale in Maine when an unfortunate accident occurred. Both Ms. Claxton and Dr. Embry sustained injuries. Ms. Claxton promptly summoned assistance and was instrumental in saving Dr. Embry's life. We have every hope for Dr. Embry's full recovery and his return to his groundbreaking work. In this difficult time, the C&B Institute requests that the media respect his and Ms. Claxton's privacy…"

"So I'm Ms. Claxton?" I asked. "And I saved my fiancé's life? Are those fictions really necessary?"

"Until we sort through this mess, Magpie," Octavia said.

I stood up and faced the Claxton Empire.

"I'm not Tennyson. You knew who I was all along. Marissa was the only one in the dark. You conspired with Giles, or you let him manipulate you. He's a murderer and a monster. You could have stopped him. You didn't."

There was a thick silence in the room. They sat frozen around the table, Foxhall, Octavia, and Porter. My grandparents and my father. They couldn't find a word to say.

Good, I thought. I have to say a few more.

"My life was stolen from me. I didn't know who I was, but I fought to find out. I managed to find someone to test my DNA against yours, Octavia. Yours and the Senator's. It's a match. I have proof that you are my grandparents."

"My God, girl, of course you are a Claxton," Foxhall interjected. "We all knew that. DNA proof indeed."

"And that DNA proves that I am a bastard, as they say. But how, exactly, does one distinguish between all the bastards in this room?"

Porter and Foxhall looked away. Octavia sighed.

"We didn't know, my dear," she said. "Not in the beginning. We suspected something was very different about you when you dove into the pool and swam like an Olympian. Tennyson could never have done that. You, on the other hand, couldn't ride. Though you've made such progress on horseback. We know you're our granddaughter, Magpie."

Calling me "Magpie" was a nice compromise, I thought. She didn't dare call me Tennyson. She couldn't bear to call me Marissa.

"I knew the truth when we danced that first foxtrot to Benny Goodman, you and I," Foxhall said softly. "Your other grandfather must have taught you how. But I was happy to step into that dance with you."

Porter cleared his throat. "I didn't know what to believe. Marissa returning from the dead just seemed too fantastic. Too impossible."

"Who knows, Dad? How many illegitimate kids do you have? Besides me?"

"Just the one." He looked ashamed and miserable. "I'm sorry. Ultimately I realized Anne and Thomas Brookshire must have lied to me. I believed them. And I gave up. All those years ago. I'm so happy you're alive."

"No matter how many graves I've been buried in," I said. "But my being alive is no thanks to anyone else at this table. Is it?"

It was hard to get them started, but now they were all talking at once. Everyone in my family had a denial, an excuse, a rationalization, an apology, if not a dozen of each.

Octavia claimed that Tennyson had been troubled all her life. Damaged. Toxic. Nothing helped Tennyson, not drugs, money, fame, sex tapes, psychologists, or rehabs. The family always feared her life would end badly. By alcohol, an accident, an overdose, a kidnapper, an abusive man. Ever since she was a teenager, they waited for the knock on the door to tell them she was gone.

"When that knock finally came," Foxhall said, "Giles told us Tennyson had miraculously survived. She was alive, but she didn't remember anything. She was injured, but her physical wounds would heal. She was in a coma for weeks. None of us could see her, except glimpses through the window, and then she was in his intensive therapy. Giles said our granddaughter needed seclusion and time. We were deeply concerned, all of us, but it seemed as if fate was giving her, and us, a second chance. We entrusted her to the only person, and the only place, that might be able to restore her to us. Giles Embry and the Campus. We couldn't imagine he was manipulating all this—"

"You are the granddaughter we always wanted." Octavia reached out her hand to me, but I didn't take it.

"The minute I laid eyes on you at the Farm, I knew who you must be," Porter told me. "It's strange. Physically, you and Tennyson could be twins. But you are your own person. Intelligent, sensible, caring, grounded. Everything she was not. You're the other side of the coin. I'm sure much of what went wrong with Tennyson was my fault. But it didn't seem so wrong, taking this second chance. With you."

They claimed they didn't know how Giles had found me and created the whole deception. So I told them. I laid it out for them in an outline that an elementary school teacher might devise. I told them how Giles found me, and then Tennyson found out about me and decided to leave Giles. If he lost Tennyson, he knew the Claxton gravy train would go off the rails, and that sealed her fate.

What Giles did, he believed, was for the greater good of mankind. What was the life of one irrelevant heiress, compared to saving the minds of millions? And saving the career of one brilliant scientist?

"Here's the collected wit and wisdom of Giles Embry," I told them. "The greater good demands sacrifice. Science has no shame. Evil is just a word. Little lives don't matter. That's who you entrusted your daughter and granddaughter to."

I described how and why Giles engineered Tennyson's death and my abduction, her near look-alike. How he broke me and assaulted me and tried to destroy my identity. How he planned to replace the troublesome Tennyson with Tennyson Two. How he would have cemented his place in the family fortune by forcing me to marry him and have his children, preferably two.

"Giles told you this?" Foxhall asked. He opened the bottle of wine and poured a glass for each of us.

"After he strangled me, and about the same time he told me how he planned to kill me. Eventually. After I'd served my purpose." I sipped the wine. "Giles enjoyed telling me, because he was going to wipe the slate clean again. With his magic drug. He said it would only erase my memories if they were fresh in my mind, so he had to tell me everything. Besides, he couldn't tell anyone else. He couldn't publish his greatest triumph."

"I can't believe this, it's too horrible." Octavia stood up and went to the window overlooking the harbor. Foxhall followed her, putting his arm around her shoulder. "Why in the world would he want to kill you? Why?"

"He was going to wait a few years." I was making sure I remembered it by saying it aloud. "After he erased my memories and installed new ones. Building Tennyson Two Point Oh, he called it. And most importantly, after we had kids and he was safely in the will and the heir to the Claxton fortune. Your fortune, by the way." I lifted my glass in a salute. "Not mine."

"You have been through too much, my dear. I am so very sorry," Foxhall said. "We all are. But you survived."

I gazed out the window at Camden Harbor. I thought about how sweetly naïve my life had been before encountering this crew of cutthroats, and I wondered why I had ever wanted more family.

"We understand that you're angry," Porter said.

"Angry? I'm furious," I said calmly. "Giles nearly killed me! He killed my sister. And he killed others. Barnaker, Jensen, Miss Jasmine Lee, I don't even know how many."

"Now, Magpie—"

I pushed my sleeves up my arms, revealing my bandaged and scabbed wrists. I pushed my hair back to show the bruises on my neck. They had bloomed into bright smudges of purple.

"What would you have done if he'd managed to destroy my mind? Just gone along with his scheme? Handed him millions of dollars for the Campus? Congratulated him on how sweet and docile the new Tennyson was? Comforted the grieving husband when he finally killed me?" They were silent again. "I don't even care! I don't want to be part of this family. You can have the famous Claxton DNA. I want to find myself again. I want to be free and clear."

"Of course you do, my dear. But we have a rather delicate situation here." Foxhall poured us more wine.

"What's so delicate about it?" I asked. "Giles stole my life and he murdered your granddaughter. When I tell the police and the media, they won't think it's so damned delicate."

Foxhall settled back into a chair, his fingers laced together.

"He did do all that. But he also gave back to us Porter's first child. His most resilient and resourceful child. The grandchild we had hoped for all along. We want you with us."

"This is not just about the Claxtons, Marissa," Porter said. The first time he'd said my real name. "It's about tens of thousands of people. Shareholders and employees. People who depend for their livelihoods on the various entities under the C&B umbrella, all the Claxton subsidiaries, the foundations, the charities, the Institute. A scandal like this would rock all the boats, even sink them. People will suffer."

"The Campus would suffer too, Magpie," Foxhall said. "If our star researcher were embroiled in this kind of scandal it would have to be shut down. It's the jewel in the crown of the public face of C&B. And so many people have been helped by it, and so many more might be helped in the future. We need to try to save it."

"You're not going to press for charges against Giles, are you? Not here, not in Virginia, not anywhere."

I had no desire to bring this tale of two sisters, greed, hubris, deceit, and murder to the media, but surely it couldn't be simply covered up. Where was the justice in that?

"You must understand, Magpie, C&B will deal with Giles," Foxhall promised. "In fact, you have dealt him a punishment far worse than anything we could have devised. A man so physically fit, so mentally sharp—paralyzed? Crippled? His mind fogged? Perhaps forever? He will have to live with that for the rest of his life. A greatly diminished life."

If we are all lucky, I thought.

I'd had enough. I wanted to leave them all behind me in the rear view mirror. I gathered my things to go. I asked Foxhall what they wanted to do with the house and the car that I'd bought. I didn't want to give them up, but if that was the price of my freedom, so be it.

I threw the keys on the table and turned to leave. Nothing was going to stop me.

"Don't be in such a hurry to throw yourself on a pyre, Magpie," Octavia said. "Is that a Catholic trait? Because surely it is not a Claxton attribute. Claxtons have grit."

Porter shook his head sadly and said nothing. He choked up and put his face in his hands.

"You don't want your house? You don't want the money?" Foxhall asked. "You once asked me how much money there was, re- member."

"The money was Tennyson's. I am not Tennyson. I don't even want her money. My name isn't Claxton. Thank God for small favors. I didn't have much, and I don't know what's happened to it since Giles took everything from me. But I worked for every penny I ever made."

"You can't go back to teaching at that school," Porter said. "Everyone knows Marissa Brookshire is dead."

"Thank you for reminding me, *Dad*."

As if I hadn't thought about that every hour of every day.

"If you turn your back on us, you would have no money, no resources," my father pointed out.

"That never bothered you before, *Father*. Not when I was born and you turned your back on my mother. My sweet, doomed mother, who made the mistake of falling for a handsome, heartless, rich bastard. Do you think I ever cared about the money?"

"As much as we would like, we cannot undo the past, Magpie," Octavia said.

"We must face facts, my dear," Foxhall added. "This is a sad day, and a cautionary one. You cannot go back to your old life. It's been taken from you. Would that we could give it back to you. Would that we could have you both alive and well. But we can't. Tennyson was killed in January of this year in a horrendous automobile accident. Your life as Marissa Brookshire has been irreparably harmed. But your life as Tennyson Olivia Claxton could be a charmed and useful one. And a happy one."

"You can't be serious! You want me to keep this charade going?"

"As Tennyson Claxton, you would be a woman of property, of means, of stature." The Senator was back in grand speaking form. "You could live your life as you wish, on your own terms. You could keep everything, including the house here. We understand it holds great meaning for you. And you would be the sole heir. To everything."

"But you would be a Claxton to the world," Porter put in. "You'd have to be. And you are. Your DNA proves it. You're my daughter."

"What about Priscilla? I don't have her DNA. I care about her, and I don't want to hurt her."

"She's always wanted a daughter with whom she could have a real relationship," Foxhall said. "She finally found one. She wouldn't question this gift. And it is a gift. To all of us."

A gift? It wasn't the gift of love I felt, but the family's tentacles, reaching out for me.

"Blacksburg Downs is at Foxgrove Manor, and I'm sure you're missing him," Octavia said. "And Princess has become quite your faithful companion. She is morose and lost without you. As am I. Please come home, Magpie. We want you with us."

"It's up to you," the Senator said. He slid the keys back across the table to me. "I once promised you I would never let you be taken anywhere against your will, Magpie, and I stand by that. You can live a quiet life as a quiet little nobody, somewhere far away from here. Or you can live your life as Tennyson Claxton. You can complete your education. Take your rightful place in the family business. There are many advantages to coming home with us, my dear. Please come back. The choice is yours."

But, by the almighty author of thy race,
Tell me, oh tell, is this my native place?

Chapter 52

I'M SPENDING THE rest of the summer at the house in Camden. I told the Claxtons I need the summer to decide. I didn't give them any choice about that. I have a little time to think, time to make up my mind, time to change it again. Time to enjoy this old house and this pretty little town, to see if it can feel like my home again, to find out if those memories pull me in. Or push me away.

I was never charged with anything. Giles was soon flown back to Virginia. Mercy flew up to Maine to make amends, in her one-woman cavalry mode, and I closed on the house, only a couple of days late. I had the banister fixed, and the sagging shutter and the sticky doors. I painted the porch. There's still no granite or stainless steel in the kitchen. There's not much furniture, either. A bed, a couple of tables, a few chairs, some books in a bookcase, a radio. I don't want to become too attached to things I may have to give up.

Brendan visits whenever he can get away from running Far Meadows Farm and his horses. I've never told him who I really am. It's to protect him. He knows, without my having to say it. It doesn't matter. He's never called me Tennyson again. I'm his Magpie.

He drove my blue Volvo wagon up here for me, and he gives me regular updates on Blacksburg Downs. He grooms and exercises Blacksburg for me when he's home in Virginia. He had a surprise for me: When he opened the car door, Princess spilled out and ran to me on her short but swift legs, howling and moaning and rolling over on the lawn, a gift from Octavia. Obviously Princess was in need of my attention. And my love.

"Octavia said you have to take her. She just mopes around the place without you."

"Princess is a drama queen," I replied and bent down for sloppy beagle kisses.

Brendan has listened to me weep and wail. He's held me in the night, all night, night after night, and he's been there when I awoke in the cool Maine summer dawn. He will be there for me, he says, no matter who I am. What he means is: No matter who I choose to be. I believe him and I miss him when he isn't here.

I talk to Priscilla on the phone in Buenos Aires every week or so. We've promised to visit each other this fall, but I don't know if that will happen. She knows about "the accident," but the Claxtons haven't told her the whole story. Neither have I.

Mercy and Hailey came up for a long weekend over the Fourth of July. We had a wonderful time, just the three of us and Princess. I have friends again. Nobody asked me whether I really am Tennyson, though that's the name I'm using for the summer. Mercy was mortified that Giles slipped through her agent's surveillance. She told me she was very sorry that it ended the way it did, but also very thankful that it ended the way it did: With me alive, and Giles the way he is now.

Most of the time, I am alone in my little house, with the Claxton Sword of Decision hanging over my head by a thread.

I moved the dollhouse, the replica of my house, downstairs onto a tall round table in the front hall, where I can admire Grandpa Tom's workmanship. I've stopped having nightmares about the doll-house in the crawlspace. After all, they were what saved me. Sometimes I dream about Tennyson, my half-sister. In these dreams, she is not dead but hanging out in a curious half-world, where we have long, confusing conversations about horses and beagles and dollhouses. Sister talk.

For the time being, most people here in town call me by my nickname, Tenn. Some of their faces are familiar from when I lived here before, but I never talk about that time. I'm grateful for their famous New England reserve. They seem to keep their thoughts mostly to themselves. They don't ask me about the accident or the doctor or my famous family, or the infamous banister. They like to talk about painting porches, or the fishing in Penobscot Bay, or whether their boats will make it through another winter.

The national media indulged in a brief feeding frenzy over the "accident." The stories fell into a few categories. The brilliant doctor ironically struck down by his nemesis, traumatic memory loss. The mythical "Claxton Curse" and the shadowy "Claxton Empire." The remarkable rehabilitation of the sexy drug-crazed party-girl heiress. The poor little rich girl, hiding far from the media glare. I tried not to read very much of this stuff. I no longer need *The Big Show of Tennyson O.* Perhaps if I dedicate myself to charity in a foreign land they will someday forget all about that woman.

I have been thinking and walking, and pacing and stomping, all around Camden Harbor, up on Mount Battie, and down the maple-lined streets. I visit the grave in the Mount View Cemetery where the headstone reads MARISOL AND CHILD. I bring my mother flowers. On Sundays I go to Mass. But no matter where I go, I can't escape. I am followed by the looming deadline and the choice I must make this fall.

Foxhall said I would be a nobody if I choose to be Marissa. That is not true. He won't give me up that easily. It's not even true that I would be destitute, except perhaps by his lights. He said he'd provide me with a "small allowance" until I could get on my feet. A small allowance by Claxton standards would be "comfortable" by mine.

Porter, my conflicted father, also offered to provide funds for me, if I promise not to drag the family name through the media muck.

I know what life would be like if I choose Marissa. It would be quiet, once the media tired of my return from the dead and all the trouble it would cause. Unless the Claxton Empire gave me a new name and identity, like witness protection. But yet *another* name? The idea makes my head spin.

As Marissa Brookshire, there would be moments of confusion. *Didn't we go to middle school together? Where have you been all these years? What happened to your green eyes?* From time to time people might mention that I look a little bit like that crazy heiress, the one that dropped out of sight after her terrible accident. Maybe she was disfigured. Or did she have a religious conversion?

If I turn down the Claxtons' comfortable "allowances" and walk away free and clean and empty-handed, I would have to scrape by, try to earn enough money to survive, and go back to school. I could do that. I could be happy, or at least content, knowing the life I escaped. And the life I nearly lost. It might be a little life, but little lives matter.

I am positive I will never again volunteer for another scientific study.

If I walk away as Marissa, Giles Embry will never see me again or come looking for me or even remember my name. He will be paralyzed for life, his memory of recent years and schemes wiped away, his soul empty, his body shattered, a shadow of the monster he was.

This is my consolation and my favorite fantasy. But how can I be sure?

That leads me to: On The Other Hand.

If I were Tennyson, all my old money problems would go away. New ones would take their place. I could go back to school and never worry about the bills, but I'd lose all those years of my own schooling, my flawless academic record, my teaching career. Aside from the fact that living a false life is probably a sin, if I wanted to remain a Catholic and confess those sins, I would have to take instruction and "convert." Under Tennyson's name. Would that also be a sin? I'd have some confessing to do.

If I were Tennyson, I tell myself, I would use the Claxton money for the good of others. Many others. But that is easy to say, hard to do. How do I know all that money and privilege wouldn't warp me and stick to my soul, like tar that I couldn't scrape off?

Octavia and Porter tell me that Giles wants to know why Tennyson hasn't visited him in the hospital in Virginia. He doesn't remember the accident or their engagement, according to Porter, but he believes they must be friends. Why else would he have been helping her look at houses? His memory loss is severe, and so far, resistant to treatment. Though he's making progress physically and is regaining some use of his right arm, they say he will be permanently paralyzed.

The question of Giles haunts me.

Though he cannot use his legs, he is still potentially brilliant, still subject to the darkness raging inside of him. I cannot rule out the possibility that he might regain his memory. After all, I did. And nobody knows what the long-term effects of experimental drugs like Hypnopolethe might be. Giles might wake up out of the Fog. If he wakes up, he might try to kill me, whether I'm Tennyson or Marissa. If he ever has the power, I'm afraid he will kill again.

If I were Tennyson, I could find out what the Claxton Empire and the C&B Corporation, in all their hydra-headed incarnations, really do. I could demand a place on the board of directors of the Campus and have an active voice overseeing the funding, the research, the treatment protocols, the staff, the residents—and that broken monster, Giles Embry.

I am torn. It's peaceful and beautiful here, but I cannot go on the way I am now. It's almost September.

I ask myself: Who would have a greater purpose in life? Marissa or Tennyson? I'm not really either one of them anymore. Perhaps I'm both.

The clock is ticking.

Ulysses had his own choices to make, on his long journey home. Gods and goddesses tempted him with exotic places, new names, old dangers, strange fates. His journey is long past. Not mine. I'm still writing between the lines. I must choose my name and my fate and begin my new life.

Soon.

It fits thee now to wear a dark disguise,
And secret walk unknown to mortal eyes.

Also by Ellen Byerrum

Ellen Byerrum is a novelist, a playwright, a former Washington D.C. journalist, and a graduate of private investigator school in the Commonwealth of Virginia.

The Woman in the Dollhouse is her first suspense thriller. It introduces us to a young woman, Tennyson Claxton, whose mind seems to hold the mingled memories of two very different women. Her past is full of questions, her present is filled with deception and danger, and her future is a blank page—unless she can discover who she really is. Byerrum anticipates exploring Tennyson's continuing odyssey in a future novel.

She also writes the popular Crime of Fashion Mysteries, which star a savvy, stylish female sleuth named Lacey Smithsonian. Lacey is a reluctant (but well-dressed) fashion reporter in Washington D.C., "The City Fashion Forgot." Two of her Crime of Fashion novels, *Killer Hair* and *Hostile Makeover*, were filmed for the Lifetime Movie Network. The tenth in the series is entitled *Lethal Black Dress*.

Byerrum has also penned a middle-grade mystery, *The Children Didn't See Anything,* the first in a projected series starring the precocious twelve-year-old Bresette twins.

Follow Ellen Byerrum on the web at **ellenbyerrum.com** and on Facebook and Twitter. Her books are available through bookstores and from Amazon.

Lethal Black Dress

The tenth in Ellen Byerrum's Crime of Fashion Mysteries
Now available from Lethal Black Dress Press

When does an innocent little black dress become a *lethal* black dress? When that elegant black dress becomes unexpectedly "weaponized" at the most security-conscious event in Washington, D.C., the fabled White House Correspondents' Dinner.

Fashion reporter Lacey Smithsonian is delighted to finally take her well-deserved place at this legendary D.C. media-insider bash. But while people-watching (and collecting crimes of fashion for her newspaper column), she senses there's something strange about TV reporter Courtney Wallace's vintage Madame X gown, a black dress with a stunning emerald green lining.

When Courtney takes a tumble with a tray of champagne and later dies of something *other* than sheer embarrassment, Lacey taps into her famous ExtraFashionary Perception and follows her hunch: This lethal black dress was no freak accident.

Lacey juggles her unconventional investigation with her love life and future in-laws, while spies and lies and an enemy close to home bring her face to face with danger and jealousy, the "green-eyed monster." Will this fashionable style sleuth discover that green can also be the color of death?

Lethal Black Dress is now available through Amazon as a Kindle ebook and a trade paperback.